There were no Amrithi clans visiting the city in Irinah. No clans visiting the towns. No clans visiting the villages. No clans.

They were vanishing.

The Emperor's hatred had not grown suddenly, as Mehr had so foolishly believed when Maryam had warned her of his messages to his nobles. His hatred was a storm that had grown ever larger by feeding on itself, and Mehr had been protected from the full weight of it by the shelter of her privilege and of the very Ambhan walls that so stifled her. Now the storm was too great for even Mehr to ignore. Her status as the Governor's daughter couldn't protect her forever. She had Amrithi blood, and the Amrithi were being erased.

"You can have my blood," Mehr said finally. "But in return you'll owe me a debt."

"Anything," Sara said. "Oh, anything, my lady."

Mehr watched the shadows of the daiva shifting in the dream-fire's light.

"A favor," Mehr said. "You'll owe me a favor. That's all."

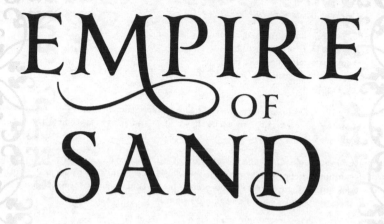

EMPIRE OF SAND

THE BOOKS OF AMBHA

TASHA SURI

www.orbitbooks.net

Copyright © 2018 by Natasha Suri
Excerpt from *Realm of Ash* copyright © 2019 by Natasha Suri
Excerpt from *Torn* copyright © 2018 by Rowenna Miller

Author photograph by Shekhar Bhatia
Cover design by Lauren Panepinto
Cover images by Shutterstock
Cover copyright © 2018 by Hachette Book Group, Inc.
Map by Tim Paul

Orbit
Hachette Book Group
1290 Avenue of the Americas
New York, NY 10104
orbitbooks.net

First Edition: November 2018

Orbit is an imprint of Hachette Book Group.
The Orbit name and logo are trademarks of Little, Brown Book Group Limited.

The publisher is not responsible for websites (or their content) that are not owned by the publisher.

The Hachette Speakers Bureau provides a wide range of authors for speaking events. To find out more, go to www.hachettespeakersbureau.com or call (866) 376-6591.

Library of Congress Cataloging-in-Publication Data:
Names: Suri, Tasha, author.
Title: Empire of sand / Tasha Suri.
Description: First edition. | New York, NY : Orbit, 2018.
Identifiers: LCCN 2018027281| ISBN 9780316449717 (trade pbk.) |
    ISBN 9780316449694 (ebook)
Subjects: | GSAFD: Fantasy fiction.
Classification: LCC PR6119.U75 E47 2018 | DDC 823/.92—dc23
LC record available at https://lccn.loc.gov/2018027281

ISBNs: 978-0-316-44971-7 (trade paperback), 978-0-316-44969-4 (ebook)

Printed in the United States of America

LSC-C

10 9 8 7 6 5 4 3 2 1

For my dad, Nishant Suri.
You would have been proud.

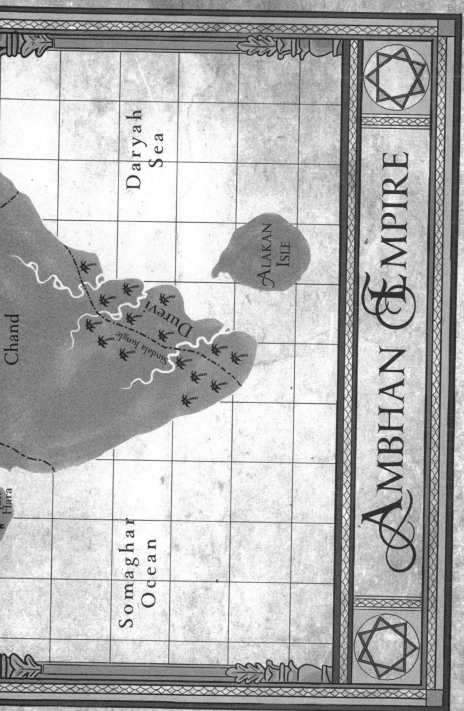

Daryah Sea

Chand

Durevi

Sundala Jungle

Alakan Isle

Somaghar Ocean

Hara

Ambhan Empire

By Tim Paul ©2018

CHAPTER ONE

Mehr woke up to a soft voice calling her name. Without thought, she reached a hand beneath her pillow and closed her fingers carefully around the hilt of her dagger. She could feel the smoothness of the large opal embedded in the hilt, and its familiar weight beneath her fingertips calmed her. She sat up and pushed back the layer of gauze surrounding her divan.

"Who is it?" she called out.

The room was dark apart from one wavering light. As the light approached, Mehr realized it was an oil lantern, held aloft by a maidservant whom Mehr knew by sight but not by name. Through the glare of the lit flame, the maidservant's features looked distorted, her eyes wide with nervousness.

"I'm sorry to disturb you, my lady," the maid said. "But your sister is asking for you."

Mehr paused for a moment. Then she slid off the divan and wound the sash of her sleep robe tight around her waist.

"You work in the nursery?" she asked.

"Yes, my lady."

"Then you should know Lady Maryam won't be pleased that you've come to me," she said, tucking the dagger into her sash. "If she finds out, you may be punished."

The maidservant swallowed.

"Lady Arwa is asking for you," she repeated. "She won't sleep. She's very distressed, my lady."

"Arwa is a child," Mehr replied. "And children are often distressed. Why risk your position and come to me?"

The light wavered again as the maidservant adjusted her grip on the lantern.

"She says there is a daiva watching her," the maidservant said, her voice trembling. "Who else could I come to?"

Mehr strode over to the maidservant, who flinched back.

"What's your name?"

"Sara, my lady," said the maidservant.

"Give me the lantern, Sara," said Mehr. "I don't need you to light the way."

Mehr found Arwa curled up in her nurse Nahira's lap outside the nursery, surrounded by a gaggle of frightened maidservants. There was a Haran guardswoman standing by, looking on helplessly with her hand tight on the hilt of her blade. Mehr had some sympathy for her. Steel was no good against daiva, and equally useless in the comforting of distressed women.

"Mehr!" Arwa cried out, coming to life in the woman's arms. "You came!"

The nurse holding on to her had to tighten her grip to keep Arwa in place, now that she was squirming like a landed fish. Mehr kneeled down to meet Arwa at eye level.

"Of course I've come," said Mehr. "Sara says you saw a daiva?"

"It won't leave my room," Arwa said, sniffling. Her face was red with tears.

"How old are you now, Arwa?"

"Nine years," said Arwa, frowning. "You know that."

"Much too old to be crying then, little sister." Mehr brushed a tear from Arwa's cheek with her thumb. "Calm yourself."

Arwa sucked in a deep breath and nodded. Mehr looked up at Arwa's nurse. She knew her well. Nahira had been her nurse once too.

"Did you see it?"

Nahira snorted.

"My eyes aren't what they once were, but I'm still Irin. I could smell it." She tapped her nose.

"It has sharp claws," Arwa said suddenly. "And big eyes like fire, and it wouldn't stop looking at me."

Arwa was growing agitated again, so Mehr cupped her sister's face in her hands and made a low soothing sound, like the desert winds at moonrise.

"There's no need to be afraid," she said finally, when Arwa had gone still again.

"There's not?"

"No," Mehr said firmly. "I'm going to make it go away."

"Forever?"

"For a long while, yes."

"How?"

"It isn't important."

"I need to know," Arwa insisted. "What if another one comes and you're not here? How will I make it go away then?"

I'll always be here, thought Mehr. But of course that was a lie. She could promise no such thing. She looked into her sister's teary eyes and came, abruptly, to a decision. "Come with me now, Arwa. I'll show you."

One of the maidservants made a sound of protest, quickly hushed. Nahira gave her a narrow look, her grip on Arwa still deathly tight.

"She won't approve," warned Nahira.

"If my stepmother asks, say I forced you," Mehr told her. She touched light fingers to Arwa's shoulders. "Please, Nahira."

"I imagine Lady Maryam will draw her own conclusions," Nahira said dryly. She let Arwa go. "She doesn't think highly of you, my lady."

"Oh, I know," said Mehr. "Come on now, Arwa. You can carry the lamp."

The nursery was undisturbed. The living room was lit, candle-light flickering on the bright cushions and throws strewn across the marble floor. Arwa's bedroom, in the next room along, was dark.

The guardswoman trailed in reluctantly behind them. Her hand was fixed firmly on her scabbard.

"There's no need for this, my lady," the guardswoman said. "Lady Arwa simply had a nightmare. I'm sure of it."

"Are you?" Mehr replied mildly.

The guardswoman hesitated, then said, "I told Lady Arwa's nursemaid and the maidservants that daiva don't exist, that they should tell her so, but..." She paused, glancing uneasily at Mehr's face. "The Irin are superstitious."

Mehr returned her look.

This one, she thought, *has not been in Irinah long.*

"I ran into the room as soon as she screamed," said the guard, pressing on despite Mehr's pointed silence. "I saw nothing."

Ignoring her, Mehr nudged Arwa gently with her foot.

"Go on, love. Show me where it is."

Arwa took in another deep breath and stood straight, mustering up her courage. Then she went into her bedroom. Mehr followed close behind her, the guardswoman still hovering at her back.

"There," Arwa said, pointing. "It's moved. On the window ledge."

Mehr looked up and found the daiva already watching her.

Pale dawn was coming in through the window lattice at its back.

Silhouetted against it, the daiva was a wisp of taloned shadows, its wings bristling darkly against a backdrop of gray-gold light. It was small for a daiva, no larger than Arwa, with nothing human in the shape of its face or in the lidless glare of its golden eyes.

"Stay where you are, Arwa," Mehr said. "Just lift the lamp higher."

Mehr walked toward it—slowly, so as not to startle it from its perch. The daiva's eyes followed her with the constancy of prayer flames.

Three floors above the ground, behind heavily guarded walls, nothing should have been able to reach Arwa's chambers. But daiva didn't obey the rules of human courtesy, and there were no walls in Jah Irinah that could keep them out of a place they wanted to be. Still, Mehr's gut told her this daiva was not dangerous. Curious, perhaps. But not dangerous.

Just to be sure, she held her hands in front of her, arms crossed, her fingers curled in a sigil to ward against evil. The daiva didn't so much as flinch. Good.

"What are you doing?" whispered Arwa.

"Speaking," said Mehr. "Hush now."

She drew her hands close together, thumbs interlocked, fanning out her fingers in the old sigil for *bird*. The daiva rustled its wings in recognition. It knew its name when it saw it.

"Ah," breathed Mehr. Her heart was beating fast in her chest. "You can move now, love. There's nothing to be afraid of."

"It still looks like it wants to bite me," Arwa said warily.

"It's a bird-spirit," Mehr said. "That's what birds do. But there's nothing evil inside it. It's a simple creature. It won't hurt you."

She took another step closer. The daiva cocked its head.

She could smell the air around it, all humid sweetness like incense mingled with water. She sucked in a deep breath and resisted the urge to set her fingers against the soft shadows of its skin.

She held one palm out. *Go.*

But there was no compulsion behind the movement, and the daiva did not look at all inclined to move. It watched her expectantly. Its nostrils, tucked in the shadows of its face, flared wide. It knew what she was. It was waiting.

Mehr drew the dagger from her sash. Arwa gave a squeak, and behind them the guardswoman startled into life, drawing the first inch of her sword out with a hiss of steel.

"Calm, calm," said Mehr soothingly. "I'm just giving it what it wants."

She pressed the sharp edge of her dagger to her left thumb. The skin gave way easily, a bead of blood rising to the surface. She held her thumb up for the daiva.

The daiva lowered its head, smelling her blood.

For a long moment it held still, its eyes never leaving hers. Then the shadows of its flesh broke apart, thin wisps escaping through the lattice. She saw it coalesce back into life beyond the window, dark wings sweeping through the cloudless, brightening air.

Mehr let out a breath she hadn't known she'd been holding. There was no fear in her. Just the racing, aching joy of a small adventure. She pressed her thumb carefully against the window lattice, leaving her mark behind.

"All gone," she said.

"Is it really?" Arwa asked.

"Yes." Mehr wiped the remaining blood from the dagger with her sash. She tucked the blade away again. "If I'm not here and a daiva comes, Arwa, you must offer it a little of your own blood. Then it will leave you alone."

"Why would it want my blood?" Arwa asked, frightened. Her eyes were wide. "Mehr?"

Mehr felt a pang. There was so much Arwa didn't know about her heritage, so much that Mehr was forbidden from teaching her.

To Arwa, daiva were simply monsters, and Irinah's desert was just endless sand stretching off into the horizon, as distant and commonplace as sky or soil. She had never stared out at it, yearning, as Mehr had. She had never known that there was anything to yearn for. She knew nothing of sigils or rites, or the rich inheritance that lived within their shared blood. She only knew what it meant to be an Ambhan nobleman's daughter. She knew what her stepmother wanted her to know, and no more.

Mehr knew it would be foolish to answer her. She bit her lip, lightly, and tasted the faint shadow of iron on her tongue. The pain grounded her, and reminded her of the risks of speaking too freely. There were consequences to disobedience. Mehr knew that. She did not want to face her stepmother's displeasure. She did not want isolation, or pain, or the reminder of her own powerlessness.

But Arwa was looking up at her with soft, fearful eyes, and Mehr did not have the strength to turn away from her yet. *One more transgression*, she decided; she would defy her stepmother one more time, and then she would go.

"Because you have a little bit of them in your blood," Mehr told her. When Arwa wrinkled her nose, Mehr said, "No, Arwa, it's not an insult."

"I'm not a daiva," Arwa protested.

"A little part of you is," Mehr told her. "You see, when the Gods first went to their long sleep, they left their children the daiva behind upon the earth. The daiva were much stronger then. They weren't simply small animal-spirits. Instead they walked the world like men. They had children with humans, and those children were the first Amrithi, our mother's people." She recited the tale from memory, words that weren't her own tripping off her tongue more smoothly than they had any right to. It had been many years since she'd last had Amrithi tales told to her. "Before the daiva weakened, when they were still truly the strong and terrifying sons and daughters of Gods, they made a vow to protect their descendants, and to never willingly harm them." She showed Arwa the thin mark on her thumb, no longer bleeding. "When we give them a piece of our flesh, we're reminding them of their vow. And, little sister, a daiva's vow is unbreakable."

Arwa took hold of her hand, holding it near the glow of the lantern so she could give it a thorough, grave inspection.

"That sounds like a children's story," she said finally, her tone faintly accusing, as if she were sure Mehr was telling her one of the soft lies people told their young.

"It *is* a children's story," said Mehr. "Our mother told it to me when I was a child myself, and I've never forgotten it. But that doesn't make it any less true."

"I don't know if my blood will work like yours," Arwa said doubtfully. She pressed her thumb gently against Mehr's. Where Mehr's skin was dark like earth after rain, Arwa's skin was a bare shade warmer than desert sand. "I don't look like you, do I?"

"Our blood is just the same," Mehr said quietly. "I promise." She squeezed Arwa's hand in hers, once, tightly. Then she stepped back.

"Tell Nahira it's safe to return," she said to the guardswoman. "I'm going back to my chambers."

The guardswoman edged back in fear. She trembled slightly.

If Mehr had been in a more generous mood, she would, perhaps, have told the guardswoman that Irinah was not like the other provinces of the Empire. Perhaps she would have told the guardswoman that what she so derisively called Irin superstition was in truth Irin practicality. In Irinah, the daiva had not faded into myth and history, as they had elsewhere. Weakened though they were, the daiva were holy beings, and it was wise to treat them with both wariness and reverence when one came upon them on Irin soil.

But Mehr was not in a generous mood. She was tired, and the look on the guardswoman's face had left a bitter taste in her mouth.

"Never mind," said Mehr. "I'll go."

"Daiva aren't real," the guardswoman said blankly, as Mehr swept past her. "They're a barbarian superstition."

Mehr didn't even deign to answer her. She walked out into the hallway, Arwa scampering after her, the lamp swinging wildly in her grip. As they left the nursery, Nahira swept Arwa up into her arms and one of the maids plucked the lamp deftly away. Mehr kept on walking until Arwa called out her name, holding out her arms again in a way that made Mehr's traitorous heart twist inside her chest and her legs go leaden beneath her.

It would be best, she told herself, to keep walking. It would be best not to look back. She did not want to be punished. She did not want *Arwa* to be punished.

"Don't go," Arwa said in a small voice. "Can't you stay just one time?"

Mehr stopped. If she turned back—if she stayed—Maryam would ensure that she would not be allowed to visit Arwa again for a long, long time.

Mehr took a deep breath, turned, and walked back to her sister regardless. She closed her eyes and pressed one firm kiss to Arwa's forehead. Her skin was soft; her hair smelled like rosewater.

"Get some sleep," she said to her. "Everything will be better when you wake up."

"Go," Nahira said. "I'll take care of her, my lady." A pause, as Arwa struggled and Mehr hesitated, her feet frozen in place by a compulsion she couldn't name. "Lady Maryam will be awake soon," Nahira said, and that, at last, broke the spell. Mehr turned and walked swiftly back toward her room. She could hear Arwa crying behind her, but as she had told the maidservant Sara, children were often distressed. The hurt would pass. Soon Arwa would forget she had ever been sad at all.

In the privacy of her own chambers, Mehr bathed and dressed, one single yawning maid helping her to oil the wild mass of her hair and braid it back from her face. She could have gone back to sleep, but that seemed pointless now. Her stepmother would be calling for her soon enough.

As the maid wound thread through her braid to hold it in place, Mehr stared out of the lattice wall of her living room. Hollowed out in the shapes of leaves and flowers, it gave Mehr a clear view of the city of Jah Irinah and the desert beyond it. She looked at the sandstone of the city, the gold of the desert, and the clear sky above it and thought: *There's a storm coming.*

There hadn't been a true storm in Jah Irinah in years, but Mehr knew when one was on its way. There was Amrithi enough in her for that. The daiva had been the first sign of it. The city was no place for its kind, and yet the bird-spirit had come. Mehr was sure it had flown to Arwa's window on the first sharp, invisible winds of the coming storm, dreamfire under its wings. Soon enough more daiva would arrive, followed by rising sand and a fall of dreamfire to cloak Jah Irinah in light.

The daiva's scent still clung to Mehr's senses like a warning, a portent of things to come. It was no surprise to her when a maid arrived, holding a message delivered by courier moments before. The message was brief, to the point.

I'm coming. Important news.

"Bring refreshments, please," she said, folding the message up. "Something simple will do."

The maid left with a hurried farewell. There were perks to being the daughter of the Governor of Irinah—even an illegitimate one. People obeyed you. Servants rushed to your bidding. Even the ones who loathed you—and there were many—were forced to veil their contempt and keep their loathing eyes lowered.

All people faced hatred. All people suffered. Few had the cushion of wealth and privilege to protect them as Mehr did. She reminded herself of this as she walked over to the bare floor in front of the lattice, pressing her feet against marble warmed by the morning sun. She was very, very lucky. The heartache she experienced every time she thought of her sister tearily reaching out to her was an agony she had no right to feel.

Better to put the agony away. Better not to think of Arwa at all.

Mehr took a deep breath, slowly filling her lungs. She straightened her spine and rolled back her shoulders, raising her hands above her head to greet the sky. When she pressed her feet flat to the ground, legs bent to a diamond angle, she felt a veil of peace settle over her. The old rites never failed to calm her.

Although the correct time for it had passed, Mehr moved through the Rite of Sunrise, hands shaping the sigils for *night* and *sun* and *sky* as her body moved fluidly from stance to stance. Subtle poses transitioned into the wider, florid movements as she mimed the sun rising. Her muscles warmed; her breath quickened. She let her heavy thoughts go.

The dance was ancient, and its age comforted her. Amrithi had greeted the dawn just like this for generations. There was an endless, unbroken history of men and women who had moved exactly as Mehr was moving now: arms upraised, then lowered, fingers interlocked, then spread in a constant rhythm that matched the rising beat of her heart. Mehr was merely a link in the chain. She didn't have to think. She was elemental.

From dawn she moved to day, and from day to dusk. There was a whole cycle of rites simply for the passing of the hours. Mehr knew them all. Lost in her body, she didn't even notice when Lalita finally entered, even though a maid had surely arrived to announce her. She only realized Lalita was there when she heard a voice humming with the rhythm of her steps, fingers tapping along with the smack of her feet against the floor. Mehr stopped immediately, falling into the finishing stance.

"Welcome back," Lalita said wryly. Her Chand guard Usha, standing in the doorway, gave a shy wave. "Are you wholly with us now?"

Mehr's legs were cramping. She must have been dancing for hours. It wouldn't have been the first time she'd lost herself in the rites. She stretched out the soreness in her muscles, her breath still a shade too fast. "Were you waiting long?"

"Oh no, not long," Lalita said. "One of your maids offered me refreshments. Such a pleasant girl." She raised a small glass of fruit nectar to illustrate. "Will you join me in a drink?"

Mehr joined her on the floor cushions, crossing her aching legs before they could resist her will.

It was hard not to look at Lalita without being reflexively astounded by her beauty. Although she was a woman old enough to be Mehr's mother, she wore her age the way she wore her loveliness: proudly, like armor. She'd once been a courtesan in Jah Ambha, the Emperor's city. Usha had told Mehr in awed, hushed tones that Lalita had danced once for the Emperor himself. But now she lived a quiet life in Jah Irinah, near the desert of her ancestors, holding small salons and entertaining only the most select of guests.

Lalita passed her a drink. Her mouth curved into a smile. Her hair was loose around her shoulders in glossy curls; her lips were painted red. But her eyes were tired, and she couldn't quite hide the tremor in her fingers as she handed over the glass.

"Are you well?" Mehr asked cautiously.

Lalita dismissed the question with a wave of her hand. "You need to practice matching your sigils with your stances," she said. "Your timing is imperfect."

"Blame my teacher."

"Very funny," Lalita said dryly. "I *am* well, dear one. But I have unfortunate news."

"Tell me," Mehr prompted.

Lalita's gaze flickered over to the doorway, where Usha stood. They shared a glance. Then she returned her gaze to Mehr, her face now grave.

"I have to leave Jah Irinah. I may not be able to return for a long time, Mehr."

"Ah," Mehr said. She swallowed around the lump in her throat. "I see."

"I am sorry for it," Lalita said softly. "But I have drawn some unwanted attention. One of the perils of my work, dear one. But I will write to you, and you must write back, you understand?"

As a courtesan, Lalita faced many risks. Mehr understood that well enough.

But Lalita was not simply a courtesan. She was also an Amrithi woman hiding in plain sight under a Chand name and a Chand identity. And that, more than her profession, placed her at risk of terrible danger. It was Lalita who had carefully, gently explained to Mehr the dangers their shared heritage posed.

Mehr looked at Lalita's hands, which were still trembling faintly. Lalita's calm, she realized, was as fragile and brittle as fine glass. It was not Mehr's place to shatter it. Instead, she swallowed her questions away, and simply nodded.

"I hate writing letters," she said, forcing herself to sound light. She saw Lalita's face soften back into a smile as some of the tension left it, and was glad she had done so. "But for you, I'll try."

"I feel very special."

"As you should," Mehr said. "You dreadful abandoner. You know my stances will only grow worse without you, don't you?"

"I dread to think," Lalita said with a sigh. She gave Mehr

a thoughtful look and said, "You will practice without me, won't you?"

"Of course." Mehr hesitated. "Lalita, do you...?"

"Yes?" she prompted.

"I thought your message was about something else entirely." Mehr shook her head. "It doesn't matter."

"Tell me," said Lalita. "Has something happened? Your stepmother?"

"Last night there was a daiva in my sister's room."

Lalita's gaze sharpened. She leaned forward.

"Was it strong? An ancient?"

"It was nothing but a bird-spirit. But I believe it was a herald, Lalita. I think a storm is coming."

Lalita looked out through the lattice wall, considering.

"The last time I walked the edge of the desert, the daiva did seem restless," she said finally. "For a benign spirit to move so far among mortals...yes, my dear. I think you may be right." Her forehead creased into a frown. "I can't quite believe I missed the signs. I've misplaced my head." She looked at Mehr. "You've taken the proper precautions?"

Mehr nodded. There was no chance of a daiva coming into Mehr's chambers. Mehr had bled on the doors and windows often enough, after all, every turn of the moon since her tenth year, just as she'd been taught.

"And your sister?"

"Her window was freshly blooded. I used my dagger."

"Then there's nothing to fear, and everything to look forward to." Lalita set down her drink. There was a faraway look in her eyes. "How old were you during the last storm?"

"Young," said Mehr. "I can't remember."

"It's been an age since I last saw a storm," Lalita said, a wistful edge to her voice. "When I was a child I loved them. My clan would spend days preparing the Rite of Dreaming. And when the dreamfire fell—ah, Mehr, it was a beautiful thing. You can't imagine it." A sigh. "But of course storms were more frequent where I was raised. There's just no soul in Jah Irinah."

Storms of dreamfire only occurred within the confines of Irinah's holy desert. But Irinah was vast, and Lalita had grown up deep in the heart of the desert, where storms fell frequently. Jah Irinah, built as it was on the outer edge of the blessed sand, was rarely graced with storms. Nonetheless, it was a common belief among the Irin that the presence of the Ambhan Empire in the city—in its buildings, its fountains, its culture, and its people—kept the storms at bay. Dreamfire, they would whisper, belonged to Irinah and Irinah's people. It wouldn't deign to fall before foreign eyes.

Mehr understood that belief. Built in the early years of the Empire, when the first Emperor ordered a loyal Governor to the conquered country to rule in his stead, Jah Irinah was and always would be a purely Ambhan city. The Empire was visible in every swooping arch, every mosaic-patterned wall, and every human-made fountain pumped with precious, wasted water. The city was built on Irinah's back, but there was certainly none of the country's harsh beauty in its bones.

Lalita was still lost in old memories, her face soft with sadness. "The Rite of Dreaming usually needs more dancers, but we'll manage." She looked at Mehr. "We'll greet the storm together."

"You want me to dance the rite with you?" Mehr said, not trying to hide the disbelief in her voice.

"That is how Amrithi greet storms, Mehr," Lalita said, amused. She patted Mehr's hand. "Don't worry. I've taught you everything you need to know."

"I thought you were leaving."

"For this," said Lalita gently, "I can delay my journey a little longer."

How many times had Mehr looked out at the desert and

imagined living on its sands in a clan of her own, dancing the Rite of Dreaming for the storms of dreamfire that so rarely crossed its boundaries? She'd always known it was an impossible thing to hope for.

"My mother..." Mehr stopped. There were so many feelings hurtling through her. She didn't know how to put them into words. "The Rite of Dreaming is danced by clans," she said finally, her voice brittle. "And I have no clan." She swallowed. "This isn't for me. But I thank you."

The amusement faded completely from Lalita's face. The expression that took its place was full of knowing compassion.

"Neither of us are good Amrithi, my dear," Lalita said gently. "I have no clan anymore either. But we can be clan to each other." She pressed her fingers to Mehr's knuckles in fleeting comfort. "You're a woman now. You've learned your rites and your sigils, and shown your ancestors the proper reverence. You *are* Amrithi, Mehr. The rite is your inheritance, just as it is mine. When the storm comes I'll be here to dance with you. I promise this."

Mehr felt an upswell in her heart. But she kept her expression calm.

"I appreciate it," she said.

Lalita leaned back, took another delicate sip of her drink, and swiftly changed topic. She eased the conversation onto lighter ground, relating gossip from the racier circles she traveled within in Jah Irinah that Mehr had little access to. Lalita darted artfully from topic to topic, telling Mehr about scandals among the city's merchants, and news of new fresh-faced courtesans rising in fame or infamy. She told Mehr about the restlessness among factions of the nobility, and the trouble they'd caused in response, or so she'd heard, to rumblings from the Emperor's court.

"The young ones," she said, "the ones who want to prove themselves and earn glory for their names, are causing no *end* of trouble in the city."

"What are they doing?" Mehr asked.

Lalita gestured vaguely with one hand, a line of irritation forming between her brows. "What do men do, when they want to cause trouble? Harassing traders and merchants, barging their way into pleasure houses. They claim to be the Emperor's eyes. They say it gives them the right to do as they please." Lalita's gaze sharpened. "They may have the right. But your father will know far more about the Emperor's business than I do."

Hungry, ambitious young nobles trying to curry the Emperor's favor by striving to fulfill his perceived desires were a nuisance, but a nuisance her father could quash. Nobles acting on the Emperor's orders—as the nobles that Lalita had so carefully chosen to warn Mehr about claimed to be—would be infinitely more dangerous. Governor though he was, her father could not stand in the way of the Emperor's direct commands.

"My father doesn't speak to me about such things," Mehr said finally.

"I know, dear one," Lalita said. Her voice was soft. "But ah, enough of serious business. Let me tell you what I learned from a patron last week..."

After one inspiring story about a hapless merchant and two business-minded dancing girls, Mehr was almost relaxed. She was laughing when a guardswoman entered, a grim expression on her face.

"Lady Maryam has asked for you to attend her, my lady," she said.

That put a complete stop to Mehr's laughter. She straightened up, offering the guardswoman a cool look that was returned in kind. Her stepmother's servants had no particular love for Mehr.

"Give me a moment," Mehr said. Knowing Maryam would have demanded Mehr be brought to her immediately, she added, "I must say good-bye to my guest. I'm sure Mother would agree."

As Mehr stood, Lalita stood with her.

"Mehr," Lalita said, a hint of hesitation in her voice. "We will talk more when I return for the storm, but do try to be . . . careful. Your father will keep you safe, my dear, but these are difficult times."

Mehr nodded. She was very conscious of the guardswoman waiting for her, listening to Lalita's every word.

"When you return for the storm we'll speak properly," Mehr agreed. "I'll make sure we're not disturbed, if I can."

"Thank you."

Usha came over and placed Lalita's hooded robe around her shoulders.

"I'll see myself out," Lalita said lightly. She touched her fingers to Mehr's cheek. "Be brave," she said. "Nothing harms like family. I know."

"I'm always brave," Mehr said.

"So you are," Lalita said, ever so softly. "My dear, I hope you never change."

CHAPTER TWO

The guardswoman led Mehr down increasingly elegant marble-floored corridors to the Receiving Hall. Used solely for entertaining the wives of visiting courtiers, the Hall was no place for a private conversation between family members. No doubt Maryam had chosen the Hall for exactly that reason. She wanted to remind Mehr of her place. This was Maryam's household. Mehr was just an unwanted interloper: an illegitimate child, a heathen, a *visitor*.

Mehr hardly needed the reminder. She knew what she was.

The guardswoman crossed the threshold of the Hall and bowed low as she announced Mehr's arrival. After a short pause, the guard gestured at her to enter. Mehr steeled herself and stepped into the room with her head held high.

The room was sumptuously decorated with silk tapestries unfurled on the walls and rubies inlaid into the domed ceiling. Mehr swept across the Hall, ignoring the watchful, judgmental eyes of her stepmother's many attendants. She kept her own gaze fixed on the raised dais in front of her where Maryam waited.

Lady Maryam, wife of the Governor of Irinah and scion of one of the great Ambhan families, looked down at her step-daughter from her raised seat and offered her a cool smile. Mehr gave her a small bow in return.

"Mother," she said. "How may I serve?"

"Sit down, Mehr," said Maryam. "We need to talk."

Maryam was a true bloom of Ambhan womanhood. Her hair was sleek and dark, wound into a gold-laced braid that fell to the small of her back. Her skin was light brown, her eyes hazel, her face fine-boned and delicate. She looked exactly as fresh and maidenly as she had on the day Mehr's father had brought her to their home, dressed in wedding silks with his seal hung around her neck. Even the hate in her eyes when she looked at Mehr, kneeling on the cushions before her, hadn't altered one jot in the last eight years.

There was a tray of pastries and a jug of spiced wine in the arms of a servant at Maryam's side. Maryam allowed the servant to pour her a drink and set some of the pastries in front of her as she continued to stare down at Mehr with a look that could have curdled milk.

Maryam sampled the wine. Everything else she left untouched. Mehr and the servants waited in complete silence.

"I thought we had an understanding, Mehr," Maryam said finally. "Arwa's upbringing is my responsibility."

"I know that, Mother."

"Not yours. Mine."

"I understand perfectly," Mehr said.

"Then why," Maryam said, eyes narrowed, "did you go to the nursery last night?"

"Because Arwa needed me," Mehr replied calmly. "It was a small thing, Mother. Nothing of consequence."

"How easily you tell lies," said Maryam. A look of absolute bitterness flitted across her features. "I know what you did. Filling her head with heathen madness is not a *small* thing, Mehr, and I won't stand for it. I have worked so very hard to ensure that Arwa is better than her mother's low blood. I have raised her with all the care I would have shown a child of my own flesh, if I had been so blessed. And I have done well, Mehr. She is *good*."

"She is," Mehr said softly. This, at least, they could agree upon.

"Because I have made her good," Maryam said sharply. "Because I have raised her and molded her, and taught her to be grateful that she is a noblewoman of the Ambhan Empire." *Unlike you*, Maryam did not say. She had no need to. "Did you know, Mehr, that every night before she sleeps, she kneels by me at my altar to worship the Emperor and Maha and give thanks to the mystics for their prayers? No? Of course not." Her voice was a blade. "You know nothing about her, because she does not belong to you. She is *mine*."

Maryam paused, then, to make a faint gesture at one of her servants. The servant filled her glass to the brim with a murmured apology. Maryam waved her away, her gaze still fixed on Mehr.

"Tonight, no doubt, Arwa will ask me about your blood and your knife and your shadow monsters, and I will have to shame her for believing your heathen lies. She will be grieved, and that will be your doing."

Mehr bowed her head. She was not ashamed, not of what she had done, but the thought of Arwa suffering because of Mehr's foolishness... Oh, it pained her.

Silence fell, and as the quiet deepened around them, Mehr realized that Maryam was waiting for her to apologize. An apology would not be the end of it, of course. No matter what Mehr said, Maryam would continue to vent her fury. Mehr had faced Maryam's anger often enough before to know that.

If she apologized now, if she groveled and pleaded, Maryam's fury would settle—eventually. The punishment she would inflict on Mehr would be lighter. Mehr had played the part of the remorseful child often enough in the past to know that.

But the memory of the daiva's prayer-bright eyes—and Arwa's

tears—wouldn't leave her be. She couldn't do it. Today, with dreamfire rising and a storm hovering on the horizon, she couldn't allow Maryam to belittle everything she held holy.

"They aren't monsters," Mehr said quietly. So quietly. In the silence of the Hall, her voice carried far enough.

The air grew tense. Along the walls, Maryam's attendants went very, very still.

"Is that all you can say?" Maryam asked. "I give you the chance to apologize, and all you see fit to do is offer me more nonsense?"

"Not nonsense. Just the truth, Mother." And because it wasn't all she could say, because she had already fanned Maryam's fury into a wildfire and groveling was no longer an option, she went doggedly on. "They are the Gods' first children. They're ancient, elemental, sacred—"

"Do you want me to believe your bloodletting is sacred too?" demanded Maryam.

"It is," Mehr said, and watched Maryam's beautiful face twist in revulsion.

Maryam visibly restrained herself, drawing in a deep breath, straightening in her seat. When she spoke, her voice was tight and controlled.

"Your father may allow you to indulge in your mother's heathen customs, but you will *not* inflict them on Arwa." Maryam touched the seal hung around her throat. Inscribed with the Governor's genealogy in ancient Ambhan script, it marked Maryam as his other half, his partner in all of life's duties, his bride and his property. It was a reminder of the power Maryam had that Mehr did not. "When I married Suren I vowed to raise you both as proper Ambhan women. I wanted to help you rise above your roots—*both* of you. But I knew from that moment I first set eyes on you that your mother had already rotted you with her barbarian ways." Maryam leaned forward, intent. "I have failed to save you, Mehr, but I won't fail Arwa. I won't allow you to drag her down with you. Is that clear?"

"Very," Mehr said. "I won't disobey you, Mother."

"If only I could believe you," said Maryam.

Maryam took another sip of her drink. She watched Mehr over the rim of the glass, her eyes sharp. She was ready to pass judgment.

"No more contact, I think," she announced. "When you've shown me you understand how to obey your parents, Mehr—as a true Ambhan daughter should—you'll be allowed to visit Arwa again."

Mehr felt her own rage rising. This was why she should have groveled. This was why she should have held her pride in check. Wielding truth had unpleasant and unavoidable consequences.

"I have the utmost respect for you, Mother," Mehr said. *Lie.* "But if Arwa needs me, I won't turn away from her." A beat. "She's my blood, after all."

Maryam flinched as if she'd been struck. Mehr felt an ugly rush of satisfaction tangled with shame. Maryam could claim Arwa as her own as often as she liked. It would not change the truth. Maryam had never borne the child she'd so longed for. As the years had passed, it had become clear there would be no little Ambhan daughters carved in Maryam's image, and no sons to carry on the family name. There would only ever be another woman's child to raise and mold into her own as best as she could. For all Maryam's efforts, Arwa would never be the child she truly craved.

"You value blood ties far more than you should," Maryam said. "Blood wasn't enough to make your birth mother stay, after all, was it? No." Her voice trembled. She swallowed and held her head high. "Like it or not, we are family. And you will obey me, as is your duty."

A wound for a wound. Mehr supposed there was some fairness in that. She sucked in a breath and held on to the iron in her spine, refusing to relent or apologize.

Maryam's mouth thinned.

"Leave us," she said to her attendants.

The servants filed out obediently. At the wave of Maryam's hand, the guards closed the doors.

"Stand up," Maryam said. She stood herself, smoothly adjusting the heavy weight of the silk shawl draped over her shoulders. She stepped down from the dais.

Mehr stood as Maryam walked over to her. "Why did you send the servants away?" she asked.

"Because some things aren't for their ears," Maryam said. Her skirts, diaphanous layers of netting and embroidered cloth, whispered against the floor. Closer now, Mehr could see the tension lining her face, the way her hands bit into the slippery weight of her shawl.

"You didn't bring me here for privacy," Mehr pointed out. "You brought me here to humiliate me."

"How bold you are," said Maryam, venom in her voice. "Things change, Mehr."

Crossing the last bit of distance between them, Maryam roughly took hold of Mehr's chin. She stared up into Mehr's eyes without blinking.

"Look at you," Maryam said softly. "Every year you grow more rebellious. You think I don't see the look in your eyes? I know what you are, Mehr. I've accepted that trying to improve you is a pointless task, but perhaps you'll pay me some heed when I tell you this: Your stubbornness is putting us all at risk, especially Arwa."

Mehr could feel the sharp bite of her stepmother's nails. She didn't try to pull away. She told herself the pain was nothing.

"You don't understand politics," Maryam went on. "And why

should you? Your father has kept you sheltered, as is right and proper. But I am your father's other half. I share his burdens, and I know too much. I cannot allow you to continue blundering about in ignorance, harming us all." She lowered her voice. "The Emperor, praise his name, has sent messages to his nobles across the Empire. He believes their efforts to drive heathens out of the Empire have been . . . lacking. He has asked them to search out your mother's people in earnest and force them to the edges of society, where they rightly belong." Maryam was still holding Mehr in her grip, nail to flesh, keeping her pinned fast. "Mehr, by the Emperor's grace, you were born an Ambhan woman, and the walls of your father's household shelter you from their sight and from harm. But even you are not so well hidden that your heathen rituals may not draw . . . attention."

Mehr's mind was full of noise. Her jaw ached.

"Why has the Emperor's hatred grown so suddenly?" she whispered, forcing the words out through the grip of Maryam's hand.

"It isn't for us to question the Emperor," Maryam said sharply.

Mehr bit down on her tongue to hold back an audible wince of pain as Maryam's nails dug in deeper.

"No one has to know about the taint in your sister's lineage," Maryam said. "She is already my child in all the ways that matter. If you stop reminding the world of your heathen background, your father and I may be able to arrange good marriage prospects for her. Arwa could have the life she deserves. Or not. It's up to you, Mehr."

Finally Maryam released her. Mehr resisted the urge to touch her face.

"May I go?" she asked.

"You may go and think on what I've told you," Maryam said. "But be warned. If you don't make the right decision, I will have to convince your father to stop indulging you." Her eyes were flinty. "No more dancing. No more heathen rites. His guilt won't control him forever, Mehr."

You can try, thought Mehr. This time she chose to be wiser, and held her tongue even as her heart hurt in her chest. Maryam made a dismissive gesture with one hand, and Mehr turned without offering her even the semblance of a respectful fare-well. She swept through the doors, not bothering to hide the red marks on her face. Let the servants say what they liked. She'd had enough of her stepmother and her games to last a lifetime. Now all she wanted was to be alone.

Over the next few days Mehr got exactly what she'd wished for. The servants gave her a wide berth, mindful of the fact that Mehr was at odds with her stepmother. No one wanted to face Maryam's displeasure by showing Mehr any favor. Arwa was kept away from her just like Maryam had promised. Mehr spent most of her time in her own chambers, waiting for the bruises on her face to fade and watching the horizon.

The daiva had been a herald of a storm. Mehr had been right about that. Every day the storm rolled in closer, building in waves against the sky. She watched the dreamfire glowing against the horizon, its deep ruby and amethyst flames flickering white at the edges. This was the first storm to reach Jah Irinah in a decade, and it should have been a privilege to witness it.

And yet, all Mehr could think of was Maryam's sharp words and Lalita's gentle warning. She couldn't help it. The memory of Maryam's nails tightening on Mehr's jaw tangled together with the memory of Lalita's voice as she warned Mehr to be careful, leaving a strange, painful dread in Mehr's heart.

The Emperor was looking for her mother's people. The Emperor wanted his nobles to drive out her mother's people in earnest. People like Mehr.

Like Arwa.

Mehr worshipped the Emperor and the Maha, the Great One who had founded his bloodline, when it was expected of her, of course: on the Emperor's birthday, on the anniversary of the Empire's founding, or whenever Maryam demanded it. But she had no altar in her chambers, and no particular love of the Emperor in her heart. Her mother had hated him, in her own quiet way. She had refused, when Mehr was small, to worship him at all. *I will never pray for him*, her mother had said, with a black look in her eyes that Mehr had never forgotten. *He has no right to an Amrithi's prayers.*

As a child, Mehr had not understood the weight of blood and history that lay behind her mother's hatred. It was Lalita who later taught Mehr how the Maha, the first Emperor, had conquered Irinah and raised his temple upon its back. She told Mehr that the Amrithi had rebelled with the help of the daiva. When the daiva had begun to weaken, fading, the Empire had crushed the Amrithi with terrible swiftness. The Amrithi had been reviled for their resistance ever since.

Every time Mehr thought of the Emperor, she remembered that history and felt an echo of the darkness she'd seen in her mother's eyes inside her own heart. She thought, too, of the way noblewomen would look at her when they visited her father's palace, and the things the servants would whisper when they thought Mehr could not hear them. *That one stinks of her mother's blood. She's not really Ambhan. Look at her face. Look at how she behaves.*

They believed, just as the Emperor did, that there was no place for heathens in the Empire. If Ambhans were the highest of the high, blessed by the Emperor's grace, obedient to the laws of an orderly and civilized culture, then Amrithi were the lowest of the races: barbarians, faithless wanderers, who had no respect for contracts or Ambhan law. The people of the Empire's other provinces—even the Irin, for all their superstitious respect for the daiva—belonged to the Empire in a way the Amrithi never could.

To be visibly Amrithi was to be outcast. Amrithi had no real place in the Empire. *Mehr* had no place. And if the Emperor's hate for her mother's kind had truly sharpened into a deeper and more active loathing, then Maryam was right to be afraid. Mehr had put them all at risk, simply by being who she was.

The Amrithi were hunted by the nobility and hounded to the edges of society, forced to live far beyond the borders of Irinah's towns and villages, where they could not taint the Empire or its citizens with their alien culture or their heathen rites. Some survived as Lalita did, by hiding their heritage and building new lives. So far, Mehr had been protected by her father's position and by the walls and veils that defined her life as a sheltered noblewoman. But if the Emperor was encouraging his nobles to persecute Amrithi more aggressively, if their eyes were beginning to seek out her mother's people in vicious earnest...

Well. Mehr would do whatever she had to in order to keep Arwa safe.

Lalita had found a way to hide her heritage and thrive, taking on a Chand name and practicing Amrithi rites only in secret, behind closed doors. Mehr could do the same if she had to. She *would*. For her sister's sake, she would do a great deal. But she had fought very hard to hold on to her heritage, and she would not discard it or make herself small without good reason.

She would need to speak to Lalita and ask her exactly what was happening in the city and in the Empire beyond it. She would bribe the servants who could be bribed, and listen for whispers not intended for her ears. She would arm herself with the knowledge she needed to protect herself and her family.

But first, she'd dance the Rite of Dreaming. That, at least, she refused to sacrifice. She'd hungered for it for far, far too long to give it up now.

Her memories of the last storm to reach the city were vague. She had been nine years old, and her mother had taken her out onto the roof to watch the dreamfire fall. Her mother had lifted her up—she'd been so strong!—and shown her the clouds of lights ghosting across the desert sky.

She'd told Mehr stories about the desert: how it was a special and holy place, the place where the Gods had gone and laid down their bodies for their long rest. In sleep, their dreams were the force that kept the world whole, and shaped the earth's balance, its many cycles of birth and death, suffering and joy, rise and ruin.

She'd told Mehr what the Amrithi believed: that the dreamfire was their immortal dreams manifest, a sign of their power at work on the land where they slept. *When the Gods dream, Mehr, they make and unmake the universe. Dreamfire is the light of their souls—see how beautiful it is, my dove? The dreamfire is pure creation.*

Her mother had lowered her down then, and demonstrated the first simple stance in the Rite of Dreaming: hands held aloft, palms cupped together, body bowed and sharp like the arc of a falling star. With her palms cupped against the sky, it had looked as if the dreamfire were pouring into her hands like water.

Her mother had watched Mehr's delighted awe and smiled.

There, you see, she'd said. Mehr still remembered the huskiness of her mother's voice, how soft it had been. *When you're grown, we will dance the Rite of Dreaming together. We'll dance with the Gods, you and I.*

And Mehr had looked at the dreamfire, traced it with her hungry eyes, and begun to dream of the moment when she would dance with the dreamfire too, as an Amrithi woman grown. In all the years since, the dream had not faded. Instead it had grown inside her, deepening its roots in her soul.

She would dance the rite as an Amrithi. Just this once. She had earned this, at least. She thought of the way it would feel to lift her arms again and hold dreamfire in her hands. There were no words for how that would feel. Only pure, uncharted emotion, bigger than sky.

In preparation for the storm—and because she clearly needed something to distract herself from the pointless, twisting worry in her chest—Mehr decided to organize everything she would need when the dreamfire finally fell. Apart from her dagger, she kept her few Amrithi possessions in a wooden chest tucked away with the rest of her clothing, where it was unlikely to attract her stepmother's attention.

Mehr removed the heavy chest from storage on her own, placing it by her divan. Inside the chest, preserved and fragranced by bundles of dried herbs, lay Mehr's garb for the rites. She lifted each item out reverently.

There was a short, fitted bodice, a fanned skirt, and long lengths of cloth dyed a vibrant indigo that deepened to darkness at the fabric's edges. Mehr lifted the folded cloth out, then reached carefully for what lay beneath it: small stone flowers, strung on coils of white thread, ready to be wound through her hair, and a faded band of red silk. She held the silk up to the light, admiring the delicate patterns stitched onto its surface in white thread—images of sky and stars, of the heavenly bodies in motion.

The bodice and skirt had been gifts from Lalita. "If you need replacements, you ask me," Lalita had told her. And Mehr had nodded, understanding, because she could hardly ask her stepmother's seamstress for help, could she?

The sash and hair ornaments had belonged to her mother. Mehr had found them in her mother's chambers, in the early days after her mother left, carefully folded and wrapped in linen. She had no proof, but she liked to believe her mother had left them for her, as an apology and a farewell.

She fanned the cloth, the bodice, and the skirt out on her

divan. She kept the stones in her palm, tracing the edges of the flowers with her thumb. She felt restless, full of joy and sadness at the same time. It wouldn't be long until the storm reached Jah Irinah. On that day, she would finally be able to dance the Rite of Dreaming as a grown woman, Amrithi and Ambhan, light in her hands and her heart.

Then Lalita would leave, and Mehr would be alone.

A sound from beyond the bedroom made Mehr snap sharply out of her reverie. She placed the flowers on the divan and stepped out of her room. She found Sara waiting for her, a characteristic look of nervousness on her face.

"Lady Mehr." The maidservant offered a shaky bow.

"What are you doing here?" Mehr asked.

"Nahira sent me, my lady."

"Does Arwa need me?"

Sara shook her head quickly.

"Oh no, my lady. Lady Arwa is well. Nahira sent me to … to request a favor."

Mehr frowned.

"What could Nahira possibly need from me?" she asked.

Sara swallowed, biting her lip. Her reluctance to speak almost radiated off her.

"Go on," Mehr urged.

"Your blood, my lady." Sara's voice was small. "She wants your blood."

Mehr was stunned into silence. She was saved from responding by Sara, who seemed determined to finish speaking before her courage failed her. She went on hurriedly, tripping over her words. "The dreamfire frightens her, my lady. She knows a storm is coming. But the daiva—there are so many of them out there now, my lady—they frighten her so much more than the dreamfire." Sara took a deep, steadying breath. "Your blood has kept Lady Arwa safe. Everyone knows nothing creeps into her rooms at night. She sleeps soundly. And Nahira—she is old, my lady, and superstitious, you must understand—Nahira has asked if you will protect her too."

Sara had her hands on the edges of the shawl draped around her shoulders. Mehr watched her fingers as she spoke. She was twisting the cloth into knots. Her words were a buzz of noise in Mehr's ears.

"You are lying to me," Mehr said coolly.

"No, my lady!" Sara's voice was high and frantic.

"Shall I summon Nahira now and ask her?" Sara's silence was answer enough. Mehr went on. All the fury Mehr had been holding back rose up as a hard frost in her veins, her voice. "Nahira sleeps in Arwa's bedchamber. She doesn't need my blood to protect her, and she would know better than to ask for it." Right now, when Mehr was in disfavor, asking for her help was a dangerous act. Nahira was too much of a survivor to make such a basic error of judgment. "You know what the other servants say about me. You know what I'm capable of. So why, Sara, have you decided to make me your enemy?"

Sara tried to turn and bolt from the room, but Mehr was close enough to catch her hand and hold her still.

"No," Mehr said. "Speak to me first. Then you can run."

"I'm sorry," Sara said, teary. "But some of us are so afraid, my lady. Not the Harans or the Numrihans—they don't understand, they laugh at me and call me a superstitious barbarian—but we Irin, we know what's coming. I grew up outside the city, my lady. Near the Northern Oasis. I know what a storm is like. I know how the fire falls and the daiva follow it. So many daiva, my lady, and our blood doesn't protect us from them. What will we do if an evil daiva creeps into our quarters with the storm? Gods forbid, an ancient? What will we do?" Her voice turned entreating. "A little blood, my lady, that's all I need to protect the servant quarters. *Please.*"

Mehr let go of her. But Sara didn't run. She stood her ground, terrified but determined. In the face of her fear—and her stubbornness—Mehr's own anger faded. She didn't have the strength to be cruel.

"You shouldn't have come to me," Mehr said heavily. "It was a foolish thing to do. Be sensible, Sara. Find an Amrithi clan and barter for some blood. You work for the Governor, you surely have the coin."

Sara looked down at the floor, as if she couldn't bear to meet Mehr's eyes. Her voice came out in an incomprehensible whisper.

"Speak up," Mehr ordered. Her patience had worn thin.

Sara swallowed.

"I haven't seen a clan in years, my lady. That's all."

"Near Jah Irinah?"

"Anywhere, my lady," Sara said. She still wouldn't meet Mehr's eyes. "It's as if they've—vanished."

Mehr turned away from her. Without consciously deciding to do so, she walked over to the perforated wall and stared out at the desert beyond. The sand was glowing with the warmth of encroaching dreamfire.

She thought of the feel of Maryam's fingers on her face, of Lalita's trembling hands, her tired smile.

She had told herself she would seek out new knowledge. Well, here it was. Mehr already knew that not all was well in Irinah, and not all was well for the Amrithi. Lalita had always done her best to make sure that Mehr was aware of the dangers the Amrithi faced. But it was different, hearing what had become of the Amrithi from Sara's lips. Lalita's knowledge came from the highest echelons of society: from pillow talk, from salons, from the constant threads of rumors and gossip that wound their way through the city. Sara—raised near the Northern Oasis, far beyond the city's borders—had gleaned her knowledge of the fate of the Amrithi not from gossip and connections, but from the bare reality of life on Irinah's sand that Lalita had worked so hard to escape from. Sara knew what Lalita—always so careful to avoid crossing paths with the people or haunts of her past Amrithi life—couldn't have known:

There were no Amrithi clans visiting the city in Irinah. No clans visiting the towns. No clans visiting the villages. No clans.

They were vanishing.

The Emperor's hatred had not grown suddenly, as Mehr had so foolishly believed when Maryam had warned her of his messages to his nobles. His hatred was a storm that had grown ever larger by feeding on itself, and Mehr had been protected from the full weight of it by the shelter of her privilege and of the very Ambhan walls that so stifled her. Now the storm was too great for even Mehr to ignore. Her status as the Governor's daughter couldn't protect her forever. She had Amrithi blood, and the Amrithi were being erased.

"You can have my blood," Mehr said finally. "But in return you'll owe me a debt."

"Anything," Sara said. "Oh, anything, my lady."

Mehr watched the shadows of the daiva shifting in the dreamfire's light.

"A favor," Mehr said. "You'll owe me a favor. That's all."

Lalita

Lalita stood in the dark of a hallway in her home. She could smell the incense of the approaching storm, mingled with the jasmine scent of her own hair, recently washed and oiled, now bound at the nape of her neck in a hasty knot. Her neck was damp with sweat. She breathed in and out in a steady, slow rhythm even as her hands trembled at her sides.

Below her, echoing up from the central courtyard of her home, came the sound of a woman weeping.

"Tell us where your mistress is." The man's voice echoed up from below, mingling with the sound of tears. "Or I swear, I will make sure your whole family is hounded out of the city for protecting Amrithi scum. Is that what you want?"

"I don't know, I don't know!" howled a voice. "I don't know where she is!"

Farida, fool girl, could have told them that Lalita was likely to be on the roof, watching the storm approach, or in her study as she had been that morning, writing a message to Mehr. Instead the maidservant wept and claimed to know nothing, all the while begging for mercy. Lalita would have liked to believe Farida was showing her an astonishing level of loyalty, but it seemed far more likely that fear had entirely obliterated the girl's mind.

Lalita closed her eyes. Controlled her breathing. There was a rhythm to maintaining a semblance of calm in the face of danger. It was something akin to a rite.

When Lalita left Irinah, for the first time, she was just fifteen. Her grandmother had given Lalita the last of her coin and taken Lalita's face between her hands. Lalita remembered, still, her dark eyes and the uncomfortable curl of her lip, scarred from a decade-old encounter with a lowly Ambhan official who'd taken it in his head to make an example of an Amrithi woman who dared to attempt trade with a village under his purview.

Hala, she'd said. *Little one. You're the cleverest one of my blood, but your mind will only take you so far. No matter what you do, they will discover you one day. Don't argue, child. Listen to me. When you make a mistake—when they find you—don't try to save your money or your possessions. Don't try to be clever. Save your skin first, Hala. Run.*

Lalita was not Hala anymore. She had not been Hala in a long time. But she recalled her grandmother's words, as she stood still in the hall of her haveli, dressed in her Chand garb and her Chand name, and thought of all the mistakes that had led her here, into a dark corridor, with nowhere to run to.

Lalita's first mistake, of course, had been returning to Irinah. But homesickness was a curious thing. For a small handful of years, she'd basked in the comforts of Ambha, its distant white-peaked mountains, its lush lakes and sweet air. Its wealthy men. Then she'd begun to yearn, despite herself, for Irinah: for its dreamfire, its daiva, for the scents and sights of home.

Irinah was not a safe place for someone like her. She'd known that. There was too high a chance of her being recognized as an Amrithi, too high a chance of a daiva seeking her out for her ancestry, for her blood. And yet Lalita had come home.

She'd always prided herself on being a practical woman, but it was homesickness that had brought her back. Homesickness, and the feeling that she was losing herself, day by day: that somehow her hidden self was slipping, ever so steadily, from her grasp.

"Don't you know who we are, girl?" said another voice. Male, again.

"No, my lord," Farida whimpered.

Her second mistake had been ignoring Usha's warning.

One of your kitchen boys was questioned by a nobleman, Usha had said. *Somebody knows, or thinks they know the truth about you. You should run now, while you still can.*

But Lalita had not held her grandmother's advice as close as she should have. She had wanted to say farewell to Mehr. She'd needed time to arrange the transport of her possessions. Excuse after excuse had kept her feet firmly on the city's ground, when in truth she'd simply wanted to cling to the life she'd worked so hard to build. Ah, she was a fool.

"We're no petty lords. We have a higher purpose than most of the nobility," he boasted. "We're devotees of the Saltborn. Do you know what that means?"

Farida whimpered out a no.

"We serve the Emperor's will. You know who the Emperor is at least, don't you?"

There was a chorus of ugly laughter.

She was not sure how many men stood below her. She didn't dare look through the lattice window facing the courtyard, for fear they would see her. She wondered if these boastful lords— these squabbling Ambhan children, who had no higher purpose in life than wreaking destruction on their Emperor's behalf— would have thought to set guards on all the exits from the household. She considered whether men who had never worked for their survival would think to look in the servants' corridor she now stood in, a narrow passage lit by one latticed window and guttering candles set into alcoves along the wall. She hoped not.

Her third mistake had been carelessness. She'd grown soft

after living all these years in Jah Irinah. She'd made no secret of her visits to the Governor's half-Amrithi daughter. She had danced her rites in her room alone at sunrise, and kept her Amrithi dagger close. Taking on a Chand name had only provided her a thin veneer of security. She should have given up her rites. She should have discarded her dagger. She should have left Mehr well alone.

But Mehr's mother had been her friend, once—her only friend, in fact, when she had returned to Jah Irinah as a young courtesan heartsick and hungry for home. Ruhi had asked her to care for Mehr—begged her—and Lalita had loved both mother and daughter too well to refuse. She'd never found the will in her heart since to untangle Mehr from her life.

There was more shouting—and more sobbing—from below her. Through it, Lalita heard another noise. To her right, the candle flickered. She heard the scuff of a footstep. Lalita turned sharply, her hand reaching instinctively for the dagger in her sash.

The flash of a familiar face in candlelight. Usha.

Ah, Gods.

"I killed a man at the exit from the kitchen," Usha said, her voice very soft. "Go there now."

"Come with me," Lalita whispered.

Usha shook her head.

"They need a distraction," murmured Usha. "And I need to make sure they let Farida go."

In the flickering light Usha's face was resolute, her jaw firm. There was a spatter of blood on her cheek.

There are too many men, Lalita thought. *And only one of you.*

Lalita thought absurdly of the way her grandmother had taken her face in her hands, a lifetime ago. She wanted to place her hand on Usha's jaw and give a shape to a farewell that already felt wrenchingly, terribly final. She wanted to tell Usha to save her skin first, to leave Lalita to the fate she'd built for herself, and *run*. Her hands were trembling. She didn't reach out.

"I can't leave you here," she said instead.

Usha smiled wanly.

"I'll be fine," she said.

There was a commotion below them; a scream, and then silence.

If the noblemen found Lalita, she would be the one screaming. She knew very well what Ambhan noblemen thought of the worth of Amrithi. She knew the cruelty they could inflict, before they forced her from the city and the life she had so carefully, laboriously constructed for herself. She thought of her grandmother's scarred lip, her warning, and shivered.

Usha gestured with her free hand, the other one tight on her scimitar. *Go.*

Usha slipped away, toward the courtyard, and Lalita headed to the right. The exit from the kitchen was ideal. It led out to a poorer district of Jah Irinah, winding and crowded and likely to be unfamiliar to the noblemen who had come to punish Lalita for tainting their city with her heathen presence. They wanted to protect the people of Jah Irinah from her, but—thank the Gods—they knew very little about the lives of the ones who were not of their rank.

She reached the kitchens. Pushed open the door and stepped out into the street. The body of the man Usha had killed lay against the wall, in a pool of its own dark blood. She murmured a curse, averting her eyes, and finally let the panic she'd been holding at bay take her. She sucked in a breath and began to run.

Her final mistake was tangled in with all the rest: She had wanted, so very deeply, to perform the Rite of Dreaming at Mehr's side. She'd wanted to do so for Mehr's sake, because she loved the girl dearly, as if she were her own child. But most of all she had wanted to dance the rite for herself. The Rite of

Dreaming was a rite for worship and joy, for history and family, but most of all, it was a rite for dancing with clan. Lalita had wanted, just for a moment, to perform the rite with someone who was clan to her. Just for a moment, Lalita had wanted to belong.

She'd always understood that keeping even the barest bones of her heritage demanded a terrible price. But she had kept her heritage regardless. That was her gravest error.

Now all that was left for her was to survive.

CHAPTER THREE

On the morning when the sky above the city began to bleed from pale blue into the dark jewel tones of dreamfire, Mehr knew the storm had finally arrived. She went onto the roof with one disapproving guardswoman to accompany her. She couldn't stay long. The guardswoman was muttering darkly about Lady Maryam, gazing up at the sky with obvious trepidation. Mehr took a brief moment to stare at the dreamfire, to snatch in the scent and the sight of it, then returned inside.

Once she was back in her chambers, a maid handed her a message from Lalita, confirming that she would be at the Governor's residence by evening.

Worry knotted Mehr's stomach and wouldn't fade. Maryam's words wouldn't leave her. It would be a relief when Lalita arrived.

After the rite was done, she would speak to Lalita about the things Maryam had said to her, the whispers Sara had confided. She would find a way to keep herself and her family safe.

The hours passed and the sky darkened. Rather than waiting impatiently for Lalita, Mehr dressed. She put on her fanned skirt and her blouse. She wound indigo cloth around her body, draping it so it would move easily with her body and also protect her from the storm. The red silk she drew around her waist—and tucked her dagger securely into a fold, where she could feel the promise of it against her skin.

She marked her hands and feet with red. Her eyes she lined with black, and touched her forehead with ash also rimmed with red. She looked at herself in the mirror in her bedchamber. The woman who stared back at her had eyes like midnight and skin like rosewood, a solemn mouth and a forehead tipped vermilion. Sky and earth and blood.

She was ready.

She practiced the first few steps. She moved in the flickering shadows that fell through the screen wall. The sky was shifting, bright and changeable. The glow sharpened into white lightning against color. Eventually Mehr gave up on practice and simply stared at the whorls of dreamfire waiting to fall and the great winged shadows that flitted through them.

Time passed. It was night, deep night, and Lalita still hadn't come.

Mehr could think of a dozen reasons why Lalita hadn't yet arrived. Perhaps she had fallen ill. Perhaps she had been forced to leave unexpectedly. Perhaps, perhaps. But all those excuses felt flimsy, when Mehr remembered the wistful yearning in Lalita's voice, when she spoke of dancing the Rite of Dreaming at Mehr's side. She remembered Lalita's exhaustion. Her careful words.

I have drawn some unwanted attention.

The air shimmered. With frightening suddenness, the dreamfire poured from sky to earth like water, coils of light exploding into facets of brightness. It drenched the city in its glow. The air crackled.

The dreamfire was falling.

Mehr's heart was in her throat.

The dreamfire was falling, and Lalita was not here.

Mehr touched the hilt of her dagger, taking comfort in its

presence. Words and warnings swarmed in her head. Something had happened to Lalita. She knew it.

We can be clan to each other, Lalita had said. Well, Mehr wouldn't abandon what little clan she had. She walked to the entrance of her chambers and looked out into the corridor. Empty. No one would be leaving the household today, not while the storm hung over the city. They were all hiding from it, most likely.

Good. That would work in her favor.

She swathed herself in a heavy robe and slipped boots onto her red-stained feet. If Lalita was in danger, if she couldn't come to Mehr, then Mehr would go to her. She would go out into the city and find Lalita. She wouldn't let her be hurt.

That, of course, was easier said than done. She couldn't simply leave the women's quarters. As one of the noblewomen of the Governor's household, she was protected by high walls and maids and guards. When she went into public, she went with an armed entourage and traveled securely in a palanquin veiled with gauze. Outside the palanquin she wore a heavy robe to conceal her features. The robe she wore now, in fact. From a distance it was like the robes all women wore, regardless of status: plain and neat and suitable for concealment and for protection from the elements. Only closer inspection revealed the fine quality of the fabric and the swatches of rich color that lined the interior of the sleeves and the hem. It would still provide the anonymity Mehr required. She would have to do without the rest. There would be no palanquin or armed entourage today.

If she wanted to leave the household quietly, she would need help.

She slipped through the marble corridors on light feet, barely breathing, trusting that her dancer feet would know how to move softly. She made her way to the nursery.

She was in luck. Sara was leaving Arwa's chambers, her arms

full of clothes. Mehr held a finger to lips, bidding her to be silent, and gestured at Sara to follow her.

When they were alone, she asked, "Have you used the blood?"

"Yes, my lady," Sara said. Her eyes were dark and watchful. Perhaps she knew what was coming. "Is that all you wanted to ask, my lady?"

Mehr shook her head.

"I am sorry, Sara," she said. She drew the hood of her robe over her face; dark netting covered her view of Sara's stricken expression in a dim haze. "It seems I'll be needing that favor far sooner than I expected."

Because of the double-edged sword of her status, Mehr knew very little about the world beyond the women's quarters. But Sara did. She guided Mehr swiftly away from familiar chambers into the winding passageways of the servants' quarters. Here there was no marble. The walls and floor were bare and windowless, the corridors lit by torches. The farther they walked, the more strongly Mehr could smell the scent of the kitchens, a rich odor of burnt oil and spices.

"This way," Sara whispered. She gestured at Mehr to follow her.

They crept down a staircase and came to a barred door. "We receive deliveries here," said Sara. When she caught Mehr's questioning look, she went on. "Supplies, my lady," said Sara. "For the kitchens."

Of course. With so little food able to grow in the desert, Jah Irinah relied on imports from more fertile regions of the Empire. Mehr knew that. What she hadn't considered—had never thought to consider—was the need for a delivery entrance near the kitchens, and its usefulness to her as an exit from her home. She'd never thought about it because she'd never had to.

She grimaced inwardly at her own ignorance. Despite her best efforts, she knew so little.

No more. Tonight was a step in the right direction: out of the comfort of known things into the whirling, terrifying chaos of the light.

Together they hoisted the bar holding the doors shut and lowered it to the floor, struggling to muffle the sound of metal clanking against stone. By the time they were done, they were both breathing heavily. Under her heavy cloak, Mehr's skin was covered in sweat. She ran a hand over her forehead, staining her knuckles with red and black ash.

"Please don't make me go with you," Sara said quietly. Her jaw was firm, her eyes hard with desperation. No matter what Mehr said, she would *not* go. What lay beyond the door terrified her more than Mehr ever could.

"You've paid your debt," said Mehr. She pressed a hand to the door. "Keep the blood close. It will protect you."

She shoved the door open. Light poured in. Dust, glowing like slivers of candlelight, crept over the curve of her boots.

Sara stepped back. Mehr strode outside.

She was consumed instantly. The light moved around her wildly, whipping sand up from the earth to abrade her skin wherever it was exposed. She drew her hood hastily down over her face to keep the dust from getting into her eyes or her mouth. She couldn't let herself be afraid. There was no going back now. Instead she steeled her resolve and started walking.

Mehr hugged close to the perimeter of the Governor's residence, searching for the hint of a familiar path away from the palace toward the city streets. It was a more difficult task than she'd expected. She'd thought the dreamfire would light her way, but now that she was standing in the midst of it, she realized it was worse than darkness. She could barely see a few steps in front of her. Everything was light, and the light was blinding. If there were guards nearby—and there had to be guards—Mehr had no way of avoiding them. She had to trust that the fact that she was equally invisible to them would protect her. As long as she didn't walk headfirst into a unit of men, she'd be safe.

It took her far longer than she would have liked, but eventually Mehr found her way to one of the long, deserted streets of the city proper. Near the Governor's residence the houses belonged to the wealthy, and it showed. Here the light was thinner, and Mehr could see that the wide, paved streets were lined with large white havelis, mansions with courtyard gardens and ornately carved verandas. Mehr had been to Lalita's home twice before, and both times she had traveled by palanquin through streets just like these. Those journeys had been long and stifled, with the curtains shut around her and her cloak heavy as a shroud. But she'd been curious enough, hungry enough, to fold back one of the curtains and drink in the sights with her eyes. She'd memorized those journeys. She should have known the way.

The city was so changed around her that her memories were little use. She walked through the storm for a little longer, pushing hard through the beating force of the wind, before she finally accepted that she was no closer to Lalita's home than she had been when she'd been standing in her own chambers, watching the dreamfire fall.

The dreamfire was everywhere now. It was in the air she breathed, in the sweat at the nape of her neck. She could feel the strength of it churning the city into a storm. The buildings were drenched in light, debris flying through the air as if the world had tipped on its side and sent everything sprawling. Even the earth felt like it was moving beneath her feet. It was dizzying, terrifying.

Exhilarating.

She was lost, but everything inside her was aflame with

nameless joy, the feeling of a perfectly danced rite or the bright recognition in a daiva's eyes. She was lost, but her body knew this storm. It knew it was home.

She breathed in steadily. She tried to keep her mind clear of euphoria. Joy wouldn't help her right now. Frustration wouldn't either. She had to *think*.

She couldn't trust her memories, or her knowledge, or her own emotions. But she could trust the dreamfire. She could let its current guide her, move her like water, like blood.

When you dance with the Rite of Dreaming, you dance with the Gods. Her mother had told her that. Right now it felt like only divine intervention would get her where she needed to be.

The thought of dancing the Rite of Dreaming filled her with fear and exhilaration in equal measure. There were rites that Mehr had danced so often that she knew them in her bones. The Rite of Dreaming was not one of them. She had never performed it, not truly, not in a storm with the light of dreamfire pouring over her like rain. She had no fellow Amrithi to perform it with.

There were so many reasons that the rite was beyond her grasp. But here, in the heart of the dreamfire storm . . . for Lalita's sake and for her own, she would try.

Mehr knelt down and slipped off her boots. She pressed her bare feet hard against the ground. All rites required the feel of the ground on skin, the ritual connection between soil and sky and flesh. Without it the dance had no meaning, no heart. But the ground was rough on her soft soles, and she knew the longer her feet were exposed to the elements, the more she'd suffer. She bit down on the inside of her cheek. This wouldn't be easy.

She sucked in a slow, even breath. She straightened up, finding her balance. Then she raised her arms slowly, cupping her palms together, allowing her back to bend like the arc of a falling star. The first step in the rite.

The wind howled around her, threatening to throw her off

balance. Dreamfire poured into her cupped hands. Her head tipped back, and her hood fell. She felt the wind catch her braid, making it lash out behind her. She closed her eyes tight.

Here was the moment when she was supposed to take another person's hands in her own. She was supposed to part her palms and press one against a fellow Amrithi's hand, catching the light between them. She was supposed to move with her clan in a seamless dance, a sharing of light and dreams and creation.

With no one to reach for, Mehr lowered her arms. Eyes closed, she held one palm out against the air. Wind and dust rushed over her skin.

Take me to my clan, Mehr thought. It was a desperate prayer. If dreamfire was the power of the Gods making and unmaking the universe, shaping creation in their great sleep, then perhaps they could create this small thing for her: a path through the chaos. A road.

Take me to Lalita's home. Let me help her. Please.

For a long moment nothing happened. She felt the wind howl and rake over her, felt the sand bite at her face like a dozen tiny needles. She felt her own smallness. Who was she, to expect the dreams of the Gods to bend for her? She was nothing. A rich man's daughter, an illegitimate get, a girl too foolish and too willfully strange to stay within the safe confines of a privileged life. Not an Ambhan, not an Amrithi. Nothing.

The dreamfire coiled softly around her wrist. And tugged.

Her first instinct was to wrench herself free, but Mehr resisted it. She let the dreamfire draw her along. Awe and terror clogged her throat.

The dreamfire was guiding her, for good or ill. She'd asked for this. Now she had to follow it.

She could feel the dreamfire begin winding over her limbs, clutching at her wrists and her ankles. It was all heat without the strength of flesh. It couldn't force her to follow it, couldn't drag her along if she resisted its urging. One wrong move, and the tenuous bond between her and the dreamfire would tear apart.

New as the Rite of Dreaming was, Mehr had been dancing all her life. She was very, very good at avoiding mistakes.

She whirled on firm, sharp feet through street after street. Her skin burned. Her eyes stayed shut against the ferocity of the wind. She shaped no sigils with her hands, no carefully chosen stances with her feet. But she followed the urging of the dreamfire, moving with each tug of light. Her whole focus was on the dreamfire and the dreamfire alone.

She could hear voices on the wind—the whispers of daiva. She felt the soles of her feet begin to ache, then felt the ache sharpen to agony. But she didn't stop.

She didn't know how long she danced. She only knew that her breath was growing short, that her mouth was full of sand and she didn't know how much longer she could go on. Then, with a suddenness that astounded her, the dreamfire let her go. She stumbled to a stop, falling to her knees and drawing her hood hastily back down over her face so that she could suck in a few deep lungfuls of air untainted by dust. When she felt more herself, she raised her head and peered through the light.

Miracle of miracles. Mehr was outside Lalita's home.

Lalita's haveli built from honeyed sandstone, with a veranda marked by the subtle beauty of stone vines and flowers. She felt their shapes with her fingers as she blindly traced her way up the steps and under the cover of the columned entrance.

She'd made it. Somehow. She turned and looked back out at the storm.

She couldn't believe what had just happened to her.

Mehr swallowed. She couldn't let her mind linger on it now. Emotion could come later. Right now she needed to find Lalita.

She pressed a hand flat against the door, testing, expecting it to be securely barred. It creaked open.

Dark foreboding welled up in her chest. She touched the fingertips of her free hand to her dagger and slipped quietly inside.

The hallway was unlit. The lanterns hanging on the walls had guttered, but only recently, and were still giving off coils of smoke. Mehr pressed the door shut behind her.

Mehr walked deeper into the building. No guards forced Mehr to halt. There was no sign of Lalita, and no sign of any of the household staff. The rooms lining the hallway were black and silent. She slowed to a crawl, eyes and ears open. She could barely see. All she could hear was the roar of the storm and the steady thump of her own heart.

She was near the inner courtyard now, the garden that lay at the center of the haveli. She still hadn't seen a single soul.

Her sore, aching feet pressed down into something wet.

She froze, her pulse frantic in her ears. Then she kneeled down and touched the ground. The liquid was too thick to be water. She raised her fingers up.

There was blood beneath her feet.

She drew her dagger out of her sash.

There was a trail of blood leading down the hall to the inner courtyard. She followed it. She'd come this far. She had a duty to fulfill. She reached the doors to the courtyard and opened them wide.

On the steps leading down to the courtyard lay a body. Mehr ran toward it, then kneeled, furious and afraid.

Not Lalita. The body wasn't Lalita's.

"Usha," Mehr said. "Usha, can you hear me?"

Usha looked up at Mehr. Even that small movement was a struggle. Her gaze was unfocused and her face was spangled with dust.

"Lady Mehr?" she whispered. Blood oozed from her lips.

"We need to get you out of the storm," Mehr said.

Usha shook her head weakly. "Shouldn't...be here."

She clearly couldn't get up on her own, but Mehr didn't know where to touch her. Her clothes were ripped, her skin dark with blood and bruises. When Mehr tucked her dagger away again and carefully took hold of her under the arms, Usha gave a bitten-off cry of agony.

Usha was badly wounded. That at least was obvious. Mehr moved her as gently as she was able, whispering grim apologies as she went. Once they were inside the haveli, Mehr slammed the courtyard doors shut behind them, blocking out the storm. Usha lay silently on the floor, eyes closed.

Lalita's guardswoman had always looked invulnerable: confident enough to be kind, her strength draped around her like armor. But the armor was gone now. Wounded, she was all too mortal. Her body was curved protectively around the steadily darkening stain on the front of her tunic. Her breathing was labored and her skin gray.

"What happened here?" Mehr asked. She could hear her own voice trembling. "Who hurt you?"

Usha was silent for a long time. Then she said, "*Go.*"

"I'll find help," Mehr said. She was worse than useless to Usha on her own. She knew nothing about treating wounds.

Usha seemed to have understood, at least in part.

"Go," she said vehemently. "Before... find *you.*"

Mehr raced through the house. No gentle, careful footsteps now. She threw open the doors to the street and shouted for help. The storm swallowed up her voice instantly. Useless. There was no one outside to hear her anyway. The rich residents of the surrounding homes were hidden away behind their shutters and their gates. When she forced her way through the wind, slammed her fists against another door, she was met with silence. The storm had probably swallowed the sound of her fists too.

She threw herself against the doors of another haveli, then

another. But no one would answer. She screamed at the dream-fire. Screamed again, harder still, because she was furious and this was useless, *she* was useless. She couldn't help Usha. They were on their own.

Mehr found her way back into Lalita's haveli. She went back to Usha's side. She kneeled down on the floor beside her. Usha didn't look any better, but at least her eyes were open again.

"The other servants," Mehr said softly, meeting her gaze. "Are any of them going to come back?"

"All left," Usha said in a shaky voice. She was shivering. "Ran. Cowards."

Mehr nodded. She grabbed the hem of her robe and slipped it off, covering Usha's body in its dark weight. Usha murmured a thank-you, but her shivering didn't abate. She pressed her face against the long, fanned sweep of Mehr's skirt. Mehr pressed a hand to her forehead and Usha gave a sigh. The feel of Mehr beside her seemed to comfort her.

I'm sorry, thought Mehr. *I'm so sorry, Usha. I don't know how to help you.*

Mehr said none of it. It wasn't Usha's job to give her absolution.

"Where is Lalita?" Mehr asked quietly.

"They came," Usha murmured. "Knew they would."

"Who came, Usha? Please."

"Salt," she whispered, and closed her eyes. "*Tired.*"

She didn't pass away then. It would have been easier if she had. But she said nothing more over the hours that followed. Her breath rattled in and out of her lungs. Her lips foamed blood. Mehr watched as she gritted her teeth against the pain, her eyes glassy, all her attention focused inward. Mehr thought of her dagger, thought of ending Usha's suffering. It would have been easy. It might even have been kind.

As the dreamfire quieted beyond the haveli's walls, as Mehr kept vigil, Usha's breath finally faded into silence. Mehr stayed with her until the very end, her dagger a heavy presence at her side.

It didn't take long for her father's men to find her. Ever since the storm had calmed and the sky had lightened with morning, Mehr had been walking listlessly through the streets of Jah Irinah. In her blood-spattered Amrithi clothes, her feet bare, she was a hard sight to miss.

They surrounded her on their horses, their steel armor gleaming sharply in the light. Their commander dismounted. His gaze flickered over her, taking the sight of her in.

"Lady Mehr," he said. "Are you injured?"

She shook her head.

"The blood is not mine," she said. Her voice sounded hoarse to her own ears. She swallowed. "I'm unhurt."

The commander nodded, mouth thin, and looked away from her. Around him, his men were wearing identical expressions of embarrassment. Noblewomen rarely showed their faces to men outside their own families. They wore hooded robes in public; they traveled in veiled palanquins when they left the safety of the home. For Mehr to be barefaced before them, before *everyone*, was a breach of her dignity. Worse still, without the protection of her veil, dressed in her Amrithi garb, she was painfully, undeniably foreign. Half Amrithi. Heathen. Outsider.

The sight of her shamed them. It should have shamed her.

She was too numb, and too tired, to care.

The commander arranged for a palanquin to carry Mehr home. She was met at the women's quarters by a group of grim-faced guardswomen, who ushered her inside without words.

Mehr was allowed to bathe and redress in a clean tunic and pajami. She didn't argue when one of the maids gathered up her Amrithi clothes and took them away. She had no energy to fight. It was hard enough to simply obey as she was poked and prodded, as her hair was combed roughly and bound back into a hasty braid, as she was ushered along the familiar halls of the women's quarters toward a corridor that led to her father's chambers.

At the end of the corridor lay the room Mehr had most dreaded visiting in her childhood, the room where she'd been brought to be scolded and punished for misbehavior. The Governor's Study. She could still remember the terror it had once inspired in her. An echo of that old dread rippled through her now, as a guardswoman opened the door and ushered Mehr inside.

The difference between the women's quarters and the Governor's Study was impossible to ignore. The women's quarters were Maryam's domain, elegantly decorated with silks and jewels and cool marble, but the study belonged entirely to Mehr's father. Every inch was stamped with his mark. The furnishings were dark, the walls unmarked and austere. There were great thick books and sheaves of paper piled on a table set at the center of the room. No fine gems and delicate touches here. This was a purely masculine space. Here, Maryam's power ended and the Governor's power—the power of swords and steel, currency and politics and *men*—began.

Her father and Maryam were seated, waiting for her.

"Sit," her father said. His voice was rumbling, soft.

Mehr kneeled down woodenly. When she met her father's eyes she saw him flinch before recovering himself.

Governor Suren ruled one of the most barbaric yet holy reaches of the Empire on the Emperor's behalf. He had hundreds of men at his command. He was built broad and imposing, and his eyes were sharp as steel. In the rich jet and ivory of his clothing, his hair swept back in a turban, he looked every inch the statesman and soldier. He was not a man who showed weakness easily.

But Mehr looked so very, very much like her mother.

"You've disgraced yourself," said her father. He said it without inflection, without feeling. It would have been better if he had shouted.

"A woman is dead," Mehr said quietly. "And my friend is missing. I left to try to help them."

And what a waste it had been. She'd failed. In her father's face she saw that knowledge reflected back at her.

"I know where you went. I know how my guards found you," he said. "Your face bare, your skin—tainted." A heavy breath. "I have given you so much freedom, Mehr. I have been generous. And you—you have used my kindness to ruin yourself."

"You've brought scandal on us," Maryam added. Her voice trembled. "And you've disgraced yourself." Mehr saw her father's fingers touch Maryam's tenderly. Mehr looked away from them both.

"What does it matter, if I am disgraced?" Mehr asked numbly. Her father was silent. Maryam was silent. They left her room to dig her own grave. She wet her lips, which still tasted of sand and the rich iron of blood. "What will disgrace do to me, Father? Are you afraid I will stand in the way of Arwa's marriage? That I will drag her down with me?"

From the periphery of her vision, she saw Maryam's eyes narrow.

"It doesn't matter," Mehr repeated. "Arwa and I were born ruined. You know it to be true. You know what people think of Amrithi." *You know what your own wife thinks*, she did not say. She raised her arm up, holding it to the light. "My skin was tainted a long time ago. But ah, perhaps Arwa's skin will spare her my fate."

"Don't say such things," her father murmured.

"I was born ruined and without the legal protection of your name," Mehr said. Bitterness bubbled in her blood. She lowered her arm. "My mother kept true to her people's laws. She never wed you. She never wore your seal, and you never wore hers. And now she is gone." Mehr's voice cracked. "In the eyes of the Empire we are less than nothing, Arwa and I. You should never have raised us here. You should have known that no matter what we would do, we would be judged as tainted by our blood. In the eyes of the Empire, we are less than nothing, Father."

"I allowed your mother to keep her customs," her father acknowledged. "But in raising you as I have, I have kept mine. Make no mistake, Mehr: You are my daughter. You have been raised in my household, fed with my food, clothed from my coffers. You are your mother's daughter..." He faltered. "But you are also mine. And half your blood is Ambhan, noble and strong."

Mehr said nothing. When it was clear she couldn't or wouldn't respond, her father continued.

"You try to stay true to your mother's customs," he said softly. "For that I don't fault you. But when you left your quarters, you betrayed your duty as *my* child. And that betrayal, daughter, comes with a price."

He leaned forward and pressed an item into her hands. She looked down. Pressed against her palm was a circle of carved stone, marked in Ambhan script with the names of the men of the family who had come before her. She saw her own name, set at its heart. Her blood ran cold.

Her seal. This was her marriage seal.

"You are not only Amrithi. You cannot eschew all vows and contracts as your mother's people do," he said, in that same terrible, soft voice. "I have raised and treasured you as an Ambhan noblewoman, and like all my countrywomen, you have the right to make one contract." He closed her fingers around the seal. "The choice is wholly yours, Mehr. But it is a choice you must make."

Mehr's throat closed.

"Maryam has agreed to chaperone you," her father went on. "She will accompany you to her family holdings in Hara. If no courtiers there suit you, she will take you to Numriha. Find a good man, Mehr. Give him your seal. Wear his proudly. I believe you will find a way to be happy."

He spoke of other provinces of the Empire: Numriha, with its mines and its artisans; Hara, lush and green, fed by rivers and ocean alike. Mehr had heard of them, and knew guards and servants within the women's quarters who hailed from them, but she had never seen them in person. She had never left Irinah.

Her father hadn't mentioned Ambha. That, she understood. Ambha was no simple province. It was the jewel of the Empire, its beating heart, where the Emperor ruled. The greatest of the nobility, the old Ambhan bloodlines, all hailed from Ambha itself. No province had ever been ruled by a Governor who was not of Ambhan blood, born from the great Ambhan families who served in the Emperor's court to this day.

It was certainly no place for a half-Amrithi daughter.

Mehr raised her head.

"I watched a woman die today," Mehr said. Her voice sounded like a stranger's. "A good woman. I held her in my arms as she passed. I watched her go. And now you're exiling me? Sending me away from everything I know?"

"What you did in the storm, Mehr, the way you behaved, the rite you performed…" He paused, and shook his head. "I do it out of love," her father said gently. "Beyond Irinah, you can begin again."

"Begin again," Mehr echoed. "I see."

Leaving Irinah would place her beyond her tangible heritage. There would be no daiva to seek her blood, and no dreamfire to answer her prayers. Beyond Irinah she could hide her Amrithi heritage. She could give up her rites, her dagger, her dreams. She could claim to have a Chand mother, perhaps, to explain her dark skin and the distinctly un-Ambhan cast to her features. There would certainly be men willing to believe the lie for the sake of allying with the daughter of the Governor of Irinah.

She could begin again by erasing herself.

"You're not safe here anymore, Mehr," said her father.

Mehr looked hard into her father's steel eyes, eyes that were nothing like her own.

"You should never have kept me and Arwa," Mehr said. "You should have sent us away with our mother. We don't belong in the Empire."

Her father didn't flinch. But it didn't matter. Mehr knew she had struck him a blow.

"You're confined to your chambers indefinitely," he said. He looked away from her. Mehr squeezed the seal tight between her fingers.

Maryam looked at Mehr with a hard expression on her face and clasped her husband's hand tight, in a gesture that was both protective and possessive.

You'll be gone soon, Maryam's eyes said. *I'll make sure of that.*

"Go now, Mehr," she said, in a voice far softer than the look in her eyes. "Your father and I have a great deal to discuss."

Mehr stood and left without another word.

CHAPTER FOUR

Alone in her chambers, Mehr lay down on her divan and wept. She thought of Usha and of Lalita, of blood on her clothes and the sand beneath her feet; she thought of the dreamfire clutching her wrists and ankles, of awe and terror and the absolute helplessness of watching someone die. The tears poured out of her uncontrollably. She wept and wept and wept. Eventually exhaustion dragged her down into a restless sleep. When she woke, hours later, she felt as fragile as glass.

Earlier she had flung her seal to the other end of the room, too heartsick and furious to look at it. She collected it now, threading it onto a length of silk and hanging it around her neck. She washed her face clean with a damp cloth, rubbing away the salt and sleep marking her cheeks. She looked into her mirror. A worn, tired face stared back at her.

The seal was heavy. It had to be, to carry the weight of her family's history. It was marked with dozens of names, minuscule carvings that traced Mehr's lineage back over three hundred years, generation upon generation, to the first soldier who had followed the Maha from Ambha into the neighboring lands of Chand and Numriha and Hara, conquering them all in turn and forging the Empire. One of those ancestors had been at the

Maha's side when he had conquered Irinah and made it the seat of his everlasting temple.

She touched the grooves on the stone with gentle fingers. She understood that in giving her a seal marked with his ancestors, her father had tried to show how much he loved her. Illegitimate daughters had no right to ancestral names. Yet here against Mehr's skin was a heritage lovingly offered, the unspoken right to call herself a daughter of Suren, a granddaughter of Karan, a child of many men and as many nameless women.

She knew her father loved her. But Mehr knew, too, that love would not be enough to sway him from his decision.

Mehr would have to marry.

A daughter belonged to her father's household until the day she reached adulthood and her seal was placed in her hands. Ambhan noblewomen did not make contracts; they did not own property or offer their loyalty or their service. They were treasured and sheltered, protected by their men. But their right to choose their own husband was sacred, and the choice could not be taken from them.

When her fifteenth, sixteenth, seventeenth years had passed with no mention of marriage or her seal, Mehr had been grateful for her father's kindness. Amrithi did not make contracts, but as a noblewoman, Mehr had always known she would eventually be required to wed, but she had hoped to find a husband in Irinah. She'd hoped to stay close to Arwa and to the desert she loved. At the very least, she'd hoped for time. Time to watch Arwa grow. Time to come to terms with the business of tying her soul to another man's soul, and leaving the life she had so carefully carved for herself in her father's household.

All that had changed now.

In finally giving Mehr her seal, her father had placed a bitter message squarely in her hands: *Marry whom you choose. You're not mine to keep any longer.*

It's time for you to be gone. He had ensured that she would never have the husband and home in Irinah she'd hoped for.

She knew what was coming: carefully chaperoned meetings with lowly courtiers and wealthy merchants, first in Hara and then Numriha. Mehr wouldn't choose any of them. Not at first. And then, inevitably, Mehr would relent. Give in. No Ambhan woman could be forced to marry, but there were many ways in the world to make a person bend. Time would wear her down. She would choose one of the men and give him her seal. Once he placed his own seal around her neck, once their lineages and their bodies were joined, she would be bound for life to an alien land. Exiled for good.

The thought of leaving Irinah left her hollow and full of unanswerable fears. She would not be able to keep her Amrithi traditions, she knew that now. She would be forced to discard her mother's culture to keep herself—and her family—safe from the Emperor's displeasure. But what kind of marriage would she have, built as it would be on deceits large and small? What kind of man would she find herself wedded to?

What if she never returned to Irinah—never saw its desert and its storms? What if she never saw *Arwa* again?

It was a painful thought, sharpened to a knife edge by the knowledge that she had been losing Arwa slowly for years. Maryam had made sure of that.

Grief welled up hot in her blood again. She bit down on her lower lip, holding it in. Maryam had been right after all. Her father had finally stopped letting his guilt control him. Fear had taken its place. Mehr understood his fear. She had felt it in her own bones. The Amrithi were not safe in Irinah. Clans had vanished; Lalita was gone; Usha was dead. Mehr was simply not Ambhan enough to be safe in this household, this land, any longer.

But she was Ambhan enough to be sent away. Ambhan enough to marry and leave Irinah, and pretend to be the good noblewoman she was not.

When Mehr lay back down on the divan, when she curled up like a creature inside its own shell, the edges of the seal pressed into her skin. Mehr breathed against its weight, slow and steady, and tried not to feel like a chained animal, tried not to feel like she was drowning. She tried to feel nothing at all.

A week passed before anyone disturbed her grieving, full of nothing but sleep and tears and the slow wait for her heart to knit back together. She had half expected Maryam to come and gloat, but it was Nahira who hobbled into her bedroom one dull evening without so much as a greeting.

"Oh, no need to stop your wailing for my sake," she said, when Mehr scrambled off the divan and onto her feet. "But now you're up, you'd best make yourself presentable. I've brought you a visitor."

Mehr hastily wiped her face clean. She heard a sound from beyond the door, and then a delighted cry.

"Mehr!"

Arwa rushed toward her and leaped up into her arms. She knocked Mehr off balance instantly. They both fell back on the divan, but Arwa held on tight, muttering joyful nonsense against Mehr's ear. She was warm and smelled of rosewater and her knees were sharp where they dug into Mehr's sides. Mehr pressed a palm to the back of Arwa's head, like she had when Arwa was a baby and needed the support of firm hands to hold her steady.

"Hello, little sister," she murmured. Her heart was light, so light. "What are you doing here?"

"She insisted on coming to see you," Nahira said. "Complain, complain, that's all the girl does. Right now for a moment of peace I'd have taken her to the Emperor himself."

"Where have you *been*?" Arwa cried out, oblivious to her nurse's grumbling. Her eyes shined. "It's been ages and ages, and

I kept waiting for you to come see me, and you didn't." Her grip tightened.

"I'm sorry," said Mehr. "I would have come, but I was..." She hesitated. "I was in trouble."

"How?"

"I disobeyed Father and he told me to stay in my chambers."

"You're too old to be punished," Arwa said stoutly.

"I'm not *that* old, Arwa."

"Is that why you were crying?" Arwa asked. "Because you were punished?" She brushed her fingertips against Mehr's cheeks.

Mehr shook her head. "I'm fine," she said. Her sudden lightness was fragile. She didn't want to shatter it, and she certainly didn't want to pour out her troubles to her little sister. "Tell me, Arwa, did you see the storm?"

It was an obvious attempt to change topic, but Arwa responded with an eager barrage of information.

"I shouldn't have seen it," Arwa confided. "I was supposed to be asleep, but it was so loud that I woke up." She told Mehr about how she had peered out of the window at the dreamfire, watching it twist against the skyline. The maidservants had been in their own quarters. Nahira had been asleep. Arwa had stood all on her own for ages and ages, hours and hours, watching the storm color the sky and the daiva fly through it, until Nahira had finally woken up and dragged her back to bed.

Mehr listened to her silently, marveling at her sister's quicksilver nature. Mehr had been a serious child, thoughtful and quiet, and slow to forget. Arwa was not that sort of girl. She was easily swayed by kind words or cruel, and the beauty of the dreamfire had smoothed away her fears by blinding her with pure wonder.

"You're not afraid of the daiva anymore, then?" Mehr asked her, when Arwa finally seemed to run out of breath.

"I don't know," Arwa said. She frowned. "I don't want one in my room again. Do you think there's going to be another storm, Mehr? I'd like that. It was *so* beautiful."

"It was," Mehr agreed. "But no, I don't think there will be another storm. Not for a long while."

And whenever it came, Mehr wouldn't be here to see it. But Arwa would be. Now that she had heard Arwa's bright, burbling joy, now that she'd seen Arwa's shining eyes and breathless smile, she could take comfort in that. Irinah was as much Arwa's land as it was Mehr's. Blood and bone, they belonged here.

She looked up and found Nahira watching her with hooded eyes. Waiting.

"Come," Mehr said, urging Arwa off the divan. "I have something to show you."

She led Arwa to the array of pots and dyes, bright colors and dark sticks of kohl on the dresser, and told Arwa she had free rein to play with them as she liked. Arwa dug into them with glee. Once she was suitably engrossed, Mehr went to Nahira's side.

"Does Maryam know you're here?" Mehr asked. She kept her voice low, so as not to attract Arwa's attention.

"She doesn't know, and she won't be told," said Nahira. "Don't whisper, girl. Your sister isn't listening." When Mehr continued to look conflicted, Nahira sighed and led her out into the living room.

They sat down on the floor cushions. "The Governor has visitors. Important people, I've been told."

Mehr nodded in understanding. That explained why Maryam would have no time to worry about Mehr. Important visitors—courtiers, perhaps, from Jah Ambha itself—required the attention of the entire household. If Mehr had not been grieving in isolation, she would no doubt have seen the preparations take place. "What do you know?" she asked.

"I know you created a scandal," Nahira said. "Of course

everyone knows that now." She reached into the folds of her shawl. "I know that one of my girls brought me this, and that I would not expect you to part with it lightly." She took out Mehr's dagger. "I know you are in trouble," Nahira said softly. "What do I not know, child?"

Mehr took the dagger. Her hand trembled.

When her Amrithi clothes were taken, her dagger must have been taken with them. But she hadn't noticed. She hadn't cared. How could she have forgotten something so vital, so precious?

When she'd gone out into the storm she'd lost a piece of her old self. That was the only explanation she could think of.

She placed the dagger on the cushion beside her and lifted her seal up, away from where it had been concealed under her clothes. She showed it to Nahira.

"I'm being sent away," she said.

Nahira nodded. Her expression was unreadable. "Tell me the rest," she said.

Mehr told her haltingly about everything that had passed over the last few weeks. She told her about Lalita, and Maryam, about the storm, and Sara's debt to her, and holding Usha as she had died. She didn't cry, and was grateful that, for once, the tears stayed at bay.

Nahira listened silently. When Mehr trailed off she held open her arms.

"Come here," said Nahira.

Mehr leaned forward, letting Nahira embrace her. She drew Mehr to her firmly but not roughly. Her old hands gripped Mehr like iron, but her fingers on her shoulders were so very gentle. Mehr had forgotten how well Nahira understood the complex needs of grieving children. It had been so long since anyone had treated her as a child. She let out a shuddering breath. The coil of tension wound up inside her loosened.

"Hush now," Nahira said. "All is well."

Mehr nodded. When Nahira released her, Mehr tucked her seal away, straightening. She didn't want to be hunched over and miserable any longer. She wanted to be strong. Nahira watched, waiting until Mehr had regained her composure.

"You know you put Sara at great risk," Nahira said finally. Her voice was disapproving.

"I know," said Mehr. She had made a bad choice and dragged Sara along with her. The fault—and the guilt—were all on her shoulders. "Has she been found out? Is she—well?"

"Oh, she's well," said Nahira. "But only by pure luck. People are not tools to be used, Lady Mehr. Don't start following the example of your elders now. You certainly never have before," she added in a mutter.

There was a crash from Mehr's room, then a guilty silence. When Mehr began to move, Nahira shook her head and motioned at Mehr to sit back down.

"She hasn't hurt herself," she said. "The girl's hardier than that." Sure enough, Mehr heard more guilty scuffles emanate from the bedroom.

"I'm never going to see Arwa again," Mehr blurted out. Nahira said nothing, and Mehr clenched her hands into helpless fists. "I don't want marriage. Not yet."

"Well, you can't wait forever," Nahira said, ever practical. "You're older than most girls are when they wed. Think of that."

"Amrithi don't wed at all," Mehr said, somewhat churlishly. "Perhaps I should follow my mother's example."

"You're Ambhan enough that marriage may suit you."

"It doesn't matter if it will suit me or not," Mehr said bitterly. "I have my father's orders."

Nahira made a tutting noise. "You think you have no choice? My lady, marriage is the *only* choice your father's people hold sacred for their women. Use that to your favor. Make a wise decision, and you'll see so much of the child you'll be sick of her."

"What is a wise decision in marriage?" Mehr asked, even though she knew Nahira would laugh at her. And she did. Nahira's laugh was a harsh bark, nearly a cough. She shook her head.

"No one knows, child, though they may claim they do. We Irin marry who we will, and end our marriages when needs be. We don't make a fuss of such things. But an Ambhan marriage is a special beast." Nahira leaned forward conspiratorially. Her Irin eyes were narrowed. "You belong to your father," Nahira said. "And you will belong to any husband you choose. His duties will be your duties, his burdens your burdens. Your immortal soul will be bound to his."

Mehr knew, of course, what an Ambhan marriage was meant to be, but it was strange to hear it spoken aloud. Stranger still to think of marriage when she wore her own seal around her throat. She thought of its weight, its ribbon, the feel of it like a rope around her neck. A chill ran through her.

"Do you truly believe that?" Mehr asked.

"Ambhans do," said Nahira. She gave an exaggerated shrug. "What does it matter, what I believe? I can only tell you this, child: A good choice for you would be a man who doesn't enjoy wielding power over his people."

A man who would give her a long leash.

She thought of her father. He was the only man she had ever truly known. No brothers, no uncles, no cousins. Her father had kept her well concealed for her own safety. Her world was so small. Her heart faltered.

"Are there any men like that?" Mehr asked.

Nahira patted her cheek firmly.

"Don't be foolish," she said. But she said it kindly. "Now, go and help your sister clean up. Try not to scold her if you can."

"I was never very fond of my kohl anyway," Mehr said.

She had barely gotten to her feet when she heard another crash. This time it wasn't the sound of Arwa wreaking chaos, but the reverberation of the doors being slammed open by a guard. The guardswoman was breathing heavily, weighed down by her ceremonial attire. Beneath her golden helm her eyes were afraid.

"Lady Mehr," she said. "You need to come with me immediately. Your father has summoned you to the Lotus Hall."

Despite the guardswoman's urgency, Mehr refused to leave immediately. She dragged Nahira back into her bedroom and left the guardswoman pacing between the floor cushions like a caged tiger. Arwa watched quietly, wide-eyed, as Mehr undressed and Nahira rummaged through her clothes, cursing under her breath. Mehr was too tense to muster up a single word.

The Lotus Hall was the political heart of the Governor's residence. It was in the Lotus Hall that the greats of the Emperor's court were welcomed and lavished with Irinah's treasures. It was in the Lotus Hall that all the political games of the Empire took place.

The politics of the Lotus Hall were the politics of the Empire, and thus it belonged to the realm of men. Married women often attended and watched events unfold, seated veiled in a screened area behind the Governor's dais. The women shared their husbands' duties and burdens, and therefore had good reason to observe politics at work. As an unmarried woman, and an illegitimate one at that, Mehr had only been to the Lotus Hall very rarely.

Why her father wanted her there now, Mehr couldn't fathom. But she wouldn't go unprepared.

The guardswoman had her ceremonial golden garb, symbolic of the wealth of the Empire and Irinah's illustrious place within it. Mehr needed armor of her own.

With Nahira's help, she put on an underskirt of pale rose and a long, layered robe of gossamer white silk. She had no time to apply cosmetics, but she was sure her veil would hide the tiredness in her eyes.

Mehr swept out of her room with her head held high. She drew her veil over her face. The veil was thin enough around the eyes for Mehr to see, but her surroundings were colored in shades of white and silver. The guardswoman started toward her.

"Ready, my lady?"

Mehr nodded.

"Take me to my father," she said.

The guardswoman led Mehr out of the women's quarters. The corridors were wider, grander. There were male guards lining the walls. They were careful not to look at her directly, but Mehr could still remember the weight of the commander's eyes on her, the embarrassment thinning his mouth. She was glad for the anonymizing weight of her veil, the grandeur of her clothing. In her armor she was Suren's daughter, and no eyes could touch her.

The guard led her to a side entrance to the Hall. She opened the door. Hesitated.

"This will lead you behind the Governor's throne," murmured the guardswoman. She hesitated again. "Emperor's grace upon you, my lady."

She stepped back, allowing Mehr to pass.

Mehr took a deep breath and went through the door. On her left were women—a dozen at least, wives of courtiers dressed in their finery with their faces carefully veiled. On her right was a long partition screen, thin enough for the color and noise of the Hall to pour through it. She took a step forward. Another. Through the screen she could see her father's shadow. He was seated on the other side, on a raised dais facing the Hall. Above him, hung from the ceiling and visible through the screen, was an effigy of the Emperor, ornately gilded in facets of mirror glass

in hues of bronze and silver. Its position above him was sym-
bolic. Although the Governor ruled Irinah, he was merely the
Emperor's representative, appointed by the Emperor to act in the
Emperor's—and the Empire's—best interests.

"Sit by me," a voice said quietly. Mehr looked down. Maryam
was kneeling on floor cushions at the Governor's right-hand
side, separated from her husband's by the screen. Her face was
veiled, but there was no missing the ferocity in her voice. *"Sit."*

Mehr kneeled down deliberately to her father's left instead.
A ripple of unease ran through the women behind her. But
Mehr could not, would not, flinch. She sat tall, her hands clasped
before her.

"Daughter," her father said. His voice carried across the Hall.
His words weren't meant just for her. "My firstborn. Our visitors
requested your presence."

Mehr could see clearly through the thin mesh of the screen to
the Hall beyond.

The Lotus Hall lived up to its name, with alcoves shaped to
mimic the open folds of a flower, its mirrored walls shimmering
in the glow of the lanterns like rippling water. Above it all, the
effigy of the Emperor glowed most brightly of all, haloed with
light. She could see the courtiers crowded into those alcoves
with their swords in their scabbards and their hands in fists. She
could see the guardsmen in their ceremonial attire, golden and
still, barring the doorways.

She could see the visitors.

There were five of them. They were dressed in identical
heavy robes, suitable for the desert but certainly not for the finery of court. They wore thick cloth wound around their heads
and shoulders. Some had the cloth drawn up over their faces,
concealing everything but their eyes. Others were barefaced. It
was one of the barefaced visitors, a slight figure in a dark robe,
who looked up at the sound of Suren's voice and fixed their eyes

unerringly on Mehr's shadowy figure through the screen. The visitor's eyes were light, their skin Irin dark. Mehr realized with a jolt that the visitor was a woman.

"We're glad you're finally with us, my lady," the woman said, speaking to Mehr as if the screen and Mehr's veil and the sudden disapproving muttering rolling through the crowd were no barrier at all. "Please, allow me to make proper introductions on behalf of my brothers and me." She swept a bow. Her eyes never left Mehr's figure.

"We are the Empire's mystics, my lady, come from the desert to speak to you on behalf of our master, the Great One, the Maha, who bids us to pray for the Empire's glory." She smiled. Her teeth were so very white. "We have heard a great deal about you, Lady Mehr."

"You do not speak directly to her," Suren said. His voice was hard as iron. "My daughter is a noblewoman under my protection, and as such you will not stain her honor by breaching the veil. You speak to me."

"Your desire to protect your women is a great virtue, Governor," the mystic said. She looked away from Mehr. "I meant no offense." When Mehr's father made no response, as the mutterings from the watching courtiers grew more pronounced, the woman gestured at one of her companions to come forward. "Perhaps it will ease your mind to know we come at the bidding of the highest power," she said.

The other mystic stepped toward the dais, only to find his way barred by a guardsman. He turned to look back at the woman. When she nodded, he reached into the folds of his robe and took out a sealed scroll. The noise of the crowd grew. They could all see what Mehr could see. The scroll was marked with the two entwined seals: the Emperor's and the Maha's. Law and faith. Even Mehr, raised in seclusion, knew their marks. Her breath caught. She felt the roar of the crowd fill her ears like water.

The guard accepted the scroll with shaking fingers and took it up to the Governor's dais. Suren did not try to quiet the courtiers. His focus was on the paper in his hands.

The woman's voice cut through the mutters of the courtiers. She seemed to take no notice of the displeasure of the crowd. She stood straight and tall, a faint smile still lifting the corners of her mouth. "Among our order is one son highly favored by the Gods. He has served faithfully, with all his soul. Our Maha told the Emperor how wisely this son has served him, and they both wish to reward his loyalty with a suitable marriage."

"A marriage," Suren repeated. His voice was colorless. "I did not know your kind married."

"The Maha decides what we are and what we do, Governor, for we are his tools and his devotees," the woman said. "Like all people of the Empire, noble to beggar, everything we have and everything we are has been granted to us by the faith and law of the Empire. We do not question. We merely serve. Just as you serve upon your throne, Governor, at the Emperor's decree, we come to you seeking a specific marriage for our brother because the Maha and our Emperor have said it must be so."

Mehr felt, more than saw, the way the nobles quailed back from the woman as she spoke. Around her the women were deathly silent. They all heard what the woman had not said:

Whatever the Emperor and the Maha gave, they could also take away.

The woman held out her hands, palms open. "Your daughter's name reached the Maha's ears on the wings of a storm, Governor. So here we are, my brothers and I, to offer her a great honor."

Mehr felt a thud in her lungs, her bones. She felt like the ground had collapsed beneath her. She was suddenly finding it hard to breathe. She watched her father through the screen. He carefully rolled up the scroll. He placed it on his lap.

"I am afraid my daughter is unsuitable," Suren said. "She is illegitimate. Her blood is impure. She is by no means worthy of a favored mystic of the Empire."

"We know of your daughter's blood," said the woman. "It is no impediment. The Empire is vast, Governor, and the Emperor loves all his subjects. Even those with barbarian blood have their part to play." The woman gestured at her own face, a smile still playing on her mouth. "I am not pure myself, Governor. But I serve, nonetheless."

There was a beat of silence. *Speak*, Mehr thought. *Speak.*

Tell them I walked barefaced in the streets. Tell them I'm a disgrace. Convince them.

Please, Father.

"My daughter's consent would be required," Suren said finally.

"We would never violate an Ambhan woman's right to choose the path of her soul," the mystic said. "A chaperoned meeting will be arranged." The woman bowed again. The other mystics followed suit. "We pray, most sincerely, Governor, that your daughter will find the Emperor's choice suitable."

In the furor that followed, a guardswoman quickly ushered Mehr and Maryam from the Lotus Hall and guided them to the Governor's Study. No doubt she acted on Suren's orders.

Two guards stood on watch at the doors. As Maryam paced the room in silent, seething fury, Mehr lifted her veil away from her face. Her clothes were too heavy. The walls of the study were closing in on her. She wanted to go outdoors and let the night air cool her blood. She wanted Lalita, and her rites, and the rosewater smell of Arwa's hair. She wanted comfort. She didn't want to *think*. Not yet.

"I told you to be careful," said Maryam. Her voice sounded like it was echoing across a long distance. Mehr's ears were still too full of the crowd to hear her. "You brought this upon us. You drew attention to yourself, threw yourself headlong into disgrace and now you've brought those monsters to our doorstep—did you even consider what the Emperor's displeasure could do to us?—listen to me, Mehr!"

She grabbed Mehr's hand. Mehr resisted the sudden, bubbling urge for violence. She wanted to rake her nails over Maryam's skin like claws. She wanted a daiva's ferocity and a daiva's taste for blood. The hunger was painful; the rage made her mouth water. But Mehr did nothing. She simply let her stepmother hold on to her.

After all, Maryam was right.

"If you refuse this match you'll murder us all," Maryam hissed. The hate and fear blazed on her face like dreamfire in flesh. "Do you understand? Your father, your sister, all the servants—they will all die because of you. So for once in your life, Mehr, make the right decision. For once, *do as you're told*."

The door opened. Maryam released Mehr hastily and retreated to the corner of the room, her back turned. Her shoulders were shaking.

"Maryam," Suren said gently. "My love. My apologies. I need to speak to Mehr alone."

Maryam swept out of the room wordlessly. The door slammed behind her.

CHAPTER FIVE

In her eighth year, on the Emperor's birthday, Mehr had—for reasons she could no longer remember—decided she did not wish to pray. Nahira had scolded her. Her mother had made a lackluster effort to change Mehr's mind, then thrown up her hands and sent Mehr to her father for punishment instead.

Mehr had kneeled on the floor of the Governor's Study, hands clasped tight in front of her so that she wouldn't be tempted to fidget with the hem of her skirt and give away how nervous she was. Her father had watched her silently for a long moment. Then he'd said, "Why won't you pray?"

Mehr had looked down.

"Mehr," he'd said. Just once.

"Mother doesn't pray," she'd whispered.

At that, her father had sighed.

"I see," he said. "I should have known. Well, you are not your mother, and there are some things she cannot teach you, Emperor's grace upon her."

He'd kneeled down in front of her then, and taken her hands in his own. His hands had been so much bigger than hers. They'd swallowed hers whole. But they had been warm, and gentle, and Mehr had suddenly been less afraid of her father's anger.

"Who rules Irinah?" he'd asked. "You must answer, Mehr."

Mehr had relaxed a little. That one was easy. "You do, Father," she'd said.

"No, Mehr," he'd replied. "I *govern* Irinah. I act on the Emperor's behalf. I have a great deal of power, but in the end, like all people, I am his servant." He spoke gently, deliberately. His gaze on her, the cadence of his words, had made her feel shamed and small. "Who rules the Empire's soul?"

"The Emperor," she'd whispered.

"No. Try again."

"The mystics?"

Her father had shuddered. He shook his head. "Not quite, daughter. The mystics, like me, are a tool. They serve the Empire through prayer, but they do so on behalf of their master. Whom do the mystics serve, Mehr? Has your mother told you?"

"I don't know," Mehr admitted softly.

"When I was your age, my own mother taught me an old adage. *Give your sword to the Emperor and your soul to the Maha,* she told me, *and you shall walk in the reflected light of their glory.* The Maha founded the Empire, Mehr, and therefore, all Emperors since have walked in his footsteps. One cannot exist without the other. The rule of law and rule of faith are tied together. We nobles serve the law and administer the state. The mystics serve the faith and ensure that our Empire remains blessed." His grip had tightened, just a little, just enough to make Mehr meet his eyes. "Everything we have," he'd said, "my governorship, this palace, your clothes and your toys, the food we eat—all of it relies upon the benevolence of our Emperor and our Maha, because we are Ambhan, and that is the way of our Empire. When you refuse to pray, you reject the reflection of their glory that blesses us. Do you reject who we are, daughter, and all we've been blessed with? Do you want to live in disgrace and darkness?"

No one would care, she had thought then, if one little girl did not pray. But her father clearly cared, so she had said nothing, and only sniffled a little, as frightened children are prone to, and shaken her head.

"There's no need to be afraid," he'd said softly, then, "Be an obedient daughter. Pray and serve, and all will be well."

Now, Mehr looked at her father, Governor of Irinah, leader of men, and thought of how he'd looked when the guard had handed him the scroll marked with the two entwined seals; how helpless he had appeared in that moment, despite his raised throne, his armed guards, his glittering palace. Everything he had was a reflection of imperial benevolence. Everything he loved could be snatched away from him in a moment—with nothing but a few words and a simple piece of paper.

"They insisted on a chaperoned meeting as soon as possible," said her father. "I could say nothing to dissuade them."

"When?" Mehr asked.

"Tomorrow morning."

Mehr leaned back against the wall. She felt dizzy. Her father stayed where he was, standing erect with his hands clasped behind him and his gaze fixed on the middle distance.

"They made a mistake, making such a grand gesture before so many courtiers," he said, almost to himself. "The nobility will be displeased. No matter what pretty words they may use, the mystics are perilously close to defying our laws of faith. To risk the freedom of a noblewoman to choose her marriage, to risk her sacred choice..." He shook his head, unseeing. "The Emperor will not be happy when his nobles threaten to revolt."

Perilously close to defying the laws of faith was not the same as breaking them in truth, and threatening to revolt was not the same as actually doing so. That much was clear to Mehr. If the mystics had openly demanded that Mehr give up her right to choose her own husband, she was sure her father would have defied them openly in return. The angry whispers of the nobles might have bloomed into rebellion. A noblewoman's right to choose her husband was far too sacred to be stolen, and if the mystics had attempted to do so, it would have been an insult not only to her father's honor, but to the honor of all the nobility who held their women precious.

But the mystics had framed the marriage as an honor, a blessing from both the Maha and the Emperor. Their pretty words had left Mehr with a mirage of choice, and left the nobles with their honor bruised but not broken. There would be no rebellion from them.

"I hope you know this is not what I wanted for you," her father said.

Mehr said nothing. Her father's jaw clenched.

"I have arranged for a group of my most trusted men to accompany you across the border tonight," he continued. "Maryam has family in Hara who will keep you safe. You will need to prepare swiftly—take only what you absolutely require."

There was a beat of silence. "Do you have any questions for me, Mehr?"

Mehr looked at her father. He looked older, she thought. Just a short time in the company of the mystics had aged him. There were lines of tension etched into his forehead and around his eyes. His knuckles were white with tension. Desperation had stretched his strength thin. She wondered if it had thinned his good sense too. She was sure he hadn't consulted Maryam. For all her faults, Maryam was no fool. She would never willingly defy the Emperor.

"Only one," she said. "What will happen to you if you send me away?"

Her father finally looked at her. Mehr continued.

"The woman called herself one of the Empire's own mystics. A *mystic*, Father. A servant of the Maha himself. What will happen to you if you disobey the Emperor and the Maha? What will happen to Arwa and Maryam?"

"You are my daughter," he said simply. "You're under my protection. I won't allow them to have you."

Arwa is your daughter too, she thought. And for all that Mehr hated her, Maryam was his wife. If he sent Mehr away, they would face the Emperor's justice.

And the Emperor, Mehr knew, was not known for his mercy.

"This is unwise, Father," she said.

Her father turned his eyes on her. His expression was full of a terrible, blinding helplessness that made Mehr's stomach lurch.

"I am your elder," he said, his voice trembling with barely leashed feeling. "It is not up to you to decide when I am being unwise."

Mehr lowered her head. The rage she'd felt when Maryam had grabbed her was still there, simmering under her skin. It rose in her now, burning away her fear and leaving her mind sharp as a keen blade.

She couldn't compel him to be wise. Her father had never made wise decisions out of love. If he had been wise, he would never have fallen in love with her mother. He would never have had Mehr or Arwa. He would never have kept them, raised them, or allowed Mehr to keep her mother's rites. He knew the place the Amrithi occupied in the Empire. By loving an Amrithi woman and raising half-Amrithi daughters, he'd risked losing everything.

He knew that the mystics, as representatives of the Maha, keepers of the soul of the Empire, were dangerous. He knew the Emperor was even more dangerous still. But he would risk everything to fight them, because right now he could see nothing beyond the haze of love and hatred and guilt clouding his mind. Perhaps later he'd feel regret. But his guilt would do his family no good.

The mystics hadn't dressed like powerful people. But she had seen the way the courtiers flinched away from them and the proud assurance in the female mystic's voice and bearing. Mehr knew deep in her bones that no matter where he sent her, if they wanted her, they would find her.

Mehr understood, too, the great cost of defiance. Maryam had educated her in that. But the stakes in a rebellion against the Maha and Emperor were infinitely higher than the ones in Mehr's small, bloody wars with her stepmother. If her father defied the Emperor—if even a fraction of the nobility joined him—the numbers of people who would suffer for his choice would be unimaginable. She thought of those veiled wives, those women who shared their husbands' burdens, who had listened to the female mystic speak in terrified silence. She thought of their children, and their servants, and the people who relied on their patronage. She thought of the fabric of the Empire; the way it was woven of ever so fragile human lives.

Mehr couldn't allow her father to try to save her. Not when the cost was so high. Not when there was nothing to be won.

She straightened up. Still dizzy, she pressed her feet hard against the floor, grounding herself. She had to think of this as a rite, and give it all the due reverence she would give her dances.

"You gave me my seal," Mehr said. Respectful, steady. "You gave me the choice of whom I will marry. Father, as an Ambhan woman, as your daughter, I say this with love and due honor: You cannot revoke my right to choose."

Her father shook his head and muttered a curse under his breath.

"Sacred, Father," she said. "This choice is sacred. And I choose to stay."

"Those—creatures—aren't a choice, Mehr. They're an abomination." His jaw clenched again, spasmodic, even as he tried to calm himself. "You are sheltered, daughter. I have kept you well protected, and that is as it should be. But you must accept that you know nothing about evil. You must *trust* me."

Mehr had never heard anyone speak of the mystics in such a manner. After a lifetime of being told they served the Empire, to give them thanks for their prayers, her father's words shook her. But she couldn't allow herself to tremble. She had to remain strong.

"I choose to stay," Mehr repeated.

She would not bend. She would not cower. Her father cursed again, clenching a hand over his face, and Mehr stood straight and tall and waited for him to look at her. Her rage was a clean blade. She held it close.

"You don't know what choice you're making," her father said finally. "You know nothing."

"Then tell me what I should know," said Mehr. "Tell me the truth about the mystics, Father. Why do you fear them, when so many others give thanks to them?" Her father was silent. She pressed on. "Give me the knowledge to make a wise choice."

He shook his head. For a moment she was sure he would refuse, and that she had lost. But then he began to speak.

"We nobles speak our fears to one another in secret, Mehr," he began slowly. "They are not for our women, or for the common folk. But we serve the Empire, and we know what the mystics are. They pray for the Empire's continued growth and glory. Their prayers have power, Mehr. They bless us with good fortune and ensure that ill fortune never touches us. They ensure that our armies are never defeated and our crops grow without blight. For that, we give them thanks." He paused. "But when they are angered, when the Maha demands they inflict justice on his behalf... Ah, Mehr! I have seen cities put to death at their word. I have seen plague and famine and slaughter fall on men at their whim. I have seen things you cannot imagine."

There was awe in her father's voice, mingled in with the hatred. A chill ran through Mehr. She thought of Usha lying dead, of missing Amrithi clans, of the mystics who could sweep away cities at a whim, who had come for Mehr, just Mehr, with her tainted Amrithi blood.

"The Emperor hates my mother's kind. Why would his mystics want me, if he hates what I am?"

"I don't know," her father said curtly.

Your daughter's name reached the Maha's ears on the wings of a storm, the female mystic had said. Her words echoed in Mehr's ears.

"I'm sorry, Father," Mehr said quietly. "I know you never wanted this for me. And you're not at fault." Mehr was the one at fault—Mehr was the one who had brought the mystics down on them. Maryam had warned her. Lalita had told her to be careful. Her father had tried to send her away. If she had listened to Maryam, if she had changed herself, made different choices...

But it was too late. The mystics were here.

"You should send Arwa away in my place," Mehr said. Her voice came out of her brittle as glass. "Let Maryam accompany her. Please, Father. She has Amrithi blood. She isn't safe in Irinah anymore." She paused, and swallowed. "Send her away so she can begin again."

Beyond Irinah, Arwa would never cross paths with daiva or storms or Amrithi again. She would lose her inheritance from their mother swiftly, painlessly. She would never know how much she had lost.

If that was the price of Arwa surviving, thriving—well. So be it.

Her father barely seemed to be listening.

"I can't allow it, Mehr," he said, his voice low. "I can't."

"I told you," Mehr said. Her voice shook. But she didn't look away. "It's my choice. My sacred choice. And I choose to stay."

Mehr had no idea what her father said to his wife, but Maryam was ready to leave before dawn. Although her eyes were rimmed with exhaustion, she sat on her dais in the hub of the Receiving

Hall and ordered her servants around with deadly calm, arranging for clothes and jewels to be packed and for a suitable palanquin to be prepared for the long journey to the borders of Hara. Maryam herself was dressed in the simplest clothing Mehr had ever seen her wear, nothing but a plain tunic and trousers, a heavy shawl wrapped loosely around her head and shoulders. She had two guardswomen in attendance, ready to accompany her. Everything was in order.

The only problem was Arwa.

Arwa did not want to go. She was in floods of furious tears, and nothing—not Nahira's firm words, not Maryam's gentle cajoling, not bribery in the form of sweets and gifts—could calm her. Mehr watched from the edge of the bustle in the Hall, still in the glittering weight of her Lotus Hall finery, as Maryam stroked Arwa's hair and murmured gently against her ear. Arwa didn't calm. She clung to Maryam. She screamed.

When Mehr couldn't stand it any longer she crossed the Hall, slipping between hurrying servants. She stopped before the dais and gave her stepmother a perfunctory bow. Maryam glared daggers at her.

"Let me talk to her," Mehr said. "I can calm her, Mother."

"Leave us be," Maryam ordered, her hand still on Arwa's hair, still and proprietary. "You're only upsetting her."

"I can help," Mehr said. "And—I would like to say good-bye."

"You aren't needed here," she said. "And you should be in your chambers. You're still in disgrace, Mehr, like it or not." Arwa had quieted a little. She was trying to lift her head. Maryam's grip tightened, then softened again, as she stroked Arwa's hair in a motion meant to soothe her. "Would you like one of my guards to show you the way out?"

The guardswoman to Maryam's left took a small step forward. Her eyes on Mehr were hard. She was just waiting for Maryam to give the word, her hands flexing eagerly at her sides.

The women's quarters were Maryam's domain, the place where she ruled with the same assurance as a Governor ruled in the stead of his distant Emperor. Her servants were loyal to a fault, and their dislike of Mehr was an obedient shadow of Maryam's own. But some—like the guardswoman standing before her—looked at Mehr with a hatred that rose not from loyalty or expediency but from a true rejection of Mehr's nature, her choices, her blood.

Mehr looked back, then forced herself to look away.

The rage in Mehr hadn't faded over the last few hours, merely hardened like diamond flesh. It was the only thing keeping her whole, keeping her standing strong, but it also made her hungry to hurt the guardswoman before her, or better yet, hurt Maryam all over again. Viciousness burned in her blood. Only the sight of Maryam's hand against Arwa's hair cracked the armor of anger inside her.

Maryam's love for Arwa was a harsh thing, by turns tender and possessive. Mehr knew Maryam would continue to deny Arwa the Amrithi traditions that were her right. She would mold Arwa into the child she wanted. But she would also keep Arwa *safe*, which was more than Mehr could do for her sister, no matter how much she loved her.

The desire to make Maryam hurt the way she was hurting was pointless. It wouldn't win her a moment with Arwa; it wouldn't allow her the opportunity to say good-bye. All the power lay in Maryam's hands. Rage would keep Mehr going until all this was over, but for the task of swaying Maryam to her will, the truth was a better tool.

"You're leaving," Mehr said softly. "And when you return, I'll be gone. You've won. She's yours." She kept her gaze fixed and her head high. They weren't reluctant mother and daughter any longer. As of now, they would be nothing to one another, and as close to equals as it was possible for them to be. "Let me talk to my sister," Mehr said.

Something flickered in Maryam's eyes—an emotion Mehr couldn't read, or name. She raised her hand and gave Arwa's cheek a brush with her knuckles.

"Come and take her," she said. "Bring her back when she is calm."

Mehr walked up to the dais. Maryam took her by the shoulder and drew her down, fingers digging hard into Mehr's skin. Her breath was soft against Mehr's hair.

"You won't need to fear for Arwa," she whispered, too softly, Mehr hoped, for Arwa to hear her. "I'm going to raise her as my own. She will be my good Ambhan daughter, loved and sheltered, and one day she will forget she ever had a sister. I promise, Mehr: I will make sure she doesn't miss you at all."

Maryam's grip loosened. Not meeting her eyes, Mehr took Arwa into her arms. Arwa was too heavy to be carried easily, but she wrapped her arms and legs around Mehr, and that made it easier. Mehr could feel her tears dampening her shoulder. She turned and walked out of the Hall toward her own chambers.

"Hush now," she murmured against Arwa's hair. "Hush, my dove, hush."

But Arwa would not hush. So as Mehr walked down familiar corridors to her own chambers, she began to sing an old lullaby, the kind that had always comforted Arwa when she was very small. Her voice, along with Arwa's sobs, echoed through the corridors.

As Mehr slipped into her own chambers, her sister still held in her arms, she heard Arwa's voice pipe up. "What are you singing?"

"A lullaby," Mehr said. "Our birth mother used to sing it to us."

Mehr carried Arwa into her room. She sat down on the bed. Arwa didn't let go of her, but she began to hum a shaky copy of Mehr's song. Then she stopped. "Am I singing it right?" she asked.

Mehr sang the lullaby over again and Arwa's voice followed hers. Her little sister's voice was hoarse from crying, but she had a good ear for music and picked the tune up quickly. By the time she'd mastered the simple lullaby, she had stopped weeping entirely.

"I don't want to go," Arwa said.

"Maryam will be with you," Mehr said. "You'll be quite safe. And it will be an adventure."

Arwa sniffed and wiped her nose with her sleeve. "I still don't want to go," she said. "Why can't you come too?"

"I'm meeting a suitor," Mehr said. "I'll be having my own adventure."

"I can't come?"

Mehr pinched her cheek, making Arwa scowl. "You're not old enough, little sister."

"I don't want to go without you."

"Oh, Arwa," Mehr said sadly. She saw Arwa's scowl begin to melt, her lower lip trembling. She stood up. "Don't. You're—"

"I'm not too old to cry," Arwa said fiercely. "I'm not. Don't say it."

"I have something to give you," Mehr said. "For your journey."

She found what she needed lying in the living room, and brought it back to the bedroom. She placed it on Arwa's lap. "Be very careful," she said. "It's very sharp."

Arwa touched the hilt of the dagger. She brushed her fingers carefully over the large opal, the gilt work. She let out a small, awed sigh.

"It's an Amrithi blade," said Mehr.

"Was it our mother's?"

"It's mine," said Mehr. "I want you to take it with you. If you cross any daiva on your way to Hara..." Mehr shrugged lightly. "Try not to show it to Maryam, hm?"

Arwa was still looking at the blade in her lap, her eyes wide and reverent.

"Don't you want it anymore?" Arwa asked. "It's—special. Isn't it?"

"I want you to feel safe," Mehr said tenderly. She wrapped her fingers over Arwa's, showing her how to hold the dagger safely. Then she helped her wrap it in silk and tuck it safely away. "When your adventure is over, bring it back to me. How about that?"

"Okay," Arwa whispered.

"It's not good-bye forever," Mehr said. She kissed Arwa's forehead. "You'll come home to me, little sister. I promise you that."

Maryam and Arwa left just as light broke over the horizon. Mehr watched them from the rooftop, wrapped in a heavy shawl to keep out the cold. She watched until they were a speck in the distance and then longer still, until there was no sight of them at all.

She slept a little. Not much. When she woke, the women's quarters were quiet. Instead of breaking the silence by calling for one of the maids to help her dress, Mehr put on her simplest tunic and trousers. She left her hair unbraided. In an hour or so the maids would come to her anyway in order to prepare her for the meeting with the mystic. They would dress her up lavishly all over again and mold her into exactly the Ambhan woman she needed to be.

Right now Mehr wanted to be herself. Nothing more. She wanted to walk around in her own clothes, in her own unvarnished skin. She had precious little time left to do so.

She went out into the living room, bare feet silent against cool marble. The weight of her hair brushed softly against her shoulders. Through the perforated screen she could see clear skies and sunlight. How strange, that the world still looked so normal when Mehr's world was collapsing around her.

She stretched her limbs, which were stiff with tiredness. She took slow, even breaths, moving her body through gentle exercises to warm the blood. Then she raised her hands above her head and began to dance. Even though her body had grown unused to activity, even though her muscles were sore and her heart was sorer, falling into the first stance felt like coming home.

Before the storm, she had danced every morning and evening, keeping each rite that Lalita had so painstakingly taught her fresh in her memory. Dancing again made Mehr feel like the girl she'd been before the dreamfire and the blood. She missed that girl. She missed her old petty worries, her confidence, her strength.

But she wasn't that girl anymore. She moved from the first stance into the Funeral Rite.

She should have danced for Usha on the night she'd died. By now Usha had been cremated as was Chand custom, her ashes scattered to the desert winds. Mehr had failed to honor her for long enough. She whirled, head lowered. She moved like grief moved, in endless circles that felt like they had no beginning or end, circles that swallowed up her senses until there was nothing but swirling grief and weightlessness. Her hands shaped sigils that spoke of life and loss.

She remembered the first time she had met Lalita and Usha, when she'd been nothing but a child and her mother had been focused on newborn Arwa's care. She remembered Lalita's beauty, the sheen of her hair. Her gentle voice. Lalita had dressed like a Chand woman, hair loose with a sari draped neatly around her body, but Mehr had known what she was.

I am your mother's friend, Lady Mehr. And I would like to be yours, if you'll accept my teaching.

Of course Mehr had said yes. She'd been a lonely child, and her mother had already begun to fade away from her, steady as ink stretched thin with water.

She remembered how Usha had hovered, at first, nothing but a silent presence at Mehr's early lessons with Lalita. She'd terrified Mehr—so large and scarred and strong, with that armor and that hard face. It had taken Mehr a long time to see how warm she was, and how kind. She'd been so very kind.

Good-bye, Usha. You dream with the Gods now.

When the first maid arrived, Mehr was covered in sweat, her hair tangled. Instead of giving Mehr a significant look, as the maids usually did when Mehr troubled them unduly, the girl simply lowered her eyes and went to work. Mehr supposed there was no value in disliking her any longer. Maryam was gone, and her favor could no longer be won by slighting Mehr.

It occurred to Mehr that now that Maryam was gone, she was the most powerful woman left in the Governor's residence. It was an uncomfortable thought.

Mehr was not used to the kind of overt power Maryam had always possessed: the kind that came only with the right title, the right husband, the right blood flowing through your veins. All her power had been won by struggle. She had always fought so very hard to maintain what little control she had over her own life. She'd managed to continue practicing her Amrithi traditions—despite Maryam's great displeasure—by using her father's guilt to her own ends. She had bowed and scraped to Maryam, put aside her own pride time after time, simply for the chance to keep Arwa in her life. Now, for a brief moment, she was the highest-ranking woman in the household. All the power she'd never possessed was in her grasp.

And once she was wed to the mystic, it never would be again.

If Mehr had made different choices—if she had left Irinah as her father had wanted, and married a man in Hara or

Numriha—she would have had power of her own. A household of women to run, a husband's burdens and a husband's power.

What kind of power would she have as a mystic's wife? She couldn't grasp the shape of her future. She couldn't imagine the forces that would mold her life once she stepped beyond the walls of her father's household, out into the desert and the vast unknown.

Other maids arrived. Mehr bathed, and the maids combed, oiled, and threaded her hair. They brought her a robe and underskirt in warm ivory. As Mehr was dressing, Nahira entered and barked orders at the maids, sending them scuttling off in search of pins for her veil and for the silk shawl currently slipping from her shoulders.

"What are you doing here?" Mehr asked. The night had been long, and sleep scarce. She felt exhausted. She had no idea how Nahira was standing at all. But even though her old nursemaid's heavy gait was more pronounced, her hair was neat and her eyes as sharp as always.

"I've come to supervise," Nahira said. "You clearly don't know what's needed."

"I've never been introduced to a suitor before," Mehr agreed mildly.

"Look at you," Nahira tsked. "Have you slept at all?"

"Have you?" Mehr countered.

Nahira made a dismissive sound. "Your sash is loose," she told Mehr. Nahira cinched it tight with one deft hand, noting each fault with Mehr's clothing out loud. The maids scurried about, fetching and carrying and adjusting Mehr's long robe and sash, looking steadily more vexed as time went on.

"I thought you might go with Arwa," Mehr said tentatively. Nahira snorted and shook her head.

"Me? No, my lady. I'm too old for such things. I sent Sara in my place," Nahira said.

Mehr started at that. Why Sara, of all the maidservants Nahira could have chosen? She remembered Sara's face in the flickering lantern light. All of this had started with her.

"Sara," Mehr repeated.

"She'll look after Lady Arwa well enough," Nahira said. "And perhaps it will keep her out of trouble." The look she gave Mehr was significant. Nahira had always been protective of Mehr, shielding her from the greater strength and will of her stepmother, until Mehr had been better able to shield herself. She was no less protective of servant girls like Sara, who walked through life without the carapace of wealth and privilege that kept Mehr safe from so many of the world's harms. "Now stay still, girl. Who braided your hair? What a mess."

Mehr was growing tired of being fussed over. She could feel a headache building. Her head was swimming with faces: Sara, Arwa, the mystic woman with her light Ambhan eyes and her Irin flesh. She shook her head when the next maid approached, hands raised.

"No more. I'll do it."

Nahira shook her head at that, narrowing her eyes.

"Your veil is crooked," Nahira said. When a maid started forward, Nahira waved her sharply away. "Leave it to me," she snapped. "Fools. All of you."

"No more!" Mehr snapped. She gave the maids a hard look. "Leave us."

The maids trailed out, unruffled by Mehr's abruptness. Mehr waited until they were gone, then stepped out of Nahira's reach. She placed herself in front of her mirror and reached for the pins of her veil.

"Lady Mehr," Nahira said reproachfully.

"I can fix my own veil," Mehr said. For now it was thrown back over her hair, leaving her face bare. She met Nahira's eyes in the glass. "You need to tell me what has you so worried."

There was a surprised silence. Mehr huffed out a sigh.

"I recognize worry when I see it," Mehr said impatiently. "Please, Nahira. I don't have much more time."

Nahira's mouth thinned. "You should have left with your sister," she said. "You should have *run*. Fool child."

Mehr didn't respond for a long moment. She made a show of adjusting her jewels, her hair, her veil again.

"How could I have run from the mystics? Emperor's grace, Nahira, we pray to their master. Running from them would have done me no good. Where could I run where they wouldn't find me?"

"You shouldn't walk into this pit of vipers."

"They're the Empire's vipers," Mehr snapped back. "Better I walk into a pit than have us all thrown into one."

She turned to face Nahira. She reined in her temper.

"Don't make me doubt myself now," Mehr said. "I've made my choice. There's nothing I can do to change it."

She thought Nahira would argue with her, and part of her—a large part of her—welcomed the idea. She wanted the opportunity to vent some of her rage, which felt too big to carry. It was a terrible weight upon her shoulders.

Instead Nahira walked over to her and took hold of the seal hung on its length of ribbon around her throat. She adjusted it slightly, so the seal lay centered just against Mehr's breastbone. Her fingers were trembling.

"There," Nahira said. "You look perfect."

Mehr swallowed around the lump in her throat. Her anger left her abruptly, and left her small.

"Thank you," she said quietly. "For everything."

There was nothing more either of them could say. The door opened. A guardswoman stepped in.

Mehr had run out of time.

CHAPTER SIX

Mehr's father was already present and seated at the corner of the meeting room. He gestured at Mehr to sit. She kneeled down on the floor cushions facing the entrance and took her time arranging the folds of her robe and her veil. She tried to rid herself of nerves.

The room was a good choice of venue. It was small, but its windows were wide enough for the morning sunlight to pour in. Even with her veil over her eyes, she would be able to see the mystics clearly when they arrived. She wondered if her father had chosen the room for exactly that reason, as a kindness, or if he was simply obeying convention. Perhaps this was the room every Governor's daughter had met her suitors in. Mehr had no idea. Neither her mother nor Maryam had ever told her what to expect from courtship, and Nahira knew little about the intricacies of courtship among Ambhan nobility.

"Daughter," said her father. She looked at him. His face was tired, his mouth thin. "Will you meet your suitor?"

"I will," she said.

He signaled the guardswoman. Moments later she returned, ushering in the female mystic and a tall man dressed in dark robes. Mehr chose to focus on him rather than the woman. He was her suitor, after all. The man who—if a miracle didn't take place—was going to be her husband.

Like so many of the other mystics Mehr had seen in the Lotus Hall, his face was swathed by cloth. Only his eyes and the bridge of his nose were revealed, but his head was lowered, hiding his gaze. The little of his skin she could see was dark. She couldn't tell if he was young or old, ugly or handsome. He was simply male, broad-shouldered and intimidating with footsteps that were soft, too soft. He had a predator's tread.

She watched him walk over to the floor cushions directly across from her. He kneeled down without making a sound. Seated he towered over her, big scarred hands pressed to his knees, his wide shoulders hunched. She found herself wishing for a partition screen between. Even with her veil in place she felt vulnerable and small.

The female mystic seated herself in a corner of the room in the position of a chaperone, just like Mehr's father. The sight of her made laughter bubble in Mehr's throat. She held it back. Mehr's suitor patently required no chaperone. He was no young noble or merchant's son. He needed no protection, no guidance in the rules of courtship. He was a beast and interloper and apparently he would have her, rules be damned.

But it seemed both the mystics and her father were determined to adhere to convention. The woman cleared her throat.

"I, Kalini, servant of the Maha and the Emperor, have brought the Maha's favored, Amun, as suitor for Lady Mehr." She spoke the words in a deep, sonorous voice. If there was one thing the mystic knew how to do, it was to give a ritual its deserved weight. "Does the lady consent to this meeting?"

If Mehr refused now, the mystics would be obliged to leave. If they refused to do so, her father would have every right to defend her honor. He would love the excuse to vent his rage, she was sure of that. The choice was in her hands.

Mehr possessed so very many choices. The choice to run, the choice to stay. The choice to say yes or no, the choice to place

Arwa's neck under the sword alongside hers, or face her fate alone. Layers upon layers of choice, and every single one felt like another cloth pressed over her mouth, slowly suffocating her.

"Daughter," prompted her father.

"I consent," Mehr said. Of course she did.

"The suitor may speak," said her father.

The silence stretched, filling the room from end to end. Time moved in slow, unbearable increments. And then finally Amun spoke.

"Lady Mehr," he said. "I am honored to meet you at last."

He didn't sound honored. His voice was like glass: colorless, smooth, entirely lacking in warmth. She wanted to recoil from it.

"I am the one who is honored," Mehr said demurely, lying through her teeth. "I am unworthy of the attentions of such a favored servant of the Maha."

"You have been misled by my holy sister's kindness. I am a lowly servant in truth."

"Not so lowly, I think, if the Maha and Emperor have chosen to bless you with the gift of marriage," said Mehr. "Unless marriage is a common gift granted to your kind? I had thought mystics were celibate, and dedicated to service."

"We are whatever the Maha bids us to be," Amun said. "But marriage is a unique gift. I am blessed."

He didn't sound like a man who considered himself blessed. Mehr could read nothing in his voice, nor in his lowered, shrouded face. He was a negative space, a void.

The mystic woman, Kalini, was beginning to frown. Her displeasure was much easier to read.

"You must consider yourself blessed too," she put in. "To gain the Maha's attention is a beautiful thing, Lady Mehr, a wondrous thing."

"Yes," Amun said. His voice was still colorless, his words

careful. "You must consider what makes you special, Lady Mehr. You must consider what has set you apart and brought you to our illustrious leader's notice."

Kalini sighed. Mehr saw Amun's fingers curl slightly against his knees.

"Do you have any questions for me, Lady Mehr?" Amun asked abruptly. "I will answer anything you ask as honestly as I am able."

With Kalini's eyes on her, she weighed her words carefully. She had to avoid giving insult or showing weakness. Soon her life would be entirely in the mystics' hands. She didn't want to give them any further reason to harm her than the simple fact of her blood already offered.

"I don't know what questions a woman should ask a prospective husband," she said finally. And she had no more time left to find out.

"Neither do I, my lady," said Amun. "In this I cannot guide you."

Mehr bit her lip. She considered her options.

"Would you be a good husband to me, if I chose you?"

"What makes a good husband, my lady?" he asked immediately.

Mehr was suddenly quite sure that if she could have chosen her own suitor instead of being drawn into the mystics' net, she would have selected the kind of man who did not answer a question with a question. She wanted a truthful man, a straightforward one. She wanted someone who would not make a game of her life.

Nahira's words rose up in her head, unbidden: *A good choice for you would be a man who doesn't enjoy wielding power over his people.*

"Compassion," she said. She shouldn't have said it, but she couldn't take back the word now. "I don't know what a good husband should be, but I know I would like a husband who is compassionate."

Amun raised his head. Mehr found herself staring into eyes the color of a moonless night, deep and dark.

"Then I will do all in my power to be a good husband to you," he said.

She reminded herself to speak—once, twice. Her heart had leaped strangely.

"And what do *you* expect from a wife?" she asked. Not kindness, surely. "I know what is expected from the wife of a nobleman, but I know nothing of the life of a mystic."

"I have been told Ambhan women share their husbands' burdens."

"Yes," Mehr agreed.

"Then you would share my burden," he said. "And my burden is service. To the Maha, and to the Emperor."

All the human feeling absent from his voice was tucked in those eyes. He stared at her, unblinking for a long moment. Was there a warning in his gaze? She didn't know. She couldn't be sure. She wondered if he knew she was staring directly at him, unblinking herself, her heart in her throat.

"Our service is holy. Our prayers are vital to the Empire," Kalini said. Mehr looked at her. For a split second, she had almost forgotten the woman was there. "Our prayers ensure that the Gods show the Emperor and the Empire the favor they rightly deserve. It is a truly glorious burden, Lady Mehr."

Prayer, service—those words meant nothing. Kalini was not trying to help Mehr understand what lay in store for her. Her intention had been to sever that momentary connection between Mehr and the male mystic, and she had succeeded. Amun had lowered his eyes.

"I imagine it is," Mehr managed. She wanted Amun to look at her again. She said, "Amun, do you have anything to ask me in return?"

Amun did not look up.

"*I* have some questions for you, Lady Mehr," Kalini said. She smiled. Her smile said: *You will not win this fight.* "I know my request breaks protocol, but if your father permits..."

Suren's face was a stiff mask. He nodded, once.

"What happened to your mother?" Kalini asked.

"She was exiled by my father when I was ten years old."

"Why was she exiled?" asked Kalini. The woman leaned forward. "Was she a traitor to Ambha and our Emperor? You must answer me honestly, my lady."

"Nothing so dramatic," Mehr said, keeping her voice even. "I was young, Mystic, but I know my mother was unhappy living in Jah Irinah. She wanted to leave the city and return to the desert." Mehr tried to feel nothing. It was the only way she could continue. "She rejected my father and the comforts the Empire had graced her with, despite her blood. So my father did the only thing he could to protect his daughters from the taint of her choices, and forbade her from ever returning."

"Your mother was faithless in the way of her people," Kalini agreed. "You must be thankful, Lady Mehr, that your father chose to protect his children, despite their ill blood."

Mehr inclined her head. Whatever her father had done—whatever bitterness she felt toward him, for his part in the loss of her mother—he had protected Mehr and Arwa as best he could. For nine years, he had even given Mehr the freedom to be her mother's daughter. She was grateful for that.

Speaking about her mother's departure and exile dredged up memories Mehr would rather have left undisturbed. She remembered so much, too much. She remembered how her mother had faded after Arwa's birth. She remembered how her mother had stared out at the desert all those long months the way a maimed bird stares at the sky. When her mother had been exiled, Mehr had cried and begged her father to let her go too: *Please, Father, let me go.*

But her father hadn't let her go, and Mehr had watched the desert day after day, waiting against all reason for her mother to come home. Only Lalita's patient coaxing had—slowly, eventually—pulled her out of her stupor.

Mehr did not often dwell on the details of her mother's departure. It pained her to do so now for an audience. Her dredged history sickened her like poison. And there was no kindness in Kalini's eyes.

"I have one last question for you, Lady Mehr. Would you make a vow to the Empire, to our Emperor and the Maha to prove your loyalty? Would you vow to serve them with your body, your heart, your soul?" Kalini's gaze was intent. "It would put my fears quite to rest."

She spoke politely enough, but there was an avid hunger in her eyes that made Mehr's stomach churn. She looked again at Amun, who was still as a statue carved in jet. He did not look at her, but she felt the weight of his regard. He was listening. He was waiting, so tense that he barely even seemed to breathe.

"How dare you," Suren growled. His hands were in fists. He looked ready to rise to his feet. "Such an impertinent question is not to be borne!"

"It's a simple question," Kalini said mildly. "It was not intended to cause offense."

"My daughter is an Ambhan noblewoman," her father said, in a voice filled with barely leashed fury. "Noblewomen are a treasure of the Empire; their souls are in our keeping. They do not make *contracts*." He nearly spat the word. "To ask her to make a vow beyond marriage is a barefaced insult." His voice grew darker. "If the nobility learn your master seeks to pervert the honor of their women, there will be a revolt. I can assure you of that."

"I apologize," Kalini said, touching a hand to her chest. "You named your daughter tainted, Governor. I did not know you extended such an honor to her. That was my error, and I apologize."

Before her father could explode, Mehr hurriedly cut in.

"It is I who must apologize, Mystic," she said. "I would vow if I could. But my father has spoken. I am an Ambhan noble-woman and the vow is not mine to give."

"Thank you, my lady," said Kalini. "I appreciate your honesty. My most vital task is to protect the interests of the Empire. You must understand why I am compelled to treat you impertinently."

"I understand perfectly," Mehr replied.

"Well then," Kalini said softly. She gave Amun a look under her lashes. "We're done," she announced.

Mehr blinked. "What?"

"Lady Mehr, do you choose this match?" asked Kalini.

"I would like to speak to Amun a little longer before making my decision," Mehr said, in the most respectful voice she could manage.

"One meeting is not enough," Suren said. "Courtship is a lengthy process, Mystic. One meeting—"

"Is all that we have time for," Kalini cut in. "We need the lady's decision today, Governor. Needs must. The Maha requires our swift return."

Mehr wasn't ready yet. No time had passed at all. She had barely spoken to Amun, and he had barely looked at her, never mind spoken in return.

But this meeting had never been about introducing Mehr and Amun to one another. It was a formality, allowing the mystics to avoid transgressing sacred rights without allowing Mehr out of their grasp.

It was Kalini she'd spoken to. Kalini who had interrogated her, and smiled, and decided Mehr's fate. Amun had decided nothing. Perhaps she hadn't been able to read his face, his voice, because he felt nothing at all.

"Do you have any questions for me?" Mehr asked him. "Anything at all?"

Amun gave her the briefest glance, his dark eyes hooded.

"Lady Mehr," said Amun. "In the name of the Maha, I ask you: Do you consent to marry me?"

"Is that the only question you have?" she asked quietly.

"It is," he replied.

He was an absolute stranger to her. But that didn't matter. Long before Mehr had walked into this room, she'd made her choice.

"Then I consent," she said. "I will be your wife."

When Mehr's father had married Maryam, their wedding had taken place in the bride's birth household, as was traditional. Neither Mehr nor Arwa had been present. But Mehr had attended a few marriage ceremonies for nobles in Irinah, and she knew that her impending wedding was meant to be a joyful occasion, celebrated for weeks on end with feasts and dance and music. The wedding of the Governor's firstborn daughter—illegitimate though she was—should have been an especially lavish celebration.

The household was quiet. Suren had invited Mehr to eat dinner with him, and Mehr had accepted. They sat together and shared small dishes of rich, slow-cooked meat and lentil broth. As they ate, Mehr's father told her there would be no time for celebration. She would have a simple wedding ceremony in two days' time—all the time that the mystics, in their benevolence, had allowed. No poems would be recited, no music would be played, and no gifts would be shared between families. The ceremony would consist of nothing but a simple exchange of family seals. In time, Amun would remove Mehr's seal from his own neck—*when*, exactly, her father didn't say—but Mehr would wear her husband's seal for the rest of her natural life.

Mehr could not understand why the mystics wanted the marriage to proceed so quickly. She had a terrible suspicion that they did not want to allow her or her father time to find a way to save her from the fate they had decided for her.

Her father spoke in stilted, awkward sentences that eventually petered out into silence. Usually it was up to a mother to tell her child about marriage, but Mehr's birth mother was in exile, her stepmother was gone, and Lalita was missing. Mothers were in short supply. In their absence, her father did his best, but the responsibility ill-suited him. Feeling rather uncomfortable herself, Mehr did nothing to encourage her father when his voice faded and he returned to his meal.

Mehr wasn't particularly hungry, but the meat was soft, the lentils faintly sweet, and it was easier to concentrate on her food than to consider what lay in store for her. She would have been content to continue picking at her meal in peaceable silence, but her father had other ideas. He looked at her.

"Your mother," he began.

Mehr set down the dish she was holding with a thump.

"No, Father," Mehr said. "I don't want to talk about her." They had never discussed her mother's departure. She had no idea what he wanted to say, and she didn't care. Whatever it was—an apology, an excuse, an explanation—it had come far too late. "I spoke about her to the mystics because I had no choice. Will you force me to speak like they did?"

She had never spoken to her father like this before. But there was no anger in her father's expression, only resignation.

"Your mother," he said, gently, "never told me why she feared and hated the Emperor. I thought I understood her reasons, but now I see I knew nothing."

What little appetite Mehr had left was gone. But she ate another bite, giving herself time to get her emotions back under control.

"I will send a messenger to inform Maryam about your—marriage," her father said.

Mehr nodded silently. She tried not to think of her sister journeying away from Irinah never to return. She tried not to think of Maryam's soft, spiteful words. *I promise, Mehr: I will make sure she doesn't miss you at all.*

As if sensing the direction of Mehr's thoughts, her father spoke again.

"Arwa won't return here," he said. "No matter what happens I will keep her out of harm's way. On my honor, I promise you that."

His eyes were flinty. Some of his old strength showed itself in the shape of his shoulders, his raised head. She found herself believing him.

Would he send Arwa away forever, to be raised far from him and from Irinah in safety? Would he allow Maryam to stay with her, or give Arwa away entirely, leaving her to be raised by strangers? Would he truly choose to lose both of his daughters in one terrible blow? Mehr didn't want to ask. There was no answer he could offer that would not in some way break her heart.

"Thank you," Mehr said softly, instead.

She looked down at her meal. No. She couldn't eat any more. She couldn't sit here any longer either. Her father's guilt was an oppressive weight. She could feel him looking at her still, things unspoken hovering in the air around him.

Your mother—

"Mehr," he said. She raised her head reluctantly. "If you would like to write a message to Arwa, I will ensure that it's delivered."

It was a small kindness, but it brought a lump to Mehr's throat.

"I don't know what to tell her," Mehr confessed.

"Think on it," he said. "The messenger won't leave until morning. You have time."

CHAPTER SEVEN

Dear Arwa—
No.
Dear sister—

Mehr stopped, took a breath, and began again.

Starting the letter was hard. How formal should she be? How honest? Finishing it seemed like an impossible task. Mehr had never had much cause to write lengthy letters, and her feelings for Arwa were far too huge and complex to reduce down into words. But Mehr struggled on. She stained her fingers black and wasted copious amounts of ink, but the letter was finished in time for the messenger to carry it alongside her father's missive for Maryam.

It was an inadequate letter, full of useless platitudes and soft, meaningless chatter. It wasn't the message Mehr had wanted to write, but being honest about all the love and fear curdled up inside her wouldn't have helped Arwa. So she lied, and wrote that her husband-to-be was handsome and kind, that her wedding was going to be beautiful. She wrote that she was happy.

She hoped Arwa would read her letter and believe every word.

There was no time to think about the letter after that. The household was in chaos. There was simply not enough time to plan a wedding, even one that had been reduced to nothing but its bare bones. From the murmurs of the servants, Mehr knew that a feast was being planned, suitable entertainment was being arranged, and the Lotus Hall was being decorated in fresh flowers, sourced by some miracle despite the withering desert heat.

Her father may have said that there would be no music or dance, but this was the wedding of the Governor's daughter. All the noble guests—and there would be guests, despite the short notice—would expect the Governor to provide a respectable celebration in honor of his daughter's marriage. The servants understood that. They recognized the unspoken expectations of his station, and their own.

Mehr's station gave her the privilege of taking no part in the preparations. She sat in her room, worse than useless, as the maids fussed over her. All she could do was wait and wait, agonizing over what was to come.

Nahira took it upon herself to make the experience infinitely more difficult by hovering over Mehr with all the ferocity of a tiger protecting her cub. The seamstress arrived to fit Mehr for a hastily made bridal robe, and Nahira nearly made her stab Mehr with a needle by scolding her until she was a nervous wreck. The maids came with questions; Nahira sent them scattering. Mehr tolerated all of this. But when Nahira began explaining what happened between a husband and wife in the marriage bed in extensive, excruciating detail, Mehr found that she'd reached her limit.

"I know what men and women do," Mehr snapped. "Gods, Nahira, Lalita was—is—a courtesan. She told me enough."

Nahira huffed, making low sounds under her breath that didn't sound particularly complimentary.

"Is my hearing going?" Mehr said. "I didn't quite catch that."

Nahira gave her a level look. Then she said in a clearer voice, "Your father should have told you about that. Not her."

Mehr shuddered. "I'm glad he didn't. I can't imagine a conversation I'd like less."

"If Lady Maryam hadn't left, then she would be the one sitting here telling you about the marriage bed." Mehr grimaced and put her face in her hands. Nahira patted her shoulder. "There you are. It could always be worse."

After that Nahira was quieter, perhaps aware now of how fear had altered her behavior and made a fool of her. The quiet left Mehr far too much room to think, and she regretted having snapped at her old nursemaid. There was nothing Mehr could have done to alleviate Nahira's worry except allow her to fuss, and she had even denied Nahira that comfort. But Mehr hadn't wanted to think of her wedding night, and Nahira had forced her to do so.

Now that she had begun thinking about it, she couldn't make herself stop. As the evening of her wedding came, as her maids dressed her, as they marked her with scent and lined her eyes with kohl, as her lips were daubed red, she thought of the night ahead. She was going to be intimate with a stranger. Not only would his duties be her duties, his burdens her burdens, but his body would become an extension of her own. Marriage was a matter of the soul, but Mehr had willfully forgotten that it was also a matter of flesh.

It's too late to run, Mehr reminded herself.

Nahira didn't hug her good-bye. She pressed Mehr's hands between her own, her grip firm and her mouth thin.

"Good-bye, Lady Mehr," she said. Her voice trembled. She swallowed. "Take care."

Mehr nodded, unable to speak. She had to be brave, and if she spoke she would cry.

Guards guided her to the Lotus Hall. Rather than slipping behind the partition screen with the other women, Mehr was led to the main entrance. Through her veil, she could see the vastness of the room and smell the sweet perfume of the flowers wreathed along the walls. Noblemen watched her from the edges. Behind the partition screen, the women watched Mehr too, their bodies reduced to blurred shadows. With all eyes on her, Mehr began walking to the center of the Hall, where her groom awaited under the wedding canopy.

Mehr was drenched in gold. Flowers were wound through her braid. The weight of her robe was ridiculous. But Amun was dressed in the same dark, heavy robes he had worn the entire time he had been in Jah Irinah. All the mystics, who stood in a ring around the canopy, were dressed similarly. It shouldn't have surprised Mehr that they were making a mockery of her marriage. It was no different from what they had done so far, after all.

Before she could reach the canopy, her father stood in her path. He took her arm.

"Blessings on you, daughter." His voice was rough.

"And you, Father."

Holding on to her, he guided her last few steps toward the canopy. Then, reluctantly, he let go of her arm and stepped back into the crowd.

I release you, the act said. *You belong to another man now.*

The act was only symbolic. But Mehr, of all people, knew that rites and rituals had power.

She did not want to belong to Amun or to the Great One he served. But she stepped under the canopy regardless.

Kalini was presiding over the ceremony, of course. If the wedding had been a true celebration and not the farce it was, her father would have selected a senior member of the local nobility to preside over the ceremony. Being selected would have been a great sign of his favor. Her father had himself led numerous wedding ceremonies in the past, as was his right as a respected member of the nobility and Governor of the province.

Mehr saw Kalini take a step forward from the rest of her kind, heard her sonorous voice ring out, echoing over the Hall as she began the traditional marriage chant. The words washed over Mehr. They didn't matter. All her focus was on Amun.

His face was still covered, but she could see the bridge of his nose and his dark eyes. She looked at him and thought of the marriage bed. She couldn't help but think of it.

There was a lull in the chanting.

"Lady Mehr," someone prompted. Mehr started. One of the mystics was looking at her. "Your seal," he said.

Face burning, Mehr slipped her seal from around her neck. Amun mirrored her movement, lifting his own seal up on its length of wound silk. Before, it had been hidden under his robe, but now Mehr could see that the surface of it was bare of all names but his own and marked with a winding symbol like a whorl of sand that Mehr didn't recognize.

Mehr crossed the last handspan of distance between them and raised her own seal up. Amun leaned down, allowing Mehr to slip it over his head. As the ribbon slid over his neck and the circle of stone touched his breastbone, Amun went very still. He took a soft, pained breath. Then he straightened up and swiftly slipped his own seal around Mehr's throat.

Mehr heard the chanting rise through the Hall as the nobles and servants and guards all took up the call, acknowledging the moment the vows were agreed, the marriage bond formed. But they were all drowned out by the sharp pain spearing through Mehr's chest, a burning like cold fire that raced from the edges of her new seal directly into her skin. Her first shocked cry was masked by the chanting. She wanted to cry out louder and demand help, but Amun was looking at her and opening his eyes wide in warning. He gave a small, pointed shake of his head.

There was no time anyway. The last part of the ceremony had already begun. A long length of gold cloth was lifted up by the servants and drawn around the edges of the canopy. In seclusion for the first time, hidden by thick and masking cloth, Mehr was supposed to greet her new husband by lifting her veil and showing him her face. Instead she tried to reach for the seal on her chest.

"No," Amun said sharply, keeping his voice low. "You don't want to touch it yet, my lady."

"Why not?" Mehr asked. Her voice was a furious whisper. "What just happened?"

"Not here. Finish this first." The cloth rustled around them, the chanting continued, and Mehr didn't move. "Finish this," he repeated. "Lift your veil, and we can be done with this farce."

"You first," she said. He glared at her. "I deserve to see your face. Surely I have earned the right." A beat. Mehr clenched her hands tight. "Do you want to stand here forever, husband? Because I promise you I won't relent."

Beaten, Amun reached for the cloth around his face. The deft removal of one knot allowed it to fall, pooling around his shoulders. He raised his head in the dim light and let her look at him.

Mehr's breath caught.

Dark skin. Dark eyes. She should have guessed. When she'd seen his dark hands—dark like her own—she should have known.

If she had seen his face before—those distinctive features, the high cheekbones, the fierce shape of the jaw, the full mouth, all strangely like her own features yet not at all—she would have known what he was in an instant.

Amun was Amrithi.

There were marks on his cheeks. She thought they were scars at first, but when he turned his head they gleamed blue in the light, and she wasn't sure anymore.

He reached for her veil and lifted it up just long enough to see her face. Then he let it fall back into place.

"Mehr," he said in a louder voice. "My wife."

Now that he had acknowledged the marriage, the ceremony was done. The gold cloth lowered around them, allowing the sound of muted cheering to pour in. They were married.

The feast was strained. The nobles present attempted to put on a good show, but Mehr was too nervous to do more than pick at her food. Beside her, Amun ate nothing.

As the night dragged on and the men drank more spiced wine, the feast grew louder and merrier. Mehr and Amun were left to sit in their own sea of silence. Mehr's chest itched, still tingling even though the original burning pain had passed. It was hard to resist touching her skin or the seal itself, but she held fast.

Finish this, he'd said. So she would. She would get through this. Then when they were alone, she would demand her answers.

But the night stretched on and on. The noise of the guests was growing unbearable, and Mehr could feel Kalini's eyes on her, constantly assessing her. When Mehr thought she could stand it no longer, Amun rose. He held his hand out to her. Mehr let out a shuddering breath and took it.

They retired to a room Mehr had never seen before, one of the many bedrooms in the Governor's residence left long empty. The room had been cleaned in preparation for its use as a bridal suite, and the lanterns on the walls flamed brightly. The scent of incense hung in the air. The bed was scattered with soft pillows and rose petals, as if someone had foolishly assumed they would want or need romance.

Once the doors were firmly shut, Amun immediately began removing his robes. Underneath them he wore a plain sleeveless tunic and trousers. Mehr threw back her veil. Vision improved, she could see now that his bare arms were covered with the same deep blue marks as his face. They were long whorls and loops that looked like language, just like the symbols Mehr had seen on Amun's seal.

As he began to remove the sash of his tunic, Mehr froze.

Amun looked over at her. "You asked me for an explanation," he said. "It's easier to show you first."

He finished untying his sash and drew his tunic open at the chest. There were more marks across the skin of his torso, but the one that caught Mehr's eye instantly was the one on his breastbone: a pale scarred circle, filled with the names of Mehr's ancestors.

He was marked with her seal.

"What?" Mehr's voice was shaky. She took a step forward. "How—?"

"Your mother," said Amun. "When you were a child, did she tell you why Amrithi don't marry?" Mehr shook her head. "Amrithi are descended from daiva, Lady Mehr."

"I know that. But I—"

"Daiva have great strength. Great power. But their vows are binding. Their vows are unbreakable."

"I don't understand," Mehr said, even as dawning knowledge ran cold through her bones.

He looked at Mehr with something like pity. "We don't marry because we don't make vows. To do so is to risk binding ourselves permanently." He gestured at the mark on his chest. "When I bound myself in marriage to you, the vow marked itself on my skin. It will be there for the rest of our lives."

She clutched the new seal. Clutched it so hard that the edges bit into her palm.

"I didn't know that," Mehr said faintly. Her voice came from far away. Shock had made her numb. "Why didn't I know?"

"Few Amrithi are afflicted with enough of our ancestral blood to have the gift of *amata*, the gift in our blood that allows us to be bound," he said impassively. "Perhaps your mother neglected

to tell you because she thought your Ambhan blood would protect you from inheriting the strongest of our gifts."

His words cut through the numbness like a knife, leaving
Mehr stripped bare. She sat down abruptly on the bed, curling
her legs beneath her as if reducing her size would reduce the
weight of the knowledge. A vow. Unbreakable. Gods, what had
she walked into?

Amun hesitated visibly. Then he sat down on the edge of the
bed. Mehr was glad he left a large distance between them.

"This gift," Mehr managed to say. "This—curse. You think
I have it?"

Amun nodded. "You wear the vow on your skin," he said.
"You must have it. No doubt if your mother had known your
strength, she would have warned you."

"No doubt," Mehr agreed. Or Lalita would have. But even
Lalita had left Mehr in the dark.

More softly now, he continued. "Half Ambhan, raised hidden
in this place, you should have passed beneath the Maha's notice.
But you revealed your strength, didn't you? You did something
foolish that drew our Maha's many eyes." He hesitated. "Something in the last storm."

Something foolish. Yes, Mehr supposed dancing with dreamfire in the storm, barefaced and alone, qualified. It had been an
act of pure desperation. All she had wanted was to save Lalita.
Instead she had drawn the attention of the Emperor's eyes, and
with a swiftness that terrified her, his mystics had appeared, the
name of the first Emperor a terrible prayer on their lips.

Mehr nodded silently.

"Well then," Amun said. "Once he knew of your *amata* gift,
he knew a vow could bind you. And here we are."

"What do you want me for?" she asked. "Why marry me?"

"I didn't want you," he said bluntly. "But I made vows to the
Maha. I do as I'm bid."

Against her will, her gaze lowered to his arms. Those marks were vows, she realized. Every single one of them was an unbreakable promise, limned in deep blue against his skin.

Amun followed her gaze and smiled humorlessly. "I made too many vows," he said. "And now my burdens are your burdens too."

Oh. Mehr saw the cleverness of it, even as she recoiled from it. The Maha had ensured that his mystics bound Mehr by both her Ambhan and her Amrithi blood. Because she was an Ambhan woman, her husband's burdens were her burdens. She had made an Ambhan promise, but her Amrithi blood had turned that promise into unbreakable chains, a vow like a noose around her neck. Panic wanted to grip at her insides. She couldn't let it.

"If you could look away, husband, I would appreciate it." His own vows, she realized, climbed up to his hairline. Her eyes followed them with a helpless kind of horror. What had become of her own flesh? "I need to see my mark for myself."

Amun stood and walked to the corner of the room without a word. He turned his back on her.

Mehr unpinned her veil and struggled with her wedding silks. She had been dressed by multiple maids, and the costume was far too elaborate for Mehr to remove it without assistance. There was no simple sash at the waist for her to unknot. She had an inkling that Amun was supposed to help her undress. The idea of it made her stomach knot with sickened anxiety. She struggled to shift her robe just enough for her to see the mark.

It lay just above her breasts. Unlike the deep blue marks all over Amun's skin, the scar from his seal on her chest was pale, whitish. It was an ugly thing.

She adjusted her clothes, covering the scar back up. Then she raised her head. Amun was still standing with his back to her. She was thankful for that.

She leaned forward. The sound of her wedding silks rasping

against the bed made him tense visibly. His hands were clasped behind him and clenched; the muscles in his arms stood in relief.

No wonder he went to such lengths to keep himself entirely covered. His voice was a good mask, but his body was painfully expressive.

"Has the Maha done this before?" Mehr asked. "Has he bound women like me with a marriage vow in the past?"

Amun shook his head, back still turned.

"He has never needed to before," said Amun. "And he has never had to bind a woman like you."

A noblewoman with Ambhan and Amrithi blood. A woman who could not be stolen away without the use of a binding palatable to the nobility, a marriage sealed with a vow—yes, Mehr could imagine that there were not many women in the world like her.

"What does the Maha want me for?" Mehr asked.

Amun turned back to her. His expression was blank. She knew, without pressing, that she would get no more answers out of him tonight.

"I would like to know," Mehr said, pressing him regardless. Amun shook his head.

"Lady Mehr, I don't wish to speak any longer," he said in a voice too cool, too even to be a plea. "Will you respect my wish?"

I don't have a choice, thought Mehr. She stared at him silently as he stepped away from the wall, as he sat down on the edge of the bed and removed his shoes without looking at her.

"You must be tired," he said. "The night has been long. You should sleep."

Mehr was tired, it was true. She didn't know how the nobles had found the energy to continue celebrating. Even when she and Amun had left, their wedding guests had been deep into their cups and in a bright and glorious mood. But even tired as she was, she didn't really believe she would be able to sleep. Her mind was too full, her heart was far too heavy.

She lay down anyway. Amun lay down beside her. She stiffened. He must have felt her tense, because he turned over to look at her. The lantern light bled shadows across his face, hiding his expression from her.

"I only want to rest, Lady Mehr," he said. "No more than that."

She knew they were both expected to do far more than just sleep, but Amun had already rolled back over and tucked himself tight against the other side of the bed. If he wasn't going to mention it, then Mehr wasn't going to either.

A shudder ran through her. Her marriage should have been a sacred thing, but the mystics and their Maha had twisted it into a mockery of itself. The marriage bed—the consummation— was about becoming one flesh, one soul. Now Mehr lay next to her husband with her soul already marked by trickery, her skin and his burned with the perversion of their marriage vows. She didn't want to become any more bound. She was terrified, and she was done.

Mehr folded her hands over her stomach. She was uncomfortable in her clothes, weighed down with hidden clasps digging into her spine, but she couldn't do anything about that now. She squeezed her eyes shut. She could hear Amun breathing. Trying to sleep next to someone felt strange to her.

"You don't need to call me *lady* any longer," Mehr said. "I'm your wife now."

Amun said nothing. She didn't know if he had fallen asleep or if he was awake and had simply chosen not to respond. She thought the second option was more likely than the first. She closed her eyes tighter, pretending to sleep along with him, until pretense finally turned into reality.

CHAPTER EIGHT

It was early morning when Mehr woke. Amun was sitting on
the edge of the bed with his back to her. As she sat up, he turned.
His tunic was loosened and the collar had fallen open. His neck,
she noticed, was bare. She sat up straighter, the weight of his seal
rubbing at the skin of her own throat.

"Where is it?" Mehr asked.

He held a hand out to her. The whole length of her seal, ribbon and all, was curled up in his palm. Mehr let out a shuddering breath.

"You shouldn't have removed it," she said. "You haven't earned
the right."

Nahira's unwanted talk of the marriage bed had at least done
Mehr the favor of dispelling her ignorance in this one matter:
Newly married men wore their wife's seal until the marriage
was consummated. Once husband and wife were bound in flesh
as well as soul, a man no longer needed to carry the burden of
his wife's past around his neck. A wife was a newly born creature, after all: an extension of her husband's flesh and his will,
her old self no more than a ghost for the pyre.

"We'll be disturbed soon," he said, as if he hadn't heard her.
He was moving the seal restlessly between his fingers. The

ribbon was twined around his wrist. "The feast ended hours ago."

"Husband," she said.

"Your maids will come. Or Kalini. Either way, you should prepare."

"*Amun.* Will you listen to me?"

He looked away from her.

She grabbed his wrist. His arm tensed, all wiry sinew and hard muscle, then relaxed abruptly. The seal slithered easily into Mehr's grip. She took it from him and laid it on the bed.

"Do you understand what removing your seal means?" Mehr asked.

"I do."

"You want to pretend we consummated the marriage," Mehr said quietly. Under her palm, the seal was warm from his skin. "Why?"

For a long moment Amun said nothing.

"A marriage is a twofold binding," he said finally. "Soul and flesh. Until we consummate the marriage..." He lowered his eyes. "It would be better," he said, "if the Maha believes he has absolute power over you, Lady Mehr, as he does over me."

Mehr hadn't resigned herself to being bound. She hadn't truly accepted that it was true, scarred skin or no. Now the ground was shifting under her feet. She wasn't sure what this meant. What he was offering her. She swallowed.

"I have the vow on my skin. Are you telling me I'm not truly bound by it?"

"It's not complete," he said. "You would know if it were. You'd feel it like another heartbeat." A ghost of a smile on his lips, no joy in it. "You'd feel it burrowing."

She covered her mouth and looked away. When she had control of herself—or a semblance of it—she turned back.

"Why are you helping me?" she asked.

"Did you want to marry me?" His gaze was intent. "When Kalini asked if you chose this match—did you want to be my wife?"

"No." Mehr couldn't hide the truth. She would still recant her vow if she could in a heartbeat.

"Having your will stolen from you is a violence, Lady Mehr. I chose my vows, but you . . ." He paused. Jaw clenched. "I don't appreciate being used as a weapon against another human. A tribeswoman." There was an old, deep anger in his voice. "I don't appreciate being ordered to force myself on a woman."

"I had a choice," Mehr said, head held high. He wouldn't, *couldn't*, take that away from her. "I chose to protect my family. I accept the consequences of that."

"A choice like a knife at your throat is an illusion," Amun said bluntly. "Here is the choice I was given, Lady Mehr: to marry you and bed you, or face the consequence of breaking my vow. Unbearable pain, death, eternal suffering for what remains of my soul in the aftermath. Would you call that a fair choice?"

Mehr said nothing.

"I told you that I do as I'm bid. But I do *only* what I'm bid. No more than that. I was ordered to wed and bed you, but I wasn't told when to complete the bond." Amun lowered his head. "I can't save you from the Maha's will," he went on. "But I can give you time. Enough so we can grow comfortable with one another, before we are forced on each other. You understand?"

She understood.

This was as much a violation of him as of her.

She felt sick. She remembered her fear when he had lain down beside her last night. If he had been a different man—if he had been under the weight of a stricter vow—

But no. She wouldn't think of it.

"My clothes," Mehr said suddenly. "My—my wedding silks.

No one will expect me to still be dressed. They'll know we've lied."

"Remove them, then. I'll look away."

"I can't remove them on my own," she said.

He frowned. "How did you put them on?"

"I'm a rich man's daughter," Mehr said, trying to hide her embarrassment. "I have servants to dress me. But wedding silks are always—unusually complicated."

She must have seemed utterly useless to him. She wondered what he saw when he looked at her, and decided she probably wouldn't want to know.

"Tell me what to do." His face was blank, but the unease practically rolled off him. It did nothing to put Mehr at ease.

She directed him to unclasp the loops of cloth that bound the back of her robe together. To be forced into even this small intimacy with a man seemed ridiculous to her. Torturous.

"I can do the rest on my own," she said. He let go immediately and walked away from her, arms crossed. Mehr slid the first layer of silk off, leaving her arms and shoulders bare. She clutched the cloth to her chest.

Amun's prediction turned out to be correct. The maids arrived not long after with a morning meal, and took in the sight of Mehr's state of undress with obvious pity. Kalini arrived soon after, striding past the guards at the door and the maids, giving Mehr only a brief, sidelong glance before turning her attention on Amun.

"Show me," she ordered.

Amun opened the front of his tunic without complaint. Kalini leaned forward, a crease forming between her eyebrows.

"It looks different from the others," she announced.

"It's a different kind of vow," Amun said. Nothing disturbed the calm of his features. His voice was like glass.

Kalini looked at Mehr. "Now I need to see yours."

No *my lady* this time, Mehr noted. She clutched the silks tighter to her chest.

Kalini raised an eyebrow. "Show me now or show me later," she said. "But you *will* show me, I assure you. It is your duty."

The maids were watching. Mehr wanted to refuse. But Kalini's eyes were unblinking. There was something animal about her that made Mehr's blood curdle.

Mehr lowered the silk, just enough to expose the mark. Then she lifted it again.

Kalini gave a satisfied nod, turning away. "The Maha will be pleased with you, Amun." To Mehr she said, "You'd best prepare. We leave at sunset."

Kalini left as swiftly as she had arrived, leaving deafening silence behind her. Mehr didn't look at Amun, and didn't look at the maids. Her face was burning.

"I'd like to bathe and dress now," she said, with all the dignity she could muster. She stood, the maids surrounding her like a shield. "If you'll excuse me, husband."

She heard Amun's soft footfalls as he left. She didn't watch him go.

Once Mehr was dressed, Kalini began hovering over her like a constant, malevolent shadow. She directed the servants, ensuring that no finery was packed, just the bare essentials: tunics and trousers, one simple single-layered robe with a matching sash and shawl, and a few sturdy boots. Whatever Mehr's new life would consist of, it clearly wouldn't involve the need for jewels and silks and beaded slippers.

There was no opportunity to give anyone a proper farewell. Under Kalini's watchful eye, her father embraced her, but there was no comfort in it.

"Take care, daughter," he said. He brushed his knuckles over her hair. Mehr nodded, squeezing her eyes shut to hold back unwanted tears.

"I will, Father."

Kalini gave Mehr a robe like the one all the mystics wore.

"Put it on," she said. "You'll need it in the desert."

Mehr slipped it over her head. The material was thick—no doubt good for blocking out both the sunlight and the cold. She drew a length of cloth around her head, trying to mimic the way Amun wore it. She didn't succeed but her face, at least, was covered.

Kalini guided her out of the women's quarters. They joined the other mystics and made their way out into the city toward the desert. No one spoke. The mystics surrounded Mehr in a ring, concealing her, simultaneously shielding and caging her. Amun stood to her left. He didn't look at her.

It wasn't until they reached the desert itself and began making their way across uneven, shifting ground that Mehr realized they had no transport. No palanquins, no horses, no howdahs on elephant back. Wherever they were going, they were traveling there on foot.

Hours passed. The sky darkened and the city receded behind them. Mehr was thankful for the cool nighttime air, if only because there was precious little else about this journey to be thankful for. The ground was growing even more uneven, the sand rising in thick waves of deceptive depth. Her dancing had made her stronger than the typical noblewoman, but it hadn't prepared her for anything like this.

Without warning, her foot sank deep in the sand and stuck fast. As she stumbled forward, a hand caught her arm and steadied her.

"It will get easier," Amun said in a low voice. As soon as she'd righted herself, he let go of her. "The desert has its own laws. Once we're farther from the city, you'll see."

He was right. Long after Mehr had passed the point of exhaustion, when Jah Irinah had dwindled into nothing behind them, the desert...changed.

Mehr couldn't pinpoint the difference at first. But slowly walking became easier, her footsteps consistently meeting solid ground instead of rolling sand. Mehr looked around her. As far as the eye could see, the sand was still thick and uneven, near impassable.

The desert has its own laws.

Mehr looked down.

The sand was reshaping beneath her footsteps. With every step, it was flaring out in circles, flattening to match the shape of her tread. Her breath caught. The way it moved, coiling out in spirals beneath her feet, reminded her of the way dreamfire had clung to her ankles on the night of the storm. The sand was quietly, vibrantly *alive*. In the darkness it gleamed like embers, rich with storm and starlight. The awe filled Mehr up from head to toe. For a moment, one ridiculous moment, she felt like she could walk in this desert forever. This was what the Irin believed the Ambhans had driven out of Jah Irinah: beauty in the earth, ethereal and strange, born without even a storm of dreamfire to bring it into bloom.

As the night deepened and the temperature plummeted, Mehr began to see faint lights from villages on the edges of Jah Irinah in the distance. But the mystics steered clear of them and stopped to make camp deep into the desert, where the lights were fainter than starlight. Tents were erected and a fire was lit. One man paced the edges of the encampment, his dark robe melting into the black of the night. The rest waited in silence.

He trudged back to the fireside and kneeled down. "All's quiet," he said. Then he peeled the cloth back from his face.

It wasn't long before the other mystics followed suit, baring their faces and sharing provisions between themselves as they talked in low voices. Without their faces covered, they were not as alien or as fierce as they had appeared to be in the city. Mehr watched them from the far edge of the fireside, the night cold against her back. They were men. Just men, some with fair skin and some with dark, their faces unmarked, their smiles easy. They were nothing like Amun, who stood at the far edge of the camp, his face still covered and his eyes fixed on some far point in the distance.

"You should come closer to the fire," a voice said.

One of the mystics was looking back at her. He was young, his skin the color of parched earth, and his eyes were kind. He gestured at the ground beside him. "You must be cold."

Mehr moved closer, taking the spot he had offered. The conversation went quiet as she joined the circle but picked up again when Mehr simply raised her hands to warm them against the heat of the flames. The mystic at her side snapped his flatbread in two and offered her a piece. Too hungry to refuse, Mehr took it from him. "Thank you," she said.

"You can take that off, if you like." He gestured at the cloth around her face. "It might be more comfortable."

"I don't think it would be right," said Mehr. The mystic looked at her askance. "Ambhan noblewomen don't show their faces to people who aren't family." It was strange enough to be talking to this man, who was no blood to her, no husband, no guard—nothing. "I mean no offense by it."

"Just family?" he asked. Mehr nodded. The mystic appeared to consider this, chewing meditatively. "Well. Then there's no problem at all. We're all family here. Brothers and sisters in service to the Empire."

I have a sister, Mehr thought. *A true sister*. But she said nothing.

"We were all orphans, or as good as that, before we came to service," he went on earnestly. "My mother wasn't married when I was born, and her family rejected her—and me. I was blessed to be given a home and a purpose by the Maha. He made me more than a bastard."

Bastard. It was an ugly word, and one that Mehr had heard far too often in the past. It curdled in Mehr's stomach. But she said nothing, only nodded in encouragement so that he would continue.

"Now we are one," he said. "A whole." He shaped a circle in the sand with one finger. The sand rustled at his touch, then settled with a shiver like an indrawn breath. "I'm sure you'll grow to be happy with us," he added gently.

Did he think she would be happy with them because she was like him—illegitimate, a *bastard*? Or was he simply trying to comfort her? From the soft look in his eyes, she thought his motivation had probably been pity.

Mehr stiffened, suddenly angry with herself. She'd clearly done a poor job of playing the obedient new bride. She must have been exuding misery, trudging through the sand with her shoulders hunched and her hands in fists, not talking to a soul. She would have to make a conscious effort to hide her emotions in the future. There were so many ways, after all, that they could be used against her.

"If we're family, I should know your name, shouldn't I?" Mehr said.

"Edhir," he replied.

"Edhir," she repeated. "My name is Mehr."

"I know," he said, and instantly looked embarrassed.

One of the other mystics laughed. Kalini was talking to one of them now on the other side of the fire, a smile playing on her mouth. Her eyes met Mehr's through the flames. Mehr looked down.

She didn't know how to keep herself safe among these people. At least within the walls of the women's quarters she had possessed a measure of power. She'd known the dangers she faced. Now only unknown dangers lay around her, ahead of her, and she had no idea how to protect herself. She tried to distract herself from dark thoughts by sifting the sand between her fingers. As it touched her skin, it almost seemed to brighten.

"It's beautiful, isn't it?" Edhir said. His voice was quieter now. The color on his face had deepened. He wanted earnestly to be kind to her, it seemed. But Mehr was not sure she could trust appearances.

"It's like nothing I've ever seen," she said.

On his other side, another mystic leaned forward to look at Mehr. He was older than the rest, with features weathered into permanent grimness that he tried to soften with a grin. He didn't succeed.

"Our little family is named for the desert," he said. "Has the boy told you that yet?"

Edhir made a sound of protest.

"The boy fancies himself a scholar," said the older mystic. "Always reading. He's barely talked to a woman."

"I have barely ever talked to a man," Mehr said, drawn into defending him against her will. "I can hardly judge him."

The mystic barked out a laugh. "As you say," he said. "My name is Bahren. Emperor's grace on you, sister."

Mehr nodded stiffly. She could hardly offer her name again, when they knew everything there was possible to know about her already.

"Tell me about your family's name, Edhir," Mehr said.

"*Our* family's name," Kalini called out. Mehr didn't react.

"Please," she said instead, looking at Edhir.

He was hesitant, now that the attention of his brethren was focused on him. He began in a halting voice.

"In the old mantras, they say the desert existed long before the Gods went to their long sleep. In the early age of the world, it was created by an old, grieving Goddess who mourned her children, who had died and left her." He was warming to his topic, his voice growing stronger. "Mother's tears, some called it, because the sand was born from her sorrow. Others named it—"

"Get to the point, Edhir," another man muttered.

Edhir coughed. "They called it the Salt. For tears, you see? And we call ourselves the Saltborn, because—the Maha says—without the Salt, we wouldn't be what we are."

He smiled. Mehr managed to murmur out some appreciative nonsense. She saved herself from having to offer a better response by biting into the flatbread, softened by the heat of her fingers. Her mind was whirling. She hoped her hands weren't shaking.

Salt.

How do you forget a death that happened in your arms?

Mehr lay in the darkness of the tent with her eyes wide open. The entire camp was asleep. She was sharing a tent with Amun, a single blanket beneath them, their robes thrown over them for warmth. The temperature had dropped even further, and Mehr was very cold. But there was nothing she could do about it. All she could do was lie still, and wait. And remember.

Who came, Usha? Please.

Salt.

She shivered.

Salt. Saltborn. Usha had tried to warn her. Mehr did not know if the mystics had been the ones to kill Usha, but their name had been on her lips when she had died. They were responsible in some way, tangled up irrevocably with her death and with Lalita's abrupt absence. That, at least, she was sure of now.

She wanted to turn to Amun and ask him if he knew what had happened to Lalita. But she bit her lip. She wasn't an utter fool. So Amun was a good enough man not to want to hurt her—what did that matter? It didn't mean he was trustworthy. It didn't mean she could show him all her weaknesses without consequence. He was still bound to the Maha; he had still made vows that held him fast, that covered his skin like chains made flesh. What kind of man bound himself to people like these? Could anyone truly understand a man like that?

Whatever had happened to Lalita, Mehr would have to find out on her own.

But Mehr couldn't think of Lalita. Usha's death was a splash of red across her memory. Every time she closed her eyes she saw it all over again. There was no room in her tonight for anything else. So she kept her eyes open. She listened to one of the mystics pacing the edges of the camp, his booted footsteps crunching steadily against the sand. She listened to Amun's steady breathing, her own breath warming her hands, which were clasped in front of her.

Then she heard another sound. Light footsteps. Chimes.

"Are you well?" Amun asked.

Mehr realized that she had sat up.

"I'm fine," she said. All was quiet again. She had thought she had heard a dancer's tread, a distinctive way of moving that reminded her of Lalita and her mother, and made her yearn for a home she'd never had. She must have imagined it. Her mind had begun slipping into sleep, perhaps, chasing dreams. "I didn't mean to disturb you."

"You didn't."

Mehr didn't have to look at Amun to hear how alert his voice was. All this time he'd been wide awake, and she hadn't even known it.

Mehr lay back down. She ached all over. Her body was one long bruise. She tried to imagine getting up and packing away the tent and doing this all over again in just a few hours. Even the thought exhausted her.

"How many more days of this?" she asked. "How long until we reach your Maha, husband?"

"At least a week," Amun said.

Gods, a week. She had no idea how she'd make it through so much time in the company of these men, with Kalini's eyes always on her, with Amun a constant, silent shadow at her back. She shivered and curled up tight.

She would just have to find a way.

CHAPTER NINE

Mehr would have liked the days to pass in a blur, but every hour dragged by with torturous slowness. The desert was unrelenting. The darkest hours of the night were bitterly cold, and the brightest hours of the day were scalding hot. Those were the hours when they rested, setting up their tents at nighttime or crouching in the shade of dunes when the heat of the sun rained down. In the hours in between, they walked. And walked.

Mehr was deathly tired of walking.

Worse still, she knew it was her slowness that was lengthening the journey. She wasn't equipped for desert travel. Whenever they stopped she slept like the dead. She was constantly thirsty. Her ration of water never felt like enough to sustain her. The ache in her limbs hadn't lessened over time, only deepened from constant exertion and lack of rest. She would have given absolutely anything for her own bed and a night of uninterrupted sleep.

On one sweltering morning, when the sun seemed particularly fierce above them, Mehr's legs simply gave way. She tripped or stumbled—the result was the same. The mystics were all too far ahead of her to help, so this time she fell with no one to catch her, hitting the ground with an embarrassing thump. A moment later she felt Amun's hands on her, helping her up. The other mystics were watching.

"I hadn't expected a woman with Amrithi blood to be so weak," Kalini called out. "I thought you were *born* for desert travel. How foolish of me."

Mehr gritted her jaw, furious with herself.

It would have been easier if she believed Kalini was trying to be cruel. But it seemed to Mehr that Kalini was simply testing her, assessing her worth with cool eyes. She had judged Mehr unworthy, and frankly she was right to do so. Life in Jah Irinah had made Mehr weak. Her mother had grown up in the desert, but Mehr could barely survive in it for a few scant days.

She thought wryly that it was clear why Lalita had abandoned her clan and built a new life beyond Irinah. The desert was a hard place, and the life of Amrithi had to be a rigorous one. It was certainly not the sort of life a woman like Lalita would choose for herself.

Mehr wouldn't have been able to continue walking, no matter how much Kalini goaded her, so she was relieved when Bahren intervened on her behalf, insisting they make camp.

"What is speed worth if the girl sickens?" he pointed out. "Use your head, Kalini."

Kalini sighed and shook her head. "As you say," she said. Shrugged. "Let's waste an hour or two, if we must."

The rest wasn't long enough. It was never long enough. The last mystic in the group, a quiet and self-contained man named Abhiman, gave Mehr some of their water before the journey continued again. That, combined with the little sleep she'd managed, would have to sustain her. Mehr drank the water gratefully, and began walking again.

Three days passed before the monotony of the journey was broken. Dawn rose on the horizon as they walked, the five mystics and Mehr. Pale light filtered across the sand, setting the grains on fire.

This was the part of the day Mehr's body found most bearable. It was cold, but not as cold as it was at deep nighttime, and Mehr was as well fed and well rested as she was going to be for the day.

She had grown to love watching the skyline change, darkness bleeding from black to gray to the brilliant blue-white of daylight. The mystics were talking, arguing about the journey ahead. Mehr saw the daiva before any of them.

It rolled across the dunes, flat against the ground, moving so gracefully that it looked at first like the shadow of a passing cloud. But the sky was clear. Amun turned to look at Mehr sharply. His eyes were wide.

"Daiva!" cried out Edhir.

"Don't panic," Bahren barked out in return.

But the daiva was no small, weak spirit. The one that had flown into Arwa's room a bare handful of weeks ago had been a soft, benign creature, carved out into the shadowy form of an animal, as the weakest of the daiva were. This vast darkness unfolding beneath the sand was no young spirit, but something old and clever and simply *different*. As it approached, Mehr couldn't help but think of Sara's fear of ancient spirits, the panic in her eyes. A shiver ran down Mehr's spine.

As the daiva passed beneath the mystics, it seemed to flinch. Its edges fractured. It coiled away from them, warded off by the power of their presence.

"Come here, Mehr," Kalini said. She held out her hand. "We'll keep you safe."

Mehr hesitated. She saw Amun shake his head, saying something furiously. She saw him take a step forward—and suddenly the dark being shot through the air, forming a barrier between them.

The daiva's formless darkness surrounded her on all sides. It rose up above her in a high arc, blotting out all but the thinnest blade of sunlight. The sand whirled beneath Mehr's feet. She drew the cloth tighter around her face and held her ground. She could hear the mystics shouting beyond the barrier. From words snatched through the howling darkness, she knew they couldn't reach her, but they were trying.

Mehr gathered her courage and gave the daiva a small bow. She flattened her palms together, in a sigil for respect and greeting. In response, the howling quieted, the darkness shifting silently now around her, loping and curious.

"Mehr!" Kalini shouted. "Answer us! Are you hurt?"

"I'm fine," Mehr responded.

The darkness shuddered, pausing in its motion like an animal that had scented prey. The dark drew closer. Its surface rippled, peeling back to reveal the hard silvered contours of a jaw, a mouth. A golden eye.

Once the daiva had been strong enough to walk the world like men. Mehr knew that. This daiva wore no mortal face, but its features were constantly re-forming, from animal to some faint semblance of human and back again. It was looking at her. It had responded to the sound of her voice.

"Do you understand me?" Mehr said quietly. Far too quietly for the mystics to hear her.

The daiva gave a slow blink. Yes. Yes it had.

Mehr hadn't known that daiva recognized any language beyond their own. All the daiva Mehr had ever known, after all, had responded to sigils alone. But this one was old, old and strong, she was sure of that now. It was nothing like the soft things that flitted along the edges of Jah Irinah. Perhaps in all its long years, its lifetimes upon lifetimes, it had learned something of the languages beyond its own tongue. Perhaps it had once worn a human visage, and lived among mortal men. Mehr lowered her hands slowly, mouth dry. Her heart was beating a frenetic rhythm.

"Spirit," she said, trying to infuse her voice with the appropriate respect. "I have no blade, but I think you know what I am."

She held her arms out, palms open and fingers spread in a

gesture of welcome. She saw the eye give another slow, considering blink.

The daiva took hold of her wrists. It held them like a human would, with a simulacrum of fingers curving around her skin. Its daiva-flesh was warm. It shaped her human flesh curiously, as if it wasn't sure what to make of her.

Mehr held her breath. She wondered if it would try to speak like a human. She wanted it to. But instead it tugged her hands, ever so gently, and began to raise them. It was trying to form a sigil, to speak to her in its own language.

Without warning its grip vanished. Its hands disintegrated around her, collapsing back into formless darkness. Its edges grew jagged; its face fractured like glass, a snarl bared on its simulacrum of a mouth. It was struggling, but Mehr had no idea what it was fighting, what force was dragging it away from her and reducing it back into shadow. She stumbled back, her hands in fists at her sides, as it began to inch away from her, growing ever smaller by the second.

Barrier gone, Mehr could see that the mystics were ringed around her, watching the daiva crumble. Standing directly in front of her was Amun.

His feet were pressed hard to the ground, knees at an angle, his back straight and tall. She watched his arms move, great sweeping motions that drew the daiva as if it had a chain around its neck that compelled it to follow. His hands were shaping a constant line of sigils, one flowing into the other with a seamless grace that Mehr had never been quite able to achieve.

He was dancing an Amrithi rite. But it was no rite Mehr had seen before. As she watched he turned, head lowered, hands sweeping the air and skimming earth. It was a move like the fall of a scythe—a transition for death dances, for grief and the fallen and harvest and forgetting. Not for this. Not for dragging a daiva across the sand, every inch of it vibrating with hollow rage.

Mehr stepped forward. She wanted to shout at him to let it go, let it go now. But Amun was lowering himself into a crouch, hands shaping the sigil for *Go*. It seemed the daiva had no choice. All its fragments scattered into the air. The darkness hung around them like falling rain for a long moment, a heartbeat—and then it was gone.

Amun rose from his crouch, falling into the last stance. Bahren let out a long, colorful string of curses and went to grab the fallen packs of provisions, which had somehow been discarded in the chaos.

Mehr walked over to her husband. She heard nothing, saw nothing. All she could see was Amun's face in the achingly clear morning light.

"What did you do?" Mehr said. She was helpless to hold back the words. Helpless to hold back her horror. "What did you *do*?"

Amun had thrown back the cloth around his face. In the light, the blue marks on his cheeks glowed livid. Cold fire. His mouth wore a bitter smile.

"What I was told to do," he said.

Mehr didn't get the chance to speak to Amun alone until nighttime. The mystics kept Mehr close for the rest of the day, surrounding her on all sides in a human barrier. They were tense and silent. They held no weapons, but weapons were no good against daiva, and they were not afraid of being attacked by mortal men. They were the blessed servants of the Maha, after all, and above such danger. Even the most desperate thieves knew that attacking the Maha's people was worse than a death sentence. The fear the mystics provoked kept human dangers at bay.

Amun walked ahead of them all. If any daiva came, they would face him first. After what Mehr had seen him do, she knew he was weapon enough.

It was miserably cold and dark when they made camp and

settled down to sleep. The tent was barely warmer than the desert outside, but Mehr was grateful for its protection.

Amun was on guard for the first few hours of the night, so Mehr waited for him, curled up under the blanket for warmth. When he came in she sat up. Amun had brought an oil lamp in with him. He set it down on the ground, light flickering over his face. He leaned down to blow out the flame, and Mehr gestured at him to stop.

"Is anyone else awake?" she asked.

"Abhiman," he said, letting the flap of the tent fall down behind him. "He's walking the perimeter. Speak if you like. He won't hear you."

"What did you do to the daiva?" she asked.

"You saw what I did."

"The rites don't have that kind of power," Mehr said. But even as she said it, she wasn't so sure. All her life she'd believed the rites were a matter of prayer, of ritual and faith. But on the night of the storm, she'd reached out a hand and the dreamfire had reached back.

When she'd danced the Rite of Dreaming that night, had she manipulated the dreamfire—the magic of the Gods—the way Amun had manipulated the daiva? Not by intent, certainly. "We don't have the ability to control the daiva. Do we?"

Amun shrugged. "You saw what I did," he repeated.

"But *how*?"

"I learned," he said shortly. He had no desire to tell her more, that was clear enough.

"What you did—however you did it—was wrong. The daiva deserve our respect."

"Is that what your father's people believe, my lady? That daiva deserve our respect?"

Oh, Mehr had already grown to dislike that opaque voice of

his. His face was unreadable. She couldn't tell if he was furious or calm.

"Call me by my name," she snapped. "I've told you before, I'm not a noblewoman any longer. Surely you know that. It's your fault, after all."

"Then don't call me husband," he replied, just as fast. She realized, then, that he was angry. Good. "Call me Amun, and I will call you Mehr. Consider it a trade."

"It's what you are," Mehr said sharply.

"I'm not…" He stopped. Swallowed. "I don't want to think of myself as that."

She thought of the weight of that word, *husband*, and the duties bound up with it. Mehr resisted the urge to touch the seal at her throat.

"Fine," she said. "As you wish. I will call you Amun."

She wrapped her arm around her knees, drawing her legs up to ward off the chill. She could feel Amun's eyes on her, still watching her. There was a beat of silence.

"You're cold," he murmured. He reached for her wrist. Mehr felt the brush of his fingers on her skin and thought of the daiva, of its fingers shattering around her, and flinched away from him.

Amun's face changed before her eyes, hard blankness breaking for a moment to reveal the feelings beneath. His expression was awful—a deep, painful angry thing, his features twisted with loathing.

Mehr had wanted to see some emotion in his face. She saw it then, in the flickering light.

His face became shuttered. He turned away from her. Blew out the lamp.

Mehr clutched her own wrist. "I'm sorry," she said.

"There's nothing to be sorry for."

She heard him shift, lying down on the ground. She didn't

have to see him to know that he had his back to her. She opened her mouth to speak. Closed it again. He didn't want or need her apologies. He wanted her silence. He'd shown Mehr, unwittingly, the secret that lay at the heart of him. He'd shown her his weakness.

Under the mask he wore, Amun was full of poison. But none of it was aimed at her. No. Mehr knew what it looked like when another human being stared at her with hatred. What she had seen in Amun's face was a knife turned inward.

She had seen it in his eyes, then. How he hated himself.

Even in the darkness, the sight of his face was imprinted on her memory. She'd been denied knowledge, any knowledge at all for so long, but in his face she'd found a light to burn away the edges of her ignorance and keep the cold at bay. His self-loathing made a cold, terrible kind of sense. In all the days that had passed, she had never seen the mystics offer him company or a kind word. If Mehr felt lonely, after mere days in their company, she could only imagine what Amun felt. To be so utterly unwanted, to be scarred and silent, to be treated in large and small ways as less than entirely human . . .

That kind of torture had the strength to shatter anyone. But Amun was not shattered. He was whole and strong, lying next to her on the floor of the tent, wide awake, breathing his careful, even breaths. Despite his self-hatred he had reached for her hand. Despite it, he had offered her a little time, a little mercy. He wanted goodness and tenderness—he *craved* it, starving with loneliness as he was—and that fissure in his strength was a tool at Mehr's disposal.

I could use him, Mehr thought, a thrill running up her spine. It felt like something akin to hunger. It would not take much. The Maha had bound him with vows written into his skin and his soul. But Mehr could bind him too. All it would take was a little kindness.

She could place a hand on his back now. She could apologize again. *I'm sorry.* Let her voice soften. *I didn't mean to hurt you.*

She could turn him to her own ends so easily. And she deserved a shield, didn't she? She was so very alone out here, among enemies and strangers. Would it be so wrong to ensure that Amun was on her side?

A voice echoed through her head: *People are not tools to be used, Lady Mehr.*

Nahira had told her that when she had discovered how Mehr had used Sara, bribing her with blood for a momentary escape into the storm. She'd warned Mehr off that path, and yet here Mehr was again—hand raised, words hovering on her lips— ready to bind Amun with the insidious power of kindness.

People are not tools to be used, Lady Mehr.

Mehr had used Sara in order to try to save Lalita's life, and however foolish that had been, she had at least had noble intentions. There would be nothing noble in manipulating Amun. She swallowed around the guilt rising in her throat. Like it or not, survival was not a noble cause. It was a necessity. Mehr would do whatever preserving her life and freedom required, fine morals be damned.

But there was no doubt in Mehr's mind that manipulating Amun as she'd imagined would change her irrevocably. She didn't want to be everything she hated about Maryam. Whatever choices the mystics had stolen from her, this one choice belonged wholly to her. She could be like the people who had manipulated her and used her—the mystics, the distant Maha, her stepmother—or she could be something else.

She had to find another path.

She curled her toes against the soles of her boots, grounding herself. And then she took a leap of faith.

"I think I owe you a debt, Amun," she said carefully. "You

were honest with me about your vow, and about the vow I had made. You tried to be merciful."

She heard him turning, heard the whisper of his clothes, his breath.

"It wasn't mercy," Amun said. "Mercy would have been finding a way to ensure that we never wed. It was—decency. Nothing more than that."

"Then let me pay my debt with a similar mercy," Mehr replied quietly. "Let me be decent to you. And honest." She clutched her knees tighter to her chest. "You're not as good at hiding yourself as you think you are, Amun," she said into the darkness. "Your face, and your voice—in those, you hide your feelings well. But your shoulders. Your hands..." She trailed off, remembering his hands sweeping sigils through the air. "They reveal you," she finished. "I see it, and I believe Kalini does too. No doubt your Maha reads you just as well." Mehr swallowed. "You shouldn't allow yourself to be so vulnerable," she went on. "Not to me. Not to anyone. Weakness is a temptation. Give people the opportunity to use you, and they will, I can promise you that."

Silence.

"Do you know what it is truly like to be used?" he asked.

There was no threat in his voice. Still, she shivered.

"I know I could use what I've seen to truly use you," Mehr said frankly. "But I won't."

"Why?" He sounded honestly curious.

"Because I'm choosing to believe in your decency." And if he proved her wrong, if he turned her leap of faith into a fall into darkness, then she would find a way to gain the upper hand on him again. She would find more weaknesses, more fault lines in his nature that she could leverage to her own purposes. She would do what needed to be done without regret. "I've chosen to repay your decency in kind."

"I never asked you to do so," he said.

"But I have." Mehr shrugged.

She heard him sit up. Her eyes had adjusted a little, now, to the darkness. She could see the outline of his body—the breadth of his hunched shoulders, the tilt of his head.

"What do you want from me, Mehr?"

She felt light-headed now. Perhaps she had been a fool to talk to him without playing the demure maiden. She could have used her knowledge to build his trust in her slowly, to make him reliant upon her for kindness, for company, for affection. That would have been wiser. She had no other allies here, no one but him. If he turned against her, if he chose to distrust her, if he decided he no longer wanted to help her...

She tightened her hands into fists, pushing the panic away.

"I would like it," she said, "if you continued to be decent."

Amun said nothing.

"It's a fair trade," Mehr said evenly. "Honesty for honesty. Mercy for mercy. Tell me what the mystics want from me. Tell me why your Maha has gone to such great lengths to acquire me, and in return—I promise I will be someone you can trust. A friend, just as you've been to me."

She saw him shake his head. Even in the gloom, she could see that.

"Your trade isn't fair," Amun said. "The mystics have absolute power over me. And you..." He let out a breath. "I have nothing to gain from telling you, and everything to lose."

"Then why be merciful at all?" Mehr challenged. "Why defy your Maha and give me time before completing our marriage vow, if the cost for you is so high?"

"I just want you to recognize that this is no game," Amun said in a low voice. "You can't barter with the Maha's people for power, and you shouldn't try. None of us are worth trusting. You've told me not to show my own weaknesses. First you should follow your own advice."

"Are you telling me not to trust you?" Mehr asked.

"I am telling you that I have lived all my life as the Maha's creature, and I know what it means to serve. I know my own nature." His voice was suddenly savage. "I know that if you look for goodness, you will find it is finite. If you trust me, I will betray you. That is what it means to be the Maha's creature. That is what I *do*."

Mehr had seen his marks. She'd seen the way he obeyed Kalini, seen him banish a daiva, seen the feral bitterness in his face. *You can't trust a creature in a cage.* This she already knew. She breathed deep and slow, feeling the weight of his seal around her throat. Her mark felt like it was burning against her chest, a deep cold pain.

"If your goodness is finite, then it seems I must make use of it before it fades," Mehr replied. She was trembling. She had to resist the urge to step out of the tent and run until her feet failed her. "You've bought me a little time, Amun, just a little time before our vow is done and I am the Maha's creature too. You have told me there's no way to escape the vow." A deep breath. "If I can't avoid my fate, then at least give me the knowledge I need to choose how I spend my freedom. Tell me what the Maha wants from me. Not because I've bargained, not because I've used you. Tell me because you are *good*."

He let out a sudden, helpless laugh.

"You are a strange creature," he said wonderingly. "A very strange creature."

Mehr let out a breath. She didn't trust him. She didn't. This was just her body, her exhausted body reacting viscerally to the sudden break in his voice, that fall in gentleness. Her fingers uncurled. She felt an unraveling in her chest, as if she could breathe more easily. Even before he next spoke, she knew she'd won.

"Meet the Maha first," he said. "And then I will tell you everything you want to know."

Rahima

The sky was very black, the stars bright as small moons, when the Amrithi woman approached Rahima's hut. Rahima saw her first through the shutters, when the woman was still in the distance, striding across the sand. In the nighttime wind, her hair was a black flame, flying loose behind her. At first Rahima mistook her for a daiva. She thought perhaps one of the ancient ones had crawled out of myth and come for her, and she prayed to the Gods for mercy. But as the woman drew closer, Rahima's fear abated.

The woman was flesh, dark-skinned and graceful. She moved across the sand with the ease of someone raised in the desert. But her clothing was strange—more Chand than Ambhan or Amrithi or Irin—and she was moving her hands in an odd, sweeping motion as she walked. In response, the sand was rippling behind her, erasing her footsteps entirely.

Rahima stepped carefully out of her hut. She squatted down on the ground by the door, clasped her hands, and waited.

The Amrithi woman stopped. She lowered her hands at her sides and looked about, from Rahima, to the husks of ruined huts around them, then back to Rahima again. She was close enough for Rahima to see her face, which was hollowed with exhaustion.

"There used to be a village here," the woman said. Her voice was hoarse.

"The trade routes changed," Rahima said. "Ambhans stopped coming. Everyone left."

"I remember a water well," the woman said. "And a storehouse, full of rice and grain. A clan used to pass through here..."

The woman wavered on her feet.

"I have gold," the woman said. "Or blood, if you prefer."

Rahima stood up.

"Come inside," Rahima said. "I've got water. Food. A place to sleep."

The Amrithi woman followed her in. She sat on the floor at Rahima's direction, and waited as Rahima poured her some water into a cup and gave her a little food to dull the edge of her hunger. Rahima placed a lantern on the floor between them.

As the Amrithi woman ate, Rahima watched her. The woman was not young, but not old either. Rahima was at least two decades her senior. Old enough to be her mother. If the woman remembered the storehouse and the visiting clans, she must have visited the old village years before its demise. Only Rahima's house had survived the passing years and unkind storms, thanks to her diligent maintenance.

"Your kind haven't been here for a long time," Rahima said. "The last Amrithi I saw...why, it was a girl and her grandmother. We traded food and blood. That was three years ago."

The vial of blood was still buried beneath Rahima's door, to keep the daiva at bay. The grandmother had warned her it would lose its power after a month at most. But Rahima had seen no Amrithi since. What could she do but keep the blood close and pray for her own safety?

"Ah," the woman said. She understood. "You'd like more blood then."

"It used to be easier to keep the daiva away," said Rahima. "A clan would come here before every storm. They never wanted much. Food, mostly. Medicine sometimes. We never had to worry. But those days are gone now."

The woman said nothing. But there was something inviting about her silence.

"I haven't had company in a long time," Rahima said, half in apology for how she would not, could not, stop speaking. "My son, the last time he visited, he told me to come to his village. But I told him no, this is my place."

She told the Amrithi about her son, and his wife and child. She told her about the heyday of the village, before the trade routes had changed and the road had been swallowed back up by the desert, leaving Rahima's village to wither and die. She spoke about her life here, alone in what remained. She spoke until her mouth was dry, then poured herself a cup of water to clear her throat.

The Amrithi woman was watching her.

"There's something you want to say to me," the Amrithi woman said. "Isn't there?"

"My village betrayed the Amrithi," Rahima blurted out. "That is why the village died. We were cursed. The daiva are punishing us."

It was a relief to say so. She had carried the weight of that guilt for so long.

"My husband was the one who told the mystics about the clan," Rahima said. She ladled water into the Amrithi woman's now-empty cup with a trembling hand. Drops splattered on the floor. "They came to our village and offered gold for information. My husband told them about an Amrithi boy who could make the storms move for him. We saw the boy do it once. The mystics gave my husband gold. After that, we never saw the boy again. Soon your people stopped coming here at all."

The woman sipped the water and said nothing.

"The trade routes changed," Rahima said, pressing on. "My husband sickened and passed. My son said we should take our gold to one of the bigger villages. But I said I would die here, and he left. I thought...maybe if I stay here alone, if I suffer without my family day in and day out, and pray to the Gods for mercy, the daiva will be less angry. They will forgive us. The villagers would come back again."

The woman said nothing. Her silence no longer seemed so inviting. Rahima reached for her hand and clasped it.

"You could speak to the daiva," Rahima said, clutching the woman's hand. "You could ask them to forgive us."

The woman exhaled. Then she met Rahima's eyes and smiled, a flat and unfeeling smile.

"If people were cursed for betraying Amrithi, the whole Empire would be in ruin," the woman said.

Rahima shook her head. "You don't know. I hear them at night! They cry in the boy's voice. They tell me we should all be punished. I..."

Rahima fell silent and miserably wiped tears from her eyes.

The Amrithi woman stood. She moved to the corner of the room, back to the wall.

"I don't know if you want absolution from me," the Amrithi woman said, "but I'm not in a position to provide it." The woman leaned against the wall and closed her eyes. "If you'll allow me to rest," she said, "I'll provide you with my blood in the morning."

Rahima murmured agreement and went back to her own bed to weep.

When she woke, the woman was gone. She'd taken some of Rahima's food and water with her, and one of her robes too. There was a gold necklace on the floor where the woman had slept. Rahima looked outside, but the woman was already long gone, the sand unmarked, the sky painfully blue. She hadn't left any blood.

CHAPTER TEN

After their conversation, Amun stayed close to her side. There was no other discernible change in his behavior. He didn't grow friendly or talkative, didn't relax in her company or show her any particular gentleness. He simply shadowed her, slowing his pace to match hers as they walked through the desert with the mystics vigilant around them. Every day he walked beside her. Every night he slept by her side, his back to her. They didn't repeat their discussion. Mehr felt the silence grow between them, heavy with the weight of words unsaid. All Mehr could do was hold on to her faith that the silence would break. She had to hope that once she met the Maha, Amun would tell her everything she needed to know, as he'd claimed he would. She had taken Amun's measure, weighed his weaknesses against his strengths, and she was sure—almost sure—that he would keep his word.

Thoughts of the Emperor and the Maha haunted Mehr constantly. For so long, her only image of them had been a faceless effigy on an altar, the world held in its upraised palm, symbolic of the powers of all the Emperors who had ever held the throne. It was hard for her to envisage either of them as flesh and bone. Her father had at least met the Emperor, had served in his court and earned his governorship by winning imperial favor. She knew the Emperor was a mortal man. But the Maha...

The Maha, the Great One, first Emperor of the Ambhan Empire, had lived far, far longer than any mortal could. His apparent immortality was proof that the imperial bloodline was blessed by the Gods. His temple stood on the sand where the Gods slept, his mystics prayed for the Empire, and the Empire had grown and flourished with fortune on its side.

When Mehr tried to imagine him—the man who ruled the soul and faith of the Empire—she imagined a man with no face, smooth and unblemished and timeless.

She wouldn't have to wonder about the Maha for long. Their journey was almost at an end. Mehr could not tell one cliff or sand dune from the next, but the mystics knew the temple was close. Edhir was beaming, chattering away like a child and making no secret of his excitement. None of the mystics seemed to have the heart to hush him. Bahren simply smiled at him, his weathered face softened with joy. All of them were alight with expectation, the tiredness of their journey fading from their faces, their backs straighter and their eyes brighter, their strength returned.

Even through her dread, Mehr felt that same light inside herself. It was hard not to feel the influence of their joy; it was harder still not to think longingly of a warm bed, fresh food, and clean water. The journey had broken her down into nothing but exhaustion and hunger. More than anything—more even than answers—she wanted the opportunity to feel like herself again.

They came upon the temple just after sunrise after traveling hours through steadily receding darkness. The temple was barely visible at first glance. The same color as desert sand, it was hidden in plain sight. But as they drew closer, Mehr saw the shadow of towers and domes rising against the horizon, the silhouette of her new home forming before her eyes.

She stopped to take the sight of it in. Amun went still by her side. She could hear the soft brush of his robe against the sand as he shifted on his feet.

"Is something wrong?" he asked.

"No." The temple was nothing like the Governor's residence or the smaller, graceful havelis of Jah Irinah. It was crude and austere, unornamented with nothing but its sweeping, uncompromising lines against the skyline to lend it grandness. For three hundred years, the temple had stood on the desert. Long enough for its edges to be rubbed raw by storm and sand. Mehr knew, as all Ambhans knew, that the Maha had chosen to build his temple on the desert as a demonstration of how greatly blessed the Empire was. Looking at the temple now, Mehr couldn't deny the Empire's great and almost otherworldly power. "It's nothing."

"We'd best catch up," he said. When she turned to look at him, she saw his gaze tracking the mystics, who were still walking ahead of them. His hands were clenched at his sides. She nodded and started walking again.

They were met beneath the shadow of one low dome by three men who drew them inside and shut the doors behind them. As the mystics started to chatter and embrace, their voices low with relief, Mehr took her first few steps into the interior of the temple. With the doors shut, the natural light was quenched. Here there was nothing but the flicker of lamplight to illuminate the bare walls and long corridors. She kept her eyes lowered, breathing softly against the folds of cloth around her face. As long as she kept quiet and let the mystics talk, they would most likely ignore her. And Mehr needed a moment alone to find her strength.

The temple around her was far from beautiful, but it felt like the desert: arid but somehow vibrant. *Alive.* The floor was not the pale marble of home, but the burnished gold of sand under sunlight. She wanted to reach down and feel it with her fingers. It was hard not to believe that it would exude heat the way the desert did during the daylight hours. Her gaze flickered up to the walls, a deeper hue of bronze, and to the hooks where the lamps hung, swinging in a breeze funneled through the winding corridors. She didn't know where the breeze had come from. It smelled sweet, like water or soil in rain.

She glanced back at the welcoming party. The men were still laughing, embracing, but one lone man was standing quietly by Kalini's side. Mehr saw him whisper something in Kalini's ear. Kalini caught Mehr's eye; she crooked a finger at her. *Come here.*

Mehr obeyed, stepping back over to her.

"We need to leave," Kalini told her. "The Maha has requested your presence."

Kalini strode past her. Mehr looked back, just for a moment, seeking out Amun's gaze. He was still standing at the entrance, his back to the closed door and his arms crossed. He wasn't looking at her.

"Quicker," Kalini called out. Mehr looked away and followed her.

What had she expected him to do? Run after her? No. Not that. But she had expected him to raise his eyes, to look at her as she left his side for the first time in days. She already missed the reassurance of his presence at her side, the solidity of him, the coolness of his shadow over her. Her face was hot. She clenched her hands up tight. What a fool she was.

She didn't need Amun to reassure her. She needed to rely on herself, first and foremost. To do otherwise would be to cultivate an unforgivable weakness. And Mehr could not allow herself to be weak.

"You will need to dress appropriately before entering the Maha's presence," Kalini said, leading Mehr down a dizzying array of corridors. "Use the bathing room. I'll send someone to collect you."

She gestured at Mehr to stop, and showed her into a room with one high unshuttered window, open to the light. The floor was tiled, the air cool.

"I don't have anything with me," Mehr said. "My clothes. Kalini—"

Mehr turned, but it was too late. Kalini was gone.

Mehr gritted her teeth, holding back the curses she couldn't allow to spill from her lips. Kalini wanted her to dress for the Maha? Well, that was a doomed project. Mehr had been wearing these clothes in sweltering heat for days on end. There was no way on earth that she could transform them into acceptable garb. The Maha would have to be disappointed.

Mehr undressed and folded her clothes in the corner of the room. Someone had clearly anticipated Mehr's arrival, because a low basin of water had been prepared, with a pitcher and soap by its side. Mehr crouched down and took the pitcher in her hands. She skimmed it through the water, then raised it, pouring the liquid over her head. The water was shockingly, gloriously cool. She blinked it out of her eyes, watching dirt-clouded water pool around her knees.

She didn't know how long she had, so she made a clumsy attempt at untangling her hair before giving the task up. She focused instead on scrubbing herself clean, sloughing away the grime of the journey. Then, after a moment's hesitation, she grabbed the tunic she'd worn beneath her robe and daubed the underarms with a little water and soap.

She heard a cough. She looked up, tunic still held in her hands. There was a woman at the door, a young woman with a bundle of clothes in her arms. She gave Mehr an embarrassed smile and held the bundle out. "Kalini sent me to bring you this," she said.

Mehr took the bundle from her, her own tunic clutched loosely in front of her in a semblance of modesty.

"She told me to tell you not to cover your face," said the woman. "He wouldn't like that." Another lopsided smile, and the woman dashed away. Mehr looked down at the bundle. A tunic, a sash, a pair of trousers. No shawl, no veil. She let out a long, slow breath and started getting dressed.

Mehr needed no mirror to know that she looked nothing like the Governor's daughter any longer. She'd grown thinner on the journey, her body all muscle and bone. Her skin had darkened in the sun. She wore no ornaments, and her clothes were clean but plain and ill-fitting. She'd bound back the tangle of her hair with frayed thread, but she knew it had done little to improve her appearance. She thought of the way the mystics spoke of the Maha, thought of Amun's blue marks and bleak eyes. Nervousness gripped her insides. Being herself was not enough. She wanted fine clothes and jewels and a veil to protect her from the Maha's eyes. She wanted an armor of beauty, strong and glittering. But she had nothing. She was unarmed.

Kalini led Mehr out of the darkness of the corridors up onto a wide balcony open to sky. The sudden change in light left Mehr blinded for a moment. Dazzled, she stood still and listened to the howl of the wind. She could smell water. Before the desert, she hadn't known water had a scent. She did now.

Her vision cleared. At first she thought her eyes were tricking her, that she was seeing one of the wavering illusions common in the desert heat. But then she took a step closer to the edge of the balcony, breathed in that scent of water, and knew that what she saw was real after all.

Like the havelis of Jah Irinah, the temple had an inner courtyard. But the courtyard was massive, its breadth equal to the size of a village. It had to be, to encompass the oasis lying at its heart. The oasis was huge, and surrounded by vegetation and signs of irrigation. Its water glimmered in the light. Mehr had never seen such a large natural body of water. She'd never expected to see so much lush life here. It took her breath away.

She heard footsteps. Kalini bowed low to the ground beside

her, her head pressed to the floor. Mehr's mark, the one etched into her skin above her breasts, began to ache.

Mehr bowed down, following Kalini's example, her limbs doing what was necessary for survival even as her senses sharpened, taking in every detail of the world around her: the sharp acid sting on her skin, the heat of the sun. The sound of those footsteps going still.

It was his boots that she saw first. They were sturdy, hard leather, unmarked by the outdoors. The hem of his robe was a deep, lustrous blue, dark like the robes of the other mystics but made of a far finer material. If there was one thing Mehr had learned as the Governor's daughter, it was how to identify finer things.

"Stand up," said the Maha. Mehr and Kalini stood.

Mehr looked into the Maha's face.

It was not the blank mask she had half feared it would be.

On the surface, the Maha looked like a mortal man. He wore no turban, no mark of noble status. His hair was cut brutally short in the military style, but what little of it she could see was peppered gray. He was old—she had guessed, of course, that he would be old—but every inch of him exuded strength and charisma that belied his age. His eyes were as sharp as knives and unclouded by time. His bones were hard, but his mouth was shaped into a kindly smile. He reminded Mehr absurdly of her father.

"Kalini," he said. He kissed her forehead. Kalini closed her eyes, savoring the touch of his mouth. "You've done well."

"Maha," she said. She pressed a fist to her chest. "It was my honor."

"Did Amun give you trouble?"

"No, Maha," said Kalini. Her mouth firmed. She seemed to steel herself. "There was a daiva."

The Maha gestured at Kalini to continue.

"It was dealt with," Kalini went on, a pleading note in her voice.

"Amun performed the rite. No other disturbances occurred. It didn't harm the girl."

"The others?"

"Were also unharmed, Maha. Amun banished it swiftly."

"You should have been more vigilant, Kalini," he said.

"Yes, Maha."

"Blood first," he told her. "The rite should always be a last resort."

Kalini lowered her head, chastised. The Maha placed his fingertips against her forehead, at the same spot where he had pressed his lips. Mehr saw Kalini's shiver. The sight made her stomach knot.

"Go now. I wish to speak to your new sister alone."

Kalini bowed again, forehead to the ground. Then she stood and left.

The Maha turned his sharp eyes on her. Mehr was uncomfortably aware of her bare face, and of the ache of the mark on her skin.

"How do you like my temple, Mehr?" he asked. His voice rolled over her like a storm. She felt the mark flare to a biting pain. She sucked in a sharp breath and saw that kindly mouth twitch.

"It's like nothing I have ever seen, Maha," said Mehr. Careful words were required, she thought. "A holy place indeed."

"It truly is," he answered. "Look out there." He swept a hand out in the direction of the oasis. "An oasis so vast and fruitful shouldn't exist in such a desert. But this marvel thrives because our prayers ensure that the Gods dream a world that is kind to us. The Gods bless our Empire with good fortune. The world turns its tide in our favor, over and over again." He looked at her. "Do you know how Durevi was won, Mehr?"

"No, Maha," Mehr said. Durevi was the newest province of the Empire, but so distant from Irinah that Mehr had never paid its fate much heed. Her father's household had celebrated its conquering—there had been prayers, and sweets—but she knew no more than that. "I am sorry, Maha."

The Maha ignored her apology and curled a hand around the balcony's edge, his eyes still fixed on Mehr's face. The longer she looked at him, the less human his face appeared. There was a light within it: a glow that came from beneath his timeless flesh, as if his skin were a lamp concealing a flame.

"By prayer," he said. "My mystics prayed fervently for the success of our army and the destruction of the Durevi royals, and the Gods blessed us swiftly. A wave of sickness came over the army. The royal family were consumed by madness and took their own lives. Our men entered the kingdom unchallenged, and Durevi was won. Now it is part of our Empire, blessed by order and civilization, and thankful for it." He laughed then, softly, as if he had amused himself.

The sound—ah. There was no denying the power his voice had on her now. She could feel it under her *skin*.

He carried on in the slow, soft voice of a man speaking to a particularly ignorant child. "You will not understand this, child, because you have been born in my Empire blessed by glory and grace, but there is only so far that an army can extend its supplies, its weaponry, its men. There is only so far it is possible for one ruler to expand his territory. The Empire has surpassed those limits, time and time again. All empires fall, Mehr, but *my* Empire will not. Do you understand why?"

She swallowed through the knot of fear in her throat and fixed her eyes on the oasis, grateful for the opportunity to avoid the Maha's piercing face.

"Prayer, Maha," she said, forcing the words out. "Because of prayer."

Mehr could hear the smile in his voice. "Indeed."

Mehr remembered what her father had said, when she'd asked him why he feared the mystics.

Ah, Mehr! I have seen cities put to death at their word. I have seen plague and famine and slaughter fall on men at their whim.

She had not doubted him, and yet…

She hadn't expected the Maha to be as he was, human and yet entirely inhuman. She hadn't expected the feel of his power, the sound of his voice, the terror deep inside in her bones.

"That is how we serve," the Maha said. "Our prayers bring blessings to the Empire. Our prayers turn our enemies to dust. Truly, there is nothing more holy than service."

She felt the Maha come to stand beside her and tried not to flinch away. His physical closeness made bile rise in her throat.

For a long moment he stood by her quietly, watching the wind sweep the surface of the water. Then he said, "How do you like your husband?" Without missing a beat he spoke again, his voice casual, conversational. "Look at me, Mehr."

She felt the mark flare hotter. Felt herself tugged, like a puppet on strings, to do his bidding. Invisible hands coaxed her head to turn to his. Ice ran through her veins.

She could have resisted. The compulsion wasn't all-consuming. But the shock of it made her turn unthinking, her heart beating wildly in her chest. She looked up at the Maha with wide eyes, unable for an agonizing moment to hide her fear.

He saw it. She knew he saw it. He'd ordered her to look at him for one reason alone: to show her what he could make her do. To *make* her fear.

"Do you know why I dislike veils, Mehr?" He waited. Mehr stiffly shook her head, not looking away from him, compelled to obey. "I dislike them because they are so often used to conceal the truth. You, for example, child. You were hidden from the world by veils and walls. They concealed your nature from my many eyes. They kept you from service to your Emperor and your Maha. And what is service, child? *Tell me.*"

"Holy," Mehr said dully. She felt her jaw work, felt the compulsion thrill its way up her throat like fire.

"Veils kept you from holiness," he agreed. "When you left your veils and walls, when you left your father's home and entered the storm that graced your city, you revealed yourself. I have eyes in many places, Mehr, who seek truth for my sake. Praise the Emperor that they found you. Praise be, that you revealed the full strength of your blood." He smiled at her. "Because you stand before me as you do, unveiled and in service, I do not need you to tell me what you think of your husband. I see the truth of it burning in your eyes."

She didn't know what to say to him. She wanted to recoil in horror and in revulsion. She wanted to press her hands over her face and blot him out. She thought with longing of the veil she'd worn in her father's household: a noblewoman's veil, all soft gauze, that concealed her face in its entirety. He looked at her as if her flesh were itself a thin gauze and her heart a bright and bloody flame.

He can't see my thoughts, she told herself desperately. *He can't see my secrets.*

Mehr had always prided herself on her ability to conceal her true feelings. It wouldn't, couldn't fail her now. Her secrets were not written on her skin. Let him have her fear, let him have her revulsion. She would not show him the truth of her unfinished vow, the lie of it, the hope of freedom she couldn't shake. She could keep those from him. She had to.

Mehr heard the scuff of gentle footsteps. The Maha looked away from her, his gaze lifting beyond her shoulder.

"Amun," she heard him say. "Your presence wasn't requested."

"It is my duty as her husband to be by her side." Amun's low, unreadable voice had never brought her as much comfort as it did then, coming from the balcony entrance. She turned and saw him bow low, head to the floor as Kalini had done. His face was uncovered, marks gleaming a fierce blue in the light. He rose. "And it is her duty to remain beside me in return. I came to fulfill our mutual duties."

"I'm glad to see you take your vows so seriously," said the Maha. He sounded amused. Much to Mehr's relief, he stepped away from her, allowing Amun to stand by her side in his stead. "I take it you have enjoyed your reward? Answer me honestly, Amun."

"We've lain together many times." Amun's voice was a blank canvas. "She wears my mark."

True. And not true. They had lain together, but not in the way Amun clearly intended the Maha to believe they had. She wore his mark, but it was incomplete, burning and churning her flesh like a small flame. Amun had not lied to the Maha, not disobeyed—he'd simply twisted his words so carefully, so cleverly, that he'd concealed the truth with a veil of misdirection. Knowing now how the Maha hated dishonesty, knowing the power of his voice, Mehr could only marvel. And bite down on her tongue to keep her own silence.

The Maha gave a soft laugh. He placed a hand on the edge of the balcony, raising his face to the sun.

"She pleases you, then?"

"She pleases me greatly," Amun said.

If Mehr bit down any harder, she'd soon taste blood.

"A gift to you, and a gift to all of us," murmured the Maha. "What a gem you are, child." The Maha looked at her again. "You want to serve the Emperor, don't you, Mehr?"

"I share my husband's duties," Mehr managed to say. She felt Amun's sleeve brush hers.

The Maha straightened and reached for Mehr. Amun tensed.

"Don't move," the Maha said, and both Mehr and Amun froze as he reached for Mehr's chin and tilted her head up. From a distance his eyes were the light hazel of Ambhan nobility, but this close Mehr could see that the dark pupils of his eyes had points of light within them, light as sharp and jagged as shattered glass.

Whatever the Maha was, he was not entirely human. Mehr was sure of that.

"You have the Amrithi look," he said, tilting her head to the side for a closer inspection. Mehr's skin burned where he touched it. "Once there were many of your ilk among us. But there are so few of you now, and still so much work left to be done." He paused, looking at her. "You will need to learn quickly."

"She already knows a little," Amun said. "She's teachable."

"Good." He released her. "A storm will be upon us soon. Make sure she knows her duties before then."

"Maha."

Mehr thought he would let them leave. Instead the Maha turned his attention on her again, gaze intent.

"Are you glad to be among us, Mehr?" he asked, his voice dangerously kind. "Does it please you to serve the Empire? Speak truthfully."

"No," said Mehr. "I'm afraid." In horror, she smacked a hand over her mouth to stop herself from speaking on. She hadn't intended to be truthful. She'd had no choice.

"The fear you feel is simply the first step toward awe," the Maha said gently. "And awe is what is required for true worship. Embrace it. Let it subsume you, and you will learn your place."

The Maha brushed a hand over her head, smoothing her tangled hair. Mehr held her breath. Held still.

"Yes," he said tenderly. "I do believe you'll learn soon enough."

He spoke as if he could transform her feelings along with her will, as if he could make her fear turn into awe, reshaping her nature to his whims. In that moment, staring into the refracted light of his eyes, Mehr's fear deepened and grew, stretching its dark limbs. She was afraid that he could.

CHAPTER ELEVEN

Amun took Mehr to his room. It was high in one of the temple's many spires, a circular room with windows on all sides. When they entered, Amun unbarred the shutters, letting in the vast blue of the sky. Mehr waited for him to finish, then walked over to the nearest window. She leaned out and held her face to the sun. There was no perforated screen to hold her back; she could lean out unimpeded. She drew in deep lungfuls of air, one after the other, trying to calm the panicked beat of her heart.

To think, only hours ago she had been longing for the journey through the desert to end. She'd hungered for shelter and water and a clean place to sleep. Now she had everything she'd desired, and she wanted nothing more than to return to the desert again. The journey had been hard, facing the Maha's terrible, cutting kindness was infinitely harder.

Amun was silent behind her, but she could hear him breathe, slow and even, and that sound alone was enough to make her head hurt with anger.

"You should have told me," she said, and knew her anger had leaked into her voice, colored it like blood in water. "You should have told me what the Maha—*is*."

"I apologize."

Mehr was glad for the air against her face. She wished it were cooler. She felt like the Maha was still there, still with her, his presence a hot brand under her skin. She'd almost forgotten the mark of her vow during her journey through the desert. She wouldn't forget it again.

"Why do you serve him? Why would you...?" She stopped. Took one deep breath. Another. "I want to ask you why you made vows to him, Amun, but I believe I know the answer." She remembered the Maha's gaze, the softness of his voice, the way Kalini's eyes had closed when he'd pressed his mouth to her forehead. "If he had wanted to make me love him, I think he could have." She turned to face Amun, still gripping the window with her hands as if it could make her steady and strong. "But he didn't want me to love him. He wanted me to be afraid. Didn't he?"

The light illuminated the bareness of the room. The sight was a bitter contrast to Mehr's old, lavish quarters. There was a bed and a trunk for clothing. A single oil lamp hung on a hook by the door. There was nothing else. Just Amun, standing still and watching her with dark eyes.

"He did the same to me," Amun said. "When I first began my service, the day after I took my first vow. He showed me what the mark could make me do. He taught me to fear." Deep breath in. Deep breath out. "He didn't lie to you. Fear is the first step toward awe. Toward worship."

"I don't want to worship him." Her fingers hurt from how hard she was gripping the window.

"He isn't easily denied." Amun's voice was implacable. "The Maha wanted your fear, and now he has it. He wants your awe, and he will have that too. You won't deny him that, Mehr, because as long as he gets what he wants, he won't look beyond the surface and see what he does *not* have: your sealed vow."

Mehr watched him inhale and exhale, and realized he wasn't breathing steadily because he was calm, but because he wasn't. The Maha had shaken him just as much as he'd shaken Mehr.

Amun was controlling his body, his breath, with a will like iron. He was holding in the torrent of feeling.

"I sent you to him unprepared, and for that I am sorry," Amun said. "But I believed your ignorance would protect our secret, and I was right." He swallowed. "I won't lie to you again. Now that you've met him, we can speak honestly."

Although his voice was hard, he had turned his face away, his neck and jaw in shadows. His hands were clasped behind him, his shoulders eloquent with tension. In the desert she'd told him how much emotion his body revealed. He clearly hadn't taken her words to heart. She could only find it in herself to be glad of it as she let out a shaky breath of her own and pried her fingers loose from the edge of the window. In those shoulders, in that turned head, she could read everything she needed to know.

He was controlling himself for her sake. He knew exactly how she felt. He'd been in her place, helpless in the presence of the Maha. Owned. He was *still* owned and helpless. But instead of lashing out as she had, he had led her up the narrow staircase to his room with wordless, endless patience. He'd opened the shutters to let the world in, giving her a small taste of the freedom she craved to quiet the fear in her heart.

He was being kind. Mehr swallowed, her throat closing. She was dangerously close to weeping.

"You shouldn't," Mehr said, hoping her voice was steady. "Honesty is all well and good, but what if he had asked me about the vow?"

"He didn't."

"You took a risk, and we were lucky," Mehr acknowledged. "But he could have asked me anything, and I would have been honest with him. I couldn't help myself. My voice wasn't my own." The knowledge was bitter on her tongue. She copied Amun, breathing through the fear. "I can't lie to him, Amun. You should keep your secrets safe from me."

"I told you I would be honest with you. That wasn't a false promise."

"You can't be," Mehr said helplessly.

"I can," Amun retorted. "You can learn to resist him."

"As you do?"

"Better than I can, Mehr. I'm fully bound by my vows. I can only... alter the shape of my obedience. Or suffer, if I choose to resist." A bitter smile shaped his mouth. "Your vow isn't sealed. You can still fight."

She remembered the Maha's voice. The ghost of hands on her face, compelling her to face him. She shivered.

"I'm not sure I can," she said tightly.

"I know you can."

"You don't."

"I do." He turned his gaze on her again, his voice so earnest that it shocked her into silence. "I have faith in your strength."

His gaze was unflinching. Her heart fluttered strangely in her chest. She looked away first.

"Fighting him would only hurt me," she said, thinking of what her defiance to Maryam had always cost her. She thought, too, of what the Maha would do if he discovered the secret she shared with Amun. Her father had told her the Maha's wrath had destroyed entire cities. What would he do to a servant who betrayed him? "You will have to teach me how you defy him."

The longer she played the subservient role, as Amun did, the longer she would maintain her small measure of freedom—as small and as vital as the open shutters around her, the sight of the wide blue sky.

"I show the Maha obedience, always," Amun said. He spoke softly, as if afraid his voice would carry. "I defy him only in the margins. Every line of every vow I wear, I obey." His fingers brushed his sleeve, as if he could feel the shape of the vows marking his skin beneath the cloth. "But all vows have their limits. Words can be misinterpreted. To choose not to obey isn't an option. But *how* I obey...that I can control. Do you understand, Mehr?"

"Yes," she said. "Of course."

You don't allow him to break you, she thought. *You bend instead.*

Could she mimic him? Could she learn to play subtle games to protect herself from the Maha's grip? Amun believed she could. Mehr would have to believe the same. She had to believe she was strong enough to learn the truth and hold it safe inside herself, because the alternative was to allow her circumstances to drown her.

"Truth, then. Why does he need Amrithi?" Mehr asked. "Why does he need Amrithi like you and I—who the daiva recognize as their own? How does binding us serve the Emperor?"

Amun hesitated for a moment. Then he strode over to the door, pushing it wide.

"Come," said Amun. "The best way is to show you."

Mehr didn't think she would ever make sense of the temple's layout. The corridors were all winding, uniform darkness. To Mehr they were an undecipherable maze, but Amun led her through them confidently, moving through the gloom without the need for a lamp to guide him. She wondered, not for the first time, how many years he had been in the service of the Maha. He walked through the temple the way she had once walked through the women's quarters. It was as if he'd been born to this place.

She walked behind him, matching his footsteps. Every few seconds he turned his head, listening and looking.

"Do you expect us to be found?"

"We will be," he said.

He was soon proved correct. Two men came out of the shadows and began to follow them. Amun gave no reaction. Mehr watched them from the corner of her eye, head tilted down. In Amun's presence her bared face no longer troubled her, but these men were strangers. Having no choice but to show them her uncovered face shamed her, and that shame wasn't something she could easily shake. Her fingers twitched at her sides. She wished she had a shawl to reach for to draw around her head.

Amun stopped at a narrow door. He unbolted it. He and Mehr stepped out into the desert. Behind them, the two men followed.

The sand stretched out before them, a clear expanse all the way to the horizon. The men stayed near the entrance as Mehr and Amun made their way out into the open. The gentle wind, warm from the heat of the day, caught Amun's dark curls. He brushed his sleeve over his hair, frowning.

"We can stop here," he said. "They won't be able to hear us."

He positioned himself between her and the guards, his broad-shouldered frame concealing her almost entirely.

"Does the Maha expect me to run?" Mehr tilted her head at the men, knowing they wouldn't catch the gesture with Amun standing in their line of sight.

"No," he said. "He doesn't think you will run. But a valuable item should always have a keeper, or so I've been told." Amun took a step back. He folded his arms. "Do you know any rites?"

"Some," Mehr said.

"Show me the Rite of Fruitful Earth. Are you familiar with it?"

Mehr hesitated. She had never danced in front of anyone outside the women's quarters before. To do so in front of strangers felt alien to her, and wholly unfamiliar.

"This isn't a test," Amun said softly, misreading her. "I can choose another rite if you prefer."

Mehr shook her head.

"No, this will do well enough."

Doing her best to block out the world around her, she fell into the first stance.

The Rite of Fruitful Earth: It was a rite for the farmer with arid fields, a rite for people with no crops and only parched soil to sustain them. It was not one of Mehr's favorite dances, but she knew it well enough to perform it now. She moved between stances, her footsteps a whisper against the sand, her arms rising and falling as she found her rhythm. She shaped the first sigils with her fingers. When she shaped *life*—a flick of thumb to the fingertips, like the lighting of tinder—she felt something surge through her, from her feet up to her eyes. Her vision wavered, shadows flickering at the edges. She went abruptly still.

"Continue," Amun said. He sounded so much like Lalita did when Mehr faltered during practice that she found herself obeying without question.

After a moment, he joined her. He moved fluidly from the first stance straight into her own, mirroring her movements without the same cautious deliberation Mehr gave to shaping the rite. Sigils flickered over his fingers. Mehr felt power surge through her again, but this time she didn't stop dancing.

Finally, she fell into the last stance and felt the power release her.

"Look," said Amun. Following his gaze, she lowered her head.

Her breath caught in her throat.

Between their feet, the sand had transformed into soil. In amazement, Mehr kneeled down and touched the earth. It was cool and soft, heavy with its own richness. Between the clods of soil were the first pale green shoots of new vegetation. She touched the edge of a leaf. Real. It was all real.

"How?" she whispered.

Amun kneeled down too, his body still concealing hers. He touched the soil too, soft and reverent.

"The daiva draw their strength from the dreams of their mothers and fathers," he said. "This temple lies at the heart of the desert, the place where the Gods sleep and dream most strongly, which makes the daiva infinitely stronger also. Here they can truly answer our prayers."

"So," she breathed out. "We Amrithi. We can make the daiva shape our world. To our will."

"In small ways, yes." The green was withering beneath them, soil desiccating back into gold-hued sand. "The daiva only have so much strength. For a price, some of us can do more."

Amun's expression was grave. Whatever the price was, she knew it had to be high. Before Mehr could ask him anything more, Amun rose to his feet, brushing the sand from his robe.

"Stand," said Amun. "As long as we practice, they won't approach us."

Mehr stood, giving her new guards a sidelong glance as she did so. The men had edged farther back. Clearly like many of the servants in her old home, they distrusted Amrithi customs. Amun caught the direction of her gaze.

"The Maha expects you to be taught before the storm comes," he murmured. "They won't risk his displeasure by disturbing our lesson."

"Tell me about the storm," said Mehr. "Why must I be prepared for it? What does the Maha want you to teach me?"

"A very specific rite," said Amun. He fell into the first stance. Mehr followed. "Adjust your posture to match mine," he told her. He looked over her stance with a critical eye, then proceeded to offer her criticism after criticism. Her shoulders were too high—then too low. Her feet were not properly placed. The angle of her knees was not quite right. Mehr felt like a child in the schoolroom again.

"The storm, Amun," she said impatiently.

He was all reluctance. But Mehr waited, her eyes fixed on him. She would not relent.

"Reshaping the world takes a greater power than the daiva

possess," he said finally. "The Maha desires for the Empire to defy the natural order of the world and continue in everlasting glory. He desires the same for himself. For that, he must harness the one force in the world that shapes the natural order. A power only present during storms."

A force that shaped the natural order. A force that came only with the storms.

Dreamfire. He was talking about dreamfire.

"No rite can compel the dreams of Gods," Mehr whispered. "That is impossible."

"Raise your hands." Mehr did so, numbly playacting at the lesson along with him. "Show me your next stance."

"*Amun.*"

"The Maha's spies saw the dreamfire respond to you, Mehr," he said. "Dreamfire is the power of the Gods shaping the world. Don't you understand what you did in that storm?"

"I was praying, not compelling," she said tightly. "Gods are not daiva, to be compelled by vows. Gods are *Gods.*"

"But you can compel them," Amun said, "whether you choose to or not. The *amata* gift gives us the very rare ability to compel the dreams of the Gods. That decides your value to the Maha."

She couldn't. Surely she couldn't. But Amun had promised to tell her the truth, and although she wanted to believe he was lying to her, she knew he was being honest. The Maha had taken Mehr, tricked her into vowing away her life, because of the gift of her Amrithi blood. No wonder he had called her a gem. She had the power to place the world in his hands.

The truth was awful. It revolted her, deep in her gut, her bones. She had always known the daiva were holy beings and worthy of reverence, that the Gods were as permanent and powerful as the earth or the sun or the night. To bend the dreams of the Gods was to destroy the very order of the universe. She couldn't imagine a greater heresy.

Mehr had always been taught to show the daiva reverence. *Respect your blood*, she'd been told—by her mother and by Lalita after that. *Respect the daiva, because when you pass on, they will remember your actions, and your soul will pay the price.*

She had thought the way Amun banished the daiva in the desert, without respect, without cajoling, had been anathema. What he told her the Maha expected of her—of them both— was far, far worse. What price would her soul pay for such an act?

"Your stances need work," Amun told her. "We should begin again. Here." He gestured at her left arm, held his own at an angle. "Follow my lead."

Mehr had no interest in playing at the rites. Her mind was far too full. She didn't understand how any Amrithi could allow themselves to be willingly bound to this task, tied to the Maha's whims for a lifetime. She certainly didn't know how Amun could allow it.

"Are other Amrithi used by the Empire this way?" she asked.

"No." Amun's voice was curt. "Not any longer. Once, there were many Amrithi pairs here, or so I've been told. Now we are the only ones the Maha owns, and it took him years to find you."

"That can't be," Mehr protested. She knew the mystics had tried to take Lalita. She knew Amrithi tribes had been vanishing. Where could they have gone but straight into the Maha's searching grasp?

Amun shot her a look through lowered lashes.

"You recognize that what I do is heresy," he said flatly. "It horrifies you."

Mehr said nothing. It was true.

Amun took her shoulder. Mehr stiffened. To all appearances he was correcting her stance again. But Mehr could feel his breath against her cheek, hear his voice, as soft as the beat of a daiva's wings.

"Heresy is a crime against our blood. Binding our souls,

forcing us to bend the fabric of the world..." His breath was soft, so soft against her skin. "Death is preferable. Or so the Amrithi of the clans believe."

"No." Mehr's denial was reflexive.

"I've seen it, Mehr. I *know* it." He raised her arm slightly, his touch light. His voice became even lower. "We carry knives for a reason."

Mehr wrenched away from him. Amun flinched back.

"I'm sorry—"

"Don't be," said Mehr. Deep breath. "I asked for the truth. I can't blame you for sharing it."

She thought of Usha bleeding and dying. She thought of Lalita. She thought of all the clans that had vanished. She thought of her mother.

The men were watching. The sand was shifting in the wind, golden-bright in the glare of the sun. And Amun was watching her, waiting for her, an apology shaped in every line of his body, his night-dark eyes.

"Be thankful you were raised without a tribe," Amun said. "It will make this burden easier to bear."

Mehr had never had a tribe. But she'd loved people, and now she had lost them all.

She wondered if the people she loved—Lalita, her long-exiled mother—had fallen to their own daggers. She thought of the way she'd pressed her blade into Arwa's hands. How she had done it to keep Arwa *safe*.

She should have embraced ignorance. She should have been thankful for it.

CHAPTER TWELVE

As the daylight began to wane, the two men finally interrupted Mehr and Amun's lackluster training and gestured for them to return to the temple. Mehr was glad to stop. She had no heart for the rites now, not after everything Amun had revealed to her.

The men waited for Mehr and Amun to enter the temple before barring the door behind them. "We will need to practice again later," Amun told her, as one of the men paused to light a lamp. "You still have a great deal to learn." He hesitated. "I will speak to Edhir tomorrow. He may be able to tell me exactly when the dreamfire will fall."

Mehr made a noise of agreement.

They made their way through the dark corridors, not speaking to one another. Mehr couldn't bring herself to utter a single word. She had no desire to ask any more questions, and innocent conversation felt like it was beyond her reach. The truth was a heavy weight in her skull. She couldn't think beyond it. She couldn't even muster up surprise when they entered a large hall filled from end to end with people. Some looked at her curiously. She looked back.

Mystics, divided by gender, were kneeling on the floor. Lamps flickered along the walls. Before them all, wreathed in incense, stood an altar. Upon it was a carved statue, faceless, wearing a jewel turban, a world etched into one upraised palm.

"You need to sit with the women," Amun said. He stood stubbornly next to her, even as mystics jostled past them. She knew he wouldn't move until she responded.

Mehr nodded. That was all the response she felt able to offer. She joined the throng, kneeling down on cool stone on the women's side of the hall. She wished she had a pillow or a low divan to perch on, but there was no such comfort here.

The Maha was standing before the altar. He didn't kneel as the mystics did. He stood tall, as proud as the effigy of the Emperor. She watched as he clasped his hands, closed his eyes. She saw the women kneeling on either side of her bow their heads. Mehr stared at the Maha's own head, blinking away the sting of incense from her eyes. She was heavy. Heart heavy, soul heavy. But there was rage building inside her, growing ever stronger as the voices rose around her and the prayers began.

Mehr had always avoided prayer. The rites had always been her preferred form of worship. But this was an Ambhan temple, and Mehr had no guilt-stricken father to indulge her any longer. She was the Maha's property, and she would have to play at praying the way the Ambhans prayed: with mortal words and mortal song.

Mehr began to murmur along with them. Harmonies cut sharply through the air. She clasped her fingers tight enough for her nails to press grooves into her skin. She was heavy, so heavy with hate. The voices rose together in song, higher and higher, echoing off the domed ceiling of the hall. The voices sang of love and beauty and wealth, of a throne wreathed in gold. The mystics prayed for the Empire. They prayed for Hara and Numriha and Irinah and Durevi, for the provinces of the Empire, for the provinces still to come: the unclaimed countries that would one day be subsumed by the Empire's glory. They prayed for Ambha itself, the jewel of the known world.

They prayed for the Empire to grow, ever larger, ever more wealthy and powerful. They prayed for the immortality of the imperial line, for the Maha to continue strong and everlasting as their leader and their guiding light.

Every single thing they prayed for would come to pass.

Mehr fixed her eyes on the statue upon the altar. The effigy was faceless by necessity: It stood for all Emperors past, present, and future. Son followed father, life followed death, generation after generation sat upon the throne. But there would always be an Emperor. There would always be an Empire. There would always be the Maha, ancient and glorious, the source of all imperial power.

Mehr bowed her head when expected, clasped her hands when the mystics clasped their own, and thought not of the Maha, but of the Emperor.

For all that he was mortal, all her life he had been like a God to her—distant, powerful, untouchable. His displeasure was death; his favor was a promise of a life of contentment and luxury. Her father served him with unflinching loyalty and had been rewarded with Jah Irinah and all its arid, raw beauty.

Mehr had been told the Emperor hated her mother's people. The Emperor's hatred of the Amrithi for their old rebellion against the Empire and their heathen ways had been held over Mehr like a knife. She had been told to hide her customs, her beliefs, to forget her mother. To let *Arwa* forget their mother. Because if she attracted the Emperor's gaze...

She clenched her hands tighter. Well. Now she knew the consequences.

But she knew something else now too. He had never hated her mother's people. He had just never considered them people at all. They were the kindling wood that fed the fire of the Empire's strength.

The Amrithi were the Empire's tools. They were there to be put into service, to harness the dreams of Gods to shape the Ambhan Empire's golden immortality. Mehr had always been told that the Gods dreamed sweetly for the Empire. Now Mehr understood why they did so. Their dreams had been compelled. Their dreams had been stolen.

Bitterness welled up in her.

There was a lull in the prayers. As the song quieted and the Maha began to chant, silken ancient litanies to the sleeping Gods, Mehr raised her eyes again and stared at the statue of the faceless Emperor until her eyes burned.

The Empire was rotten to the core.

Finally, after years cloistered away in privilege, Mehr's eyes were open.

Mehr could not help Lalita. Either she had escaped the Maha's reach—and Mehr could only hope, dream, that she had—or she had turned her blade on herself. Whatever the case, she was firmly beyond Mehr's reach.

The only person Mehr could help now was herself.

After prayers, the mystics moved as a group to a large canopied veranda open to the air. Mehr could smell cooking fires and was reminded suddenly, achingly of her old home. The kitchens in the Governor's residence had smelled just the same, of oil and spices and burnt sweetness. But no place in her old home had been so full of strangers, or so open to the velvet darkness of the night. She wrapped her arms around herself and followed the flow of the crowd.

Even here, the mystics had divided themselves along gender lines. Mehr could not seek out Amun, and that was probably for the best. She was growing far too reliant on him for company.

He was her bastion of safety, the only one she could trust in this forsaken place. But Mehr was not safe and couldn't allow herself to fall into the trap of believing she was.

As the crowd kneeled in rows, younger mystics ran down the line, spooning out food onto plates at a lightning-fast pace. Mehr kneeled before a plate of lentils, still steaming with heat, and a flatbread crisp to the touch. She barely tasted any of it. She ate far too quickly for that. Her hunger was a furious thing.

Now that prayers were over, the noises that filled the temple were of clattering plates, quick footsteps, and chatter. None of the noise drew near Mehr. The mystics kept their distance, leaving her be. She was surrounded by her own small sea of silence.

On the journey, Edhir had always tried to engage Mehr in conversation, eager for company his own age. Bahren had made strained efforts to be kind to her. Now that she was at the temple, she wondered if she would start being treated the way Amun was. The thought of being invisible to all these people was oddly comforting.

Comforting, but short-lived. A woman thumped down on the ground across from her. She wore the same dark robes as all the mystics, but her curling hair was bound back with vibrant green thread. It took Mehr a moment to recognize her: She was the one who had interrupted Mehr when she'd been bathing. She gave Mehr a grin, a dimple etched in her cheek.

"Do you like that?" she asked. She pointed at one of the dishes on Mehr's plate. "Anni and I made it." She made a vague gesture over her shoulder at one slim, dark-skinned woman who was walking over to join them. Behind her were a handful of others.

The one called Anni smiled and gave Mehr a weak wave as she kneeled down. The other women sat down on the ground behind her, ducking their heads shyly.

Mehr nodded cautiously. "It's lovely."

"My name is Hema," the woman said, showing no cautiousness

whatsoever. Her gaze was direct and steady. "Anni and I work in the kitchens most of the time. So you have us to blame for the meal."

Mehr swallowed, trying to find her bearings. She'd been so thoroughly wrapped up in her own misery that she hadn't expected anyone to approach her. She should have. After all, she was a stranger among the mystics. She was a new commodity, a new tool in the Maha's arsenal. That made her a curiosity.

Mehr could use that in her favor. She had nothing to barter or bribe with: nothing but her newness, and the novelty that provided. In order to survive here, she would need to learn about what it meant to live in this place. Hema's interest in her was not an opportunity Mehr could allow herself to lose.

"*Blame* isn't the word I would use," she said. She forced herself to keep her voice light, welcoming. There was a trick to this. She'd grown rusty at friendly conversation, but she could remember if she tried hard enough. "I'd rather thank you. I haven't had anything so pleasant to eat in a long while."

"You're most welcome," Hema said graciously.

Anni leaned forward. "Is it true you're from Jah Irinah?" she asked tentatively. "From the Governor's own household?"

"Yes," Mehr said. It was no secret, surely. "I'm the Governor's daughter."

She was suddenly faced with a barrage of noise. It took her a moment to make sense of the jumble of questions being aimed at her. The women had only given the appearance of being shy. They wanted to know everything—absolutely everything—about Jah Irinah.

"What do the buildings look like? Are there gardens—and water fountains? I heard you have so much water there you can *decorate* with it."

"What is the food like? Is it different from here?"

"Are the buildings really covered in jewels? Rena told me they were—"

"I didn't," the one called Rena said indignantly.

"Rena, you did!"

Mehr looked from one speaker to the next, trying to look beyond the dark robes that marked them as her enemy. *Girls*, Mehr thought. They were just girls. Many of them looked younger than Mehr, maybe only a handful of years older than Arwa.

She still wanted to hate them the way she hated the Maha, but it was extraordinarily hard to dislike people who were so earnestly curious about water fountains and havelis and the fine clothes that noblewomen wore. Mehr answered them as truthfully as she could: Yes, there were water fountains—Ambhan nobility loved to surround themselves with beauty. Yes, the havelis were grand. No, they were not encrusted in jewels.

She described some of the beautiful things she had seen her stepmother wear over the years: gold brocaded, sash-bound tunics; robes so long that they required a maidservant to hold the ends as she walked. She described the fine mesh of the veils noblewomen wore, the turbans of the men.

The girls drank it all in hungrily. When Mehr finally allowed her voice to falter, some of them leaned forward, just a little. One entreated her to continue.

Good.

She'd woven an image of Ambhan life beyond the temple walls—an image of opulence and beauty, rich with color and light—and the girls had fallen under its spell. She had something they wanted now. Tales were not much to barter with, but they were better than nothing, and far more than she'd had only moments before.

"I like to sew," Anni said. "If you could draw that robe I could try to make it. I've saved a lot of cloth."

Mehr shook her head with a faint smile. "I'm a terrible artist. But I would be happy to describe it to you again, if you like."

That seemed to please Anni.

"I lived in Jah Irinah once," Rena confided. She had dark, serious eyes. "But that was a long time ago. I remember very little anymore." Her voice was wistful.

"You left?" Mehr asked.

"The Maha brought Rena here," Anni said. "He brought all of us here."

They told her then, each of them, their own stories of life in the Empire. Like Edhir, they had all been unwanted children once. Illegitimate or orphaned, they'd had no place in an Empire that valued bloodlines and order, and their lives had been defined by poverty and fear. The Maha had saved them. Mystics had taken them from their home provinces and given them sanctuary in the temple, where the Maha had fed them and clothed them and given them a purpose. When they were friendless, alone, and desperate, the Maha had raised them up, and they loved him for it.

The reminder of how lucky Mehr and Arwa had been was sobering. Mehr's life had not been perfect, but she had never hungered as the girls had hungered. She'd never doubted that she would be fed and clothed and sheltered. If she had suffered and been saved as the mystics had, perhaps she would love the Maha as they did. Their love was the trembling, hopeful adoration of a kicked dog under a kind hand. It was a love born from pain.

Of all the women, only Hema said nothing. She'd simply sat and listened, a smile playing on her mouth. She reminded Mehr a little of Lalita. She had that same confidence, that same sly mirth in the shape of her lips, as if the world were one glorious amusement to her.

"We're lucky to be here—we never forget that, do we, girls?" Hema said, and the other girls fell silent, hanging on her words. "But that doesn't mean we're not curious about the world outside."

"Perhaps you could go to Jah Irinah one day," Mehr suggested. She watched their faces. She saw the shadow pass over them.

"No," Anni said, speaking for Rena, who was playing with the hem of her sleeve, her head lowered. "Our place is here. This is where we serve."

"I apologize," Mehr said, looking from one face to the next. At least she knew now: She wasn't the only one caged here. She softened her voice, allowing vulnerability to creep into it. "I still know very little about what it means to serve the Empire as you do."

"Well, we'll be happy to teach you," Hema told her. "We can show you all the beauty we have here." She leaned forward conspiratorially. "It may not compare to Jah Irinah, but I promise, despite first appearances we have plenty of it. The oasis, for instance." There was a chorus of agreement. "We share our own room near the water," Hema continued. "You'll have to come and see it."

They were watching her expectantly, a dozen eyes fixed on her face. It was unnerving.

"I would love to, if I can," Mehr said finally. She doubted she would be allowed to slip away to meet them, but it would be pointless to reject their offer. Better to make them think kindly of her than turn them away entirely.

Hema smiled at her, pleased. "Good," she said.

Many of the mystics had vanished. Under the canopy were dozens of abandoned lengths of cloth and plates. Hema looked around, gave a sigh, and rose to her feet. Mehr watched with some amusement as the other women followed her lead again. Hema, she thought, was like an empress holding court.

"You could help us tidy, if you like," Anni offered shyly. "We could always use another pair of hands."

Mehr rose to her feet. Before she could respond, she felt a hand clamp tightly onto her arm.

"Unfortunately she isn't available," Kalini said curtly.

The girls visibly cowered away. Only Hema was foolish enough to stand her ground. She narrowed her eyes. "Kalini," she protested. "I don't think—"

"The Maha expects this one to learn her place," Kalini said, cutting smoothly through Hema's own protest. "Have you forgotten yours?"

Hema crossed her arms.

"Don't talk to me like that," she said. "I hate it."

Mehr looked between them. With her pale eyes narrowed in her dark face, her mouth severe, Hema suddenly looked a great deal like Kalini.

Kalini huffed out a breath. "We'll talk later," she said, and began dragging Mehr bodily away, her hand a vise on Mehr's flesh. Mehr stumbled after her, thinking of the girls, of Hema's crossed arms and Edhir's shy smiles, and the way Bahren had always spoken to her—gruffly, gently, as if he had no desire to frighten her.

The mystics had proven to be far more human than Mehr had expected. Only the Maha was completely beyond her understanding. Only the Maha was an evil fire under her skin, setting his fingers like a stranglehold around her will and her soul.

"You have duties, Mehr," said Kalini. "Sacred duties."

"I know."

"Do you? You shouldn't be allowing yourself to grow distracted. Especially so soon. I will have to speak with the Maha about you," Kalini said calmly, still dragging Mehr roughly after her. Mehr resisted the urge to scowl at Kalini's back.

Kalini led Mehr to Amun, who was standing in the shadow of a doorway. Kalini shoved Mehr forward, abruptly releasing her arm. "Take your wife, Amun. You misplaced her."

Kalini walked away. Mehr rubbed her arm absently, as Amun took a step out of the darkness.

"Did she hurt you?" Amun asked. His fingers twitched at his sides.

"What could you possibly do if she had?" Mehr asked, then bit her lip. That had been cruel and entirely unnecessary. Her only defense was the fact that she could feel the unkindness of her world pressing down on her from all sides. Mystics who showed her gentleness, who showed her humanity, couldn't change the unforgiving shape of her circumstances. If anything, the friendliness of the women had only made the hurt of it all sting afresh.

But Amun didn't need her to make her excuses. She brushed past him, still gently massaging the skin that Kalini had bruised with her hand. "She didn't hurt me. I'm fine."

Amun caught up with her. She could hear the soft thud of his footsteps.

"We'll need to train a little longer."

"Outside?" Mehr asked.

Amun shook his head.

He led her to another hall, already prepared with a couple of oil lamps. A burly older mystic was napping in the corner. He cracked open an eye when they entered, then closed it again.

Amun stood across from her. He pressed his feet to the ground, straightening his back and turning his knees to a diamond angle. "Mehr," he said softly. "We only need to practice until the bell tolls. Then we sleep. If you need a moment, if you can't continue..."

Amun fell silent. Mehr faced him. Heart heavy, soul heavy, she met his dark eyes.

"I'm ready," she said.

When she danced, her body moved as light as air.

Arwa was standing in the desert, barefoot in the sand. She was holding a weapon in her two hands. Mehr's dagger. Their mother's dagger. The opal at its hilt glowed like a small moon.

Her face was still and smooth, and no matter how hard Mehr reached, she couldn't touch it.

"You killed me," Arwa said. "It's your fault."

Mehr finally brushed her fingertips to Arwa's cheek. Just her fingertips. Arwa's face crumbled and scattered to the wind. In its place a black veil remained, a veil of dark smoke that coiled around Mehr's wrist with curious fingers. The veil fluttered in the wind, ragged at the edges. Through its mesh, Mehr saw a gleam of gold.

A daiva's eyes met her own.

"Greetings, sister," it said.

Mehr shot awake. She didn't look at Amun as she slipped out of bed, still dressed in her tunic, her old green shawl from her pack wrapped around her for cover. She let the shawl slither from her shoulders to the floor and stepped over to one shuttered window.

This one didn't face the desert. She unbolted it and felt the cool air brush her like a caress. She leaned forward and stared down at the oasis that lay at the heart of the temple. Its clear, calm surface reflected the light of the moon back at her.

She didn't return to sleep for a long time.

CHAPTER THIRTEEN

Mehr slept again, eventually. When she next woke, she saw pale dawn light pouring in through the shutter she had left carelessly open during the night. Amun was gone. He had smoothed the sheets on his side of the bed down flat, making it look like he had never lain in the bed at all.

Mehr stood and stretched her limbs, curling and uncurling her toes against the ground. Even though her sleep had been restless, she felt less like the burden of her circumstances was going to crush her. She'd eaten a good meal and slept in a warm, comfortable bed. Those were small things, but at least they were good things. As long as she focused on them and pushed the knowledge Amun had given her to some far corner of her mind, she could breathe easily. She held on to those small comforts as she stretched her hands above her, preparing her body for the familiar motion of a rite.

Falling into the Rite of Sunrise felt like coming home. Dancing alone, cool floor beneath her and the heat of the sun on her face—this was her place of solace and safety. She didn't need music to accompany her. She didn't need the sound of other footsteps striking the ground along with hers, creating a music of their own. She found the rhythm of the rite in the beat of her heart, the thrum of her blood, the in and out of her breath from her lungs.

She heard it when Amun returned. His footsteps echoed up

the stairs. She considered stopping, then decided against it. He'd already seen her dance. What did she have to hide?

He entered the room as she moved her body through a flourishing arc, her arms tracing the path of the sun through the sky, her fingers shaping sigils that transformed, one to the other, with each punch of her heels to the ground. He said nothing. He was silent even after she moved into the last stance.

"Good morning," Mehr said, a little breathless. She saw that his hair was damp, his clothes fresh, robe gone. He must have gone to bathe. He was already sitting comfortably on the edge of the bed, his elbows pressed to his knees.

"You look happy," he observed.

"I am." The rite had left her peaceful. She no longer felt like vanishing into darkness. She could look at Amun without wanting to flinch away from his guilt-stricken eyes. She didn't know how long her renewed strength would last, but for now she held the warmth of it close like a blanket. "The rites comfort me. They always have."

"How strange," he murmured.

She stretched her arms, her neck, working the kinks out of her muscles. "At home, I danced rites every day." Memories rose up in her mind's eye. Lalita leading her through steps, patient and smiling. Arwa peering into Mehr's room, watching for a few brief moments before one of her nursemaids found her and snatched her back up. Bittersweet memories. "I've missed them."

She thought of telling him about Lalita. About how Lalita was a mentor, an almost-mother to her. About how she'd lost her. But Amun had a faraway look on his face, a shadowed look, and Mehr found she wanted to peel back his layers instead. "Why do you find it strange?" she asked.

He gave a shrug, his broad shoulders rising and falling. "I only perform the rites because I'm bid to," he said. "They have never made me happy. They are just a duty I have to fulfill."

"I find *that* strange," Mehr said. "I've always found dancing to be a comfort." She drew closer, forcing him to look up at her. "So you've never performed the rites simply for the joy of it?"

As he stared up into her face, some of the shadows seemed to vanish from his expression. He shook his head. "The first time I danced with the dreamfire I was a child. When the dreamfire responded to me, I was...happy." He shrugged. "But I didn't know what having the *amata* gift meant. I know better now. There's no joy in the rites for me. But I'm glad..." He paused, then said, "I'm glad they comfort you. You look...different, when you dance."

"How do I look?" Mehr asked.

Amun looked at her face like he was reading it, like her expression was ink and her skin the page it lay upon.

"You look strong," he told her. "You look sure of yourself."

"I haven't been as strong as I'd like," Mehr admitted, sitting down beside him. "I wanted to lash out at you yesterday. You gave me what I wanted, but more than anything, I wanted the truth to go away. I apologize."

"Don't," Amun said instantly. "I expected you to be angry. Who else can you be angry with? I would have preferred it if you had lashed out at me, Mehr. Instead you were silent." He huffed out a breath. "I wish you hadn't been silent."

"Sometimes it's wise to be silent." Surely Amun, of all people, knew that. He was always silent around the mystics. With the Maha, he had shaped his words carefully, artfully. "I would have been cruel to you. Cruel without reason. I didn't want to be."

"I didn't know how to help you," he said.

Mehr felt an unfamiliar tenderness well up in her, looking at the stubborn shape of his jaw, his hands clenched over his bent knees.

"Oh, Amun," she said gently. "You couldn't have helped me. But next time I'm upset, I promise to shout at you. Is that fair?"

He shot her a sidelong glare that spoke far more loudly than words. Mehr smiled back.

"Mehr," he said. His voice was halting. "What I told you last night. If you have any questions..."

Her insides were tight, panic unfurling in her heart again. She took a deep breath. "I can't talk about this yet."

He murmured an acknowledgment. Then he said, "Tell me about your old home. Tell me what it was like to dance in Jah Irinah."

His words were an obvious attempt to distract her, and Mehr accepted the opportunity gratefully. She told him about her old quarters, about the perforated screen facing the desert, about the way she had danced and danced, hours spent in joyful loneliness under the checkered light that poured through it. She told him that her mother had taught her, that another Amrithi had taught her when her mother had left. She told him how the love of the rites had sustained her like air. She told him more than she'd intended to. But she was lonely, lonely and scared, and Amun was *kind*.

"I've never been able to dance like you," she admitted. "Your knowledge far surpasses mine."

When he performed the rites his movements weren't beautiful. His dancing had none of the poetry of Lalita's, or the wild, raw abandon her mother had possessed when she'd performed a rite. Amun was economical, powerful—there was a precision in his performances Mehr had never seen before. In his dances, Mehr recognized the flaws in her own.

"I've had a great deal of practice," he said. "Every waking hour not spent in prayers, I have spent on the rites. For most of my service, it has been the one duty the Maha has tasked me to focus on." A shrug. "Anyone would grow in skill under that regime."

"What does make you happy, then?" Mehr asked. "Surely something must."

She was afraid for a second that he would tell her nothing made him happy. But instead he ran a hand through his damp hair, setting the curls into absolute disarray. She recognized that gesture now, from all the times he'd caught her dressing in their shared tent, or trying to untangle her long hair with her fingers. He was embarrassed.

"Come now," Mehr cajoled. "Everyone has something that they enjoy. Perhaps you're a secret painter, hm?"

Amun was clearly amused despite himself. "What would I paint here, Mehr? Sand or more sand?"

"You see more women than most painters would ever dream of," Mehr said with a laugh. "You know my stepmother had her miniature painted for my father once? She commissioned one of the finest artists in Jah Irinah. He couldn't see her face, of course— my stepmother is too well bred to reveal her face to a stranger—so the poor man worked entirely from her description of herself."

"Was it accurate?" Amun asked, in a tone that told her he already knew the answer.

"Of course it wasn't. So my father was blessed with a min-iature of a stranger's face to carry around with him. A stranger who was a good deal more sensuous than my stepmother has ever been, I might add." Mehr clucked her tongue. "What an imagi-nation that man had."

Amun grinned. The flash of his teeth, the crinkling of his eyes, left Mehr startled. He guarded his expressions so vigilantly that the curve of his mouth struck her with the force of a phys-ical blow.

"And you, Mehr. Did you ever demand to be painted?"

Mehr snorted. "Me? No. I wasn't ready to wed, so I didn't have anyone to impress. Besides, any painter given my descrip-tion would still have insisted on making me moon pale with hair like a fall of silk." She made a dismissive gesture. "I don't need false flattery."

"They paint what they think you want to see," Amun noted, with insightfulness that—again—struck Mehr.

"They paint what they think I want the world to see," Mehr said. A woman beautiful in the eyes of the Empire. A woman with purely Ambhan flesh. "But they would be wrong about me. I like myself perfectly well as I am."

"You don't want to look Ambhan?"

"Me? No." If Mehr had looked Ambhan, perhaps her step-mother would have looked at her and seen a child she could mold to her own ends, instead of an Amrithi heathen and living reminder of Suren's exiled mistress. If Mehr had looked Ambhan, perhaps she would have lost what remained of her heritage to Maryam's manipulations. The thought viscerally sickened her. To be Ambhan in an Ambhan world, to have light brown skin and lighter eyes, and straight hair and fine bones, was to be beautiful and to belong. But Mehr had never wanted to belong to that world. She'd simply wanted a place to call her own. "I'm content with what I am, Ambhan and Amrithi and all. Would *you* want to look Ambhan?"

"You're half Ambhan," Amun said. "I am not."

"Answer my question anyway," Mehr said. "Humor me."

"It would be nice to vanish in a crowd," Amun said after a moment of thoughtful silence. "But no. I am what I am."

I am what I am. He hadn't said that he liked himself, and in a way Mehr was glad for that honesty. She remembered the fractured hatred she'd seen on his face that night in the desert. She knew *like* would have been a lie.

But she wanted to see his smile again. She wanted to see his face—that dark, serious face, inked in fluid blue lines—crack open with emotion that wasn't bloodied and sad.

"Amrithi or not, you'd never vanish in a crowd," Mehr said, absently. "You're too..." She made a vague gesture with her hands, trying to encompass his broad strength, the way he towered over her even when hunched over and seated. "You take up a great deal of space."

"Space," Amun echoed.

Mortification flooded her. What had possessed her to say that? She knew how much Amun hated to be noticed. She knew how he held his strength back carefully, how he tried to fade into the background. She'd let her words run away from her. She'd spoken without thinking.

Amun was giving her a level look, expression unreadable. His arms were held stiffly at his sides. She was sure she had offended him. She looked back at him blankly, trying to frame some semblance of an apology, when she saw his lips twitch.

He was trying not to laugh at her.

"I am what I am," he said again, softly now, almost fondly.

The sound of a loud bell echoed throughout the temple. Mehr nearly jumped out of her skin. Somehow, for a single moment, she had forgotten where she was. She had forgotten how dire her circumstances really were. For a single moment, there had been nothing but her and Amun, and Amun's smile.

Amun's expression shuttered quick as lightning.

"Time for prayers," he said. He stood and went toward the stairway.

Mehr grabbed her shawl and raced down the stairs after him.

It was Kalini who led the morning prayers, standing before the effigy of the faceless Emperor with her head lowered and her hands clasped. Mehr was glad that there was no sight of the Maha. Kalini's voice didn't have the power to curdle Mehr's blood the way the Maha's did. In her presence Mehr could contain her fear. She kneeled with her hands clasped and tried to ignore her aching knees until prayers ended.

Breakfast was not as elaborate as dinner had been. Mehr joined a queue of mystics and was handed a flatbread and a handful of sweet, dried dates, which were rich with flavor but tough as leather. Mehr ate hurriedly as she walked through the corridors by Amun's side.

Amun led her up the stairs of another tower to a room where, he told her, Edhir would be working. Mehr had grown used to the bareness of the temple, so she took in the chaos of the room around her with wide eyes.

The room was crammed from end to end with books. Charts and maps covered every spare inch of space on the walls. Mehr's father, wealthy and privileged though he was, had never owned so many books. Her fingers itched to trace the spines. Instead she took them in with her eyes. Books of alchemy, of weather, collections of maps of distant lands. Maps of Irinah. There were scrolls, too, laid out on a table and bound shut with long lengths of silk.

There were mystics scattered all over the room. At the edge of one table sat Edhir. Without his heavy robe, hunched over a scroll unfurled to its full length, Edhir looked younger than ever. The hands holding the scroll were gloved. As they approached him, he raised his head and gave Amun an uneasy look. For Mehr, he managed a smile.

"Emperor's grace upon you this fine morning," he said to her. His gaze slid nervously to Amun. "And you," he added.

Mehr looked at Amun along with him. His face was as hard and cold as a thing carved from rock. His eyes were dark hollows, with none of the softness in them that Mehr had somehow grown to expect. She looked away quickly. If she hadn't experienced his gentleness earlier and seen that smile tug the corners of his mouth, she never would have believed he was anything but the cold brute he appeared to be in that moment.

"Emperor's grace upon you also," she said to Edhir. He gave her a grateful look as she stepped between. "What is this?" she asked, pointing at the scroll in front of him.

"A map of the Empire," he said.

"How beautiful," Mehr breathed. It was highly detailed, colored in lush blues and golds, marking the Empire from Irinah to Ambha and beyond. Even lands beyond its borders were inked in. She had never seen such a fine piece of work before—certainly no map as vast and detailed as this one.

"She needs to be prepared for the next storm," Amun said abruptly, breaking Mehr's focus. "The Maha said it will be upon us soon."

Mehr did not think she'd ever heard Amun speak directly to Edhir. It startled her. She wasn't alone in that. Edhir's eyes were wide. The other mystics were watching, some covertly, some not so covertly.

"Yes," Edhir said, after a moment's hesitation. "It will be."

"When?"

Mehr wanted to wince at Amun's behavior. If this was how he talked to the mystics, then it was probably wise that he was so often silent. He showed Edhir none of the ease or careful gentleness he so often showed her. Instead he spoke abrasively, his voice unashamedly cold and unfeeling.

Edhir's jaw tightened, but he made no complaint. Instead he stood and made his way to one of the many shelves lining the walls. He lifted a mounted sphere from one low shelf and brought it over to the table. It was a strange tool—Mehr had never seen the like of it before. The sphere was faceted glass, etched with symbols, and surrounded on all sides by movable dials and calipers, all etched with small, intricate measurements. Without a word Edhir began adjusting the calipers and dials around the sphere, his eyes narrowed. Another mystic brought over a scroll and unfurled it. This one was covered in lines and equations. Catching Mehr's questioning look, Edhir said, "This is a map of the stars."

"I didn't know stars could be mapped," Mehr said honestly.

"Oh, they can," Edhir said, distracted. He adjusted another

dial in slow increments. "The Maha, praise him, discovered that by tracing the movement of the stars, we can predict storms."

"How is that possible?" Mehr asked. She leaned forward, her eyes fixed on the sphere. Now that she was looking more closely, she could see that the symbols were etchings of the celestial bodies: the moon and sun and dozens of stars, all arrayed across the sphere's surface. As Edhir moved the dials, the facets moved too, the sphere turning in a smooth arc.

"Everything in the world comes from the dreams of the Gods," Edhir said, still moving the dials with care. "Almost everything they've dreamed is perfectly designed, and adheres to its own laws. Just as we obey the law and the faith, the seasons, the tides of the great ocean, the movements of the stars, all follow the order set down by the Gods. But in Irinah, when the dreamfire falls, the order—bends." He stopped to look down at the map at his side, then adjusted one dial a mere increment to the left. "Look."

Mehr looked. Mehr did not know anything about the order the stars obeyed, but she knew there was something subtly wrong with the surface of the sphere. There were hairline gaps between its facets, a strange order to the stars.

"As we grow near a storm, the celestial bodies begin to change their behavior," Edhir explained. She could hear the enthusiasm in his voice, the sheer love he had for his subject. "Their patterns alter. We've theorized that the storms are a time when the world the Gods have dreamed is at its most fragile, softened so it can be remolded. But—it's only a theory," Edhir said, looking up, a flush rising on his cheeks.

"It's a wonderful theory," Mehr said, trying to reflect his enthusiasm back at him. Bahren had told her Edhir fancied himself a scholar. Looking at him now, Mehr realized Edhir was more than just a pretender to that title. He was clever and—praise the Gods—unable to resist sharing his knowledge with an interested listener. "We must talk again, brother."

"How long until the storm?" Amun asked impatiently.

His voice was a dull blade, and it forced the light from Edhir's eyes. Edhir blinked, swallowed, and said, "Two weeks. That's as much accuracy as I can give you."

Amun nodded sharply and turned to go.

"Our thanks," Mehr said, and followed him. She realized all eyes in the room were still on them. She stood straight, avoiding those eyes, and swept out after him.

Amun was walking so fast that Mehr nearly had to run to keep up with him. "Two weeks," he repeated. "That's no time at all."

"*Amun*," Mehr said. Hearing her voice, breathless as it was, he slowed down. Marginally. Walking by his side now, Mehr said, "You could have spoken more kindly to Edhir."

"What would have been the point?" Amun's voice was cool, glassy. "You want to be kind to them now, Mehr?"

Them. She preferred his stony silence to this sudden upwelling of bitterness. She preferred it to the reminder that they were alone, with no one to trust but each other. She crossed her arms.

"People are more helpful when you treat them well," she pointed out.

"He'll do what his duty requires."

"I'm not talking about his duties. Amun, he had maps," she said, speaking as quietly as she could without being inaudible. "Not just maps of the stars or of the Empire, but maps of Irinah itself. If we ever want to escape, we'll need some way to find a safe route through the desert."

"There is no escape for me," Amun said woodenly. "I'm bound."

Mehr bit her lip. Then she said, carefully, "But I'm not. Not entirely."

"Not yet," Amun said. There was a pause. Then Amun said, "Do what you must. They don't need to like me. Just…don't involve me, Mehr. Please." There was a long pause. Then, abruptly, Amun said, "I can't hope. It would—hurt."

Mehr suddenly felt very foolish.

"As you wish," she said softly. She said no more.

Amun couldn't escape the Maha, bound as he was. No wonder the thought of escape—the possibility of something he could never achieve—pained him.

For all that she wasn't entirely bound, Mehr had precious little chance either. Before Mehr had even spoken, she'd known that the idea of escaping the Maha was at best a foolish girl's fantasy. With eyes always on her, how could she possibly slip away from the temple without being noticed? How could she leave Amun here, knowing what the Maha was and how being bound to him felt?

And even if she did escape, how long would she survive? Without a map, without food or water or a robe to protect her from the sun, she would perish in short order.

But hope was insidious. It had its claws in her now, and it wouldn't let her go.

Edhir has maps, she thought. *And Hema works in the kitchens. She'll have food. Water.*

A way to look again at the maps of Irinah, a way to hide food and water, and find a robe to protect herself, and a way to set Amun free along with her. That was all she needed now.

She wanted to laugh. Ah, she'd set herself an impossible goal, hadn't she?

"I'd hoped to work on your technique longer," Amun said, after a long silence. "But you will need to be taught the rite immediately."

"Tell me about this rite," she said, pushing her hopes to the back of her mind. "For a start, what is it called?"

"I don't know if it has a true name," said Amun grimly. "But the person who taught it to me called it the Rite of the Bound."

CHAPTER FOURTEEN

They returned to the same dim hall they had practiced in the evening before.

"We won't perform this rite in the desert until the dreamfire falls," Amun told her. "The daiva don't like it."

Mehr could well imagine how little the daiva cared for a rite intended to bend their mothers and fathers to mortal will.

Even though it was daylight outside, the hall was timeless nighttime. Lanterns flickered where they hung upon the walls. The light illuminated Amun's face in fractured shadows. He turned to look at the doorway, where another mystic already stood, watching them.

It was no surprise to Mehr to see the man there. Wherever she and Amun went, mystics followed. The Maha had many eyes.

"Leave," Amun said shortly. "We're at the Maha's business. We need to be alone."

The mystic nodded and stepped out of the room. Mehr was sure he was still out there, hovering just beyond the entrance. But there was nothing to be done about that. She pushed her discomfort away and followed Amun deeper into the hall.

"You understand the basic forms," he said.

"I do."

"You need to be solidly tethered to the world around you," he went on, as if he hadn't heard her speak. "Your feet are earth, your hands are heaven. Your body is the bridge. Your body must be strong. Straight and tall."

"I know, Amun," Mehr said, arms crossed. She watched him pace about, for all the world like a creature trapped in a cage. "My technique isn't as terrible as you seem to believe."

He shook his head. "I didn't mean—"

"No," Mehr said. "I'm sure you didn't." She gestured impatiently. "Continue."

His footsteps slowed as he tried to will himself calm.

"Everything you know, this rite demands you discard. You cannot be grounded. You cannot be strong. You need to ignore the earth beneath your feet and the sky above you. When you dance the rite, the storm will lift you up. It will raise you and fill you up with the fire of the Gods. In order to direct the fire as the rite requires, you will need to reach beyond the mortal world, the desert salt, to the place where the Gods dream." He spoke slowly, carefully, weighing his words. "You need to touch your own immortality in order to become the vessel of their fire. And when that power has almost consumed you, you need to open yourself up to the will of the mystics and the Maha, and let them use you. That is the Rite of the Bound."

Mehr swallowed. Dreamfire was beautiful, holy, but it belonged to the Gods. For all that the Amrithi were far-distant descendants of the daiva, and therefore long-distant descendants of the Gods themselves, Mehr knew that she was all blood and bone. There were no shadows in her skin, no gold in her eyes. She was *mortal*.

She couldn't imagine how it would feel to try to hold the dreamfire within her. Couldn't imagine, and didn't want to.

"That doesn't sound pleasant," she said quietly.

"No," he said. "It isn't." His expression was grave. "This is

what I was taught, Mehr: When a paired man and woman perform the rite, they become a channel between the dreams of the
Gods and the prayers of the mystics. They can suppress dreams
the Maha and his mystics don't want in the world, and draw forward only the dreams that are desired. They become the perfect
tool for sculpting the Empire. *That* is what I was taught, and that
is what I have to teach you too, pleasant or not."

"Why a man and a woman?" Mehr asked.

Amun shrugged fluidly. "Because the rite is an act of creation.
Apparently."

It was perverse to call this terrible rite, this destruction of the
natural order, an act of creation. But Mehr didn't say so. She
doubted he would disagree with her anyway.

"Once you've mastered the first step," Amun continued, "I'll
teach you the sigils you need to make yourself into a conduit
for the dreams of the Gods and draw forward or suppress their
dreams as the mystics demand." He hesitated. "It's important to
be confident in your technique because when the Rite of the
Bound threatens to consume you, moving to one of the true
rites may be the only thing to keep you whole."

Mehr nodded without a word. She had nothing helpful to say,
no real questions to ask. She wanted nothing more than to argue
with him. This rite—the Rite of the Bound—sounded like utter
nonsense. Rites were worship shaped by the body, by flesh and
ritual and rhythm. To put the body aside was against everything
Mehr had ever learned, and everything she understood the rites
to be. Did Amun expect her to do nothing but stand still and will
her body away?

"We begin with the breath," he said. "Close your eyes."

Mehr squeezed her eyes shut. Apparently he did.

It was the breath they concentrated on for a long time, and
nothing but the breath.

Amun told her to look inward. He told her to look deep

inside herself, beyond the rush of blood, beyond skin and sinew, beyond muscle and bone.

"There is a part of you that isn't simply mortal," Amun told her. "Reach for it."

Mehr tried. She breathed carefully, slowly, as she'd been told to. She tried to see beyond her own flesh.

She believed in the soul. She'd seen its power in the marks on Amun's skin and in the spidery white lines carved into her own chest. But to reach for it, to feel its presence and nothing but its presence, to the point of forgetting flesh—that seemed utterly impossible.

In. Out. Despite her efforts, her body was all she could think of. The cool floor, the darkness pressing against her eyelids; the sound of Amun breathing along with her, matching each inhalation and exhalation until it sounded like they were no more than one creature.

Her breath stuttered. She opened her eyes.

"I can't feel it." She didn't say *I'm never going to feel it* because she wasn't a petulant child, but the words were still there tucked away in her voice, frustration simmering under the surface.

"You will." Amun's own eyes remained closed. "I feel it in myself. You'll feel it in you eventually too."

"We're not the same, Amun."

"In the ways that matter to the Maha, we are."

That was true. Mehr touched her fingertips to the seal around her neck, reminding herself what was at stake. Then she closed her eyes once again and tried to breathe her flesh away.

She tried to wind deeper into herself. To forget the cool air, the night darkness around her. After a moment, she heard Amun begin to speak.

"The Gods created the daiva, the daiva birthed our ancestors, and our ancestors birthed us. So it goes." There was a low, singsong quality to his voice that reminded her of the way she had spoken to Arwa, once upon a time, about the daiva. *Here is a story*, his voice seemed to say. *An old story. A true story.* "And here we are, mortal men and women, with immortality in our blood. Seek out the immortality inside you, and you will find the place where the Gods sleep. You are an Amrithi; it is your right."

"A speck of immortality," Mehr muttered. "It can't be more than that."

"A speck is enough," Amun said.

Mehr breathed. Breathed. Curled her hands into helpless fists. "I don't know where to look," she said.

"Look to the part of you that dreams," Amun said.

Mehr shivered. Snatches of last night's dream flickered through her head, as blurred as candle flame. Golden eyes. Arwa crumbling to ashes. She was glad she could remember no more than that.

Dreams were a strange place. Often dark and terrible, but at least the pain they inflicted was easily lost. Easily forgotten.

Mehr sucked in another deep breath. Tried again.

Once more. Once more.

Kamal

It was an unfortunate day for bartering. The heat was blistering, the sun fat and unforgiving in the sky. As a result, the village was full of Irin who were by turns irritable and listless. Kamal—who'd volunteered for this job, curse it—was struggling to exchange his blood for anything useful.

"It's worth more than that," he protested unwisely to one villager, who promptly narrowed her eyes and cursed him colorfully.

"You take what we offer," the villager said finally, "or I tell the tax collector your kind are near here. See how long your clan lasts then."

The threat kept on irritating him like a sore tooth, long after he'd accepted the villager's paltry trade and started making his way back out to the desert proper. As he reached the outskirts of the village, a child threw a rock at him and ran away shrieking with laughter, which only served to sour his mood further. Gods curse the lot of them.

He wished one of his clan had come with him. Sohaila, maybe, who always knew how to make him laugh even when he was in the blackest moods. But Kamal was alone, and wouldn't see his clan for days yet.

He'd learned young—as all Amrithi learned—to keep clan and Empire at a safe distance from one another. Once, that had meant avoiding larger towns and the city of Jah Irinah, where Ambhan officials and merchants from other provinces were likely to reside. Now it meant avoiding every small village scattered across the desert's back. Even the Irin, who understood the worth of Amrithi blood and the danger the daiva could bring in a way outsiders never could, were not trustworthy any longer. His clan were camped two days' walk away, but he'd take a long route, just in case he'd been followed by a villager in search of glory or coin.

In three days then, if all went well, he'd be home.

He walked for a time, under the weight of a burning, cloudless sky. Then he stopped and swore into the air until he felt mildly better. He took out his water container, drank three swigs in succession, and kept on walking. There was shelter ahead—an outcropping of rock that would provide him shade until the hottest part of the day had passed. He could remain there until the air had cooled a little, then continue his journey in peace.

When he reached the shelter, he found it occupied.

A woman was sitting in the shade, her legs neatly crossed, her face swathed by the hood of her robe. Both of them were frozen for a long moment. Then Kamal took a step back and began to reach for his dagger.

"Calm yourself," the woman said. She lowered her hood, then raised her hands to show him they were empty. "There's no need to be afraid of me. I'm a fellow tribeswoman."

"What are you doing here?" he asked.

She *was* a tribeswoman, he didn't doubt that. But it had been a long time since he'd crossed paths with a member of another clan, and he didn't know how to feel at the sight of her.

Her eyes searched his face with equal unease.

"I'm looking for a clan," she said finally. "They used to pass through this area. A clan led by a Tara named Ruhi. Do you know where I can find them?"

Kamal kept his mouth shut. The woman stood and began to approach him slowly. With the sun above her, he could see her far more clearly. She was beautiful, dark-skinned and long-haired, but she was painfully thin, great shadows carved beneath her eyes.

"The clan was led, before, by a Tara named Rukhsar. Her mother." The woman frowned faintly. "Ruhi may have passed on. If so, the new Tara won't be of her blood, I expect. Do you know of the clan?"

"Where is your clan?" he managed to ask.

"Long gone," she said. "I left Irinah a long time ago. I've had no choice but to return."

, Ah. She was one of those who had left Irinah and tried to begin again elsewhere. Once, Kamal had wanted to be like her. He'd hungered to see the world. But he'd loved his clan too much to leave them, and he'd been afraid if he went into the world beyond even for a short time, he'd come back and find them dead or gone, and never be able to find out what had become of them. The thought alone gutted him.

"Why have you come back to Irinah?"

"Oh, the usual reasons." She shrugged, a faint ghost of a smile gracing her lips. "Furious noblemen, desperate to cleanse the Empire of the scourge of our blood. I left before they could punish me and drive me out here themselves. It seemed...wiser."

Kamal swallowed.

"Have you had food?" he asked. "Water?"

"Some," said the woman. Her voice cracked with exhaustion. "A little. An Irin woman assisted me. But since then I've struggled. I find life on the desert...difficult. Far more difficult than I remember." She shook her head, then said, "Just tell me if you know where I can find the clan. Please."

It was in Kamal's nature to be suspicious. Distrust had saved his life numerous times. But this woman was Amrithi, gaunt

and still, and she knew his Tara's name. He thought of the villager, her threat, the child flinging its rock and laughing. He
handed her his water container. "Drink," he said.

She drank.

"My name is Kamal," he said. "And yours?"

"Lalita."

"That isn't an Amrithi name," he said.

"I gave up my Amrithi name long ago."

She took another swig of water.

Gods save him, he couldn't allow a fellow tribeswoman to
perish out alone upon the Salt. He didn't have it in him to lie.

"Ruhi is my clan's Tara," he said, when the woman lowered
the container. "You must be blessed with good fortune, to have
found me."

The woman laughed. Her laughter sounded perilously close
to weeping.

"Yes, I must be blessed," she said. She pressed a hand over her
face. "Ah. Thank the Gods."

She lowered her hand. "Please," she said. "Take me to your
Tara."

"Walk with me," he said. "We'll see what the Tara says."

CHAPTER FIFTEEN

A frustrating morning was followed by more prayers—Gods save her—and another thinly apportioned flatbread flecked through with vegetable to stretch the meager serving of grain. They returned to the hall where Amun continued to encourage her onward with growing impatience. But Mehr couldn't do as he asked, and they were soon sick of the sight of each other.

For two days they followed the same pattern of snatched food and knee-aching prayers and careful breathing that was supposed to lead Mehr away from her own skin and failed to lead her anywhere but to frustration. Her only respite on both evenings was the presence of Hema and the other women, who sat with her and shared their food and their laughter.

Mehr told herself that spending time with the women was a pragmatic decision. Hema and her women did not have seniority within the temple, but they possessed a different kind of power. Working in the kitchens meant they controlled all the food and water in the temple. If Mehr ever hoped to escape—and she did hope, despite what her good sense told her—she would need to be able to visit the kitchens without causing concern.

Spending time with them also gave her information that Amun had not thought to share with her. By listening to their conversations, she learned about the courier mystics who traveled between

the provinces of the Empire and the temple, bringing food supplies and messages from other mystics and the Emperor himself to
the Maha.

"How do the couriers navigate the desert?" Mehr asked. She
broke apart her flatbread into manageable pieces as she spoke,
keeping her tone casual. "The desert is so vast," she said. "I can't
imagine how anyone could find their way through it."

"They use the stars," said Rena, no suspicion in her face or her
voice. "But there are trade routes too. They use those to visit the
villages."

Mehr was sure Kalini and the others hadn't brought her to the
temple via a trade route. They'd traveled over unmarked desert,
and kept their distance from villages. Mehr doubted her ability
to navigate by the stars, but she stood a chance of understanding
trade routes, and navigating using individual villages as signposts.

She would need to find a way to visit the scholars—and their
maps—again without arousing suspicion.

It was her third evening in the company of the women when
Mehr finally agreed to visit them in their shared room by the
oasis. They had been offering, subtly and not so subtly, since
the first time they had met her. Mehr couldn't refuse any longer
without showing outright rudeness.

She had so many reasons why her choice was a sound one.
She rehearsed them over and over again in her head as she and
Amun practiced in the hall and then returned to his room. If he
attempted to argue with her, if he called her foolish, she would
be more than able to argue with him. But Amun didn't argue. As
she drew her shawl around her shoulders, as she turned to leave
the room, he said only, "Be careful."

"You're not going to try to stop me?" she asked.

"Could I?" he asked. He shook his head. "No, Mehr. Do as
you will."

Mehr thought of the fragile trust that had built between

them, stretched so thin now by the weight of the storm that was coming for them. She felt a pang. She pushed it away. She was far too prone to sentiment.

She met Hema at the foot of the stairs.

"Finally!" Hema called out at the sight of her. She turned on her heel, stopping once to make sure Mehr was following. "I thought you weren't going to come."

"I was just delayed," said Mehr.

There was a mystic standing guard at the entrance to the oasis that Hema led her to. When he saw Mehr his mouth thinned. But Hema was already tutting and shaking her head, a smile fixed on her pretty mouth.

"Come now, brother," she said. "Is this how you treat family?"

"I haven't said anything," he protested.

"I can see it in your face," Hema said. Although her words were challenging, her voice was playful. "You were going to stop us."

"Not you. Just her." He jerked his chin in Mehr's direction.

"Oh, don't be so cruel." Hema put her hand on her hip. "The girl needs company."

The man shook his head, his jaw set to an angle. Mehr saw the fingers on Hema's hips curl. When she spoke again, her playful voice had an unexpected edge to it.

"You don't trust me, brother?"

The man said nothing.

"If you don't consider me trustworthy," Hema continued, "perhaps you should go to Kalini and see what she says."

Mehr looked between them, taking in the tilt of Hema's head, the tight set of the man's shoulders. It was soon clear that Hema was victor. The male mystic finally stepped out of the way. Hema gave Mehr a wink, then turned to lead her through the doorway into the outdoors.

"Kalini," Mehr began haltingly.

"She's my sister," said Hema, not waiting for Mehr to finish.

"By the Emperor's grace, the Maha saved us both when we were children. Our parents died when we were small. We would have starved without his kindness." They walked farther out into the moonlit night. "I know Kalini is...difficult. But she loves the Maha, and she loves me."

Mehr thought *difficult* was somewhat of an understatement, but she nodded, and said nothing. Sometimes silence was wise.

They walked along the edge of the oasis under the moon's glow. The ground was soft and even beneath her feet. The water smelled almost unbearably pure, sweet without being cloying. Mehr felt some of her frustration begin to ease. She'd missed the outdoors.

"It's beautiful, isn't it?" Hema was gazing out at the water. "I was offered a room deeper in the temple, once. Near the kitchens where it would be warm at night. But I said no. I couldn't give this up."

Mehr followed her gaze. The moon was reflected back on the water, a circle of white against pure undisturbed black.

Yes. It was beautiful.

The girls were all awake and waiting in their shared room, their bedrolls all stretched out across the floor in service as cushions. They welcomed Hema with joy, and Mehr with warmth and kindness. Anni stood when she saw them. "Come sit by me," she said to Mehr, and drew her over to the corner of the room.

Although the room was cramped, it was a riot of color, with lengths of fabric draped along the walls, and florid patterns chalked into the corners of the floor. There was a wooden board covered in blocks and markings on the ground between the women. Rena was leaning over it, dusting it furiously with powder. Hema sat across from Mehr and gave her a small grin.

"Our brother is probably still hovering about, so we can't have anything special to drink, I'm sorry to say." She shrugged apologetically. "Next time, maybe."

Rena began to portion out a small pile of dark and light wooden discs, all equally sized and no bigger than the palm of Mehr's hand. "We're going to play karom," Rena said. "Will you join us?"

"I don't know the game," said Mehr.

"We can show you, no problem," Anni said cheerfully.

A dozen voices piped, clamoring to describe the game. But Mehr was more used to the chaos now, and dispelled it by laughing and shaking her head, clapping a hand pointedly to her ear. "Just one of you, please!"

Eventually Rena, frowning until everyone else quieted, began to explain the rules. The game was fairly simple. Each team had a set of pieces they could use to force a central black piece to the edges of the board. Sending the black piece to the end of the board belonging to the other team would result in points; the farther the piece moved into the darker squares at the edges, the higher the score. Beyond that, there were more complex rules about how the pieces could or could not be moved, and penalties for incorrect moves. Mehr understood the gist of it well enough, but she elected to watch for the first match rather than take part.

She realized she had made the right decision when she saw how intently the girls played. They didn't play simply for the pleasure of the game. As points were gained and lost, they gambled objects between them: a thin silver chain, a beaded necklace, a length of carefully worked leather. Bread scrounged from the kitchen. Spices.

Mehr was reminded of the way Maryam had entertained visitors to the women's quarters, in the early years when Mehr had still been welcome in Maryam's private salon and able to watch the refined games of strategy that noblewomen favored. Like the women of her father's household, the Maha's female servants had their own ways of exchanging and establishing wealth and power.

Mehr gave Hema a sidelong glance. Hema, no doubt, had the

best of everything: dry spices in pouches tucked in the lining of her bedroll; jewels on chains tucked beneath the collar of her tunic; access to food, to water, to the things that made life bearable in this place. That was power. If she asked any of the girls for their winnings, no doubt they would hand them over without complaint. Mehr had seen the way they worshipped her, a worship far more real and personal than the awed, terrified way they bowed their heads before the Maha. Beyond this room Hema may have been a kitchen maid, but here she was a queen.

The powder on the board helped the pieces move more easily, but it wasn't long before all the women's fingertips were stained white with chalk, and the residue was threatening to make its way onto their clothes and bedding. Seeing a chance to do more than watch uselessly, Mehr got to her feet and went in search of water. There was a clay jug in a corner. She brought it over and helped one of the younger girls rub her hands clean. Mehr was given a grateful smile in return.

"Now you come play," Hema said imperiously. When Mehr tried to demur, Hema took her hand and drew her back down to the pillows. The jug was removed from Mehr's grip.

"I don't know all the rules," Mehr protested.

"It doesn't matter if you know all the rules," Hema said. "Anyway, this is the best way to learn."

All avenues of escape were gone. So Mehr sat with them, eyeing the board with its many shades and discs and the fine layer of powder on its surface. "It's your turn," Hema prompted.

Mehr had nothing to barter, and no one asked her to offer anything up. Somehow that did not comfort her. If she failed, the possessions of other team members were at stake instead, and although this was a game, just a game, she was still an outsider. She didn't know if they would look kindly on her failing them.

Mehr looked at the board again, leaning forward. Most of the opposite team's black pieces sat like guards, defending their corners, but a few were encroaching on the opposite side of the board. She touched her fingers to the edge of one disc. Instead of trying to score a point, she flicked the disc to the left, sabotaging the opposite team by blocking their route. Her side of the room shrieked with delight, as the other side gave good-natured yells of disbelief.

"You can be on our side next time," one girl said.

Mehr leaned back and laughingly agreed.

She had a few more turns with the discs after that, but there were enough people in the room that—once the novelty of her appearance had worn off—she was able to fade into the background. Eventually as the hours ticked by and the night deepened, some of the women curled up in their bedrolls to sleep. The game drew to a close and the last winnings were carefully apportioned out by Rena, who then wiped the board clean with water and tucked it away. Mehr got up to leave, and Hema followed after her.

"Come back again tomorrow night if you like," she said, walking alongside Mehr. Her words weren't an order, but they sounded very much like one.

Mehr would have liked to oblige. But she thought of Amun—of the Rite of the Bound, and the coming storm, and the weight of the seal around her neck—and could only offer up a helpless shrug in response. "If I can," she said.

"Mehr," Hema began. Then she paused. Pursed her lips, before she said, all in a rush: "If your husband doesn't want to let you go, you can tell me."

Mehr slowed her steps, then stopped entirely as Hema placed a light hand on her wrist. The look in Hema's eyes made her uneasy.

"We have a great deal to do," Mehr said slowly. "That's all."

Hema took a step closer. They were far enough from both the sleeping quarters and the temple that they were unlikely, at least for a moment, to be heard by anyone else.

"You can tell me if he frightens you," Hema said in a low voice. "I can try to help you."

For a moment Mehr didn't know what to say. Frighten her? Why would Amun frighten her?

"I've lived here a long time," said Hema, when Mehr simply shook her head, wordless with confusion. "I've seen what he is. You don't need to lie to me."

Amun's moods could be mercurial, but even at his most sullen there was a gentleness in him, a vulnerability in every line of his body. Mehr saw it. She was sure the Maha saw it too, and Kalini. She thought everyone saw it when they looked at him. Despite Mehr's warnings, his body was still the mirror of his heart.

But Hema did not.

Whatever Hema saw in Amun was enough to make her mouth take on a bitter curl and her forehead draw into a frown even at the thought of him.

"I know what Amrithi are like," Hema said softly. "They're not like us. They don't understand loyalty, or order, or the peace and safety the Empire has brought to many. They're just... barbarians."

Mehr froze.

"Hema," Mehr said. "*I'm* Amrithi."

"Oh no," Hema said, shaking her head. "I didn't mean you. You're not like that. You're a noblewoman, Mehr. You have an Ambhan father," she said, as if that made all the difference in the world. "You've been raised to see all the good in the Empire, haven't you? You're not like *him*."

She knew it was wrong to ask. But she did so anyway.

"What is he like?"

Hema's lips pursed.

"He's a monster," she said flatly.

Mehr thought of the other women. Her stomach curdled. No doubt they saw what Hema did in Amun. They saw something to be hated. An Amrithi. A barbarian. A monster. When they'd spoken to Mehr with bright curiosity, when they had invited her to visit them and join their game... all that time, they had secretly pitied her for being bound to him.

"He's said nothing to me," she said, equally quiet. "I have the Maha's work to do and it takes—a great deal of time."

"We all have our duties," Hema agreed. But she looked far from convinced.

She left Mehr at the entrance to the temple. Mehr returned to her room, where she found Amun in bed, at least feigning sleep. She blew out the lantern light and climbed into bed with him. She'd grown familiar with having him next to her. She traced the turn of his shoulder, the vulnerable line of his neck, with her eyes. The sight of him was strangely comforting.

She wanted to reach out. A foolish instinct. Instead she clasped her hands together and closed her eyes tight.

Everyone kept their distance from Amun. Everyone wanted to. Except Mehr.

When she'd first seen Amun she had thought him a monster too. But she had seen a true monster now, and all horrors paled in comparison to the Maha. The women bowed before him, worshipped him, but they didn't wear his mark. They hadn't been bound the way Mehr had. Only Amun understood the Maha's true nature as she did.

Mehr felt loneliness close over her like a vise. She turned onto her side, facing away from Amun. Her own motives lay bare before her. She'd lied to herself. She had gone to the women not because it was clever or cunning. She had gone because she was lonely. She missed her own family. She missed her loved ones so much it felt like utter heartbreak.

Arwa. Lalita. She squeezed her eyes shut. Hot tears slid down her cheeks.

Usha.

She felt Amun's fingertips. They were light as butterfly wings against her shoulder.

"Mehr," he said softly.

So he'd been feigning sleep after all. She dashed the tears away from her eyes, blinking them back. Although he shifted away at her first movement, he was still there, a warm presence at her back. She brushed her knuckles over the ribbon of her seal, heavy at her throat.

He was here. He would always be here. That, at least, she could trust.

"I'm fine," she said. "I'm just fine. Go back to sleep."

CHAPTER SIXTEEN

Mehr expected the next day to follow their established routine of prayer and food and breathing. Instead, after prayers Amun handed Mehr a small portion of bread wrapped in cloth and guided her down an unfamiliar set of corridors. When Mehr realized they were not going to the hall—that they were, in fact, walking away from it—she tugged at Amun's sleeve to force him to slow down.

"Where are we going?" she asked.

"You need supplies," said Amun.

"If by 'supplies' you mean more clothes, I do," Mehr admitted. She had been struggling to manage with what she had. "Some more soap would be helpful too."

"Well, we're going to get you what you need."

Other mystics had also finished their prayers and their meals and were making their way through the temple. Surrounded by other people, Mehr wasn't sure how openly she could speak. She spent a good few minutes eating her bread in silence.

"I imagine the Maha won't be pleased," she said quietly. "We should be preparing for the storm. If he believes we're neglecting our duty…"

Amun shook his head. "Practicing constantly is clearly ineffective," he said. "A morning spent on other tasks would do us both some good."

"I doubt the Maha will agree with you."

Amun didn't answer immediately. He guided Mehr beyond the communal bathing rooms and said, finally, "If the Maha becomes aware of our absence, I will take responsibility. I can tell anyone honestly that this was my decision. Don't trouble yourself, Mehr."

"And you think he'll believe you led me astray, like a lost child?" Mehr tutted in disbelief. "Don't be foolish, Amun."

"As my wife bound by Ambhan vows, you should obey me," Amun said blandly. "I'm sure the Maha will understand that."

Mehr laughed despite herself. She bit her lip when she saw the startled eyes of other mystics turn on her. "I think you take my vows too literally."

Amun gave her a quizzical look. It occurred to Mehr that Amun's experience of marriage had to be limited. Amrithi didn't wed—Mehr saw now, for very good reasons—and mystics vowed to remain unmarried while in service. How to explain the nature of Ambhan marriage to an outsider?

"An Ambhan wife shares her husband's burdens," said Mehr. "She is bound to him, soul to soul. He defines her."

"So he is her master."

"He often is," Mehr admitted. "But I don't believe a man bound in marriage can remain unchanged. My father altered after his marriage. Before he wed my stepmother he was—more tender. Kinder. She changed him. She had that power." After he married Maryam, his relationship with Mehr and Arwa had changed forever. A wall had grown between them, and it had never truly fallen since. "It's not a fair bond, Amun. I would never call it fair. But it's still a bond—a rope with two ends."

Amun was silent for a moment. He had a way of always mulling over her words, considering them carefully before allowing himself to speak.

"Do you believe any bond, even one founded on great unfairness, can have power?" He spoke slowly, deliberately.

Mehr thought of all the bonds, unchosen and unequal, that had shaped her like clay. She thought of how losing her mother had scarred her, and Maryam had hardened her, and Lalita had given her the strength to be bright rather than brittle.

"The bonds that tie people together change who they are," Mehr said. "They have to."

They walked a little farther in silence, Mehr's world heavy between them. Then Mehr touched her fingertips again to Amun's sleeve.

"Don't worry about taking the blame. If we get in trouble we'll face the consequences together," she told him. She gave an exaggerated shudder. "Frankly I'd rather walk out into the desert without water than return to that damnable rite again."

Amun's lips twitched into a smile. The sight of it made a kernel of warmth bloom in Mehr's chest. She ducked her head, her cheeks hot.

The reprieve from the rite was not only necessary but revealing. Mehr did her best to memorize the layout of the temple. She still found its winding corridors dizzying, but walking slowly at Amun's side in daylight allowed her to truly understand how the corridors interconnected, and the role that each part of the temple served. Over the course of the morning Mehr saw the communal bathing rooms, and halls of contemplation where more senior mystics sat in meditative silence, wreathed in incense and darkness, and the irrigated fields of crops that marked the shadier edges of the oasis. The mystics were young and old, all celibate and dedicated to their calling. And there were so very many of them.

Mehr realized quickly that the mystics had to rely heavily on offerings from the Empire, carried by those courier mystics who followed the trade routes, to sustain themselves. The mystics were so numerous, after all, and the crops were so sparse. The majority of their food, the cloth they wore, their medicines, their fuel—all of it had to come from beyond the desert, just as it did in Jah Irinah. Like her father's people, they didn't live with the desert, thriving on its strangeness and strength. They lived in spite of it.

An unfettered view of the temple helped Mehr face the bitter truth: Although the Emperor needed his nobles to administer the Empire, they would never come first in his heart or his politics. It was the Maha's concerns that came first. It was the Maha's need for Amrithi with *amata* that had driven the Emperor's search for people like Mehr. Law and faith were intertwined, but it was faith that held sway in the Empire.

Together she and Amun collected soap, made from fat and sweet herbs, from an open veranda where herbs lay drying crisp in the sun. They even managed to wrangle some fairly new tunics for Mehr. The mystic in the laundry who offered them up said they would need some minor alterations, but surely Mehr would be able to do that for herself? To which Mehr nodded agreeably, while internally accepting that she would be wearing ill-fitting clothes for the foreseeable future. Her life experience hadn't equipped her with skills anywhere near as useful as sewing.

"I'll help you fix them," Amun muttered once they were alone.

"Thank you," Mehr said graciously, and tried not to burst into fits of laughter at the thought of Amun with his big hands delicately darning a ripped hem.

Amun had kept his silence throughout every interaction with the mystics, hovering like a dark presence over her shoulder as Mehr wheedled the mystics they encountered into giving her what she needed. It was hardly difficult. She noticed quickly that the mystics were more than willing to help her. They looked at her with pity, and no little kindness. The sight of her mussed hair and faded clothes aroused their generosity.

When they looked at Amun—if they looked at him at all—it was with loathing. Always.

"Why do they hate you?" Mehr asked. His coldness was no excuse for the level of silent spite directed at him. "Is it because you're Amrithi?"

"You are too," he pointed out, as if that were an answer.

"I've been reliably informed that I am not Amrithi in the way you are," Mehr said dryly. "But I can't quite believe that they hate you so much for that alone."

"Then you think too well of them," Amun said. They walked in silence for a moment longer. Then Amun said, "You have a way with people. They like you. It changes how they view you."

Amun made it sound as if Mehr had a natural touch with people. She didn't. Mehr cultivated connections with people by necessity. She'd learned to be whatever she needed to be, in order to win favor and gain the knowledge she needed to ensure her own survival.

Instead of telling him so, Mehr shook her head. "Oh, Amun. If you had known me before, in my father's house, you wouldn't say so. I wasn't well loved."

"I doubt that."

"Doubt all you like. It's the truth." She clutched her new clothes tighter to her chest. She'd tucked the soap between the folds of cloth, letting the sweetness of the herbs permeate through the bundle. She inhaled the scent of it now: lush like the rose gardens of the Governor's palace. "I have no special gift. I just try a little harder with them than you do." That was to say, of course, that she tried at all.

"Do you miss your father's household? Your family?"

"They're different things," Mehr said. "But yes. I miss my family."

"I miss mine too."

Mehr gave him a sharp, surprised look. He'd never mentioned his family before.

"Will you tell me about them?" she asked tentatively.

"My mother was strong," he said, after a while. "Strong and clever with a knife. My father was gentler, but neither of them was weak. We lost our clan, so we traveled between villages and settlements, bartering blood and rites in return for everything we needed to survive. They were good people."

"What happened to your clan?" Mehr asked.

Amun shrugged.

"The rare ones with the *amata*—or the ones the mystics thought might have the *amata*—were hunted down. They used their blades to save themselves," he said matter-of-factly. "Clans like ours became afraid of trading with villages. They feared that the villagers would tell the mystics how to find them. Food became scarce. When our clan began to starve, some left Irinah to start again. The rest of us tried to survive in smaller, less noticeable groups. That was what my parents chose to do together."

Amun stopped, letting out a slow exhalation. His jaw was granite, lines of tension furrowing his brow. She hadn't realized how tense he had become, or how tightly she'd been holding her own breath inside herself, coiled like wire.

"What happened to your parents?" Mehr asked him softly.

She regretted her question almost instantly. She placed her hand on his arm, watched as he lowered his head.

"Amun," she said. "I'm sorry, I—"

"It's fine," he said. "No one has ever asked me before. That's all." But he still wouldn't look at her. "My mother didn't return to our tent one night. A week passed. My father looked for her, and when he came back he told me she had turned her knife on herself. The mystics must have discovered her. She preserved her freedom in the Amrithi way. As for my father..." He looked at her then. "Losing my mother was hard. Losing my father, too, was harder. In those early days, my grief made me an animal. I was too young and too foolish to realize that raging and howling like an animal would only make the mystics treat me as one.

The mystics think I am a monster, Mehr, because in those early days, I was."

He spoke matter-of-factly, no emotion in his voice, as if those early days were long gone and couldn't hurt him anymore. But Mehr had seen him lower his head like he couldn't carry the weight of the memories that lived inside it. She knew those days lived inside him still.

"You're not a monster, Amun."

"Not anymore," he agreed.

"You've never been a monster. I've seen monsters." *As have you*, she thought. *The Maha. Even Kalini.* "You're not one of them."

"Doubt it all you like," he said, echoing her words back at her. He smiled, but it was a bleak look. "It's still true, Mehr."

Mehr shook her head. She could have called him a fool, then, but what good could it possibly do? He was harsh enough to himself. He didn't need her help to make him feel any worse.

"I manage myself better now," he continued. "But I still don't need these people to be kind to me. I don't want them to be. I learned long ago that no one can replace my family."

"I'm not trying to replace anyone," Mehr snapped. The words stung.

He shrugged inelegantly.

"I cope in my own way," he said. "You need to cope in yours."

It wasn't an apology, but Mehr had had enough apologies from Amun to last a lifetime. She didn't need one more.

Especially when his words felt like truth.

When they returned to the hall to practice, Mehr didn't feel her frustration build as it usually did. The morning of freedom had given her the chance to let go of her anger, but in its place was a sadness that had coiled itself through her bones. The knowledge of how much Amun had lost was a terrible weight. She didn't know how he could bear it. But Amun looked calm and untroubled, as if he hadn't shared his grief with her, as if nothing had changed at all.

"Try again," said Amun.

She stood still and breathed slowly in and out, searching for a state of mind that would take her out of her own skin. She had to be calm. She had to put her feelings aside and focus on learning the first stage of the rite. She had to learn: Time was running out, and when the storm came Mehr would need to be prepared to do the Maha's bidding. Only by giving him her apparent obedience could she keep her soul unbound.

"Mehr," said Amun. "Open your eyes."

Mehr did as she was bid. Amun was frowning at her, a fine crease showing in the skin between his eyebrows.

"You're holding yourself too stiffly," he said. "You look as if you're performing a rite."

"I *am* performing a rite."

"This one is different. I told you," Amun said. "You can't be connected to the earth. You need to focus on moving beyond your body, to the immortal place inside you. The place your *amata* gift comes from."

Mehr sighed.

"Show me what I'm doing wrong."

Amun moved. The change in his posture was subtle but noticeable. He stood taller, his spine like iron, his legs bent so that his body was poised for movement. "You see?" he asked. "Your back is too straight and your shoulders are too stiff. You need to relax. Like this." He closed his eyes and let out a breath. The tension in his body eased away, until he stood before her with all the dazed stillness of a man on the edge of sleep.

"You look ridiculous," she told him.

He opened his eyes.

"When I'm in the storm, and the dreamfire lifts me up, I won't," he said. "And neither will you. Now close your eyes."

She closed them. She thought about the immortality in her blood, about the place where the Gods dreamed, far beyond mortal flesh. She squeezed her eyes tighter, and slowly exhaled—

"*Mehr.*"

"I'm trying," Mehr said, opening her eyes. "But I need you to help me. Direct me."

"Fine." His frown had smoothed. "Close your eyes again."

Mehr did. She heard the scuff of his footsteps, heard him murmur an apology. Then she felt one of his hands against her spine. Her eyes snapped open.

"What—?"

"*Relax.*"

But Mehr could not. With one hand on her upper back, the other at her hip, he was tilting her body off balance. A nudge farther and she would have nothing to hold her up but his arms.

"You'll be weightless in the rite," he told her. "This is as close as I can bring you to how it feels." A pause. "If you want me to stop . . ." he said in a low voice.

"Will this help?"

"I believe so."

"Then go on." Mehr steeled herself internally. "If you need to show me, show me."

She knew touch was the best way to teach a rite. Hadn't Lalita taught her by taking her arms and legs in hand, directing her like a doll? Hadn't Mehr's mother done the same before her?

There was a difference, of course, between this lesson and the ones of the past. Mehr had wanted to learn, when her mother and Lalita had taught her. But Mehr didn't want to learn the Rite of the Bound. She didn't want to relinquish control of her own flesh. She didn't want to commit a heresy against the Gods. When she thought of sinking into the immortality within her, she remembered the tales she'd been told, as a child, of the fate of Amrithi who didn't show reverence to their ancestors.

She didn't want her soul to pay the price for her survival. In her heart, she feared that when she found the immortality within her, she'd find the punishment that awaited her also. The scar on her chest ached at the thought.

"Relax if you can," Amun said. "I can hold you."

He was strong. She knew that. It wasn't his strength that worried her. Heart pounding, she gave a small nod.

"Trust me in this," he said.

She closed her eyes again. In small increments he eased the weight of her body, tilting her until her feet skimmed the ground and her head was thrown back, heavy with the weight of her own hair. His palm was hot against her back, his fingers outstretched. Every time she breathed she could feel the shape of his fingertips.

"Try again," he said.

It should have been hard to forget her flesh, with Amun so close to her, with her own fears stretching their bleak hands behind her closed eyelids. But without having to hold herself upright she felt dizzy, weightless. The rush of her own pulse soothed her mind to something akin to silence.

She breathed.

The place beyond flesh. The place mortal minds drifted to when they dreamed. That was the place she had to go to. She could trust her body to his hands. She could leave it behind.

She remembered how it felt when she'd moved through the storm in Jah Irinah, and the dreamfire had held her wrists and ankles, guiding her through the storm. She'd been driven by desperation. But during the next storm, she wouldn't be unwittingly begging the Gods for guidance. She would be purposefully compelling their dreams, using sigils to force their dreams to give the Empire the good fortune it needed to expand and conquer and grow as close to immortality as an Empire could. She would channel the power of the Gods through all their fire, and all their strength.

And she would choke their strength too. Suppress their dreams. Crush them back into sleep and darkness.

It was anathema, an utter heresy—and Mehr would have to learn it, if she wanted to keep what little power she had, and if she ever wanted to find a way to be free.

Breathe. Breathe. Breathe.

She didn't know how long he held her. She let herself relax, listening to the crackle of the lantern flames, the soft sound of Amun's even breath. She listened to the rush of blood in her own head. As the seconds and minutes ticked by, she spiraled deeper and deeper into herself.

"Mehr." Amun's voice. "Come back."

Mehr flinched, startled. She wasn't sure what had happened. She hadn't been asleep, but she had been—*away*. Drifting in shadow, the kind of heady silence that lay somewhere between sleep and waking.

He eased her back to standing, letting her go only when she assured him she was back to herself again.

"It worked?" She wasn't quite sure.

"It did," he said. "As long as you feel as you do now, when you perform the rite, you will know you've been successful."

Mehr could have cheered. What a relief it was to finally feel like she was making progress. But she could still feel the echo of Amun's fingers against her back, and her insides were light and strange, something close to embarrassment coiling through her.

"Is that all it is?"

Amun nodded in confirmation.

"Thank you," she said. "It made all the difference. Your help."

"I should have tried earlier, but..." He shook his head.

Mehr understood, a little. He was always careful when it came to touch. It was his hesitation, the deliberate distance he kept between them that made her so utterly aware of his strength and the leash he kept it on.

Amun was so sure he was a monster. But it was the way he handled touch—with utter care and respect—that told her he was the opposite of one.

"I was taught the rites in just the same way," Mehr said, trying to put him at ease. She told him about how she'd learned the first steps of her first childhood rites by placing her feet over her mother's. Dancing with her. As she chattered on Amun listened, his eyes half lidded, letting her words wash over him.

A thought eventually occurred to her. "How did you learn the Rite of the Bound?" If learning the rite required being held, required weightlessness—who had held him? Whom had he trusted for the task?

"There was another Amrithi here for many years," he said. "She taught me."

"What happened to her?" Mehr asked. The lightness in her went leaden. She could guess, but she wanted to hear it.

"The rite was hard on her. The rite is always hard, but she was growing old, and eventually the strain was too much. She died," he said frankly. "After that, the Maha went in search of a replacement."

And here I am, thought Mehr.

Amun had seen so much darkness in his life. His parents were gone; the woman who had trained him had died; the vows written on his soul had left him feeling monstrous and alone. She couldn't fathom how he could still look so steady and so whole, after all he had suffered. She couldn't understand how he could remain so gentle when he had never sought or received gentleness from others.

"You have so much history," she said helplessly. "So much."

The look he gave her was soft, so soft.

"We all do, Mehr."

She heard footsteps from the corridor beyond the hall. Laughter. She wondered if any of those laughing voices belonged to

Hema's women. She watched the softness leave his eyes. He'd forgotten for a moment that they were constantly watched, eyes and ears always on them. Mehr had forgotten too. But she remembered now. She watched him lean back against the wall, brushing a hand self-consciously through his curling hair.

"I'll be glad when the storm has passed," Amun said.

"As will I," said Mehr.

But she feared the storm too. It was awful, that fear. She'd always considered storms holy. She'd been awed by dreamfire, humbled and joyful. But the beauty had been stripped away, and all Mehr had left was her dread that acted as the bones of awe.

"The Maha will want to meet you again soon," Amun told her. Mehr's stomach lurched. "He'll want to ask after your progress."

Anyone could have been listening. So instead of asking Amun *How do I lie to him?* she said simply, "What do I do?"

He gestured with the flick of his wrist. *Come here.* So she did. She leaned against the wall next to him, their shoulders brushing.

His voice was a murmur, so quiet she had to strain to hear it.

"Surviving with the Maha is just like surviving the Rite of the Bound. The skill will serve you for both. You let his power wash over you. You let it take you. And then you bend it. You give it the shape you need it to have. Decide how to obey him. That's all."

Amun spoke as if the task were simple. Mehr wasn't convinced. She let out a choked laugh and pressed a hand to her mouth.

"Mehr."

"I'll try," she said. "Don't you worry."

"I have faith in you," Amun said in a low voice. Mehr didn't look at him. On the ground, their shadows were tangled together by lantern light.

She knew he had faith in her. She knew.

It was a shame she couldn't share that faith.

CHAPTER SEVENTEEN

Amun began teaching Mehr the sigils necessary for the Rite of the Bound the next day. Mehr was familiar with the language of the daiva, but the sigils of this rite were a new tongue—a cryptic, clever thing that twisted her fingers into knots. These sigils, Amun told her, were the language of the Gods. Amun demanded utter precision from her. Every movement had to be perfect. The angle of her wrist, the flick of her fingers, the height of her hands, all had to match Amun's demonstrations exactly.

"Together the sigils have a specific power," Amun explained. "They are what allow us to act as a conduit. They make the dreams of the Gods vulnerable to the influence of the mystics' prayers."

The mystics' prayers: prayers for the Emperor, for the Maha, for the Ambhan Empire's strength and its glory. It was because of this rite, Mehr reminded herself, that the Empire possessed unnatural good fortune. It was because of this rite that the Empire could expand ever larger, that the generations of Emperors had lived long and fruitful lives, the Empire's cities untouched by plague, its borders secure.

Good health, safe borders—these things sounded like blessings. But the thought of all the blessings of an Ambhan life—of the life Mehr had lived for so many years—now left a bitter taste in Mehr's mouth. Ambhan wealth had been won with Amrithi blood. No more, no less.

"How am I supposed to lose my flesh *and* remember all of this?" Mehr demanded, wriggling her fingers pointedly.

"You learn," Amun said shortly.

Mehr gave Amun a doubtful look.

"You *must* perform this correctly, Mehr." Amun sounded tense. "If you make a mistake the consequences will be unpleasant."

"Tell me what could happen," Mehr said.

"You know already."

"I like things to be clear." She gave Amun a pained smile, half grimace. Her fingers were cramping from practice. She shouldn't have wasted energy goading him. But oh, she couldn't help herself. She began massaging her hands together, working the stiffness from her knuckles. "Humor me."

His gaze flickered down, fixing on her hands. She thought for a moment that he would take her hands in his, or ask if he could—

But no. Her mind was playing tricks on her.

"If you don't control the dreamfire, channel it, direct it, then it will move like fire does, and consume everything in its path," he said. "When we dance the rite the fire is *inside* us, Mehr. To perform it wrongly is to risk immortal dreams burning your soul clean away, leaving nothing of your soul or self behind." He paused. "Or the Maha could punish you."

"I'm sure both things would be equally unpleasant." Her hands dropped to her sides. "Fine. Let's continue."

"Are you—?"

"I'm fine. I'm ready."

Amun's mouth thinned.

"Let me show you again," he said. He raised his hands.

"Watch my fingers now," he said. "Don't copy me just yet. Rest your hands. Just watch."

Evening came, and with it more prayers. Mehr lowered her head and sang in honor of the Emperor along with all the mystics, but her mind was in another place entirely. Sigils flared in her mind's eye. Her head was full of the sight of Amun's hands making shape after shape. His wide, scarred hands, dark like earth after rainfall. His hands teaching her a new language.

Mehr could learn this. She could.

After evening prayers finished she began heading toward dinner with the others. An urgent tug on her sleeve stopped her. She stopped in her tracks and turned.

"Hema wants you to meet her," Rena said. "It's important you come now, before the others notice."

Her voice was urgent, her jaw hard. So Mehr followed her.

Rena guided her through the winding corridors to a tower no different from any of the others they had passed. She urged Mehr up the steps, which were so narrow they could only make their way up one at a time. Stone skimmed Mehr's arms. She could feel the darkness pressing on her.

Hema was waiting at the top, her hands on the edge of the only window carved into the curved wall.

"I have her," said Rena.

Hema look back at them. She didn't smile, but she gave Rena a wordless nod of thanks. Rena turned and left without another word.

"Come to the window," Hema said. "You need to see it." She gestured sharply, her fingers trembling. "Come to the window, please."

There was enough room for Mehr to stand next to Hema and look outside. This window faced away from the oasis, to the stretch of endless sand visible beyond the temple's walls. Mehr leaned out, the cool breeze meeting her bare face. She looked. Her breath caught in her throat.

"Gods," Mehr breathed out.

"I know," Hema whispered. "What a sight."

It was dark outside, but not so dark that Mehr couldn't see the shadows coiling on the horizon, their edges tinged with a blush of red-gold light. Daiva. So many daiva.

The storm was coming.

Together she and Hema stood in stunned silence, watching the shadows writhe, gleaming in the growing dark. The breeze carried the scent of the daiva with it: incense, sweet as the smoke of a prayer flame. Mehr had thought the coming of a storm was beautiful, when she had lived in Jah Irinah. Here in the heart of the desert the sight of it was almost overwhelming. The daiva were a wall, a rising wave of dark mingled with light, jeweled fire and shadow. When the dreamfire fell the daiva would sweep down with it, and the temple would surely drown in them.

"Before I came here I was nothing," Hema said. Her voice was even, but its evenness was like a bandage on a bleeding wound. Her trembling fingers had tightened on the edge of the window and gone still. "All of us were nothing. Just fatherless children, hungry and alone. But here we have the power to change the world. Here we can ensure that the Empire remains ever glorious, spreading its prosperity and its goodness, preserving the immortality of our Emperors. Here, *we* are the heart of the Empire."

Mehr listened without speaking.

"You're not happy," said Hema. "But there is glory in this life."

"Why did you bring me here?" Mehr asked.

Hema did smile then, a wry, secret smile.

"When I was a little girl, my sister brought me here too and showed me just this sight," she said. "She showed me and told me that I mattered. That *I* was the heart of the Empire. My prayers. My service." Hema touched a fist to her chest. "The Empire is the glory we have created." She looked at Mehr. "This is your glory too now, Mehr. All that power you see out there? You can make it do something *good*."

Mehr squeezed her own hands into fists. She thought of Amun's vow-marked skin. The scar on her chest. The weight of the Maha's eyes. The chafe of the marriage seal at her throat.

"You believe I can make a difference?" she said, glad the shake in her voice could be ascribed to so many, many things other than anger.

"Of course I do," Hema said simply.

Hema truly believed in the Maha. They all did.

If the Maha had been kind to Mehr, had raised her up from nothing and dazzled her with his power and benevolence, perhaps she would have grown to believe in him too. Perhaps she would have wanted to don his chains, hand him her beating, bloody heart on a platter. But he hadn't raised her up. He had struck her down.

The love he wanted from her was different than the love he demanded from his mystics. His mystics were his followers and his chosen, and from them he demanded a love that was as simple as a child's, adoring and fervent.

But his Amrithi were his tools. From them he wanted a love that sprouted from the dark blood of fear, and Mehr refused to give that to him.

Mehr uncurled one hand. Placed it on Hema's shoulder.

"Thank you," Mehr whispered. "Thank you for being kind."

Perhaps the Maha had asked Hema to win Mehr's loyalty. Perhaps Hema had some other ulterior motive, some unfathomable reason for trying so stubbornly to win Mehr's trust. Mehr didn't know. But she did know that any kindness in this place was to be treasured.

Hema returned the gesture, the clasp of her hand firm against Mehr's shoulder.

"You don't have to thank me," Hema said in return. "You and I—we're not just citizens of the Empire any longer. We're so much more. We're Saltborn. We're family now."

The sight of the approaching storm left a fire in Mehr's blood. Mehr could feel the necessary stillness inside her that Amun had worked so hard to teach her, and the sigils flowed easily from her fingers. But she lacked the concentration to learn any of the new tasks Amun was trying to show her, and the knowledge slipped through her fingers like so much sand.

Amun showed no impatience. Instead he was quieter than ever, his hands feather-light on her wrists as he guided her through shape after shape, sigil after sigil. His eyes had a faraway look.

She wondered if he knew how close the storm stood. If he could smell its sweetness on the air. Now that Mehr had seen it, she certainly could. Every time she breathed in, the aftertaste of smoke filled her lungs.

It didn't take long for the news of the approaching storm to spread. Amun was standing behind Mehr, directing her arms in carefully timed increments, when he went still, his grip tightening on her wrists. Mehr froze. They weren't alone any longer.

"Kalini," said Amun.

"Continue," Kalini said from the doorway. "Don't mind us now, Amun."

Mehr craned her neck. She saw the edge of Kalini's dark robe, melding with the shadows on the floor. Behind her stood Bahren, his arms crossed.

"Mehr," Amun prompted quietly. Mehr looked away.

Their already shaken concentration had been ruined entirely, but they returned to their training regardless. Instead of moving on to new sigils, Amun returned to careful, familiar repetitions of movement that they had perfected earlier, putting on a show of competence for Kalini's judgmental gaze. Mehr knew she could have done better—nervousness made her clumsy—but she hadn't expected Kalini's eyes to narrow with such clear displeasure in response.

"Is that all you've accomplished?" Kalini's voice was full of disapproval.

"We've accomplished a great deal," Amun said.

"Don't try to lie to me," said Kalini. "The Maha told me what to look for. She's learning too slowly."

"She's learning far more swiftly than I ever did," Amun replied.

"You had years to learn. She has days," Kalini said. Her gaze cut to Mehr. Her voice was pure ice. "You need to do better. The Maha demands it of you."

"I'll be prepared," said Mehr. "I know my duty. You can tell the Maha so."

"Tell him yourself. You'll share dinner with him tomorrow night." She gestured at Bahren, who stepped forward. Mehr hadn't thought it possible, but somehow the older mystic's face had become even grimmer. "Tonight Bahren needs your assistance."

Amun hesitated, then stepped away from Mehr, walking to Bahren's side. He stilled as soon as he heard Kalini speak again. "I'll send the girl to meet you in a moment."

"I can do it alone," Amun said sharply.

"You'll finish the job more quickly together."

"I don't need her help."

"Sweet as your efforts to coddle her are, your wife shares your burdens. She made a vow. Like it or not, you *will* have her help."

"Come on," Bahren muttered. "We have work to do. Stop this."

Amun looked at Mehr, indecipherable emotion flickering through his midnight eyes. Then he turned and followed.

Mehr had no idea why Kalini wanted to be alone with her, but she didn't think any good could come from it. She wanted to cross her arms, to cower back as if her own strength could give her safety. But she stood straight and tall, folding her fear away for another time. She couldn't defend herself, not here under the Maha's thumb. But she could try to hold on to the tatters of her pride.

"I hear you've been neglecting your husband and spending your time with kitchen maids," Kalini said.

Mehr said nothing. It was no secret, surely, that Hema and her friends had cultivated a relationship with Mehr.

"You're going to leave my sister alone."

Mehr took in a deep, slow breath. She should have known this was coming.

"As the Maha wills," she murmured.

"*I* will it. And if you defy me I will personally ensure that your life is as unpleasant as possible." Kalini's voice was even, but her eyes were fierce and cold. "I hope we understand each other."

Mehr nodded, clenching her hands tight.

"Answer me," Kalini demanded.

"Yes," said Mehr thinly. "I understand."

Bahren had a set of knives. They were not Amrithi blades, but they were sharp and clean, doused with medicinal alcohol and wiped dry with cloth by Bahren in Mehr and Amun's presence. Mehr listened without surprise as Bahren told them that they would need to cut their own flesh and mark all the most import-ant chambers of the temple with their blood.

She should have anticipated that this service would be expected of her. Unlike the Ambhans of Jah Irinah, the mystics knew the power of the daiva intimately. They would want to keep the strongest of the daiva—the amorphous ones, not quite as power-ful as the humanoid daiva of the past or the young animal-spirits of the present—away from their home. What better tool to keep them at bay than the blood of their pet Amrithi?

They didn't have to ask for Mehr or Amun's consent. They didn't have to barter with them, as the Irin had once bartered with the Amrithi clans who drifted near their cities and villages. They could simply take. After all, Mehr and Amun had made a vow.

"I don't mind," Mehr told Amun, who was visibly unhappy, his shoulders hunched and his jaw tight.

"I do," Amun said shortly. But after that he kept his feelings to himself, obeying Bahren's directions in sullen silence.

Mehr really did not mind, at first. She reasoned that she would at least have the opportunity to find out exactly where the most important chambers in the temple were. Any knowledge she could gain during the night would be a worthwhile price for a bit of stolen blood. Amun had consistently refused to discuss escape since the first time Mehr had raised the possibility of it, but Mehr still carried the seed of hope within her. She held on to it as they began to move through the temple, marking the windows with their blood.

But the temple was huge, and to Mehr it soon began to feel as if every single empty hall, every storeroom or empty unshuttered window was considered important. The cut on the soft skin of her inner elbow stung from being constantly reopened.

It felt like a long, long time before Bahren declared that they were done. He gave Mehr and Amun cloth bandages to tie around their cuts to stem the blood, then told them to return to their room.

"I don't know how you managed to do this on your own," Mehr said to Amun once they were alone, wincing as she tightened the bandage an increment further. She was exhausted; her fingers were trembling with tiredness. "That was difficult enough for both of us."

"Give me your new tunic," Amun said. "You're going to need it tomorrow."

Of course. She'd have to make an effort to look presentable

in front of the Maha. The Maha would not care how hard they had worked. He wouldn't care how exhausted they were, or how long they'd been bled. He would expect them to dress and act in a way that showed him the proper respect and reverence. Mehr gave Amun the tunic and lay back on the bed, letting her exhaustion take her. She watched through half-lidded eyes as he moved around the room, picking up a needle and thread. He sat down next to her, close enough that his leg brushed her knee, and began to sew. Mehr watched, letting the silence blanket them both. She'd thought the sight of him with a needle would be absurd, but instead it was strangely comforting.

She closed her eyes to the sound of the wind howling beyond the windows, and the gentle in-out of Amun's breath.

Tomorrow there would be no such comfort. Tomorrow they would face the Maha. But Mehr didn't want to think of that. To think of the Maha was to think of all the ways she could fail—the secrets she could reveal, the freedoms she could lose. She had to be stronger and braver than she believed she could be. She had to meet the Maha's terrible eyes and lie to the man who held her soul in the palm of his hand.

"You'll need to try this on," Amun told her.

"Now?"

"When I'm done."

Mehr murmured her agreement. She could feel the heat of his leg against her knee. *You believe in me*, she thought. *I don't know why, but you do. And I'll try not to fail you, Amun. No matter what, I promise you I'll try.*

On the evening of their dinner with the Maha, they were led to a balcony facing the desert. The glow of the coming storm mingled with the gold of the lantern flames, giving the walls a rose-hued warmth. But it was the opulence surrounding them, not the light of the storm, that left Mehr stunned and silent. There was a fine, handwoven carpet unrolled on the ground, the like of which she hadn't seen since she had left her father's household. The low table was covered in an exhaustive array of food: meat in a heady spiced broth, rice plump with heat and dotted with golden raisins, honeyed figs and rose sherbet. The Maha's table was set with a true feast.

And Mehr, hungry as she was, was too afraid to touch it.

The Maha left them kneeling for a long time. When he finally entered, the food had begun to cool, the steam rising from its surface fading to thin wisps. Mehr and Amun bowed their heads, pressing their foreheads to the floor as the Maha kneeled down across from them. He didn't touch the food.

"Sit up," the Maha said. "Eat. Don't be shy."

Mehr raised her head. She looked at all that food, sweeter and richer than anything she'd had since the moment the marriage seal was placed around her neck. She couldn't touch it.

Amun ate a little. A piece of bread. A sip of fruit nectar. Mehr echoed his movements, grateful that he was here to show her the way. Her fear was choking her. If the Maha asked the right questions, if he grew suspicious of her . . .

Mehr had far, far too much to hide. She tried not to let her fingers tremble as she raised a bite of food to her lips.

"The storm closes in," the Maha said, after a time. He didn't seem to expect a response.

Mehr watched his hands, and only his hands, as he poured a glass of mint tea, green leaves swirling in the fall of steaming water.

"Tonight the Saltborn will begin their fasts." She watched him stir in a spoonful of honey. "Food, hunger—these things are of the flesh. I have been blessed by the Gods, and I have moved beyond such needs. When the storms approach, I ask my mystics to try to do the same." The spoon clicked against the edge of the glass. Again. Again. "By putting aside sustenance, they are better able to focus all their desire on one purpose: the glory of the Empire. My dear mystics." His voice was full of affection. He lowered the spoon back to the table. "Their dreams, their hopes—do you know how strong they are? Ah, children, you can't imagine it. They pray so fervently that I truly believe they should be able to sway the Gods without intercession. Their prayers should be able to part oceans, set the sky ablaze." A sigh. "But alas, the daiva's children must carry their prayers for them."

He spoke, Mehr thought, exactly like a man who was used to being listened to, and never argued with. He spoke like an Emperor himself. His voice was mild and calm, but every word he said made her mark flare with pain. She bit down on her tongue, reminding herself that the pain would pass. After the dinner, the Maha would leave her and Amun alone again for a time. One dinner, and then she would be able to focus her attention on the Rite of the Bound, and the storm that lay ahead of her.

"It is a shame," the Maha continued with utter calm, "that the daiva's children are such lazy fools."

Mehr suddenly felt very cold. Both she and Amun stayed utterly silent.

"Kalini was not pleased with your progress, Mehr. She said you were clumsy. Unskilled. What do you have to say for yourself?"

She didn't know what to say. The words were stuck in her throat. *I am doing well, Maha. I know I'm doing well.* He spoke like a teacher chiding a student, but Mehr knew what lay beneath that civil veneer. Beneath his smiles, his gentle voice, his heart was a starless night. His anger, she feared, would be a terrible thing.

"She is doing everything she can," Amun said. "Maha, I promise you, no one could work harder."

"I didn't ask you to speak, Amun," the Maha said. His voice was pleasant. Far too pleasant. "So now you will not, until you leave my presence."

There was a sharp intake of breath at Mehr's side. Then

nothing. Mehr had felt the order, a cold shadow passing under her skin. She knew Amun would not be able to help her anymore this evening.

"Speak to me, Mehr. Tell me truth."

"I am trying, Maha." This, at least, she could be honest about. She let the compulsion wash over her, forcing the words from her lips. "On my honor, I am trying as hard as I can."

"You believe you are," he said gently. "But I believe you could do better—and I am a great deal older and wiser than you are, Mehr."

She was shivering. She couldn't control herself. She wished the Maha had ordered her to be silent instead of Amun. It was hard to resist the urge to garble out apologies, to cry and beg for his mercy. He had done nothing to her, but in her bones she knew he would. He wanted her fear. He wanted it more than her gratitude.

The Maha allowed the moment to stretch thin between them. His hand drifted, with deceptive casualness, away from the tea glass and spoon toward a tray of fruit. There was a knife on the tray. It was small, with a firm handle and one sharp edge, useful for cutting fruit down into fine segments. He took hold of it.

"Hold out your left hand, Mehr. Palm up."

Mehr wanted to refuse. But he had ordered her. She should not have been able to resist an order. Allowing his voice to compel her was almost a relief. She held her arm out across the table, palm upraised. With his order racing through her blood, her arm didn't even tremble.

He held the knife over the smallest finger. The metal skimmed her skin.

"You don't need all of your fingers for the rite," he told her. "I know that." A pause. "I was once served by an Amrithi male named Gaur. He was strong. Healthy. But the smallest finger of his left hand was lost when my mystics took his blade from him. A shame, but he learned to serve despite his early failures."

Mehr held her breath. There was a whiteness buzzing behind her eyes.

"Will you do better?" the Maha asked quietly. "Or will you require encouragement?"

He pressed a little harder. A bead of blood welled up on Mehr's skin.

"I will do better," Mehr said. Her voice shook like a leaf. "I promise I will."

Even in the cloud of fear fogging her mind, Mehr knew he was unlikely to risk maiming her permanently so near the storm. She knew. But that made no difference. He could hurt her. He had hurt her today—cut the knowledge of her powerlessness directly into her flesh. Once the storm had passed, he could hurt her even worse. Skin deep, soul deep. However he liked. Her life belonged to him.

This knife would hang over her, always and always, for the rest of her vow-bound life.

He met her eyes. Whatever he saw must have pleased him, because he nodded to himself and placed the hilt of the blade in her open palm.

"I will observe your training directly from time to time, in the future," said the Maha. "Clearly I was wrong to think Amun would be a reliable teacher." He slid the tea across the table to Mehr. It was still warm, steam rising from its surface. "For now, wipe the blade clean," he said. "Drink the tea and calm yourself."

There was nothing for Mehr to clean the blade with. Under the weight of the Maha's hooded eyes, she took the blade in her bloodied, shaking hand and wiped the knife clean on the sleeve of her new tunic. Her hands refused to stop trembling. She put the blade down, lifted the glass, and drank. The liquid was scalding, a shock of sweetness and heat.

"You will both perform for me now," the Maha said, his voice silken. "Show me that you will be able to do what is required of you, and you aren't as clumsy and foolish as I've been led to believe."

Under his watchful gaze, Mehr and Amun stood. Unable to speak, the weight of the Maha's command upon him, Amun guided her to look at him with a light touch of his fingertips to her arm.

Follow me, his eyes seemed to say. *Trust me. We will get through this together.*

Mehr took a deep breath and raised her hands to form the first sigil.

CHAPTER EIGHTEEN

"You seem calm." Amun watched her carefully as she sat down on the bed in their room, as she curled her hands in her lap.

"I'm not calm," Mehr said. "I just can't allow myself to feel. Not yet."

She inspected her hand carefully. The cut was shallow. It had pained and bled far more than a cut of its size deserved to. Even now, every time she curled her fingers, sluggish blood oozed from the wound. She pressed her stained sleeve hard against the cut to stem the flow. Performing the rite, shaping its sigils, had opened the cut again and made it pain all the more.

Her poor sleeve. After all the effort Amun had gone to in order to make her tunic presentable, the fact that the cloth was irreparably ruined seemed somehow a greater injustice even than the wound the Maha had inflicted on her. Mehr ran a finger over the cloth. The stain had dried fast. Even if Mehr begged some boiled water from the kitchens and sacrificed some of her new soap to the task of getting it clean, something of the stain would be left behind—some faint hint of darkness, the smell of bitter iron.

"You're doing well," Amun said. "No matter what the Maha claims, you are."

"Then why punish me?"

"He wants you to be as skilled in the rite as I am," said Amun. "He needs us both to be prepared, Mehr, or his rite can't be performed. He doesn't have other Amrithi to perform the rite as he once did. He just has us."

It was strange to think of the Maha as fearful. It was stranger still to think that the Maha needed them: that without Mehr and Amun the great Empire, all its provinces and wealth and beauty, would fall to dust.

"You *are* prepared, Mehr," Amun said into the silence. "Don't worry."

"I'm not worried about that," Mehr lied. "Has he ever observed your training before? Ever demanded you perform for him?"

Amun shook his head. "He taught the woman with whom I performed the rite, from time to time. But not me. He trusted her to teach me."

But he didn't trust Amun. More than that, he didn't trust Mehr. She was too green, too clumsy; she was not an adequate tool. He'd used his blade to hone her. The thought left her feeling raw.

"We were lucky he didn't find out the truth about my vow," said Mehr. Now that they were back in the privacy of Amun's room, she could be honest. She could feel the weight of their shared secret. She knew how easily she would have revealed it if the Maha had cut just a little deeper.

"You did well."

"Of course. I didn't have to lie." Mehr pursed her lips. "But if he'd asked me the right questions we would have been ruined."

"You did well," Amun repeated.

He was nearly vibrating with energy. She could see the tension in his shoulders.

"Let me fix your hand," he said abruptly.

"The cut isn't so bad."

Amun didn't move. He was so tense she feared he would snap. So she sighed and relented.

"Go on then."

He moved immediately, looking for a clean cloth and water. She understood that he wanted to help her—that watching the Maha hurt her without being able to interfere had been agony for him—but there was little he could do. The cut was shallow and would heal with time, but the wound the Maha had left in Mehr's head wasn't so easily fixed. And that had been the Maha's intention, of course: to give Mehr a long-lasting hurt without compromising her usefulness. He was a clever man, and all the more terrible for it.

She let Amun take her hand without complaint. He turned her hand over gently, lowering his head to take a closer look at her skin. His fingers were warm as coals. She realized suddenly how cold she was.

She looked away from him, forcing herself not to stare at his lowered face or the blue whorls that swept from the nape of his neck down under the cover of his tunic. Instead she looked at the bare room around them. Red-gold light filtered in beneath the cracks in the shutters.

When had Amun's bedroom begun to feel like home? She didn't know. Here was the only place she felt like the Maha's eyes were not on her. She still had uneasy dreams, still woke reaching for the blade that was no longer under her pillow. But within these bare walls, these shuttered windows, she felt *safe*.

"The Amrithi he spoke of," Mehr said slowly. The cogs of her brain were still turning, sifting through the Maha's words for a pattern, an answer. Knowledge. She had to seek knowledge. "The man. Gaur. He wasn't the one who trained you, was he? You told me you were trained by a woman."

"There's only been one Amrithi pair in the temple, in my time here," said Amun, his attention still focused on her cut. "The woman who trained me, and myself. Then you and me. No more than that."

Mehr thought of the Amrithi pairs who had come before them. She thought of the great effort the Maha had gone to, in order to acquire Mehr—the way he had twisted the sacred institution of marriage, sacred to his Empire and to his people, in order to control one single half-Amrithi woman with the *amata* gift.

"The Amrithi, our gifts, our people," Mehr said softly. "We're fading, aren't we?"

Amun let out a deep breath. "I don't know," he said. "Perhaps. I try not to think of it."

Mehr closed her eyes and let out a breath. She thought of the Empire. She thought of the Maha. She thought of all those dreams that had never touched either of them. She thought of dreams of aging and death.

Death and decay followed humans with every breath, every heartbeat. Skin could be cut, and skin could heal. Bodies could hunger and be fed. But the Maha no longer hungered as humans hungered. She'd seen the light under his skin, the strangeness of it. She wondered if he could even bleed any longer.

He'd used the rite to make himself something not quite human.

Somewhere, immortal dreams of his death lay, crushed beneath the weight of the mystics' prayers and the rite. If he had managed to twist himself into something so utterly inhuman through the power of the rite, what had he done to the Empire? What had he done to the world?

A shudder ran through her. The emotions she'd been so careful to push away drew in closer. She clasped Amun's hand in her own, taking comfort in him. He was here. His hand was in her own. What a small thing that touch was, and how utterly vital it felt to her in that moment.

She heard his breath catch.

"Mehr," he said.

She should have let go of him then. She knew that. But he was so warm. She waited for him to speak again, but when he was silent she clasped his hand tighter, leaning closer to him. Under his shadow, she didn't feel the need to hold on to the iron in her spine. She could breathe.

Amun didn't move noticeably. But she felt him relax, increment by increment, until they were leaning in to each other.

As the seconds ticked by, she realized a line had been crossed between them. The careful distance they had worked, without words, to maintain all this time had been breached. She was glad she couldn't feel right then. She was glad not to be ashamed. Perhaps she would be later. But not now.

She looked up at him. There was a warmth in his face, a heat that made her think he knew just as well as she did that a line had been crossed between them, and could never be uncrossed.

"Mehr." His voice was low. Regretful. "You should let me go."

They were nearly sharing breath. Mehr did not examine the thrum of her heart, or the way the world felt as if it had gone slow and silent around them. She didn't examine the desire his words evoked in her to hold on to him even tighter.

"You're hurt," Amun said. "You're afraid."

I'm not the only one who is afraid, Mehr thought. But she said, "Do you want me to let go?"

His nostrils flared. A small, ridiculous show of emotion.

"I do."

He had always respected her wishes. So now she respected his, and released him. He pulled away.

As he stood, Mehr made a show of looking down at her hand. The wound was bound and clean. He'd done a fine job, but it didn't seem right to tell him so now. He had his back to her. His hands were clasped tight behind him. He'd never learn to hide his heart.

"I won't be able to fight the vow forever, Mehr." The words passed his lips torturously, as if he were loath to say them. "I can delay it a little longer. I think. I hope. But I can't...I can only bend my obedience." His voice was rough. "I can't shatter it completely."

His vow. To make her his wife in flesh and soul. To take her to his bed.

"I know," she managed. "I know, Amun. And I'm sorry for it."

Her heart hurt. She'd known, always known, that he couldn't break his vows, only shape his obedience. She had allowed herself to forget that. More fool her. Worse still, she had simply not considered what their shared secret meant for him.

"Does it hurt?" she asked. "The mark—does it hurt you?"

Amun said nothing. But she watched his fingers curl tighter, knuckles whitening, and that was answer enough.

"I'm sorry," she whispered.

"Don't apologize." Bitter blackness in his voice. "I will be my Maha's faithful servant in the end."

Mehr bit her tongue, holding back her own words for a long moment. It would do no good to tell him to be kinder to himself. He was what he was. And some part of Mehr shared that black despair she heard in his voice. Some part of her felt the inexorable pull of the Maha's power, dragging her down a path she did not want to walk.

"We will find a way to be free of him," Mehr said. "Amun. I promise you we will."

"There is no way to be free of him. Not for me. I've told you, Mehr."

"If you truly believed that, you would never have tried to give me time. You still give me time, Amun. You fight. If the Maha can't be resisted, why do you fight?"

"Because I'm not so cruel as all that," he said wretchedly.

"You're not a monster," Mehr agreed, although she knew he believed he was. "But you also have hope. You must have hope." Her fingers twitched. She wanted to reach out to him. She didn't. "We don't have to be what the Maha has made us. We can try to be free, Amun. Just *try*."

Amun shook his head. He said nothing.

The shutters rattled with the wind. Mehr took a deep, slow breath. Her hand had begun to throb. He'd told her, once, that hope would hurt him. She knew he feared that hope was pointless and came at too high a cost. But they couldn't continue to live like this, bound and terrorized. They had to work together and find a way out.

"We'll get through the storm first," Mehr said. "And then we will find a way to escape, Amun. I know we will."

As the Maha had told them, the mystics had all begun their prayers and their fasting. All other tasks were abandoned. The fires went unlit, food uncooked. Mehr and Amun, who both had no desire to fast, scrounged up some dried dates from the food stores. Neither of them was particularly hungry, but they would need the energy to face the demands of the rite.

When the dreamfire began to fall, the first gouts of color drifting down from the sky, one of the less senior mystics, a boy Mehr had seen sweeping the corridors from time to time, brought them clothing that was a close approximation of Amrithi costume. Fanned cloth trousers, a blouse, and a length of cotton shot through with faded color were given to Mehr to wear draped across her torso. She dressed in silence, her back to Amun, allowing them both some privacy.

She missed her own Amrithi clothing. She missed the joy it had once given her to drape herself in cloth and mark the edges of her eyes with kohl. Mehr felt nothing but nervousness now. Nothing about this storm was as it should be. She felt drab and colorless in her clothes, her stomach filled with butterflies and her skull heavy with all the things she couldn't forget: sigils, secrets, vows.

As she began to try to apply kohl to her eyes without a mirror to guide her, she heard Amun's voice.

"Let me help you."

She turned to him. Froze.

He looked nothing like his old self. No longer swathed in a heavy robe or ill-fitting tunic, he was tall and strong, his blackened eyes otherworldly, his expression serene. In Amrithi clothing he looked like the self she'd seen flashes of, through his usual garb of hunched shoulders and self-loathing. He looked clear-eyed and strong.

The sight of him—oh, it brought a lump to her throat. What could Amun have been, if he had never made vows to the Maha? What kind of man could he have grown to be among his own people?

A kind man, a voice inside her said. *Just as he is now.*

Mehr held the kohl out to him wordlessly and he took it. She closed her eyes as he applied ash to the lids, fanning the color out. "You remember everything I taught you?" he asked.

"I remember."

She heard him let out a breath.

"Then I suppose we're ready," he said.

They were followed outside by a procession of mystics, who sang in bright voices for the Empire's glory. She didn't try to look into their faces, which were concealed from the sand by low hoods. She didn't wonder if the Maha stood close, or if Hema followed her in the procession or kneeled praying inside the temple instead. She and Amun, exposed as they were to the burning light and sand, had other things to worry about.

The mystics nearest to them carried weapons. Mehr tried not to think about that either.

She covered her face with her hand as she walked, her eyes closed tight. She could feel the shudder of the dreamfire, as if the earth were reshaping around them. The sand should have abraded her bare feet, but instead it smoothed beneath her footsteps to a slickness like glass. She wished she could open her eyes and take the sight of it in, but she was afraid the storm wouldn't be as kind to her vision. She took small breaths, too, to protect her lungs.

There was song in the air. The prayers of the mystics. The cries of the daiva. Mehr shivered and went still. The dreamfire was falling. The storm was here.

For a second her eyes snapped open. She looked at Amun, suddenly panicked. She couldn't do this. She was afraid. She couldn't.

But it was too late. Mehr saw the dreamfire shower down over Amun's form, saw his steady, blackened gaze, the trust in his eyes.

The light swallowed him whole.

The storm Mehr had experienced in Jah Irinah had been nothing like this. Jeweled light consumed her body, as it had in Jah Irinah. But the way this storm cloaked her—swallowing her flesh, turning her body to pure flame—terrified her, made her body instinctively flinch from the promise of agony. But there was no agony. Instead she felt a crushing pressure, battering her from all sides, stealing through her blood.

This was the power of the Gods' dreams, in the very place where they slept and dreamed. This was the power Mehr was expected to turn to his will.

Right now, that task felt utterly impossible. She crumpled to her knees. Amun. She needed Amun. But there was too much light, too much for her to even see the mystics she knew stood all about her. She needed him, but she couldn't speak, couldn't reach out.

She sucked in breath after desperate breath, not caring about the sand any longer. She pressed her hands into fists. The cut throbbed.

Slowly, slowly, a calmness welled up inside her.

She didn't need Amun. Not for this. He'd already taught her what she needed to know. It was up to her now to find the strength to stand up and perform the rite. It was up to her to survive.

She stood up, held the fragments of that calm close, and stopped letting the power crush the strength out of her. Instead she let the power pour in.

Amrithi danced with dreamfire, Mehr knew, because it was as close to the divine as any mortal could come. Falling into the immortal place inside herself, Mehr realized in her last moment of clarity that she was committing an act forbidden to mortals for good reason.

When we dance with dreamfire, we dance with the Gods. So her mother had told her. She'd been right. But this was no Rite of Dreaming. This was not dancing with the dreams of Gods. This was being consumed by them.

Dreams roared through her. Her mind, so fragile and mortal, could make no sense of them.

She was human. She wasn't meant for this. The dreams of Gods were too huge, too beautiful, simply too much. They were everything that lived and everything that died: a great, weaving circle, the cycles of creation and destruction that molded all things. They were a knife to the hand and a field of metal and blood. They were glass and flame, earth and water, the way birth feels and a blinding tightness akin to dying. They were creation. Creation, in its headiest, purest form. She wasn't made for this. She was small, far too small to survive.

But Amun had survived this. Over and over again, he had survived. Other Amrithi—the man Gaur, with his missing finger, the nameless older woman who had taught Amun the Rite of the Bound—had done it before him.

And died, a voice said in Mehr's head. *They all died, in the end.*

Not Amun. Not yet. And Mehr would not die either. She had to live to find a way to set them both free.

Mehr breathed. She breathed as Amun had taught her in all those long, painful lessons. She breathed until she felt as she had on the day he had held her in his arms, letting her soul tip free from her skin. She breathed and drifted deep into the heart of herself, deep beyond flesh and fear and the animal terror scrabbling at her animal bones. The dreams carried her along with them.

She breathed until she knew she would not drown.

Then she stood, and felt the calm well up in her and run through her blood and her bones. She felt the dreamfire coil around her, winding over and through her, raising her from the earth into the burning winds of the storm. She began to move.

The sigils, which had meant little to her during her training, suddenly seemed to leap into life. They skimmed her hands lightly, rippling off her fingers with their own heady power. They shifted the fire running through her mind and her blood, diverting the flow of those dreams, stemming them and turning them to the call of the mystics' prayers on the wind. She felt those prayers waver through her own bones. Her scarred skin burned with the weight of the Maha's presence. She was performing the Maha's will. She was performing the Rite of the Bound.

It was a relief to know that she could do this. She kept on moving, kept breathing, maintaining the shape of the rite. She just had to make it through the storm.

Her hands suddenly faltered.

She was sure that her faltering had been a symptom, not a cause, of what came next. Her body knew long before her mind did that something had gone wrong. The fire had changed inside her. Something—an unwanted dream, a thread of brittle white flame—slipped free from her control and from the call of the mystics' prayers. Something that had been carefully suppressed by the rite was suddenly no longer crushed and contained by the force of the rite's power.

The pale flame grew, and grew, boiling and seething. She felt it pooling at the base of her skull, feeding on her fear and her desperation to be free. She felt it shudder to terrible, sentient life, tracing the shape of her bones, knitting its own terrible sinew and flesh.

She faltered again. Sigils died on her fingertips. And the pale flame—oh, it rushed through her, cloying and cold. It rose up. She felt the sand collapsing beneath her feet.

Nightmare. This was a nightmare.

Mehr stumbled. She couldn't think. She couldn't remember what to do. The nightmare had shattered her concentration. The dreams were going to bury her. She was done. Finished.

Mehr!

Amun. She could hear him. Feel him. He was there in the heart of her, in the place where they were both immortal, in the place where the Gods slept. He was there in the fire, the glow of him, the strength. Her ragged breath caught. They were dreaming with the Gods. They were dreaming together.

Amun?

Mehr. I'm here.

The scar of her marriage seal throbbed. She pressed a closed fist to her chest. Her body was distant but alive, still alive.

Amun, I don't know what to do.

Don't fight it, he told her. *Keep going. Continue the rite.*

I can't.

The nightmare was dragging her under, under. It had hands. It was drawing her down by the body, by the soul. But there was his voice. There was his heart.

You can.

She felt his faith. It coursed through her like dreamfire, like blood. Her own image wavered in front of her eyes—a woman with dark skin and dark eyes, a tangled mess of hair and the bearing of an Empress. She saw the light of her own smile. The dimple etched in her cheek when she laughed. This was how Amun saw her.

In his eyes, she was the one who was strong, who stood straight and tall and never let the world crush her. In his eyes, she was the one who was kind and good. She wanted to laugh and weep at the same time.

Together. Perhaps it was her thought. Perhaps his. She no longer knew anymore. The dream had tangled them together like two skeins of thread. *We do it together.*

Mehr raised her hands and shaped a sigil. Then another. She breathed, steady and strong. She danced with all her strength, danced because she wanted to live. She felt the nightmare loosen its grip, increment by increment, until there was nothing left but the fire and the shadow of Amun's presence.

Finally the storm began to quiet around them. She felt the dreamfire fade away until there was nothing but her aching body and the exhaustion that felt like it filled her head to toe. She stood, swaying and helpless, as the dust settled and the sky lightened with the blush of morning.

She turned, seeking out Amun with her eyes. He was farther from her side than she had expected him to be. When his mind had touched her own in the storm, he had felt so much closer. But instead he was covered in a layer of fine, glittering sand, his body on the ground. Under the dirt she could see that his face was gray and bleak, his eyes half open but unseeing. She tried to walk toward him but her legs refused to cooperate. Instead she fell, her head hitting the ground, agony bubbling in her blood.

The world went suddenly and blissfully black.

She woke in someone's arms, face pressed against musty cloth. She was being carried back to the temple, the mystics around her utterly silent. She looked up blearily. Bahren was the one holding her. His hood was thrown back, his expression grim. When he felt her stir, he looked down.

"Are you awake?"

Mehr didn't respond. Something at the corner of her eye had caught her attention. She let her head loll back, looking behind Bahren at the fading dreamfire behind him. Tangled with jeweled light was a creature as brittle and pale as bone, its eyes the flat silver of a sharp blade. It skittered behind them, flickering in and out of life as the dreamfire wavered with it.

She remembered the feel of the pale flame inside her, tracing her bones. She shivered. She'd felt this one rise out of suppressed, leashed dreams. She'd felt this one being born.

"There's a nightmare following us," she slurred out.

Bahren did not look. But she felt his grip on her tighten.

"I don't like this," Bahren muttered. "I don't like this at all."

The mystics around them said nothing, but Mehr could feel their unease. She swallowed. Her mouth tasted of ash and blood. She kept her gaze fixed on the nightmare until her vision grew hazy again, and the blackness gently retook her.

CHAPTER NINETEEN

She woke with the feeling of silk underneath her cheek. Groaning, she turned onto her back and took in her surroundings. She was on a rug, a floor cushion tucked beneath her head. To her right she could see a divan surrounded on all sides by a curtain of gold gauze. Lamplight flickering on the glittering cloth. She hadn't been surrounded by such opulence since leaving Jah Irinah.

Am I home? she thought. No. The memory of her old room had faded, but she knew it hadn't been quite like this. The divan was too large, the curtains made of far finer cloth than Mehr, the illegitimate daughter and disgrace, had ever earned. And she wasn't dreaming either, she was sure of that. The ache of her muscles was far too sharp, and her head hurt—a clear, pounding ache that told her in no uncertain terms how awake she really was.

She sat up. She was still wearing her Amrithi costume. There were fine grains of sand under her fingernails. She touched her grainy fingertips to her chest. Through all the other aches and pains, she had barely noticed the way her scar was burning softly beneath the weight of her seal. She knew suddenly where she was.

The Maha's room.

Where else? She had seen the rest of the temple, with its high walls and honeycomb corridors. Nowhere else had been so luxurious. And the Maha loved surrounding himself in finery. She knew that. Cold dread unfurled in her stomach. Where was Amun? Why was Mehr here alone, without him at her side?

She clambered to her feet. Her legs felt unsteady beneath her, but after a moment of uncertainty, where she trembled on the spot, she knew they would support her weight. She took a few tentative steps forward, skirting the edge of the divan.

Through the doorway beyond she could see a man's silhouette, his back turned. The scar flared hotter. Mehr swallowed. She thought of turning back.

"I'm waiting," the Maha said.

Mehr kept walking. The Maha was standing by a window, one of Edhir's strange contraptions on the table beside him. Its dials gleamed.

"I know you are weak, Mehr," the Maha said. He turned to face her. "But I expect to receive my proper respect."

It took her a moment to understand him. Then, cheeks burning with a rush of humiliation, she got down onto her knees. She bowed to him, her head pressed to the floor, her hands flat. She felt dizzy. She could hear the beat of her own pulse in her ears. He made her wait far longer than he usually did, but finally she heard him speak again.

"You may stand."

She stood, her legs trembling with her own weight. The Maha looked at her, his expression unreadable.

"How do you feel, Mehr?" he asked. "The storm appeared to be brutal."

"I feel well, Maha."

"The truth."

"I am weaker than I usually am," Mehr admitted, because how could she hide it? "But I am still well."

She certainly felt better than Amun had looked. She remembered Amun's gray face, his closed eyes. She held back all the questions clamoring inside her. The Maha wouldn't appreciate her asking how her husband fared. He wanted her obedience, her soul, her silence.

"If you are well, you'll be prepared to speak. So tell me, Mehr," he continued, his voice silken. "What did you do, out in the storm?"

"I performed the rite Amun taught me, so the prayers of the mystics would be heard by the Gods."

The Maha shook his head. "No, child," he said. "I want to know how you erred."

A blackness opened up in her chest. Fear without edges.

This will not end well, a voice inside her whispered.

The Maha's voice grew softer, sharper. "The dreams did not obey as they should have. I should have felt their strength pour through me." The blandness of his expression was shattering to reveal something terrible beneath: a monster Mehr had always known was there beneath his flesh, waiting for the chance to crawl out.

"Instead I felt the power try to slip through my fingers." He held one elegant hand before him. "I felt darkness arise in its place."

The nightmare. So the Maha had felt it too. Bahren had felt it when he'd held her. She'd seen his unease as he carried her, the tension in the mystics who had stood in the desert and watched the dreamfire fall.

"Amun has never failed me before," the Maha told her. "So tell me, Mehr: What did you do?"

"I did everything I was taught to," she said unsteadily. "I did as I was bid. I promise, Maha. I *obeyed*."

He took a step forward and struck her.

She felt the blow all the way through her skull. There was no pain at first. Just shock. She stumbled, raising a hand up as if to ward him off.

"What did you do?" he repeated.

He hit her again before she could respond. She fell to the floor this time, the weight of the blow sending her down with a crash. Her shoulder skidded against cold marble. She felt the cold through her hips, her knees, her elbows. Her head was ringing like a call to prayer.

"Nothing, nothing," she gasped out. "Nothing, Maha. It was a nightmare. A nightmare tried to hurt us both. I did nothing. I obeyed you. I'm bound by my vow. Maha!"

He had a hand in her hair. Her curling hair, tangled and stained with sand. His grip was unyielding. He kneeled down beside her, his shadow consuming hers.

"Tell me what you did," he demanded again. His voice was savage. Gone was his gentle malevolence, his elegant cruelty. He was no longer full of clean, pure light, the dreams that had so long fed his immortality. The dreamfire, full of the brittle and bone-like dreams he'd so long suppressed, was inside him. The nightmare shuddered behind his eyes.

She couldn't help but think of her unformed vow, in that moment. She tried to force it from her mind, as panic bubbled up inside her. And yet the truth was there, on the tip of her tongue, like a bird with its wings stretched for flight.

"Nothing," Mehr said again, instead. She was not above pleading; no, she was not. She wanted to hide the truth, and she wanted to *live*. "Maha, *please*."

He raised his free hand and she flinched from him. For some reason this seemed to calm him. She watched his hand go still, then lower. When he spoke, a tinge of reason had crept back into his voice.

"Perhaps your Ambhan blood has flawed you after all," he said. "And yet, at first, you seemed so *perfect*."

He took her chin in his hand. His other hand was still tangled in her hair.

"I must remember to be gentler with you," he said. "You're willful, but a little careful correction will guide you. And if it does not..." He sighed. But his expression was cold. "You must understand, Mehr: I have no use for flawed tools."

She could taste blood in her mouth. The urge to spit in his face was overwhelming, but some deep-seated, primal instinct made her swallow instead.

"Look at me," he commanded.

She looked obediently into his nightmare-flecked eyes, which were terribly, inhumanly wrong—shattered within, like broken glass. His face was no longer smooth and timeless. Instead, his skin was like a fissured painting, cracked and faded. When she blinked it almost seemed to shift, ever more human, ever more fragile. Decay and mortality had come for him, reached for him out of the darkness of chained dreams. They'd left their mark.

Monster, her mind whispered. *I see you. I know what you are.*

"Speak, Mehr."

"I understand, Maha," she said. She swallowed again. Her mouth tasted hot, tasted of metal and salt. She realized her cheeks were wet with tears. "Please spare me, Maha. I serve you with all my heart."

She watched as his mouth widened into a smile. Her face hurt. Her stomach hurt. Oh, how he loved to hurt her. How he loved to see her small.

"Now," he said softly. "Now you begin to fear and worship as you should. I am finally as a God to you."

"Yes, Maha," she whispered.

He was not as a God to her. In his smile—even in his eyes— she saw his humanity like a blazing light, a harsh desert sun that illuminated all and left all secrets bared. So he fed on the power of Gods—so his mystics fell at his feet, worshipped him. He was *still* nothing but flesh. He hungered for power as a human hungered. He enjoyed hurting her as a mortal man enjoyed crushing another mortal underfoot. He was a man who took pleasure in hurting a woman. His evil was born from his humanity.

She remembered Maryam's cruelties large and small. Maryam had been so petty, so utterly bitter at heart. She had punished Mehr for—what? Being another woman's daughter, with another woman's skin? Her hatred had made her small.

The Maha was no less small. He had shamed her, disgraced her, but through her fear and her pain she saw him finally with clear sight. The storm had made him angry, and his anger made him err. She had seen his true face now. He could not play at being the omnipotent master. She had his measure.

She knew exactly what he was.

His nails were digging harshly into her scalp.

"You will serve me better next time, won't you, Mehr?" he asked. His pleasure had softened the edges of his rage. The next time he was angry—and she knew, already, that there would be a next time—she would have to remember how much he liked tears.

"I will, Maha. With all my heart." She had bent her soul to the fire of the Gods. She could bend her words now, bend them to a bone-deep lie. He was nothing compared to them, after all, no matter what he believed. Nothing.

"See that you do," he said. Finally, he released her.

She managed to catch herself on her hands before her skull met the floor. Then she bowed to the floor, her forehead to the cool marble. She allowed herself to tremble, feigned being a thing bent and broken by his cruelty. She did not have her jewels or her fine clothes, but she had this power, at least: She could give him a simulacrum of what he desired from her, and hold her crumbling strength tight.

Let him think he had broken her. As long as he believed he

already had, as long as she fooled him, he would not succeed in truly doing so.

The Maha watched her.

"The next time a nightmare frightens you, my dear, remember how much worse I am. Remember the wrath of your God."

"Maha," Mehr said, allowing herself to cry, allowing her hands to tremble, so that he wouldn't see the iron blooming in her blood, her spine, in her heart. "On my vow, Maha, I will. I *will*."

Mehr thought, for one brief moment, of seeking out Hema and showing her exactly what the Maha was capable of. She thought of showing Hema her swollen lip, her bruised cheek, the nail grooves cut into her scalp. Then she discarded the idea. As tempting as it was, she knew she wouldn't be able to shatter Hema's belief in the Maha. Mehr had seen the strength of that faith shining in Hema's eyes. Not even Mehr's blood would have the strength to tarnish it. No doubt Hema would simply look at her bruises and ask Mehr what she had done to deserve them.

So she didn't approach Hema. She avoided all the mystics entirely, unable to stand the thought of having their eyes on her. She missed the comfort of her old chambers. She missed Arwa and Lalita and Nahira, her veils and her walls, the certainty she'd once had in her own worth. But she didn't try to seek out pity. Like an animal looking for somewhere quiet to lick its wounds clean, she drifted along shadowed corridors until she found an exit that led to the inner courtyard of the temple. There was a guard, but he did nothing to stop her. She felt his eyes follow her as she made her way across the sand to the edge of the oasis.

The sky was clear, unmarked by the storm. The air smelled sweet. There were crops growing. Precious little, but there was something about the fresh, tentative life that gave Mehr comfort.

She knelt down by the oasis and breathed in and out. In and

out. She could dance the Rite of Fruitful Earth and make those precious few crops grow lushly, if only for a fleeting moment. She was a descendant of the daiva, and through them, a descendant of the Gods who slept beneath the sand, whose fire had lit the skies and burned inside her. But the power she possessed was useless. It couldn't set her free. It didn't give her the strength to stop the Maha from hurting her. It was no good at all.

She looked down at her own face in the water. The oasis was perfectly still, reflective as glass. The face staring back at her was nothing like the one she'd seen through Amun's eyes. She wasn't fierce or beautiful. She was only bruised, and gaunt, and solemn. A shadow of a woman.

She dipped her hands into the oasis and splashed water over her face. The cold was shocking. She blinked water away and dabbed the blood from her lip, her cheek. Her skin was hot and swollen, but her bones weren't broken. She marveled at that— the strength of her bones.

The Maha hadn't broken her yet. Not yet.

She splashed her face again. The water's chill was fresh and crisp, like green things, like life. She cupped a hand into the water and raised it to her lips. Drank. She hadn't realized how thirsty she was. The water was sweet.

An old grieving Goddess, that was who had built the desert. So Edhir had told her. An old grieving Goddess had built the desert, and the desert had been named for her tears. Irinah. *Salt.*

But here was the oasis, old and bursting with life. Here was the oasis, and there was no salt in its water. Just sweetness, cold and pure. In the water Mehr tasted the promise of something more than bitterness. She tasted hope.

She heard footsteps. She turned, her face still dripping, the water in her lashes blurring her vision. She heard a soft intake of breath, the murmur of a curse. Her vision cleared. Bahren stood before her. He was looking at her face with pure revulsion.

She looked back at him. Was he judging her, or judging the Maha? His gaze made her skin prickle with unwanted shame.

Let him look, she thought. *What does it matter, in the end, what he thinks?*

"You were looking for me?" she asked, when Bahren simply continued to stare at her in silence. She didn't ask him how he had found her. She knew there were always eyes on her.

"Your husband has woken up," Bahren said finally.

She stood. She held her head high, unflinching. She was bare-faced and bruised, yes. But she was a woman who had faced a monster in mortal flesh, and the bruises were a badge of the Maha's shame, not her own. She was a woman who had felt the nightmare of Gods pour through her soul. She was not fragile any longer. She had moved past her own fragility into an animal stillness, a deep place inside herself where one piece of knowledge alone sustained her, and held her strong: She was going to ensure that she and Amun escaped from here. She was going to make sure they survived.

"Take me to him," she said.

Amun was lying on his own bed, two mystics speaking over him in low, serious voices. From the stoppered bottles in their hands, Mehr guessed they were the Saltborn's physicians. But they held little of her interest. Amun was the focus of her attention. He was awake, but only barely, his breath loud and unsteady, his skin bleached gray with exhaustion.

She couldn't hold the sound of shock that escaped her lips at the sight of him. Amun flinched, his eyes snapping wide. He propped himself up onto his elbows, her name dying into silence on his lips.

She watched his jaw tighten, watched his dark eyes become somehow even blacker as he stared at her, mapping every one of her wounds with his gaze. He didn't say a word. He didn't have to.

"How do you feel?" she asked.

"Me?" He looked at her, his expression smoothing out into unreadable calm. "I'm well."

She crossed the room and sat down on the bed beside him. She took his hands in her own and heard the mystics fall silent above them. Amun's hands felt warm in her own. Warm and comforting. It was suddenly very hard to keep her voice steady.

"Our brothers and sisters have prayers to attend to. I'm here to take care of you now, husband." She looked up at the mystics. "Thank you," she said.

She had not ordered them to go. They would not have gone, if she'd ordered them to. But simply sitting quiet and tall, looking at them with her bruised face, gave her more power than any sharp words would have been capable of. They looked away from her, uncomfortable, and turned to leave.

Bahren stood by the doorway as the other mystics filed out. "The Maha will want to speak with you, Amun," he said.

"Now?" Amun asked. His hand tightened on Mehr's.

A short pause. "He knows you're unwell," Bahren said after a beat. "Tomorrow morning will do well enough."

"Thank you," Mehr said, when it was clear Amun was going to remain silent.

For a long moment, Bahren did not move from the edge of the doorway, where he'd stood since guiding her into the room. There was a look on his face she couldn't understand—something grim and quiet and thoughtful. Then he too turned away and vanished down the staircase back to the temple proper.

Once they were alone Mehr realized Amun's hands were trembling. She released her grip on him. She was sure he would pull away but instead he reached up and cupped her face in his palms. His fingers were still dusted with sand. His skin smelled like incense, like the smoke of a storm and a daiva's flesh.

"Who did this to you?" he asked.

"The Maha."

Amun closed his eyes. Opened them again. His expression was shattered.

"Mehr," he said quietly. "I am so very sorry."

"I'm safe now," Mehr said. She closed her own eyes. With his hands on her, she could almost believe it.

"You aren't safe," he said, despair and self-hatred welling up in his voice like poison. "He has hurt you, he could hurt you again, and I can't protect you."

"You're protecting me right now," Mehr said. That, at least, was true. He couldn't stop the Maha from hurting her, but his touch was a balm to her wounds. His goodness was a shield for her hurting heart. She felt his touch falter. She grabbed his wrist. "*Please*, Amun."

He hesitated. Then his fingers uncurled against her cheek again, feather-soft on her bruises.

"Whatever you want," he said softly.

She wanted him to keep holding her head in his hands. She wanted this moment to last forever, so she wouldn't have to face the mystics and the Maha and the wounds that had been inflicted on her skin and her soul. She pressed into his hands and eventually found her way onto the bed by his side. She curled up against him, her head on his chest, his heart beating under her ear. He kept one hand on her cheek, his body entirely still, as if he were afraid a sudden movement would shatter her. But he couldn't, wouldn't, shatter her. There was no violence in him. Not even a little. He was her only safe harbor in the storm.

She listened to his heart beating and his shallow, pained breath. She listened for a long time before she finally moistened her lips with her tongue and spoke.

"Does the rite always affect you like this?"

"It's always terrible," Amun said. "But no. I'm young. Strong. It grows worse over time, as you get older. It wears the body out. This time it was much worse for me. Worse than it has ever been before. I don't..." A shaky breath. She felt the rise and fall of his chest. "I am sorry, Mehr."

"You have nothing to be sorry for," Mehr said. "Nothing at all."

He huffed out another sharp breath. But he didn't argue with her. "The rite is always fierce." He went on. "Painful." Hesitation. "But that anger—you felt it?"

"Of course I did."

"I've never felt anything like it before, Mehr."

"It felt like a nightmare," Mehr whispered. "A true nightmare, a thing of rage and fear."

She described then the creature she'd seen after the storm before she'd fallen unconscious. Its flat silver eyes, its brittle body. "I felt like it was born from those suppressed dreams," she said. "It felt like all the things the Maha had kept from this world breathed life into it."

Amun was silent for a moment. Then he said, "I felt it in my bones. My mind."

Mehr shuddered. Nodded.

"As did I," she admitted.

She took a deep breath. She felt the seal tied to her throat rise and fall with her.

"It was because of me," Mehr said finally. "The nightmare you felt—it was there because of me."

"No, Mehr," Amun said instantly. She felt his hand shift on her cheek. "Don't blame yourself."

"You're disagreeing because you want me to feel better," Mehr cut in, calm now. She was sure of herself. "But don't you see, Amun? I'm not truly bound. I danced the rite, I danced for the glory of the Maha, for the Empire, for the Emperor...but because of your mercy, all my will, all my blood, wasn't tied to the Maha's will and blood, as yours is."

Amun shivered but said nothing. He let her continue to speak.

"I performed the correct stances," she continued, "the correct sigils. But the rites are more than stances and sigils. They are will too. And in my heart I don't want the Empire's glory. I don't want the Maha to flourish. I want everything the Maha and the Emperor love to burn."

Her rage was undirected, amorphous. She didn't really want the Empire to suffer. She loved her sister and her father. The Empire was her home. It was hard not to love the Empire, despite herself, hard not to love it because it had raised her, because it was her history and the source of so many of her life's comforts. But her feelings had no respect for logic and couldn't be easily dispelled.

"I don't want what the Maha wants," Amun said suddenly, his voice raw. "I don't *want* to serve."

"I know, Amun," Mehr said softly. "I know. But you're bound. You've told me yourself. I've felt it. The vows you've made are so powerful, so binding, that your desires have no power. Just as mine wouldn't, if you hadn't saved me."

Mehr thought of Amrithi turning their blades on themselves. She thought of Amun's grief, and his hate for the Maha. She thought of how hard he'd tried to save her, and how hard he still tried to keep her safe.

"What did he do," she murmured, "to force you to make vows to him?"

"He did nothing to me," Amun said. But his voice was empty, so empty. She didn't believe him.

However the Maha had bound Amun—by trickery or by violence—he had tied Amun to him by chains that superseded his will and his heart. Amun, and all the vow-bound Amrithi before him, had bound the Gods in turn, turning all their sweet dreams to the service of the Maha.

But Mehr was not fully bound. Mehr's will and desires weren't yet completely superseded by the Maha's will. And through her—through her fractured will, her imperfect service—the Gods could unleash their suppressed dreams and their hollow rage. Through her, they breathed life into their nightmares and set them free.

She took a deep breath. "The Gods are so furious, Amun. I know we both felt it. They are angry at our heresy, at the Maha. I feel..." Her heart beat like a fist in her chest. "I feel as if their nightmares are a terrible beast waiting to break free."

"I know," Amun said. He sounded old, and tired. "Of course the Gods rage. How could they not? But Mehr—the Gods will rage long after we're gone. New Amrithi will take our place. It won't end."

It was the first time he'd spoken it so openly: the despair that lay at the heart of him. The truth that they were enslaved, bound—that one day Mehr would become vow-bound too. That they would die here.

"No." Mehr shook her head. "We're not going to die here, Amun. No more of this. I told you before the storm, and I meant it: We're going to escape. Both of us."

Amun had tried to give her time. A little bit of freedom, a little bit of mercy before the Maha gained control of her. But time was running short. The Maha had bound the dreams of the Gods for too long, had manipulated their dreams so the world favored the Empire above all else. Now the natural order was perverted. The world was imbalanced.

As long as Mehr was free, her imperfect service provided an outlet where the dreams could manifest freely, a place where all the dreams the Maha had suppressed over his long years could be unleashed. Dreams that would have brought the Empire plague or natural disaster, rebellions or death or betrayal.

Ruin.

The Maha had been willing to believe that Mehr had erred in the rite. But by the next storm, he would know something greater was amiss. He would know Mehr was flawed, and he'd seek out the source of the flaw—the incomplete mark on her chest. Her unconsummated marriage.

Facing the Maha had already hardened her resolve to stop hesitantly searching for escape, and to pour all her energy into the task of setting her and Amun free, no matter the costs or the risks. But now, thinking of the rite and the terrible fury it had created and now barely held at bay—looking into Amun's eyes, as he murmured her name, as he shook his head—Mehr had an idea.

They could use the Rite of the Bound.

Bending the dreams of the Gods was a heresy, a terrible, forbidden thing. But it was a heresy she and Amun had already committed under the Maha's orders. What more harm could it possibly do to the both of them to turn the rite to their own ends, to bend the dreams of the Gods to their will, instead of his?

As the idea formed in Mehr's mind—as it grew, stretching its wings, soaring in her heart—she felt a hope growing within her that no shame could possibly quench.

"It's impossible," Amun said lowly.

"No," said Mehr. "No, it isn't. Amun, we're going to use the Rite of the Bound. We're going to find freedom together."

CHAPTER TWENTY

In the morning Amun went to the Maha. He dressed with laborious, painful slowness. In the pale dawn light creeping through the windows, his skin looked gray. Bahren waited for him by the door, his back turned. Mehr stayed on the bed, her knees drawn up to her chin, and watched them both.

Bahren doesn't seem entirely happy with the Maha, she'd told Amun last night.

Bahren is old, Amun had responded. *Old and trusted. He has seen more of what the Maha can do than most. But he's loyal, Mehr. Do not doubt that.*

Mehr had said nothing to that. She didn't doubt Bahren's loyalty. But she'd seen chink after chink in his shields: his grimness when he'd carried Mehr from the desert, eyes haunted; the way he'd sucked in a sharp breath when he'd seen her bruised face by the oasis; the night of mercy he'd given Amun to recover before facing the Maha. All those small cracks added together into a clear weakness, a wound that Mehr could potentially use to her advantage.

How, she didn't know. But as she stared at Bahren's back, noting his crossed arms and the tired lurch of his head, she knew she would find a use for it in time.

"The Maha will be growing impatient," Bahren said in an even voice. He didn't turn.

Amun tied his sash carefully at the waist of his tunic. She saw the faint tremor of his fingers and bit down on her own tongue just hard enough to remind herself that she couldn't protect him. Not this time. Not yet.

"I'm ready," said Amun. He gave her a look as he left. *All will be well*, that look said. She wasn't sure if he was looking at her to reassure her or to reassure himself.

Mehr waited for a long moment, then stood up. If she left the room now and went to the bathing chamber, she would just have time to wash her face and comb a hand through her hair before facing the day. The bell for morning prayers hadn't rung yet, but it would soon, and Mehr didn't want to face the mystics looking both bruised and haggard. The bruises were beyond her control, but at least she had power over the rest of her appearance.

Although her feet felt frozen beneath her, Mehr willed herself to move. She would have to go to morning prayers whether she liked it or not. The routine of life in the temple was strict. It wouldn't relent for Mehr just because she didn't want to take part.

At least she had the comfort of knowing it wouldn't be the Maha leading prayers today. Knowing his eyes wouldn't be on her gave her the strength to make her way down the staircase to begin the day.

Once she'd made it to the bathing chamber, she focused on unraveling her knotted hair, which hadn't seen a comb in what felt like a lifetime. It was easier to focus on mundane things than to think about what Amun was potentially suffering at the Maha's hands.

It would be so easy for Amun to reveal their ruse. But she wasn't afraid he would. Or at least, she was no more afraid than she always was. Amun was brave and clever, could twist the truth into knots, and he would protect them both if he could. She was far more afraid of what the Maha would do to him. The Maha had been so full of black, bloody rage. He hadn't spent it all on her, she was sure of that.

And Amun had been shaking when he'd left her. Shaking and quiet and gray.

She feared more than anything that he'd return to her hurt. Her own bruises were bad enough. But his...his she couldn't bear.

No. Stop thinking, she chided herself. The fear and shame that were gripping her were destructive and would do her no favors. She needed to be strong. She had to put her terror away. She needed to hold on to the iron of her will, the cold sureness of steel in her bones, and consider her options.

She tied back her hair in a vaguely respectable braid. Somewhere deep in the temple, the bell for prayers rang.

As Mehr walked, following the crowd toward prayers, she kept her mind resolutely cold and clear. She thought of the rites she had danced all her life. Ever since her early childhood, rites had shaped the rhythm of her life, had been her breath and blood. She knew that the bones of all rites were essentially the same: stances mingled with sigils, the movement of the body matched with the power of mortal feeling. It wasn't enough to simply know the language of the rites. Her mother and Lalita had taught her early that the rites were nothing without an Amrithi's reverence. An Amrithi couldn't simply enact a rite. They had to feel it.

Rites were sigils for words and stances for emotion and will for fire and blood for oil to the flame. Rites were a mechanism and a magic that Mehr had always felt awed and privileged to have in her grasp. But the Rite of the Bound...

The Rite of the Bound was different. *Other.* It was a rite for slipping away from flesh, for harnessing the dreams of Gods.

It was a rite for committing a terrible, anathema act, a heresy against nature at the Maha's bidding. But Mehr knew the rite now, knew its stances and sigils, and her knowledge couldn't be undone. She had swum in the nightmares of Gods. She had felt their fire run through her. All she could do now was use the rite for her own purposes.

Instead of letting the fury of the Gods pour through her, or the Maha and his mystics use her, Mehr was going to use the rite to draw forward dreams that could save her and Amun from their fate: dreams that weakened the Maha and his temple. Dreams that broke the chains of their vows, and let them both walk free. She wasn't fully bound. She *could* set them free.

Amun could teach her how to alter the sigils of the rite for their own purposes. Together they could reshape the rite. Together, they stood a chance of gaining their freedom.

If any force could give her and Amun freedom from their vows, it would be the dreams of the Gods.

She prayed. She ate a meager breakfast, spice-flecked bread so dry it parched her tongue. With nothing to do, she returned to the bedroom and waited for Amun.

When he returned hours later, he walked in, slow and careful, the weight of the world on his shoulders. She quickly stood.

"I'm not hurt," he said immediately. But she couldn't stop herself from walking over to him.

She took his face in her hands. It felt natural to do so, and any awkwardness she would normally have felt dissipated when she felt him relax into her touch. She'd slept in his arms last night, his heartbeat an ocean in her ear. He was her husband. She had a right to this, at least: his skin, his exhaled breath, his comfort.

"See," he said finally. "I'm well enough."

She could see the blue glow of his sigil-marked flesh through her fingers. She nodded. "I'm glad," she said.

"He wanted to check my health. No more than that. He

needs me strong." There was a ghost of a smile on his lips. She felt the tug of muscles in his jaw. "He's afraid to harm me. I'm too weak."

Of course. Amun was the Maha's most valuable asset. Mehr was no good on her own. Mehr was flawed. He wouldn't risk Amun, when Mehr alone was not enough to ensure the rite's success.

There was comfort in that.

"What did he say to you?" she asked.

"He asked me about the storm. He asked me about you. And I told him the truth. That I believe you tried to serve, with all the power you possessed. And that in time, you would learn to serve as he desired."

The truth, but not the whole truth. He'd done well.

"Good," Mehr said shakily. "Then you've bought us a little more time." She lowered her hands; he turned his head away from her. "We need to reshape the language of the Rite of the Bound. I'll need your help to do that, Amun. I don't have your experience of it, or your knowledge."

Amun's expression shuttered.

"You want us to use the rite to set ourselves free," he said carefully.

"You know I do."

"Mehr..." Amun exhaled. "We can't. *I* can't."

"I can perform the altered rite," Mehr said. "All I need is your help to do it. Your knowledge."

"I can't," he repeated.

"We can use the rite to draw forward dreams that will break our bonds," Mehr said, pushing doggedly on. "We can use it to stop the Maha. Amun, you don't have to fear hope any longer. This isn't a—a children's tale, or foolish fantasy. This is real. I truly believe we can escape. We can shatter our vows."

"Vows can't be broken," Amun said, and his voice was utterly devoid of feeling.

"*Daiva* can't break vows," Mehr stressed. "We can't break vows. But Gods are—Gods. They created all things, and they can destroy them too. We've seen what their dreams can do, Amun." For the Maha. For the Empire. "The rules of nature can be changed. Our vows *can* be broken, I'm sure of it."

He looked down so she couldn't see his eyes. The light from the windows threw shadow after shadow over him, and although she couldn't read him at all, she knew his mind was moving at lightning speed, his sharp tumble of thoughts just beyond her reach. She wished she could see inside his head.

"Mehr," he said. "I'm not sure... I'm not sure I believe I can be saved."

"Then let me believe for you," she told him softly. "Let me have faith for both of us."

Silence. All Mehr could hear was the beat of her own heart.

"You know," he said in a low voice, "we're likely to fail. You must know that."

Mehr sucked in a breath. The darkness rose in her again.

"I can't think of it," she told him.

"He'll force you to lie with me." His voice was utterly blank. "I will hurt you."

Something raw and wounded welled up in her. It was a bleeding, bloody softness in her heart. She couldn't stand it. "Don't think of it, Amun."

"I have to think of it. I think of it all the time." The words sounded like they were torn out of him. "If we fail, this will happen. And we will most likely fail, Mehr. In fact, I am sure—almost sure—we will." He took a step closer to her, and suddenly there was no distance between them, and not a shadow to hide the look on his face from her anymore. "Knowing that, knowing the truth, Mehr... do you still want to try?"

She met his eyes. She'd decided to risk herself for freedom. Asking him to risk his life for the same goal when he had fought so long against the possibility of hope...ah, it felt like a heavy burden.

She had to succeed: for his sake, even more than her own.

Mehr had promised to have faith for them both, and she would. She would.

"Yes," Mehr said, looking straight back at him. "I do."

The second day after they had returned to practicing the rite, the Maha came to observe them. Mehr felt it when he walked into the hall. The scar of her marriage seal throbbed sharply. Her insides froze. Clumsy as a child, she stumbled between stances, her feet refusing to obey her. She felt the warmth of Amun's hand on her arm then, holding her steady.

"Calm," he whispered. "Calm, Mehr. I'm here."

He could not protect her. But she wasn't alone with the Maha, and there was comfort in that. Mehr placed her hand over his, briefly, in silent thanks. Then they released one another, and bowed low to the ground as the Maha swept into the room.

"Begin," the Maha said shortly. He moved to stand in the shadows as they raised their heads, stood, and obeyed.

As she and Amun moved through the sigils of the rite, the Maha instructed them. He told Mehr how to arc her wrist, how to shape the movement of her fingers and her arms. It was difficult for Mehr to follow his guidance through the white haze of her fear. Harder still, because he guided them by words alone, never raising a hand to illustrate.

When the glow of the lantern shifted the shadows from his form, she saw his skin in brief slants of light: his flesh, riven and thin, bright with light; his eyes, black in the darkness. She didn't think his body was capable of demonstrating the delicate movements he described. When she thought too hard on what had become of his flesh, her own skin itched with revulsion.

"Enough," he said eventually.

The Maha walked toward them. Mehr tried not to look at him or at Amun. She fixed her gaze on the wall beyond his shoulder, as the Maha stepped between them and placed a hand gently on Mehr's hair.

"You've improved," said the Maha. His voice in her ear. His voice beneath her skin. "Good."

His hand stroked her hair, once, gently. She hated the relief that poured through her when the touch didn't hurt.

"Thank you, Maha," Mehr whispered. "I am trying. As I promised, with all my heart."

"We'll see," he said. But he sounded pleased. He stroked her hair once more, then let her go.

Mehr's eyes met Amun's then. His expression was shuttered, but his gaze was unwavering. He was here. Thank the Gods that he was here.

"I will return tomorrow," said the Maha. "Prove your worth to me. Show me you have learned to obey, and I assure you, you will not suffer."

Mehr understood the threat. She shivered a little, ducking her head as Amun said, "We will, Maha."

With that, the Maha left. But he returned again the next morning, and four more times after that before he was satisfied that Mehr was teachable and would not fail him when the next storm came.

Mehr was painfully grateful when his visits stopped altogether. Without the Maha's eyes on her, without the threat of punishment looming over her for every error, she could breathe again, and turn her attention back to the most important task at hand:

Escape.

It was disturbing how quickly they returned to a familiar daily routine: hours upon hours of punishing practice of the rites,

broken up only by morning and evening prayers, and breaks for
food. The only marked difference in their days was that a mystic now remained to watch them during their practice sessions,
standing by the door for hours on end.

Mehr knew the presence of a watcher was a message. The
Maha didn't need to set a guard upon them. But he wanted them
both to know that his eyes were on them, and that if they faltered in their practice, if they gave him any less than perfect
obedience, he would know about it. And they would face the
consequences. Under those eyes, they practiced all the harder,
until exhaustion set in and beyond. They couldn't rouse the
Maha's suspicion. They had to be fearful. They had to be *good*.

The days were terrible, and therefore the same as always, but
the nights...

The nights were different.

"The sigils of this rite are so different because they speak a
different language from the traditional Amrithi rites," Amun
said. "This is a darker language. Not the language of daiva, but
the language of Gods." He stopped for a moment, considering.
"The woman who taught me believed it was a rite taught long
ago to the first clans by the daiva, and lost over the generations."

As Amun spoke, Mehr lit the oil lanterns hung on the walls,
using the light of the one held in her hand. The light banished
the darkness to the corners of their bedroom, leaving everything
illuminated in a warm, flickering glow. "But the Maha found
it," she prompted.

"I suppose he must have," Amun said.

When the Maha had conquered his provinces and created his
Empire, he had come to the desert to establish himself as the
ruler of the faith and soul of the Empire and—Mehr understood
now—to take control of the dreams of the Gods and establish
the immortality of his legacy.

They would never know how the Maha had learned of the Rite of the Bound, or how he had forced or cajoled Amrithi into his service. Some things were lost to time.

"Just our luck." She shrugged, a fluid movement she felt down to her toes. She winced. After practicing all day, her body was bone-tired, her muscles sore. But the nights were the only time they had to themselves, to try to untangle the rite and use it for their own purposes.

Amun stood in the circle of light, feet bare, his body straight and tall. "Are you sure you're able?"

"Don't fuss, Amun," Mehr said. "I know you're more feeble than I am at the moment." She walked up to him, facing him, mimicking his stance.

"I'm fine," he said flatly.

"You hide it well," she agreed.

Obviously choosing to ignore her, he settled into the first stance of traditional rites, rolling back his shoulders, centering himself.

"The woman who taught me..."

"You never say her name," Mehr noted.

Amun gave Mehr a level look. Continued. "The woman who taught me often trained alone with the Maha. He was—fond of her. As you've seen, Mehr, he knows everything about the rite and the language that shapes it. Because of his fondness for her, he taught her a great deal more about it than he ever taught me."

He raised his hands before him.

"It's lucky," he said, "that I was good at learning by observation."

Mehr knew he didn't want her to ask any more questions. And because she was tired and pained—and knew Amun had to be accordingly infinitely more tired and pained than she was—she kept her silence and mimicked his movements again.

"Teach me what you know," she said simply.

Amun talked her through each sigil patiently, explaining their meaning, their syntax, as best as he could. Ever since the Maha had interfered with their training, Amun's reluctant hope had transformed into a fierce, focused determination to transform the rite to their needs. Every night they worked through the sigils, learning the language, theorizing how to reshape those movements from a conduit for the mystics' prayers into the commands they needed for escape. *Vow, loyalty, breaking—or does that mean damage? Again. Try again.*

For all that their schedule was exhausting, Mehr preferred to keep active. Activity silenced her mind and stopped her from considering the fact that her bruises had turned bright and livid and still throbbed painfully when she so much as moved. Whenever mystics looked at her with speculative, pitying glances Mehr thought of the sigils. She thought of escape.

Mehr didn't mind practicing at night either. She didn't sleep well anymore anyway. When she wasn't dreaming of veiled faces, or Arwa turning to dust, or the cold of the Maha's floor, she was thinking of sigils. Sigils for freedom. Sigils for vows. Sigils for subterfuge. So many sigils, she could barely contain them.

When Mehr began to yawn, Amun insisted that they stop practicing.

"You need to rest more," Amun told her.

I'll rest when we're free, Mehr thought. But Amun was wavering a little on his feet, and Mehr couldn't forget that he was still weak from the storm. Still weak from Mehr's last failure.

"You're right," she said. But even after Amun had fallen into a fitful but—Mehr hoped—healing sleep, Mehr stayed awake and stared at the ceiling, wishing she had a knife under her pillow to keep the nightmares at bay.

She tried to imagine what she would write to Arwa, if she had ink and parchment, if she were allowed to reach out to her sister, if it were safe.

Dear sister,
Dear Arwa—
   I love you. I miss you. I hope Hara is beautiful. I hope Maryam
still loves you like you're her own blood. I hope you haven't forgot-
ten me—
   —I hope you have.

She scratched the words out in her mind's eye. What self-pity
she was capable of! She was glad Arwa would never know how
afraid Mehr was, and how small the world had made her. She
hoped Arwa would never learn the lessons she'd learned. She
hoped Arwa was happy.

She touched her fingers to Amun's side, listening to him
breathe, feeling the rise and fall of his chest. One breath at a
time. That was all they could do, the both of them. That was all
there was.

Little sister...
   I am trying very hard not to let go of hope.

Mehr knew that in order to keep hope alive, she would have to
prepare for escape as if it were a certainty. Although she couldn't
avoid prayers or practice without consequences, she tried to be
watchful for an opportunity to return to the scholars' tower and
access a map of Irinah without drawing suspicion. If—*when*—
she and Amun escaped, it would be important for them to be
able to navigate the desert.

An opportunity arose unexpectedly, one morning after prayers.
Mehr and Amun had only just left the Prayer Hall. They were
still surrounded by all the many mystics who had prayed alongside
them, when they heard a sharp yell cut through the air. A young
boy in heavy robes, a pack upon his back, ran headlong into the

crowd, stopping only when an older mystic caught hold of him and bade him to be still.

"Calm down," said the older mystic. "Breathe. Tell us what's wrong, brother."

"Daiva," he gasped. "There's a daiva—attacking the other couriers—we need *help*—"

There was suddenly a great deal of noise as some mystics ran outside, and others crowded the boy, asking questions. It was only then that Mehr saw the cut on the boy's sleeve. The skin beneath it was bare and wounded, livid with blood. His face was wan with terror.

Amun gripped Mehr's hand.

"You should go now," he said. "They're going to want our blood soon."

"The maps," Mehr said quickly. "I could go now, they're distracted—"

"Mehr. Just go."

He squeezed her hand tighter, then released her.

The crowd was large and cloying, but Mehr slipped between the mystics as swiftly as she could, and raced toward the scholars' tower. She ran up the winding staircase; out of breath, she stopped when she reached the room and looked inside. For once, luck was on her side: The room was empty.

Catching her breath, she walked over to the rows of shelves. She traced them with her fingertips, trying to ascertain where the map of Irinah was located. She probably didn't have much time. The boy would only serve to distract the mystics for so long. She needed to act quickly.

She drew down one map, then another. Neither was of Irinah, so she placed them back on the shelves in short order. The third—thank the Gods—was a map of Irinah in all its glory. She unfurled it fully on the table and took the sight of it in.

There, limned in bright color, were the villages that surrounded the Northern Oasis and the Eastern, and the trade routes that spidered across the desert. Even the temple was there, set at a distance from all other human settlements, and signified by the Maha's seal.

She drank it in with her eyes. *Remember. I must remember this.*

Only a few minutes had passed when she heard a noise echo from the bottom of the stairs. Someone was coming.

Mehr cursed inwardly. The map was far too large for her to conceal and take away with her. Her memory would have to suffice.

She had just managed to put the map away when a mystic walked into the room and paused abruptly at the sight of her. His eyes widened, then narrowed.

"What are you doing in here?" he asked.

Mehr leaned back against the shelves, her hands shaking with adrenaline. She felt light-headed with terror.

"The daiva," she said. Her voice was shaking too. Good. She could use that.

"What?"

"The daiva, is it . . . is it gone?" She crossed one arm over her body and held the other to her cheek, as if she were trying to ward off tears. "I—I saw someone had been injured and I was frightened. I thought if I hid in my room I'd be safe but I—I think I'm lost, and I didn't know what to *do*—"

The mystic didn't roll his eyes, but it was a close thing.

"It's gone," he said. "Come on. I'll take you to your husband."

"Are you sure . . . ?"

"Yes, yes," he said impatiently. "Follow me."

Much to Mehr's relief, Amun was in their chambers rather than their practice hall. The mystic left her, and Mehr sat by Amun's side.

"I saw the map," she said.

"Describe it to me," he said. He listened to her as she spoke, as she closed her eyes and envisaged the map, the trade routes, the villages. When she opened her eyes Amun was drawing on the ground with kohl.

"At least this way we can wash away the evidence if we need to," he told her, when he saw the look on her face.

Mehr kneeled down beside him and looked at his drawing. It was close, very close, to what she'd described. She rubbed some of the kohl away with her thumb, altering the edges of one route.

"Did you find out what happened with the daiva?" Mehr asked.

"Of course," Amun said. "They needed me to will it away."

"Did they take your blood?"

Amun nodded. "It was good that you left," he said.

"Show me."

He gave her his arm. She rolled up his sleeve. There was a small nick on his forearm, but the cut was clean and no longer bleeding, which was a comfort.

"There were three couriers," he said. "The boy, you saw. A daiva followed them for a full day. It shouldn't have harmed them. They had old blood of mine, and the Empire's good fortune to protect them. But the daiva attacked them suddenly. They're badly wounded. It will take time for them to heal." He looked at her. "Mystics aren't usually easily hurt."

Mehr knew the fresher the blood, the stronger its ability to defend its carrier from the daiva. She'd been taught by Lalita to mark the windows of her home once every turn of the moon. But for a long time the daiva had been weak, only strong enough to cause harm in the hallowed time surrounding the storms. No doubt the couriers had rarely required the protection of new blood.

"I know," Mehr murmured. She could remember the way the

ancient daiva they'd met in the desert had flinched away from the mystics. "Something must have changed."

Amun looked at her. They both knew exactly what had changed.

"The daiva are stronger now," he said.

Amun's expression was as opaque as ever, but Mehr knew how to interpret his face. She took his hands in her own. Mehr had given the dreams of the Gods an outlet to dream without compulsion, natural dreams full of both good and ill fortune; daiva had injured mystics; and now Mehr and Amun were learning the sigils that would set them free.

He'd been unable to even contemplate the idea of escape once. Since then he had chosen to work with Mehr toward their goal of freedom, and poured all his efforts into the task. But he was only now starting to really, truly believe they stood a chance. He no longer needed her to have faith for both of them. He was beginning to hope all on his own.

Mehr knew she should feel some sort of sympathy for the mystics who had been hurt, but she couldn't find it in her to care about their fate. All she cared about was the light in Amun's eyes.

"I'm glad," said Mehr. "I truly am."

CHAPTER TWENTY-ONE

After everything that had happened, Mehr had almost entirely forgotten Kalini's warning to keep Hema at a distance. It was only when she left the bathing room one evening and found Hema waiting for her that the memory jolted back. Mehr froze in her tracks. Hema's mouth ticked up into a solemn smile.

"Hello, Mehr."

Mehr hesitated, still. She wasn't afraid of defying Kalini, not exactly. But she could remember the look in Kalini's eyes, hard and cold and furious. It was sensible to be wary of a look like that. Besides, her interest in utilizing Hema and her women to learn more about the temple had waned as her focus on learning the sigils of the Rite of the Bound had grown.

"What are you doing here?" Mehr asked.

"Waiting for you," Hema said. "It's hard to get you alone, you know."

"I know." Mehr took a step forward, conscious of her damp clothes, her even damper hair, the sharpness of her wrists where they protruded from her sleeves. She'd grown thin over the past weeks. In contrast to her, Hema looked pristine and healthy, her skin glowing, her hair neatly pinned away from her face. "But why do you want to talk to me alone? You could have approached me at meals, any time you liked…"

"You've been avoiding everyone," Hema said bluntly. Her lips pursed. Then her voice softened. "I've been watching you, Mehr, and you seem...out of sorts. I know the failure of the storm was hard on you—it was hard on all of us—but you need to take care of yourself. The Empire relies on you."

Hema took a step forward.

"I brought you this," she said. She held a cloth parcel out. "You haven't been eating."

Mehr took the parcel. She peeled back the edge of the cloth. Inside were sweets, soft and dense, made from red dates and butter clarified to a golden sheen. The last time she saw food this rich was on the Maha's table. The thought robbed Mehr of what little was left of her appetite. She covered the food back up. "Thank you," she murmured.

Hema gave her a careful look, with none of her usual sly humor in it.

"Tomorrow night, do you think you could slip away from your husband?" Hema asked. "Rena and I, we've managed to get our hands on a good few bottles of spiced wine. The strong kind." Her eyes twinkled. "We need something to make us all smile again, don't you think?"

Mehr could hear the coaxing note in Hema's voice. She didn't want to agree with Hema. She wanted to stay with Amun and practice the rite, find the sigils they needed to demand that the Gods break their chains and set them free from their vows. She and Amun had spent the night before trying to refine their copy of the map Mehr had seen in the scholars' tower. Mehr hoped it would help them when they escaped the temple, but the task of creating it had consumed time they could little afford to lose.

They *had* to be prepared for the next storm. What Mehr didn't want or need was Hema's misplaced pity, or the pity of any of those other green girls, with their unshakable faith in the Maha and their sure, steady fear of Amun.

But Hema was looking at her with sad eyes, knowing eyes—eyes that had read Mehr's bruised face, her failing appetite, and had come to a conclusion that was almost, but not quite, the truth. Mehr had been hurt by a man, hurt over and over again, and she was holding on to her strength by a thread. Hema's look said: *I want to save you, and I'm not going to stop trying until you let me.* Mehr didn't have the energy to break herself against that look.

"I'll consider it," Mehr said, and knew she'd lost.

"I shouldn't go," Mehr said. "I know I shouldn't go."

Sweating, sore, she was curled up on the floor with her head in her hands. Amun sat across from her, legs stretched out across the floor, looking equally exhausted.

"You should know by now, Mehr. I have nothing to say."

"I'm asking you to say something."

Amun shrugged.

"Go if you want to go," he said.

What did Mehr want?

She wanted to practice the sigils. The sigils they'd strung together were almost coherent enough to be of use when the storm came. They were so very close to finding the secret to freedom. But she also knew that neither of them had anything left to give. Instead of practicing they were collapsed, exhausted, doing nothing.

"I'll achieve nothing by going to them now," Mehr said. The sigils were far more important than anything the women could give to them.

"It's your choice."

"They think you hurt me," Mehr said. "Do you realize that?"

Amun shrugged again.

"You don't care?" she asked.

"You know I don't," he said levelly.

Mehr heaved out a sigh. "Well, I do."

They were both silent for a long moment. Then Amun spoke.

"It's better they believe I hurt you, instead of the Maha. They would just wonder how you'd failed him, and blame you for it." He looked at Mehr, simple truth in his eyes. "You need people, Mehr. Go to them."

"And you?" she asked. "Do you need people?"

She thought, for a moment, that Amun would react badly. He frowned at her, his brow furrowing—and then a yawn cracked his seriousness. He gave a soft laugh and leaned back against the wall.

"I need to rest," Amun said. "That's all that I need right now."

The wine was a mistake.

Mehr realized too late, of course. The girls had gambled, and Anni had triumphantly poured them all wine into cheap clay cups pilfered from the storeroom. The cups were small. They could only hold a mouthful or two of drink. It had been easy for Mehr to take the first cup of wine offered, then the second, then the third; by the fourth she was light-headed and dazed. She realized too late that the wine was far stronger than the watered-down, sweet stuff she had drunk in her father's household. It didn't help that she had barely eaten and that she was exhausted. She'd been weak and out of sorts before the first mouthful of drink had even touched her lips.

I should go home, Mehr thought. But she couldn't seem to make her arms and legs move. Instead she sat at the edge of the room, the chatter around her eddying in and out of focus. The girls were talking about the male mystics, their voices hushed and full of laughter.

"Of course I don't go near the men," Rena said, more loudly than the rest. She sounded affronted.

"We go near the men all the time," another girl said in a joking voice. "They're everywhere."

"Except when we eat, bathe, shit, pray, or sleep," another voice said dryly. Mehr thought it was possibly Hema's. But the room was soft and the voices blurred like ink and water. She didn't really know.

"We have a sacred duty to serve with our whole hearts. Men are a distraction."

"And you keep away from men, do you?"

"It's not as if we can get—"

"Don't say it."

"Well, you should. I'm no fool. Imagine what would happen if the Maha—"

"...opposite of our calling. The poor girl..."

Someone muttered a sharp word. *Careful—the monster's wife.* Mehr heard the conversation stutter. Silence fell. She felt their eyes turn on her, one by one, and her face flushed hot.

When Mehr said nothing, the conversation soon began again. They turned to other topics, and her tension eased. The flush on her skin remained, though. Perhaps it was the influence of the wine.

She felt Hema come and settle down beside her.

"Some of us serve in a different way," Hema said. Her voice was kind. "Some of us have to be brave."

Hema touched her fingertips gently to Mehr's arm. "I hoped showing you the glory of our purpose would help."

She should have stayed with Amun. Here, among all these people, she missed his steadiness, his solidity. She resented the pity in Hema's eyes: resented it, and burned at how *wrong* it all was, how little they understood of her suffering, or his.

"What has he ever done to deserve being so hated?" Mehr asked.

A sharp silence. "He's like an animal," Hema said. She continued, a careful edge to her voice. "You know. All men are not like him."

Mehr tried not to laugh. "I was raised a noblewoman. I had no brothers. My father was the only man I knew before him." *But I know men aren't all like him. They're not as good. Or kind.*

"The way he acts..." Hema's eyes lingered on Mehr's face. The fading bruise on her cheek. "The way he treats you...we've all seen it. We..." She stopped. Thinned her lips, then said firmly, "We know you do your duty. And we feel for you."

"He doesn't hurt me," Mehr said.

"Mehr—"

"He doesn't touch me. You don't see, you understand. He doesn't touch me, not like that, not at all, *at all*." Vehement words. "He's a good man."

Mehr stopped, sucking in a breath, trying to calm the heat of her brain, her flesh. She was so addled that it took a moment for the reality of what she'd said—what she'd done—to hit her. Cold gripped her heart.

Oh, Gods.

She hoped for a moment that Hema wouldn't understand the full meaning of what she'd said. Hema was not in the Maha's inner circle, after all. She should not have been privy to the workings of his control over his Amrithi, and the details of the vow that held Mehr to Amun and to the Maha in turn.

But Hema was Kalini's sister.

Hema hadn't misinterpreted Mehr's words. Not this time. Her eyes were wide. Her face had grayed, drained of color. She'd understood Mehr perfectly.

You shouldn't have said it. The voice in Mehr's head was dispassionate and clear. *You shouldn't have thought it.*

Now the Maha will rip you both apart.

Rip them apart—and rip them away from each other.

Mehr rose to her feet and stumbled outside. She made it as far as the edge of the oasis before she was violently sick.

The wine. The wine had been a mistake, a terrible mistake.

The wine and her own utter foolishness. Her *weakness*. After all the times Amun had protected her, after all the ways they'd both fought to hide their secret from the Maha—how could she betray him like this?

She squeezed her eyes shut. They were wet, streaming with unwanted tears.

She'd thought Amun had grown fragile after the storm. But she'd grown fragile too. If the storm hadn't left her weak—and it surely had—then the sleepless nights, the nightmares, the Maha's cruelties, had all done the storm's work.

And now she'd failed herself. Failed him.

Mehr didn't move when Hema kneeled down beside her.

"Drink from the oasis," Hema said quietly. "It's safe."

Mehr cupped her hands in the water, raised them to her face, and rinsed out the foul taste in her mouth. Then she cupped her hands again and drank one, two sweet mouthfuls of water. They did nothing to clear her head. She looked at Hema. Hema was staring down at the water, her face still gray, her mouth a solemn line.

"Better?" she asked.

"Why are you trying to be kind to me?" Mehr asked in return. "I've done nothing for you." *I am nothing.*

At first Hema was quiet. Then, carefully, she placed a hand on Mehr's shoulder.

"I wanted to have Amrithi blood when I first came here. I knew the Amrithi were heathens, weren't *right*, but I wanted to be useful. I wanted to serve with more than my prayers and my adoration. Your husband has always seemed like an animal, but the lady he served with...she was better than her kind, she was beautiful, and I wanted to be her more than anything." Hema's voice was soft, contemplative. "I watched her sicken and die, and I—I pitied her. I didn't want it anymore." She shook her head. "What you do is hard enough, Mehr. But to have to serve with him..."

"You're kind because you pity me," Mehr said. Hema looked at her, eyes flashing with unfamiliar fire.

"No, Mehr. I'm kind because it's *right*. You have a hard service and you deserve the support of your sisters." She leaned forward, gripping Mehr's shoulder hard enough to hurt. "I'm kind because the kindness of the Maha saved me. He took me and mine from hunger and poverty and gave us hope. You may not have come from hunger, Governor's daughter, but you have purpose now. Your life has meaning. *You* have meaning. Can't you see how wonderful that is?"

Mehr was silent. She wished Hema would let go of her. Her heart was hammering in her throat. There was no room for words. She felt Hema's grip slacken, just a little. Saw her gaze soften. "I am going to try to forget what you told me," Hema murmured. "I am going to decide I misunderstood you. Perhaps I did. But I will hold you in my prayers and hope you do what is right. Do what's right, Mehr, and all will be well in the end. So the Maha wills."

Mehr nodded wordlessly. Hema smiled.

"Good. Good."

Mehr heard a scuffling sound behind them. She looked up and saw Anni watching them. She didn't know how long Anni had been standing there; she didn't know how much Anni had heard. But Anni looked no different from usual, just a little cold, her arms wrapped around herself to keep warm.

"Hema," Anni said timidly. "Mehr. Are you coming back in?"

Hema sighed. She released Mehr and kneeled back. "You can stay here tonight," she said to Mehr.

Mehr shook her head. "No," she said. "No. My . . . my place is with my husband."

Hema gave her a faint, approving nod.

"Drink some more water before you go," she said. "Your head is going to feel foul in the morning."

Hema accompanied Mehr to the staircase of her room. Mehr made the journey up by herself. When she entered the bedroom, she found Amun asleep, curled up on his side. For all his bulk, he looked as innocent as a child. When she sat down on the bed beside him, he woke up with a snap, eyes sharp and alert. He took in her tearstained face and sat up.

"Mehr. What—?"

"I made a mistake, Amun." She swallowed. "A very bad mistake."

CHAPTER TWENTY-TWO

She told Amun everything. He listened in silence. It may have been her imagination, but as she talked, the sigils on his skin seemed to brighten, faded blue growing a deep and livid indigo. When she finished speaking, he was breathing hard. His jaw was clenched tight.

"Amun," she said finally, tentatively. "Amun, what—"

"Get off the divan." His hands were fists. "Please, Mehr."

She got up. She made her way slowly, warily away from the bed to the edge of the room.

"You want to hurt me now, Amun?" A dark pit opened in her stomach. She felt cold. The water hadn't been enough to clear her head, but Amun's anger was a sharper shock than ice. She'd expected his anger, deserved it, but she could still hardly stand to see it. She remembered the Maha's fists and flinched internally. "I can hardly blame you."

"No," he snapped. "Hurt you? No." He lowered his head, chin to chest, breathing deep and harsh through his nose. Then he looked up. "My vows are just growing hard to bear."

Mehr pressed her back against the wall. Amun gave her a thin, pained smile before lowering his head again.

"Oh, Amun," she said softly.

"Don't talk," he managed to say. "Just for a moment. Please."

Mehr waited, and waited, barely daring to breathe.

"So," he said, once his breathing had grown more even. "One of the mystics knows." He looked up. "I'm not angry, Mehr. I knew this was inevitable. Our chances were always slim."

"We don't have to lose hope yet," Mehr said. She couldn't stand the bleakness of his eyes.

"We have a little hope," Amun observed, his voice flat. "If she doesn't speak before the storm. If we manage to break our bonds during the storm, which is unlikely... Mehr, you must see, there are too many *ifs*."

Mehr swallowed. There was no question that Hema would speak, only a question of *when* she would. Mehr knew it just as well as Amun did. Hema was far too loyal, far too faithful to the Maha, to keep Mehr and Amun's secret.

"I'll tell her I—I lay with you. I'll tell her I did my duty."

"You think you can lie to her now?" His expression was far too knowing. She had the awful sense that he could see right through her.

Lying to Hema would be nothing at all like lying to Maryam or maidservants or her father. In her father's household, she'd lied to ensure her small freedoms. She'd lied to save herself from punishment, or for the sake of power. She'd understood that nobility valued many things more highly than truth: their status, their honor, their own pride.

But Hema and the mystics valued nothing more highly than their honesty to the Maha. And Mehr had never lied to save a freedom as vast as the fate of her own soul.

"I've lied before," she said thinly. "I can lie again if I need to. Besides, this is my error. I can try to make it right."

"Not all mistakes can be made right, Mehr." It would have been better if Amun had sounded angry. He didn't. He sounded like he'd expected this all along.

Frantic thoughts ran through Mehr's head. She thought of

suggesting that they ask Edhir when the next storm of dream-fire would fall. She thought of running out and seeking Hema, begging her for silence. But all of that was foolish. All of it was pointless. Mehr could not make her mistakes right. They were going to lose their freedom, and Mehr was responsible for it.

She leaned more heavily back against the wall and closed her eyes. Her head was racing; she felt cold and sick in body and soul. She heard Amun get up from the bed and cross the floor.

She stiffened when he touched her. She opened her eyes, ready to apologize—but for once, Amun had not flinched away. His jaw was hard, his sigils livid with pain, but the hand on her cheek was confident in its tenderness. She leaned into his touch, almost despite herself. He didn't hate her. How could he not hate her?

"You don't need to comfort me," she protested. "You're hurting yourself." But when he placed his other hand against her shoulder, drawing her against him, she didn't protest. She stayed very still, feeling the warmth of him, the cadence of his breath. She'd move away in a second, offer him a respite from the pain of his vows. But not just yet.

"Don't tell me everything will be well," she said.

"I don't lie. Not to you." A pause. "But you'll survive. And I'll do everything I can to keep you safe."

"Thank you," she said. And then, because it bore repeating: "I'm sorry, Amun. So very sorry."

"I wanted to buy us a little time," he said, his breath gentle against her forehead. "And I did. That's enough."

It was painful to lose hope. But she knew, now, that Amun had never had it. His hopes had always been smaller than hers. All he'd wanted was a modicum of kindness, a small sand grain of mercy. He'd won them that. Now all they could do was face the consequences of Mehr's failure. Now all they could do was wait.

Hema had been right. Mehr did feel foul in the morning. But she'd felt worse before. The journey through the desert, with its relentless heat and sunlight, had made her feel infinitely worse. So she put her pain to the back of her mind and went to prayers, sharing her breakfast with Amun as they went to their practice hall. They didn't speak about the night before. Instead they went through the motions, performing the rite, praying with the mystics, adhering strictly to the monotonous routine expected of them. They made it through the day. And the next one.

On the third day, Bahren and Abhiman came for them. Abhiman came armed. He wore a dagger at his waist. Mehr looked at the dagger and at the look in his eyes—deadly and flat and soft. She knew why they were there even before Bahren spoke.

"The Maha wants you. Both of you."

Abhiman strode over and grabbed Mehr roughly by the wrist. Amun, fool that he was, stepped forward, his face thunderous. In a flash, Abhiman had his dagger out of its sheath, its tip a hairsbreadth from Mehr's chin. She raised her head, gave Amun a sharp look. *Please, please, don't try to play the hero. Not now.*

Amun had already frozen. He held his palms upraised. "Brother, you don't need swords to compel us," he said.

"Apparently we do," Bahren said tiredly. "Come quietly, boy. Don't make this harder than it has to be."

They were marched through the corridors. Abhiman didn't lead them to the Maha's private chambers, as Mehr had expected and dreaded. Instead they were led to the Prayer Hall.

Without the usual throng of mystics at prayer, the hall seemed somehow vaster. Beneath the statue of the Emperor stood the

Maha. He watched as they approached. His fractured eyes glowed in the glare of the torchlight. In the emptiness of the hall there was nowhere to hide from him.

Mehr reminded herself to remain calm. As Abhiman shoved her forward, she forced herself to look beyond the Maha. Kalini stood at the edge of the room, half her face cloaked in shadow. Two women kneeled at the Maha's feet. Hema, with her face to the floor, identifiable only by her short, curling hair. And Anni.

Abhiman forced her to a stop, his hand a vise on her wrist. Mehr stumbled over her feet.

"Show some respect," Abhiman said. His voice was full of disgust. "Kneel."

Mehr kneeled. Amun was thrown to the ground beside her. She bowed her head and waited.

"Come closer and kneel by your sisters, Mehr," the Maha said. His voice was terrible and gentle. There was an undertone to it that made her mark burn cold with fire. She sucked in a sharp breath and stood, moving to kneel by Anni's side. The Maha was so sure of being obeyed that he didn't give her a second glance. His eyes were fixed on Amun.

"I have been given some news that has made me unhappy," he said slowly. "Can you imagine what news that was, Amun?"

"I think so, Maha," Amun said. His voice low. Mehr didn't dare turn back to look at him. All her focus was on the Maha, standing before her, his hands clenching and unclenching on nothing but air.

"Well then, Amun. Tell me this. Have you fucked your wife?" The ugliness of the words made Mehr flinch. His voice was so soft, so terrible. "This isn't a question I should need to ask you." A beat. "Have you? *Speak.*"

Amun said nothing. Mehr could hear nothing but Hema's breathing, shallow and overloud in the vast quiet. She clenched her own hands, heart hammering.

"The longer you wait, the more your vows will hurt," the Maha said. "I am not averse to hurting you, boy."

"No." Amun's voice was strangled. Every word was ripped from his throat. "No. I have not."

The Maha nodded. He leaned down and offered Anni his hand. She took it and stood, trembling. She didn't look at Mehr. She didn't look at Hema.

"You've done me a great service, daughter," the Maha said. He kissed her forehead. "A great service, and one you will be rewarded for. But for now, you may go."

"Thank you, Maha," Anni whispered. She bowed again— deep and low, pressing her forehead to the floor—then turned and left as fast as her legs could carry her.

The sound of her footsteps died away. The Maha let out a long, drawn-out sigh. His hands flexed.

Without a word, he hit Mehr. One blow, then another, hard enough to send her skidding across the stone. She curled up, covering her face with her arms. She thought he would keep going, would beat her bloody in front of Amun and Hema and Bahren and Kalini and Abhiman, debase her with an audience. But after the second blow, as she cowered and bit her tongue and waited—he stopped, and stepped away from her.

"I will deal with you further in a moment," he promised. Mehr lowered her arm from her face and watched him turn to face Hema.

Hema was crying.

She hadn't betrayed Mehr. But Mehr wished now that she had. Instead Anni had heard more than either Mehr or Hema had suspected, that night by the oasis. She must have understood enough of their hushed conversation to know that Mehr had disobeyed the Maha, and that Hema had chosen to keep her confidence—enough to condemn them both. Now Anni had told Mehr's secret, and left Hema to face the consequences.

Oh, Hema. Now you know what the Maha is. I'm sorry for it.

"Aren't you going to tell me you serve with all your heart and soul?" His voice rang out. "Aren't you going to beg forgiveness, child? You have deceived me. Betrayed your Maha and your Emperor."

Hema shook her head wordlessly. She looked too terrified to speak. The confident, sly woman Mehr had grown to know had been reduced to this—to silence and fear, to the wait for the inevitable punishment to rain down upon her.

"If Anni had not come to me, your betrayal would have continued. I know it. I know your heart, child. And it is rotten." A sigh. "I am so disappointed in you." He paused to let his words sink in: the consummate orator. "You understand, I'm sure, that your actions have consequences. You were told when you first came here that traitors must be punished."

Someone in the room sucked in a sharp breath. Hema raised her face, her teary eyes fixed somewhere around the Maha's chin. Even now, she was loath to give offense by doing something as heinous as meeting his eyes.

"I have always tried to serve truly, Maha," she whispered. Mehr had never heard Hema's voice sound so small. She sounded like a small creature left out in the cold. "I am faithful. I only hoped..." She stopped, swallowing. "I only hoped to help Mehr be faithful too."

The Maha stared down at her, his fractured eyes glacial. He held out his hand. "My blade, Kalini," he said.

Hema let out a sob.

"Maha," Kalini said. Her voice trembled. "I beg you. Please, no."

"The *blade*, Kalini."

"Maha—"

Abhiman swore a sharp oath. Mehr turned just in time to see him snatch the blade from Kalini's grip. He bowed to the Maha and handed him the hilt before stepping back to stand again at Amun's back. The Maha gave a faint nod of thanks.

"Kalini," the Maha said gently. "You are my most faithful servant. No taint from this will touch you."

"Maha, my lord, please. When my sister and I joined you, you promised we would be safe." Kalini sounded wretched. "We both love you above all things."

"You love me, that I don't doubt. But your sister has not shown me her love as she should have. I am sorry for your loss, Kalini," he said gently, kindly. When Kalini said nothing more, he turned his attention back to Hema. "Stand and turn away from me, child."

Hema's gaze finally drifted to Mehr. But she looked right through her, her eyes full of uninflected terror. She stood, shaking, and turned. "Kalini," she said. Her voice was small, so small.

"Maha," Kalini said in a strangled voice.

"Kalini, it is my love for you that takes this responsibility out of your hands," he said soothingly. "Stand down, before I change my mind and ask you to prove your love." He waited. Kalini was silent again. The threat had stoppered her. "Close your eyes, if it makes matters easier," he suggested.

Then, without further ceremony, he raised the blade and cut Hema's throat.

Hema didn't die instantly. That was the worst of it. Mehr watched Hema sway for a moment, as if the shock held her steady; she watched Hema raise her hands as if she thought, somehow, she could stem the bleed. There was silence in the hall, utter silence, but even if there hadn't been, there would have been no way for Mehr not to hear the choking noise Hema made, as she tried to breathe, tried to scream, and failed at both. Mehr would remember that sound for the rest of her life.

She watched Hema crumple to the ground. It took her a long

time to realize the noise had stopped, and longer still to feel the hot wetness of the blood pooling around her knees.

"This punishment was not for you, Mehr. But I hope it teaches you a lesson," the Maha was saying. His voice sounded like a faraway thing, an echo through water, even though he was walking closer to her, breaching the barrier of blood between them. "The Empire expects loyalty from its people. Disloyalty must have a price."

He kneeled down before her, heedless of the blood staining his robe. But what did it matter to him? The thought was vague, hysterical, tripping through the frozen horror of Mehr's mind. He probably had many robes to spare, just as he had many people to kill, if the mood so took him. What did a little bit of blood on one robe matter, when he had such a glut of property at his disposal? What did it matter to a man like the Maha, that Hema had been kind and good and faithful, that she had been a leader of women, a sly and clever and kind friend?

"You and Amun have failed me repeatedly," he said, low and soft. "Hema earned an easy death, but you, Mehr—you have earned my disappointment. All the power of the storm wasted. Because of *you*." A shake of his head. "I would not enjoy killing you both, but I would do it."

Oh, how he lied. She looked into his eyes. There was a nightmare inside them. He would enjoy it.

"But you are the Empire's tool," he said slowly. "Harming you would only harm our good Emperor. So you will live, and be thankful. But if you betray me again, Mehr, if you tell me a single lie, have no doubt that I will make you dance until your feet bleed, and I will make sure my mystics pray for dreams that curse your sister and your father and every gentle soul in the Governor's household. I will focus all my strength on making them die the death you rightly deserve, and it will be your dance that kills them. You will be the blade at their throats, as surely as you were the blade at Hema's."

He traced her throat as he spoke, one fine fingertip following the hummingbird beat of her pulse. She almost wanted him to close his fingers around her neck. At least then she could stop being afraid of the unknown.

"Are we clear, Mehr?" he asked.

She could feel the blood staining through to her knees.

"Yes, Maha," she whispered.

His hand moved lower. He gripped the edge of the braid of cloth around her neck, the braid that held her marriage seal. He raised it, looking at the wooden carving Amun had made for her, so many months ago.

"Let me begin with a simple question. How did Amun leave you untouched? How did he lie to me?"

Her knees hurt. She could hear Kalini now, keening, a low, terrible sound of mourning.

"He followed the word, not the spirit of your orders." Her voice was dull, her mouth full of ash.

"Did he now?"

"Truth can be twisted," said Mehr.

The Maha made a noise, a soft hum of acknowledgment. "I see. Ah, Amun. I thought I'd molded you into something better than this. A shame." He looked over Mehr's shoulder. She wished she could turn, wished she could see Amun's face. But the Maha still had her marriage seal in his hand, holding her as steady as a leash held a hound.

Amun. I'm so sorry. So very sorry.

"I'm not going to be coy with you any longer, Amun." The Maha's voice hardened. "Make her your wife in more than name. Fuck her. Are we clear? On your vows, you will make this woman yours in flesh now, or may your damnable vows eat you whole." He flung Mehr to the ground and stood. Mehr scrambled back onto her hands and knees and turned, fixing her frantic gaze on Amun.

Whatever expression he had been wearing before was gone. She saw black in his starless eyes, utter emptiness in his face, as if his soul had been banished behind a wall. Perhaps it had been. He'd been given his order. He would obey it. Everything in Mehr recoiled. Her breath grew shallow with panic.

He was going to reach for her here, with Hema dead, with the floor bloodied, with the Maha and the Emperor's effigy staring down at them; he was going to reach for her, and he was going to—

Mehr swallowed, nauseous. No. She could survive it. She could survive anything if she had to. But Amun had fought so long and so hard to be good. Hurting her—doing this?—would destroy him beyond repair. She couldn't allow it.

She crawled across the floor, head swimming from the blows of the Maha's hand, from the metal scent of blood, from the pure acid of terror. She placed a hand on Amun's chest, right over the mark of that unfulfilled vow, that spidery white mark of a marriage seal that bound them both together as husband and wife, as slaves, as survivors.

"No, Amun," she murmured. "No, no. Remember yourself. Remember me. Please, Amun. Not like this. Amun, remember."

He was trying to fight. He gripped her hand; his hand shook, his grip hard enough to hurt, his palm slippery with sweat. He gritted his teeth, squeezed his starless eyes shut. She saw the sigils on his wrists and his face shift, livid. She tried to speak to him in the language of their forefathers and mothers, clumsily shaping the hand against his chest into half sigils. *Promise, trust, you.*

Love.

On the last sigil, he jerked away from her, a snarl on his

breath. His eyes snapped open. He rolled on the floor, curving in on himself just as Mehr had when the Maha had beaten her. Mehr cried out when he slammed his head against the ground, once, twice—and then his eyes rolled back, and he went still.

The Maha made a noise of disgust.

Mehr jerked her head up. Bahren, Abhiman, Kalini—they were all watching. For all her keening, Kalini's face was dry. She looked down at Mehr and Amun with an expression Mehr couldn't read.

"Fool boy," the Maha sighed. "Make sure it's done, Bahren. And Abhiman, get a girl to come in here and clean up this mess." He strode out.

"He will expect me to watch," Bahren said.

Amun's bedroom was incongruously peaceful after the horror of Hema's death. The sweetness of the oasis wafted in on the breeze. The oil scent given off by the guttering lanterns had left a palpable warmth in the air. Mehr relit the lanterns as Bahren, with surprising strength, arranged Amun on the bed. It gave her something to do.

She looked outside at the sky, dark and clean and cloudless.

"You don't need to do that. It will be done."

"He will ask me if I did."

Ah, but you can lie, Mehr thought. There was little point saying so. No doubt Bahren had no desire to have his throat cut.

"Then you'll have a long night," she said instead. "If fighting his vows makes Amun anywhere as sick as he was after the storm, he'll take time to awaken and to be—prepared." Mehr's stomach lurched.

She imagined how Amun would surely look at her when he awakened. She imagined his horror. She knew he cared for her, just as she cared for him. But their caring had grown on the knife edge of the vows that bound him, and half bound her.

They had run out of doors, run out of options. How would he react to knowing he was going to be forced to take her?

She thought of how much worse it would be with Bahren standing over them. Shuddered again.

"Nonetheless..."

"Please," Mehr said sharply. She placed a hand over her eyes. Oh, what she would give for the comfort of a veil, a screen. Anything. "Please, Bahren, let me keep a little of my honor. I am Amrithi, but I am an Ambhan noblewoman too. I had an Ambhan woman's dignity once. I had the right to cover my face. I had the right to give my soul as I wished. And now..." She let out a sob. She showed Bahren her anguish, in all its real, ugly glory, hoping it would sway him. She looked at his face between her fingers. He looked stricken.

Good. She'd struck a blow.

"Now," she gasped out. "I'm nothing. Just this man's—wife. A *belonging*. Please, Bahren. Give me this. Show me a little mercy."

He let out a breath. He wouldn't have relented if he hadn't just seen Mehr beaten, Hema's throat cut. He wouldn't have. But Mehr had found his weakness, small as it was. He was not the Maha. He was not a monster. His conscience was her ally.

Bahren let out a long, slow breath. "I don't want to be here either. Know that, Mehr."

"Then don't be," she said wretchedly. She lowered her hands. Looked at him with eyes she knew were red, wet. "Please, Bahren."

A long silence. Finally he said, "I'll wait at the bottom of the stairs. Come morning..." A huffed sigh. "For all our sakes, do your duty, girl."

He didn't wait for her to thank him. He strode out of the room. She heard his footsteps on the stairs, and then silence. He'd settled down to wait. For Mehr to do her duty.

She rubbed her eyes dry. Walked over to the door and softly closed it. She turned back to the bed. Amun lay unconscious,

forehead bruised, his sigils still so livid they shone in the flickering light. She sat on the edge of the bed and brushed one dark
curl away from his wound. He murmured, turning into her
touch. Trusting as a child.

A memory flashed before her eyes: Hema's throat cut. Hema
falling.

She snatched her hand back and stood. She went over to the
window, leaning out to meet the cold night air. She was dizzy,
and the sky was whirling with stars.

Gods. There was nowhere left to run, was there?

CHAPTER TWENTY-THREE

At first she wasn't sure if Amun would even wake up before dawn. Fighting the Maha's orders had drained his strength severely. He lay on the bed, still and gray and hurt, silent for hours. She feared for a while that she would have to seek out Bahren and ask for a physician to be sent. But eventually he began to move fitfully in his sleep, eyelids flickering as he struggled against harsh dreams. Then she began to wonder if he'd wake with the same dead-eyed stare he'd had when the Maha had laid down his orders. The idea filled with her dread.

What could she do if he woke blank-eyed and broken, a shadow of himself? Nothing, absolutely nothing. She was powerless here. So she pushed her fear away, locking it into the dark place inside her where all her grief and horror lived, waiting to be let out. She focused on practicalities instead. She took off her bloodstained robe—oh, how she would have loved to burn it whole—and put on her plainest shawl and tunic. She left her legs bare, not bothering with pajami, even as she wrapped the shawl tight around her shoulders and drew the cloth up to her face, breathing its scent in. If she breathed deep enough, perhaps she'd be able to find the scent of the women's quarters, that unique combination of rosewater and oil and perfume she'd once kept stoppered in a perfect glass vial on her dressing table. But there was no scent of home.

The shawl smelled like everything in the temple smelled: of sand and sunlight and dust. It was as if her old life were a story she'd made up, an utterly perfect dream she'd conjured to comfort herself through the bitter reality of her slavery.

But her life before had been real, just as real as her life was now, and it hadn't been perfect. She'd been an outsider in her own home, protected from the worst cruelties a legal wife could inflict on an illegitimate, mixed-blood stepdaughter only by the strength of her father's guilt. Even then, she hadn't been safe, and she hadn't been free. But she'd had Arwa, and Lalita, and Nahira. She'd had love, she saw now, in abundance. That love had given her the strength to breathe.

Now all the people she'd once loved were gone from her life, and her chains had grown heavier and heavier. She didn't know if she could survive without hope. Could she let the thought of freedom go, and live like Amun had lived for years on end, like an animal in a cage, quelled and silent, always watching warily for the next blow to fall? She didn't know if she had his strength. It would be easier to simply splinter herself on hating the Maha. Her pride made her want to. It would be the Amrithi thing to do, after all, to annihilate herself rather than letting the Maha have her heart and soul.

It would be harder—far harder, and far braver—to find a way to survive. Harder even still, to find a way to truly *live*.

Amun made a low, tortured sound as he tossed on the bed. She touched his hair, made a hushing noise, as a mother would for a child. He didn't wake. There were hours still until daylight, and Mehr feared all over again that he would not wake up in time. She curled herself up on the bed beside him, tucking her legs beneath herself. She kept stroking his hair. He made another pained noise, eyelids fluttering, and she began to sing him the lullaby she'd once sung to Arwa, to comfort her little sister when she'd cried.

It was a ridiculous thing to do; she knew that. Amun was no child. She remembered, distantly, Arwa's warm weight in her arms—her long braid of hair, her warm child scent. Amun was huge, all sinew and muscle, and smelled of blood. There was stubble on his cheeks. She touched her fingertips to his jaw. Her voice was thin and raw, but Amun still seemed to be soothed by it, his breathing softening as she cupped his face, as she sang.

She watched his eyes open.

"Mehr?" he said blearily. He reached a hand out. She took it. His large fingers enclosed hers.

"I'm here," she said softly.

"Did I...?"

"No," she said, seeing the fear dawning on his face. "No, you did nothing. You fought."

He gave a pained laugh. "No wonder I hurt so mu—" He stopped, his voice choking. His grip on her hand tightened. "I can feel it. The vow."

She waited. His grip didn't weaken. He was so gray with pain. "The song you were singing," he said finally, pain leaking into his voice. "It sounded familiar."

"It was a song my mother used to sing to me," she said. "An Amrithi song."

Amun nodded. "My... my father. He used to sing me to sleep. He was better with me than my mother. Because she had the— the *amata* gift, she was harder. More afraid. But my father... he had a—good voice. He taught me." Breath. "Everything I know. He taught me."

Mehr listened. Just listened, as Amun struggled for words, as he closed his eyes and spoke, still holding on to her as tightly as a man in the sands holds his last flask of water.

"After my mother, he was afraid to...to leave me alone. Because I was like her—he knew. He'd seen the dreamfire. With me. He tried not to go to villages. Tried to keep me safe. But we were hungry, so we went. And someone told the mystics we were there." Pained breath in. Out. "When the mystics found us...Mehr, if my mother had been with me, she would have slit my throat before the Maha could take me. But my father—he loved me too much. He hesitated and they—took him. Us."

"You were a child," Mehr whispered. "When you made your vows to the Maha...you were just a child?"

"The Maha told me if I made my vows he would spare my father pain. He said he would show him mercy. I learned from the Maha how to tell a lie with truth." A pause. Another harsh breath. "He killed him fast. It was mercy of a kind. But not the one I wanted."

All the stories he'd told her of his life before the Maha, all the careful absences in his stories, suddenly made sense. He'd told her he was young and foolish in his early days in the temple. She hadn't thought he'd meant that he'd been nothing but a child, tricked into service by a Maha who had used his fear for his father's life to bind him.

Amun had been compelled, just as she had, by the need to protect someone he loved.

Just a child. *Oh, Amun*, she thought.

His breathing had grown ragged. He was shaking. "Let me go, Mehr. *Go*."

"I can't," Mehr said. "Bahren is waiting at the bottom of the stairs."

"I expected him to be in this room."

"I asked him to leave me some dignity," Mehr said. "As an Ambhan noblewoman. But he will still be waiting."

Amun shook his head. "Mehr," he said despairingly. Then he fell silent.

"Amun," she murmured, ever so soft. She wished, distantly, that she'd let the lanterns gutter. Maybe darkness would have made this easier. "Amun. It's okay."

"It's not," he said. Deep breaths, sharp with pain. "Mehr, I... I've asked myself. So many times. When the vows hurt. When I was alone. Would I turn my blade on myself if I could? If I weren't vowed..."

"Amun," she whispered again.

"I was never—sure," he said, forcing the words out through his pain. "I thought—no. I couldn't. But Mehr, I know now. I would rather die than hurt you."

Tears pricked her eyes.

"I'm not even a little afraid of you hurting me. You've tried so hard..." She swallowed back tears. "You were trying to buy us time. And you did. You have." She covered their joined hands with her own. "I trust you more than anyone I've ever known. All will be well."

"I thought time would be enough. But that was before I knew you."

"And now you know me?" Mehr asked softly.

"Now..." He exhaled, shaky. "I think about the boy I used to be. I think about what kind of man he would have become, if the world had been kinder. If the Maha hadn't found him. That man would have... he would have courted you. In the Amrithi way. He would have told you how he admired you, for your strength—your beauty. Your heart. He would have left his clan for yours."

"I don't have a clan, Amun," Mehr said, finding her voice somehow. Somehow.

"I would have been your clan, then," he responded, so soft. "I would have loved you without vows or seals. Just my heart for yours, as long as you willed it."

"Ah," she whispered back. Words seemed too far away, too hard to grasp when there was no air in her lungs.

This, not her past, was the perfect dream, the mirage hovering on the horizon, always out of grasp: a love given freely, without vows or seals, chains or guilt. She ached for it. What he dreamed of was all she'd ever wanted, and could never have.

If she could have been free. If she could have been born a woman without duties to bind her, if she could have chosen any-one in the world to love…

"Mehr." He said her name in that low, solemn voice she'd come to know so well. "You must know that I love you. I know you can't love me in return, but—"

"Then you know nothing," Mehr said, more harshly than she'd intended. She bit down on her lip, hard enough to sting.

"Please go, Mehr. I can't…" His voice was a sudden rasp. He winced, closing his eyes.

Mehr lifted her free hand and touched one sigil at his wrist. She could feel the heat rising from it, burning him from the inside. He was so brave. Brave to have survived, brave to have shown her kindness, and braver still now to keep fighting the Maha's orders, even though it clearly hurt him beyond belief to do so.

"If I had been born a free Amrithi woman, I may have loved the man you described, that free man, without vows or fear," Mehr said, carefully shaping the words even as her insides shook. "But this is the only life I have, Amun. The only one, and I can't…I can't simply pretend I might have met you in another, kinder life." She swallowed hard, searching for words. "But in this life, this one I have…perhaps because we are trapped together, you and I—or perhaps because you're so kind and gentle, and difficult, and sly and…" The few words she had caught in her throat.

Amun said nothing as she tried to muster up the dregs of her courage. He waited patiently for her to speak. That was the kind of man he was—the kind who waited for her to find her small, inconsequential words even as a pain far greater than she could understand tried to eat him whole. A good man. The best man she'd ever known.

"I love you." She said it like a confession, and with the words a burden she hadn't even known she'd been carrying eased from her shoulders. In its place was nothing but relief: relief and a sweet lightness that almost brought tears to her tired eyes. "I love you. And if I had my free choice, if we were simply man and woman in this room together, no vows on us, then I...I would choose to love you as a wife, in body and in soul."

"Mehr." He breathed her name, looked up at her with those pained midnight eyes, dark and sweet. "We don't have a choice. You know that. You know he's taken our choices away from us."

"We always have choices," she said. "You taught me that. When you obeyed the word, not the spirit of the Maha's words, when you chose pain, over and over again, instead of hurting the both of us in...in a different way. When you decided to help me perfect a way to use the Rite of the Bound to save ourselves, even though you knew our hope of success was small and our risks were huge. You *showed* me what choices really mean."

"I can't see," he said hopelessly. "I just can't see what choices we have."

The blankness was encroaching on his eyes. She cupped his face in a hand, willing it away. "You were thinking of the boy you were, and the man you could have been. Think instead of who you are now. Push back the pain if you can," she pleaded, "and listen to me."

"I'm trying," he whispered, his skin burning hot beneath her touch.

"You just as you are now—scars and vows and sigils and all—you are the one I trust," Mehr said fiercely. "Not some imagined version of you. *You.* If you esteem me as you claim to do, Amun, then trust yourself as I do. You can let the Maha turn you into an animal, or you can choose to take the love offered to you freely. Look beyond the pain and the blood and tell me: What choice do you want to make?"

He looked at her, looked through the pain, as if he saw her and only her. His grip on her hand relaxed, fingers uncurling slowly to let her free. She pulled back her own hand, just a little, but remained still. Waiting for him. He rose up on one arm, shaking with the effort. She watched, holding her breath in her throat, as he reached a hand out, and cupped her face.

Then he kissed her.

The kiss was tentative—just a bare, brief touch of his mouth against hers, the fleeting pressure of his warm skin. They parted. Then Mehr leaned forward, into his hand and his lips, and kissed him back.

This kiss was gentle, but not tentative. Mehr marveled at that—that something so new and so alien could feel so perfect, and so much like coming home. Something hot flared under her skin as the kiss deepened, as Amun's hand moved from her cheek to tangle in her hair. Every inch of her skin felt suddenly, startlingly alive.

They were on the precipice of—something. There was a yawning pit in her stomach, a sense that if she touched him in return they would move to a place beyond fear to utter sweetness. She brushed her fingers over the line of his jaw. Amun made a noise against her mouth—and then pulled back sharply.

He got off the bed, even as his legs shook from the pain of it and his sigils stood out bright and livid on his skin. As Mehr tried to gather her thoughts, tried to quell her hammering heart, he slapped a hand against the wall and leaned his weight against it, his back to her. She could hear his ragged breath.

"No, Mehr." She got to her feet as he spoke. "Don't come here. I don't want to hurt—"

"Hurt me? You won't hurt me. What the Maha does, that isn't you, Amun. I know you." Her heart hadn't stopped hammering, but the fire in her blood had burned her despair away and left her feeling alive again.

The fire he'd ignited in her body had woken something in her heart: a small, fragile light, a thing beyond the hunger and pull of the body. It wasn't quite hope. It felt like a door opening, a narrow road not leading to the vast freedom she'd so long yearned for, but to something more possible. More real.

Something to hold on to in the dark.

She said his name again, once. But she didn't move. She'd told him he had a choice. She had to let him make it.

"Vows," he said abruptly. He turned to look at her, all his sigils feverish and bright on his dark face. "If—if we must be bound by *his* vows, I want us to make our own vows to each other." A spasm of pain crossed his face. "I want to vow true things. Things that we choose to bind us."

"Vows," she repeated. She nodded. "I can do that."

Vows. True things. Their lives had been shaped by vows layered upon vows: vows of service, vows of marriage, vows of ownership. Amun gave a gasp, doubling over, all his weight on the arm he had planted against the wall.

He couldn't speak, so she had to. She mustered up all her courage.

"I vow that I trust you. That I will keep trusting you," she said tentatively. "I vow to...to continue seeing you as the man that you are, not what other people have tried to make you." A deep breath. "I vow to know you."

He slumped a little further. Afraid he would collapse, she ran to his side and caught hold of him. But he wasn't falling. He turned in her arms, pressed his forehead to her own, as if her body gave his strength. She felt his breath soften as his pain eased. His fingers touched her face, light as dust. She shivered.

"I vow..." A laugh. "I want to vow not to harm you, but how can I do that?"

"You promised true vows," Mehr said quietly, measuring her words as best as she could. "You can't promise to protect me from the Maha, or from the mystics. But you can vow that you will never choose to hurt me. You can vow that." She touched his face in return. "I trust you. More than anything, I'm sure of that."

He let out a breath. A smile shook his face.

"I vow to be the man you trust," he said softly. "Choices and all."

Their mouths met. The touch felt sharper somehow, like the harshest midday sunlight concentrated in the press of their lips, the touch of their fingertips. Then his hand was in her hair, and her body was arching into his, consumed by the fall of his shadow, the shaking strength of him.

"I vow to love you," he whispered, when they parted. "Always."

"You can't vow that," she told him.

"I can," he said, low and reverent, and kissed her again.

She noticed how her touch flushed the pain from his body, restoring his strength. He moved easily back to the bed with her, never quite letting her go. His touch was gentle, a question in every brush of his fingers. Like this? Or this? She took his wrists in her hands, strangely sure of herself, despite her hammering heart. With her guidance, he slipped off her tunic, her shawl, leaving her bare to his eyes and touch.

"Oh, Mehr." His voice was full of light.

She hadn't been ashamed of her own skin before coming here, before her body had been marked indelibly as property. She felt some of her new shame fade at the look on his face, all wonder and want. She felt exhilarated, unafraid, even as his sigils glowed, even as the Maha's compulsion ran through his blood.

To be unafraid—that was a choice too.

She touched the sigils on his face. When he gave a shake of his head, she moved her fingers to the seal etched onto his chest instead. In the mark she saw her history—all the men who had made her, an old and illustrious bloodline that had defined Mehr, like it or not. In the mark she saw herself.

"I vow to hold these vows higher, more sacred than any vows

that have been forced from us," she said. She drew him closer still, the bed firm beneath her back, his skin warm and glowing with sweat and life. "I vow that I am your tribe and your clan and...I vow that I choose to belong to you."

He touched her seal-marked skin in return, a back-and-forth touch, so tender it nearly brought tears to her eyes. "We belong to each other," he said. "That is a true vow, Mehr."

They touched each other compulsively, curiously. She learned the language of his body and her own, as new and strange and holy as a rite, but one that needed no name, no laws. The brightness inside her grew as whispered vows gave way entirely to touch. She was sure, so sure of him. The feel of him against her, inside her—even the clumsiness of it all, the brief pain, the heat of his breath on the slope of her shoulder—all of it only made her more sure.

I vow that you're my choice, the only right choice I've ever made, she thought, feeling the vow bloom open in her heart, red as blood. *No vow, no matter what it compels from me, will be more important than the one I've made to love you.*

Maybe she spoke the words. Maybe she didn't. But in the dying lantern light, after his sigils had dimmed and he lay beside her in the growing glow of dawn, she looked into his eyes and saw the light in them, the softness of it. He knew her, heart and soul. He knew.

CHAPTER TWENTY-FOUR

Mehr lay next to Amun as the dawn lightened the sky. Amun was quiet. She could feel his eyes on her, drinking her in.

Her body felt different. Warm, wrung out with trauma and with joy. The sigil on her chest was burning, stretching its roots deep under her skin as it shifted and changed with the force of a vow made permanent. Her fate was sealed into her skin now.

She didn't think of Hema, of Arwa, of anyone or anything at all. She listened to Amun breathe. She thought of the cage that had closed in around them.

They could no longer use the rite to try to win their freedom. All their escape plans—the sigils they'd strung together, the knowledge they'd carefully gleaned, the map they'd redrawn in kohl...it was all a waste. They were utterly bound, by body and by soul.

She fanned a hand thoughtlessly over her stomach, felt the heat of her own skin.

"You don't have to fear," Amun said. His voice was hoarse. All his agony had faded, but its ghost was still there, in his eyes.

"I have a lot to fear," Mehr said wryly. "We both do."

"No." A moment of hesitation. Then he placed a hand over her hand, covering her bare stomach.

"You won't..." He hesitated. "There's no need to worry."

Mehr sucked in a breath and nodded. She hadn't even considered it. She should have sought out the herbs she needed, the
bitter greens that Lalita had shown her once and warned her she
would need someday.

"There are no children born here," Mehr said. It wasn't a
question. She knew, suddenly; she was sure. "Why wouldn't he
have his Amrithi create him new servants, if he could?" she said
out loud, wondering. "He can't, can he?"

"He tried, with her," said Amun. "The woman who came
before you. He'd tried before too." He was silent for a moment,
then said, "In the end, he decided the rite was to blame. The
dreamfire used in that way was...too much."

Amun had told her that the Rite of the Bound took a toll.
She'd felt its impact after the last storm. She hadn't considered
what other consequences the act of becoming a vessel for immortal fire could have on the human body.

"I am sorry for what has been done to you, Mehr," Amun said
in a low voice.

"Don't you be sorry," Mehr said, something savage in her voice.
She turned, pressing her face to his skin. "Not you."

The physicians came and took Amun away. He went without
complaint, quiet and lumbering like the beast she knew he
wasn't, unsteady on his exhausted legs. Left on her own, wishing keenly that he were with her still as her scar thrummed and
burned, Mehr went down the stairs. Bahren was waiting for her.

"I can tell him truthfully that you obeyed," Bahren said. He
looked profoundly uncomfortable, and profoundly tired. He
must have stayed up all night, standing guard at the bottom of
the stairs, waiting for Mehr and Amun to obey the Maha's orders.

She didn't ask how intently he had listened to them. She didn't
ask what he had—or had not—heard. He had done the kindness
of giving her a little dignity. That had to be enough.

"Thank you," Mehr said quietly. She crossed her arms, look-ing around the dark hallway. Somewhere she heard the bells ring, calling the mystics to morning prayers. Soon there would be people walking the corridors, dressed in their dark robes. The girls—Rena, even Anni (Mehr's stomach dropped; *Anni,* that traitor, that wretch)—would already be up and dressed, the morning food cooked. But Hema would not be with them.

We both watched Hema die, she thought suddenly. *We both saw her die, and it's as if nothing happened at all.*

"The Maha will want to see me, won't he?" she asked.

"He's asked for you," Bahren said.

He'd asked for Mehr, and Mehr alone. She was grateful Amun was gone and wouldn't know she was facing their master alone. She nodded and tried, desperately, to muster all the tatters of her courage around her like a screen, a veil, a wall. But it was hard to be brave. She had seen blood and betrayal and felt love even in the dark despair. She could feel Amun still, the echo of him in her sore flesh. She could feel the Maha too in the mark on her chest that burned and burned. She was a raw nerve with nothing to protect her from what she had chosen, and what had been done to her.

"I will see him whenever he wills it, of course," she said. As if she had a choice.

Bahren led her down the corridors toward the Maha's pri-vate chambers. Mehr had no fond memories of those rooms, but she followed obediently regardless. Bahren slowed until they were walking side by side. Although Mehr did not raise her head, she knew that other mystics, making their way to prayer, watched from the edges of the corridor. She wondered how many of them knew what happened. How Hema had died.

Bahren spoke.

"I don't know how you tricked him," Bahren said, his voice so low even she strained to hear it, walking close by his side. She doubted the other mystics could hear a word. "You and the boy did a foolish thing, a horribly foolish thing. I blame you less than him, because you are young and sheltered. He was wrong to lead you astray. Perhaps the Maha will show you a higher level of mercy accordingly."

"I think," Mehr said tightly, "that my husband has paid a high enough price for our foolishness."

He gave her a sidelong glance. She was reminded of his age. Once, he must have been a lost child, like all the other mystics had been: orphaned or abandoned, or disgraced for illegitimacy, trapped in poverty by circumstances beyond his control, until the day the Maha had taken him into service and raised him up. How long had he served the Maha? How much had he seen? How much did he know?

Enough that he was trusted. Enough that his word was enough to convince the Maha that Mehr's loyalty was finally, truly, embedded in her skin.

"He is always looking for more Amrithi with the gift," he said abruptly. "Your people's blood may be spread thin, but he will find more. You understand?"

Mehr said nothing, because she knew what it sounded like when a question didn't actually require an answer.

"When he finds more like you, he won't be so kind to you or the boy in the future," Bahren went on.

Mehr did not want to listen to him. After what she had suffered—after what she and Amun had *both* suffered—she did not want to consider the idea that the Maha had treated them...kindly.

They had their own room, food and water. They had clothes and small creature comforts—Amun's needle and thread, sweet soap Mehr had wheedled from a kindly elderly mystic. They had their limbs and their lives. Things could be so much worse.

Mehr had seen the darkness in the Maha's eyes. Felt it. She knew the Maha was capable of a great many things, and if she was lucky, she would not survive them.

"You should learn to be obedient," Bahren said.

"I will try," Mehr said thinly.

They walked a little longer. Then Bahren spoke again.

"Make no mistake, little sister—I chose to be here. Our people could be weak instead of strong." His voice softened as he spoke of the Maha's purpose. Like Hema, he believed in the Maha's work. In the Maha, who was beloved and terrible and had built the glory of the Empire out of nothing but sand and dreams.

Sand and dreams—and the blood of Mehr's people.

"The Maha has ensured that our Emperors are always strong and brave and wise. He has ensured that we will always be prosperous."

Mehr had significant experience in keeping her head lowered and her mouth silent. In that moment, she chose to put the skill to good use.

The Maha was waiting.

Mehr bowed low to the floor. Waited until he told her she could stand. She raised her head to meet the Maha's eyes— looked into them for a sharp, painful second—then fixed her eyes on his chin. His eyes hurt her. She felt his presence, sharp as a blade, right through her chest. For a moment it choked her; she parted her lips, catching the air until the pain settled.

"Well, Mehr," he said. He sounded pleased already. "Bahren has told me you obeyed. But I want to hear it from your lips now. Have you obeyed, or must I be more specific?"

She swallowed. "We had intercourse. Amun and I."

"Finely put, my dear," he said mildly. "That will suffice. Now show me the mark."

He hadn't asked to see it before, but Mehr should have expected it. She felt nothing at all as she loosened the sash, as she showed him the scarred skin where his mark sat.

He crossed the distance between them and placed a hand

firmly on the sigil. He didn't ask her permission. She supposed he didn't feel that he needed to. She was his possession. Not a true person, or citizen of the Empire.

The touch of his hand was terrible, terrible. It burned through her free will, leaving her hanging suspended in her skin, surrounded by a maelstrom of darkness. The nightmares that haunted the storms, the nightmares that filled his eyes, were suddenly boiling under her own skin. They were part of her.

"Are you able to lie to me, Mehr?"

"No, Maha," she said. Her voice like winter. "Not at all. Not anymore."

"You're bound to me," he said.

"I am." There was no question in his voice, but she answered regardless.

For a man who had recently slit a woman's throat, he'd looked remarkably relaxed even when Mehr had first entered the room. Now he looked positively delighted.

"I should have realized why you so enraged me," he murmured. "I didn't quite have you. But the bond by marriage is a new creation, a thing of necessity, and I thought perhaps it simply felt strange to me because of its rarity. But now—ah, yes." The satisfaction in his voice made her want to recoil. "I have you now."

He didn't let her go. Her skin hummed where his hand touched her.

"Everything will be so much better now," he told her in a voice as tender as bloodied meat. He gave her bruised face a long, leisurely look. "You will no longer be flawed, my dear, by your weak blood and your weaker heart. Your blood and your heart are mine now—and I will shape them into a tool worthy of the great honor of service to my Empire." He stroked a hand along her cheekbone. "You will be worthy of my love, and glad of it."

She thought of how he had looked after the storm, with his riven skin and eyes shattered from within. Now, stroking her face with terrible tenderness, he looked more like the man who had greeted her when she had first arrived at the temple. His eyes and his skin glowed with inner light. The fractures in his eyes shone like pointed stars.

He could afford to be tender now, cruel, sadistic animal that he was. Now that he had her—truly had her—he did not have to hurt her. His presence alone was pain enough. His touch was agony. Even his voice clawed her ears. How had Amun survived this horror since childhood? Mehr couldn't fathom it.

"Speak to me," the Maha prompted. "Tell me what you're thinking."

"That my pain brings you joy," she said promptly. She had no control. None. The words poured out of her. "That you are far older than any mortal man has the right to be. That you have single-handedly crushed my mother's people to dust for the sake of the Empire, for a throne you no longer sit on and I can't—I don't know what you are, but you are *monstrous*—"

He gripped her hard, holding her jaw painfully shut.

"Stop," he ordered softly. When she fell silent, breathing hard through her nose, he patted her cheek and let her go. "Good girl."

She stayed very still. She thought he would beat her again then. She had failed so thoroughly, to be what he had demanded. Her scar throbbed painfully. But he only shook his head and smiled, a terrible soft smile.

"Now," he said, satisfied. "Now you begin to understand true awe, and true worship. I am so pleased with you, Mehr. So pleased."

"I wish I could kill him," Amun said.

When Amun had returned from the physicians and found her sitting in their room, he'd only had to look at her to know she had faced the Maha without him. He'd listened without comment as she'd told him what had passed between her and the

Maha. When he spoke, his words were without inflection, without rage. They were just truth.

"You're not a murderer, Amun," she said.

"Every man is, when he has to be." He sat touching distance from her. The gap between their bodies felt heavy, significant. "I chose this fate. I can manage the burden of—what he does. But you, Mehr..."

"I can cope," she said swiftly. "I'm stronger than I look."

He exhaled. Gave her a swift, sidelong smile. "It's not your strength I'm worried about. Seeing someone you love being hurt, knowing their pain so perfectly... Mehr, it's hard."

Her own heart gave a pang in her chest. She leaned against him, breaching that distance between them. Her pain eased as he wrapped his arm around her and pressed his face into her hair. These small things. They had to be enough.

"I don't want to talk anymore about what he said to me." *What he did to me.* "I want you to tell me a story. Tell me more about your childhood. Tell me how you grew up."

And haltingly, gently, he did.

CHAPTER TWENTY-FIVE

What are you supposed to do when you have lost the war and every possibility of victory has been absolutely, thoroughly annihilated?

Mehr had always fought. Sometimes in big ways, but usually small: carefully calculated rebellions, little victories won under a thin veneer of obedience. Now all the fight had left her. She couldn't rebel any longer. She wore the chains of her servitude under her skin and her bones, in her *soul*. She and Amun could no longer alter the Rite of the Bound and ask the Gods to set them free, or compel the daiva to their will. Mehr's small measure of freedom had been the key, and now the key was gone.

So Mehr did the only thing left to her: She obeyed. She and Amun practiced the rite. They prayed. Mehr did not try to seek out Hema's women. She didn't track down Anni and claw out her eyes. She did her duty and kept her own eyes lowered, her body at work. She allowed herself to become colorless.

It was only when she and Amun were alone that Mehr felt like herself again. Amun didn't ask her for intimacy, and she didn't ask him either. Instead Mehr would lean against him, safe in the circle of his arms, and listen to his voice. He would talk to her—more than he'd ever talked before—about his Amrithi childhood, and his life among the mystics in the long years before

Mehr had joined him. There were no more halting silences, no more tales cut short to hide their true brutality. They'd suffered together, survived together, made their own soul-binding vows to one another. There were no more walls between them now, and Amun's company was the one comfort Mehr had in her newly bound life.

Kalini came for her when she and Amun were training in one of the spare halls, a guard watching them as always.

"Mehr, you're needed," Kalini said sharply from the doorway. Mehr startled, stumbling. It had been so long since she'd last seen Kalini.

"And me?" Amun asked.

"Just your wife," Kalini said. She sounded bored. "Come on now."

Mehr didn't question. She drew her shawl tight over her shoulders and followed Kalini from the room. Kalini was the Maha's favored mystic; what she ordered, the Maha ordered. So Mehr obeyed.

She still cried out, shocked, when Kalini shoved her hard against a wall, hard enough to knock Mehr's skull against stone and make her ears ring.

"*Silence*," Kalini ordered—but it was the blade she held point first to Mehr's neck that truly made Mehr hold her tongue.

Mehr froze, barely daring to breathe. They were too far from the hall for Amun or the other guard to have heard them. Kalini had waited until they were alone, hidden from sight in the nook of a dark corridor, before cornering Mehr with her blade.

"I told you to leave Hema alone," Kalini said. "I told you." Her grip on the blade was steady, her eyes resolute. "You should have listened to me."

The flat of the blade pressed a shade harder against Mehr's skin.

Mehr looked Kalini hard in the eyes, not blinking, never letting her gaze waver. This was an awful thing. Another awful thing, on top of so many others. Frankly, Mehr had had her fill of them. So she stared into Kalini's eyes and did not flinch from what she saw in front of her. Kalini was hard and full of hatred, and she wanted to kill Mehr. There was nothing Mehr could do to stop her.

But Mehr was not afraid. She didn't have the strength for fear any longer. Even that had been rubbed away, leaving her bare and empty and silent inside.

"I'm sorry," Mehr said, her voice quiet but even. "I should have listened to you. But what will you do to me now?"

"Isn't it obvious?" Kalini said. Her voice was flat. "Foolish girl."

"I understand the significance of the knife at my throat," said Mehr. "What I don't understand is who you want to punish. If you want to punish me, then murdering me is hardly worthwhile." She thought of Hema's death, of the agony of the Maha's soul beneath her skin, of the dark night and the endless litany of prayers and dance that there was no escape from anymore. She thought of Amun's voice, when he'd told her that he'd thought of taking his own life. She held that despair close and let it shine through her eyes, so Kalini could see it, *believe* it. "My life is a nightmare, sister. Release me from it, and my spirit will thank you. It is the Maha who will be hurt. Hurt by your betrayal, and by the loss of one more Amrithi." Mehr smiled, a hard smile. "You must know we're a finite resource. You procured me, after all."

"Don't speak of the Maha," hissed Kalini, wildness in her eyes. "You foul his name with your mouth."

"Kill me if you want to punish him," Mehr went on doggedly. "Kill me if you want to hurt your God and your Empire. Don't let yourself believe you'll be punishing me, Kalini. I will die *thanking* you."

"You liar," Kalini said, vicious, eyes wet. "You viper."

Mehr leaned forward, a calculated risk. She felt the blade nick her skin but didn't waver.

"Do it," she said. "Or don't. I no longer care."

Kalini didn't move for a very, very long time. Finally her hand began to tremble. She dropped her blade.

"Rot in your cage, then," Kalini said. She spat in Mehr's face. "I hope she haunts you. I'll pray for it when the next storm falls. Glory to the Empire and my sister's blood on your soul." Her lower lip began to tremble. *"Animal."*

Kalini snatched up her blade and strode away. Mehr waited until she'd vanished, then sucked in a shaky breath and wiped the saliva from her face.

When she returned to the training hall, Amun paused his practice, one hand still upraised in the shape of a rite. There was a question in his eyes.

"You were quick," he said.

"Kalini was called away," Mehr said with a shrug, conscious of the guard watching them. "I suppose I wasn't needed after all."

Mehr saw some of the tension ease in Amun's shoulders. His eyes softened. He thought she'd been saved from the Maha's presence. He thought she'd returned to him safe and sound.

The way he feared for her made her heart hurt. She smiled at him, pushing away the memory of Kalini's blade. She hadn't been afraid then. She wouldn't let the fear touch her now either. She would stay clean and empty and pure, and save them both from hurt.

"Come, Mehr," he said, holding his hands out to her. She took them. "We can practice a little longer, then."

She didn't tell Amun. Perhaps she should have. But when they returned to their room, he lit the oil lanterns except one, then turned to the divan and began determinedly tugging off the bedding. She watched him, silently bemused.

"Amun," she said slowly. "What are you doing?"

"Could I have your shawl?"

She handed it to him and watched as he used it to knot the blanket to the divan, hooking the other end to the edge of the unused lantern hook. "I don't understand what you're doing," she said.

He looked at her, his dark eyes still so very soft.

"We're building a tent," he said.

"No, you're building a tent. I'm just watching." A beat. "*Why* are you building a tent?"

"For fun, Mehr." Very seriously, he beckoned her closer. "Come in here. Bring the pillows in with you."

"You're ridiculous," Mehr said. But she did as he asked.

Inside the makeshift tent the light of the lanterns was softened to a glow. Mehr could see nothing but Amun's silhouette. She curled up on the pillows next to him. "I did something like this with my sister once," she said. "We pretended we were in our own little house. She played mother."

"And you?"

"I was the baby, of course." Mehr had done so many ridiculous things when Arwa was small, just to make her little sister laugh. "Children like to play pretend. I humored her."

"Just like you're humoring me?"

"Exactly like that." She placed her fingers on Amun's sleeve. "What are we doing, exactly?"

"Playing pretend. Pretending we're somewhere else." He took her hand, threaded his fingers with her own. "Somewhere out in the desert, perhaps."

It was a nice idea. Mehr wanted to allow herself to believe the illusion, to think they were out under the cool star-flecked night sky, in a tent all their own. But she couldn't.

"We're too old to be so foolish," Mehr said sharply. "We are where we are. We can't change that."

"We can't," he agreed. "But we can put aside the burden for a little while."

"I didn't think you were the sort to lie to yourself." The words were harsh, and Mehr regretted them as soon as she'd spoken.

But Amun didn't tense, didn't grow defensive. Instead he made a soft hum of agreement. He released her hand and brushed a hand through her hair, traced the line of her jaw, until his thumb came to rest against the edge of her lips.

"I never see you smile anymore," Amun said.

"I smiled earlier."

"I know what a real smile looks like, Mehr."

Mehr pursed her lips. "I never see you smile either."

"I'm solemn by nature," Amun said, and oh, he *was* smiling now. She could hear it in his voice. "You are—"

"What?"

"Not," Amun finished. "Not solemn."

Mehr said nothing. She could almost feel Amun's smile fading away. His hand moved away from her jaw. "You don't sleep well either. I know."

"I don't have many reasons to smile anymore," Mehr said softly. "You know that. I can't help it."

"I know. But I'm asking you to try to put your burden down. Just for a little while." He was warm and close. He took her hand again. "Mehr."

There was so much in his voice, in the gentle way he spoke her name, like the world was suspended inside it.

"I suppose it feels like we're somewhere else," Mehr said grudgingly. "A little."

Amun laughed softly, and Mehr felt herself melt.

Their mouths met, and Mehr felt that light inside herself again—that brightness that had built inside her when they'd kissed, on that awful night of blood and darkness. She felt the emptiness inside her ease, just slightly.

She didn't know how this light would survive their future. But for now she didn't need to know. She just needed to feel the stubble on Amun's cheek beneath her fingertips. She just needed this make-believe, this man, and the dream of somewhere else.

The storm was coming, and there was training to be done. Training that was made infinitely more difficult by the constant presence of a rotating selection of mystics on watch duty, marking their every mistake or success for the Maha's attention. Mehr was grateful for the reprieve offered by a visit to the scholars' tower.

Edhir was there in the tower, bent over one of his spheres covered in golden dials. Mehr watched him work, turning each dial in painful increments, comparing his movements to the near incomprehensible lines and numbers on the charts unfurled on the table in front of him. He looked tired and thin.

Mehr knew that her and Amun's failure in the last storm had had consequences for all of the Maha's obedient servants.

"Three days," he said to Amun tersely. "Usually you'd get more notice, but this time things are moving—differently from usual." He scowled at the sphere in front of him, as if its numbers and dials had betrayed him.

"Not very accurately put," one scholar mystic piped up, disapproving. "A day is hardly a precise measure."

"Accurate enough for them to understand, though," Edhir said, annoyed. Disdain dripped from his voice. He hunched his shoulders and pointedly did not look at Mehr or Amun. "Can you leave me be, now? I'm busy."

Amun tilted his head in acknowledgment, then turned to leave. Mehr followed after him.

She'd heard Edhir talk so to Amun before, but now she understood she too was included in that disdain. It stung, but only a little. It was not as if Mehr wanted to risk friendship any longer. She'd learned the consequences of that.

It was no surprise when the Maha sent a messenger demanding their presence for dinner that evening. Amun had been tense
before the summons but was even more so after it. He stalked
around their room like a caged animal as Mehr went through
the motions of getting dressed, brushing her hair back into a
braid, tightening the sash of her tunic around her waist.

"I won't be able to manage him," he said. "Not anymore.
Mehr, you'll have to be careful with him. He's very—"

"Angry," Mehr cut in. "I know." She tightened her sash an
increment further. All her clothes were overlarge now. "We'll
be fine," she said, trying to sound sure of herself. "Besides, I'm
not afraid."

"You don't need to lie to me, Mehr."

"But I'm not," Mehr said. In fact, this at least was true: She felt
nothing at all. She didn't feel strong or brave either. Ever since
receiving the summons, Mehr had felt numb, as if her emotions
were a limb starved of blood. "Don't worry for me, Amun. I'll
manage. Just make sure you don't anger him. I don't want to see
you harmed either."

Amun looked into her eyes, a curious, searching look on his
face. Mehr looked right back at him. *I never see you smile*, he'd
said to her. He knew her face, read it just as easily as she was able
to read the curl of his hands, the slump or rise of his shoulders.
What did he see in her face now?

Whatever he saw, he didn't question her any further. He kept
close to her side as they walked to the Maha's chambers, his
warm solidity a comfort Mehr hadn't even realized she needed.
It was only when they entered and kneeled on the floor in the
Maha's presence that he stepped away from her, leaving her to
support her own weight.

The meal was as sumptuous as ever. It was ashes in Mehr's
mouth. She kept her head lowered and picked at her food as the
Maha stared down at her silently, a smile playing on his mouth.

She could feel the Maha's eyes on her, burning and constant. When Amun tried to speak and draw his attention away, the Maha made a dismissive noise and waved a hand in Amun's direction.

"There's no need for you to speak," he said, his voice all mild benevolence. "Sit quietly, Amun. Eat your food. There's a good boy."

Amun didn't say a word after that, and Mehr did not raise her head. She thought of the sticky, sweet nuts and dates Hema had brought her to eat. She hoped the Maha would not force her to eat more than she had. She couldn't stomach it.

The Maha stood. Mehr didn't have time to tense before she felt his hand winding the long weight of her braid into a leash and tugging her head back. She winced, clenched her teeth hard to hold all noise in.

"You know I don't like it when you avoid my eyes," he said disapprovingly.

She looked up at him. Was it her imagination, or had the fractures in his eyes deepened? "I am sorry, Maha," she said.

"You must learn to do better, my dear," he said. "You will do better, won't you? You won't fail me this storm?"

"No, Maha."

His grip tightened, one torturous increment. "I'm not sure I believe you."

"I am bound." She raised a hand slowly. Touched her fingertips to her chest, where her marriage seal sat over the sigil that bound her. "You trained me yourself, Maha. And I have learned my place."

"And what is your place?"

"I am a conduit to your will. A tool." A beat. "I share my husband's service, wholly and completely. Please believe me, Maha."

It was the pleading he had wanted, really. Satisfied, he finally released her.

"Keep eating," he ordered, offhandedly. "You'll need your strength to perform for me later. I want to see how far you've both come."

Mehr returned to the task of picking at bread with one hand, her scalp stinging and sore.

That night she dreamed of the desert. Not of a tent under the stars, not of Amun lying by her side with the warm glow of lantern light on them both, but of cold sand, sharp as glass, beneath her feet, and the moon fat and glaring in the black sky.

There was a woman standing before her, with a long ragged veil concealing her face, its gnawed edges brushing the sand. There was a ring of spreading darkness around her. Mehr knew what that darkness was. She'd seen blood before.

Kalini had said she'd pray for Hema to haunt Mehr, and for a long moment Mehr was sure she'd gained her wish. But when Mehr collapsed down on the sand, heavy with the weight of her own sadness, the blood bloomed into red flowers at her knees. She reached out her fingers—reached out all hesitant and wondrous and *hoping* for something beautiful—and the flowers reached back, twining around her wrists, lifting her hands a gentle increment higher.

I remember this, Mehr thought. Not the flowers. But the feel of her wrists being taken in an inhuman grip, being raised, as the daiva that had cornered her so long ago in the desert had tried to shape her hands into words—

She woke, sharp and sudden, breathing in air as sweet as incense. Amun's hand was on her shoulder, his voice in her ear. He must have been trying to wake her.

"I can smell it," Mehr gasped out. "The storm."

"Yes," Amun said. His hand was still on her shoulder, soft and steady. "Not long now."

CHAPTER TWENTY-SIX

There was very little time for the usual preparations. The mystics attended their fervent prayers, all other tasks forgotten. Bahren came for Mehr and Amun, a dagger at hand. It was time, again, to mark the temple windows and doorways with their blood. Mehr was obedient enough, but inside she was cold. She had no room for emotions, for the terror threatening to creep over her. She had to be strong. And for that, she had to avoid feeling anything at all. She couldn't think of the nightmares uncurling beyond those blood-marked windows. She couldn't think of the way they'd seeped into her own dreams, ragged veils and flowers and all.

She moved through the day in a daze. Practiced when she was told to practice. Ate when she was told to eat. There was no cooking done, with the storm so close, as all the mystics were spared from their usual tasks for the vital service of prayer. Amun scavenged bread from the kitchen and urged her to share it with him. He broke everything in neat halves, placed bread and palmfuls of seeds into her hands. Mehr ate the food and tried not to think of how much she had hoped this storm would be the opportunity for her and Amun to break their bonds and escape the Maha's service. All those hopes felt so far away now. She tried not to think about how she would make it through the storm at all.

Last time, her weak bond with the Maha had allowed the night-mares of the sleeping Gods to break free, to resist the demands of the Maha for the Empire's unnatural fortune and his own equally unnatural longevity, enacted through Mehr and Amun's speaking flesh. But now she was vow-bound. She would allow the prayers of the mystics and the Maha's will to bend those sleepers' dreams. There would be no room for nightmares. And yet...

Like always, like she had to, she folded the fear away, away, until she was entirely numb.

Amun watched her with intent, careful eyes. But he said noth-ing about the state of her, and for that Mehr would be grateful later, she was sure.

He wasn't the only one watching. Even with the preparation for the storm at its peak, the Maha ensured that there were guards on both of them, watching them for disobedience or weakness.

The day came as fast as expected. The mystics prayed and prayed, and Mehr and Amun did what they were expected to do. They went to prepare. She took out the wooden flowered beads to string through her hair. The fanned trousers, the tunic soft, color washed away by age. She laid them out on the divan and stared at them. She could be strong. She could—

"Mehr." There was a thread of worry in Amun's voice that tugged at her like a physical thing wound up beneath her breastbone.

She didn't want him to worry. So she smiled at him, even though she knew already that he would see right through her, that he knew her face as well as she knew the way he carried his emotions in his hands, his spine, the line of his shoulders. She smiled not to show him she was happy—he was no fool, her Amun—but to show him that she was still strong, still iron-willed, and the fear hadn't broken her yet.

"Hush, Amun. I'll be well when this is all over." She swal-lowed. "We'll both be well when the storm is done."

Amun shook his head, and Mehr raised hers sharply. She looked at him, forcing herself to see through the haze of her own pain. She saw the shadows under his eyes, the furrowed line of worry between them. She walked over to him and reached up, rising a little onto her tiptoes so that she could smooth the crease away with the flat of her thumb.

Amun's mouth parted, just a little. They were so close to one another. She couldn't help but feel the pull of his dark eyes, remember the softness of his mouth. Her thumb fell to touch his lower lip. She felt the warmth of his breath.

A jolt of awareness ran through her.

This man. This man is mine. And I am his.

She dropped her arm to her side. "I need to bathe," she said, her voice hoarse. "We're running out of time."

She went to the bathing room, undressed, and kneeled down so she could pour clear, cold water over her hair. She had to let go of the jittery energy that hummed inside her. She needed the numbness back. Instead she was alive inside—as bright and fierce as the storm building and building beyond the temple walls. But the brightness had nothing to do with the dreamfire, and everything to do with the softness of Amun's mouth.

She heard a sound. Looked up.

Amun was there.

It was as if her thoughts had conjured him, with his soft mouth and his dark eyes, and his hair that curled just a little at the ends. He stood in the doorway, not moving. Just looking at her.

"Mehr." The way he whispered her name—oh.

Mehr stood, and beckoned him in.

There was no holy sweetness this time. It was hunger that brought their mouths and their bodies together. In the quiet of the bathing room, all Mehr could hear was his breath as he took her long dark hair into his hands, as she rose onto her tiptoes and fanned her fingers out against his shoulders to draw him closer.

"Don't slip," he murmured against her lips. "The floor—"

"I know you can hold me up," Mehr murmured back.

He could. He raised her up in his arms, and she held on to him, trusting him with her weight. It was a dance of a kind: her legs wrapping around his waist, his arms holding her steady against the wall, their bodies meeting. She remembered the weightlessness she'd experienced when she'd first learned the Rite of the Bound, the terror she'd felt. She felt no terror now. She trusted him too much for that.

She felt like she was flying.

After, they washed each other clean. She laughed a little when Amun poured water over her hair. "It's cold," she said.

"Sorry."

Amun worked the tangles from her hair, fingers ever so gentle.

"I made vows to you, Mehr," he said. "And you made vows to me."

"I did. You did."

He turned her and lifted her face to his, mouths almost touching. "I vowed to hold our vows above all others. To love you above all others. To belong to you, if I belong to anyone." There was a curious urgency in his voice. "Remember that."

"I will," she whispered, and kissed him. How could she possibly forget?

They dressed in their Amrithi garb. Amun threaded wooden flowers through her braid. She smudged kohl around his eyes when he closed them and stayed still beneath her fingers, trusting her utterly.

Mehr could hear the howling of the storm draw closer. Armed mystics met them at the bottom of the stairs. Even from here, even with the storm howling, Mehr could hear the thrum of their prayers. She heard them like they were drumming inside her skull.

She was their vessel, after all. She was a tool for bringing those prayers to life, for enacting the Maha's desires in the form of a rite, so that the dreams of the Gods would be compelled to obedience. It was heresy, but not one Mehr could avoid or resist.

The Maha was with her. The mystics were with her. She couldn't outrun them. But Amun was with her too. He took her hand and walked with her, strong and steady at her side. They would survive together. She had to believe that.

They walked out into the light.

The air glowed beautifully. The storm was unlike any she'd seen before, huge and wild and deep, its jeweled light a thousand shards that glimmered like broken glass. The sight of it made Mehr want to stand and simply stare, overwhelmed by its strangeness. It put her guards on edge. The guards—Abhiman among them—tightened their grips on their weapons, watching the surroundings carefully.

Mehr could feel the power of the storm. It was fire in her skin, her bones. She swallowed. It was time. She straightened, bare feet curling in the sand, and tried to slip free from Amun's grip. But his hand was iron on hers, and when she tugged, his grip only seemed to tighten.

She looked up at him sharply. In a movement that was almost imperceptible, he shook his head. *No.*

"We need to be deeper in the storm," he said. His voice was loud but calm. His eyes said, *Trust me.*

"You can perform right here, boy," Abhiman said coldly.

"The storm isn't strong enough here for our needs," Amun said.

He was lying. Mehr could feel the strength of the storm like a weight draped over her shoulders. She was shaking beneath it. All he had to do was let go of her, and the storm would swallow them both. Why was he lying?

What are you up to, Amun?

She didn't ask. She waited.

"The Maha wants you to stay close," Abhiman said, mouth thinned. "Those were his orders."

"The Maha knows we have a task to perform, and that we can be trusted."

"Can you?"

"Emperor's grace, we wear our loyalty in our skin," Mehr snapped. "Isn't that enough? Let us do what we've been ordered to do, or may the Maha's mercy for your error when we cannot serve be swift."

There was some muttered counsel, as Abhiman's eyes narrowed and he turned to his fellow mystics for assistance. They didn't have time to seek the Maha's permission. The storm would soon reach its peak.

"Go, then," Abhiman said, gesturing. "Fan out," he snapped to the others.

The mystics moved slowly, not quite keeping up to Mehr and Amun's faster pace. They weren't at ease in the storm. The whirling sand was gold and red, rose-ash and fire, turning the mystics into shadows, and Amun had still not let go of her hand.

"Mehr," he said. "Can you hear me?"

The storm was wailing around them now, a loud and mournful cry, but she could. "I can," said Mehr. "Amun, what are you *doing*?"

"I made vows to you. Remember, what did I promise?"

"Amun—"

"*Please.* I need you to remind me." His voice was suddenly raw, wild. She bit her lip and held his hand tighter in return.

"To love me. To be kind to me. Amun, what are you—"

He released her, only to take hold of her again, her upper arms in the vise of his grip, her feet barely touching the sand as his grip and the wind-lashed fire held her aloft. It should have hurt, should have scared her, but his eyes were dark and soft and she was helpless, weightless.

"I vowed to give you a good life, Mehr. I promised you. I can't forget that vow, Mehr. Can't forget, and so—I have to try. Please understand."

"Stop begging me," Mehr whispered, uncomprehending. "It doesn't suit you."

"I love you," Amun said, as if he couldn't, wouldn't, hear her. "And I can see that this life will erase you. I can see it happening already—"

"Boy," barked Abhiman. "Get on with it."

Amun flinched but didn't stop. "I've felt it happen to me. But you—you make me feel like a whole person again. I can never thank you enough. But I can try. *Try.*" He squeezed his eyes shut tight. Opened them. His sigils were burning so very bright.

"What are you doing?" Abhiman demanded, yelling as the sand whirled around them, higher and higher. He snarled an oath, only the words *disobedient* and *Maha* audible to Mehr's ears, and strode toward them.

"Remember, you vowed to trust me," Amun whispered. "And run."

When Abhiman touched his shoulder, Amun turned and struck. He wrenched Abhiman's scimitar from his grip with one hand and slammed his fist into Abhiman's face with the other. Abhiman crumpled instantly. He didn't even have time to defend himself. Amun took hold of the scimitar in a two-handed grip, shoulders squared, feet planted hard against the ground as if he were performing the first steps of a rite. He was panting. His sigils were bright, bright fire on his skin. Mehr felt her own mark flare, livid with the pain of disobedience.

The other mystics yelled, swords drawn. They began to run over. And Mehr was—frozen.

"*Run!*" Amun yelled. "I'll hold them off!"

"I can't," Mehr yelled back wildly. Shocked still. "My vows to the Maha—"

"You made vows to me! Not him." He doubled forward, letting out an audible groan of agony. He held on to the scimitar for dear life. "So run and be free for both of us. Mehr, *go.*"

The mystics were closing in. But Amun was drawing the scimitar in an arc through the air one-handed, shaping sigils with the other. She felt the tug of dreamfire following his call, watched as a wall of sand flared up into the air, as jagged as glass, keeping the mystics temporarily at bay.

They had practiced that sigil together, when they'd first decided to defy the Maha and use the storm to set themselves free. Mehr had set that hope aside.

But Amun clearly hadn't.

"*Run!*" His voice was scratched raw with pain.

Everything in Mehr screamed at her to stay where she was. Her soul was bound. She had a duty, a calling. Like it or not, she wore a cage in her skin, and it kept her at the Maha's face. And Amun—oh.

Amun.

She could not leave him to suffer alone. She knew it was wrong.

But Gods help her, Amun was screaming at her, telling her to go, to be free for the both of them, and Mehr had to try. So she drew all her meager courage around her, sand stinging her eyes, her chest burning as if a coal had been shoved between her ribs, and turned. And ran.

She ran as the sand turned smooth and slick beneath her feet. She ran as the storm grew and grew, reaching its apex. She felt the tug of her vows grow and grow, setting its thorns deep into her skin. The sand was smooth, but she felt as if she were running on broken glass. Her mouth was full of the taste of blood. Every vein of her body, every beat of her heart, told her she should turn back. The mystics were praying, and their prayers were inside her. The Maha's soul was inside her.

She had vows. She had to obey them.

Your vows are to Amun, a voice inside her said. And it was true, a true voice, a true thing. She had married him first, before the Maha had marked her. And even after that, even after the vows had been twisted into chains, they had made new promises to one another. Promises sealed in flesh, in tears, in love.

Those promises had been greater than all the rest. Even as the Maha's chains burned inside her, she felt the truth of that— clean, sharp as a blade, cutting her free.

She'd vowed to trust Amun, so she did. She ran and ran, ran until the storm swallowed her, until she was flying, until everything was light.

CHAPTER TWENTY-SEVEN

The nightmares were following her. They drifted after her under the cover of the dreamfire's light, their brittle bodies skittering along, their flat, lidless eyes watching her. She didn't have to look back to know they were there. When she'd stumbled she'd felt their fingers reach inside her skull, settling darkness inside her. So she ran faster. Around her the dreamfire grew wilder and wilder still, its howls a cry of fury.

In the dark inside her own mind, Mehr saw Amun and nothing but Amun, his sigils livid, his face warped with pain. Her own scarred chest ached. If she closed her eyes she could see the vow tying them, golden and strong. If she let it, it would lead her right back to him.

But she wouldn't go back. Amun had asked her to run, and she would. She had.

Eventually she stopped running. She kneeled down on the ground, hands flat against the sand, and struggled to breathe. The nightmares had faded bodily behind her, but Mehr could still feel their darkness clawing at her skull, threatening to drown her. She breathed shallowly, and oh so carefully pushed the fear away.

Beneath her the sand rippled softly, like water.

Her fear was not misleading her. She was sure now.

The storm was wrong.

Mehr had danced with the dreamfire enough to know what it was supposed to feel like. This storm was far too fierce, far too bright. It was as if the storm had thinned the wall between the world of spirit and the world of flesh, bringing the Gods and their fury close to the surface of the world.

She had not danced the rite. Amun had not danced the rite. The Gods were dreaming around her, dreaming freely, for the first time in centuries. Their nightmares crept around her, within her, their rage made brittle flesh. The world around her—sand, sky—wavered around, fragile and weak as glass.

Mehr lowered her head to the ground. Tears stung at her eyes. She cried because she was tired and she was afraid. She cried because she had left Amun behind. *Breathe*, she thought. *Breathe. Be strong. Don't stop running yet.*

The world rustled again. She heard the nightmares draw back even farther, skittering under the cover of the light. But it was the silence that followed—deep as the beat of a dream—that made Mehr look up.

A veiled woman sat before her, hands folded primly on her lap, legs crossed neatly under a skirt of voluminous white silk. Her veil fluttered in the breeze of the storm; beneath the thin mesh of cloth her eyes were the only features that were visible. They glowed with the steady constancy of prayer flames.

It took Mehr's fevered mind a moment to realize the woman was no woman after all.

Daiva.

The daiva looked more human than any daiva Mehr had ever seen before. Its shadowy hands, clasped so neatly in its lap, were utterly mortal in shape, with fine nails and creases at the knuckles. Only its eyes revealed its true nature. Its eyes reminded her of the ancient daiva she had seen in the desert so long ago. She wondered if it was the same daiva after all, all its billowing edges transformed into the neatness of the human form.

The daiva gazed at her tranquilly, its candle-flame eyes flickering. There was no urgency in it.

She had never seen a truly ancient daiva, only had heard people speak of them in hushed, fearful whispers, in tales of time long gone. Perhaps this ancient one had come to take her, to carry her away to the place beyond the sand where the Gods slept. Perhaps it had come to grant her peace. More likely, it had come to exact the suffering she deserved for all the heresies, large and small, that she'd committed in the Maha's service, and to save herself from it. The thought should not have comforted her, and yet somehow it did. An end. At least it would be an end.

Mehr raised a hand to touch her chest. She touched her seal, Amun's seal, hanging on frayed thread. She touched her scar, which was livid and aching. The screaming inside her, the sound of the Maha trying to draw her back to servitude, had quieted. But it was still there. The pain was a sign, at least, that she was still alive.

The daiva raised a hand, carefully mirroring her movement. Then it slowly uncurled its fingers and held them out to her. Mehr was reminded, ridiculously, of the little bird-daiva that had rustled its wispy wings on Arwa's window ledge. Just as she'd known what the bird-daiva wanted from her, she knew what this daiva wanted too.

"I have no knife," Mehr said. Her voice was nothing but a rasp, thin and tired. She shaped her hands into the sigil for *blood*, drawing her left hand back in a negation.

The daiva held still for a moment. Its little finger twitched. Then in a quicksilver motion it moved, darting across the sand until its hand was a hairsbreadth from Mehr's cheek. She barely stopped herself from flinching. It was only then that she realized she'd been weeping.

"You want my tears?" she asked, uncomprehending.

The daiva waited, watching her with its soft flame eyes. It did not move.

Tears were not blood. They were not the sacrifice of the knife, the reminder of shared blood and an old, old vow passed from progenitor to progeny. What could the daiva want with tears?

"Why?" Mehr asked. She bit her tongue, suddenly angry with herself. She tried to raise her hands, to speak respectfully in the daiva's language, but it was already leaning back, shaping sigils with quick fingers.

Flesh. Blood. Tears. A fist held to the daiva's chest. *Heart.*

The daiva shaped a circle, cinched with a flourish by fingers shaping a knot. Mehr knew that sigil. It was the sigil for that which could be made, but couldn't be broken.

Vow.

Mehr nodded.

"Take my tears, then," Mehr whispered. "I hope they are as good as blood to you." She shaped the sigil for *gift*, laboriously, afraid her suddenly trembling hands would fail her.

But she needn't have been afraid. The daiva leaned forward again, catching her tears on a fingertip. It held the hand in front of it as if marveling at it.

Gift, it echoed back at her.

Mehr felt the world shift again, sand reshaping beneath her. The storm howled fiercely, falling low upon them. She saw the veil flutter again, and the daiva reached out as if to hold her.

There was nothing after that.

Mehr woke up with the pale dawn sunlight beginning to pour across the sand.

The storm still swirled around her, dying as the sun rose. Through falling wisps of jeweled light she could see the horizon, set against a flat expanse of desert. Wherever she was, her feet and the storm had carried her a long way from the temple.

She climbed to her feet, scraping sand off her face. She was tired and thirsty, and the scar of her marriage seal hurt terribly. She touched a hand to it and felt a sudden, sharp pain run through her entire body. She heard the shadow of Amun's voice in her ear again, all bitten-off agony and desperation.

Run, Mehr!

She snatched her hand away. Mehr would have wept again, if she'd had the strength. Instead she covered her own face with her hands and breathed. And breathed.

The vows she'd made to Amun, when they'd held each other and hungered through the dark night, had been sacred things. They'd been vows of flesh and blood and heart, vows made for mortals with daiva blood, but they had been vows of hope too. Amun had risked everything for the sake of that hope.

Amun had saved her.

Mehr lowered her hands. She looked at the desert around her. She could feel the pain still, a constant tug between her ribs. If she followed it she would find her way back to him. She wondered if he could feel that bond in return, that knot like a circle without an end.

"I'm here, Amun," she said, speaking into the air. "I'm here. Look what you've done. You've managed a miracle. You've set me free." She took a step into the pain. Another. "I don't know what made you take the risk. But Gods help me, I'm glad you did."

It was hard to resist the urge to walk back to him. She thought of him still in the grips of the Maha, surrounded by mystics who hated him, crushed by the vows to her he'd obeyed and the vows to the Maha he'd defied. She took hold of her marriage seal, holding the circle tight in her hands. Then she gathered up her will and forced herself to turn away from the way back to him.

"Wait for me," she whispered. "Survive, Amun. I'll come back for you. Somehow, I will."

That day, Mehr used the lessons she'd learned from her first journey from Jah Irinah to the Maha's temple. When the sun was nearing its peak, she sought out shade and slept in snatches. When she grew thirsty, she used a little strength and performed the Rite of Fruitful Earth, snatching new green life from the earth, eating it fast to catch its moisture. She tried not to think about what she would do when true thirst and hunger inevitably came for her. She'd spent so much of her time at the Maha's temple preparing for survival after her escape, and now all her careful planning had gone to waste.

The desert hadn't been like this when she'd first traveled through it with the mystics. The sands had been clear and arid under a glaring blue sky. Now, with the storm still spinning, dying away, every surface seemed to be a trickery woven out of shadows and light. She couldn't trust her senses. More than once, she found herself walking in circles, drawn back to where she'd been hours earlier by the movement of the sand.

The storm had misled her so utterly that when she saw the shadow of a man through the dust, she thought it was no more than another mirage and kept on trudging forward. Then the shadow stepped forward into the light, boots crunching against the ground, and she realized the man was no illusion after all.

The man froze when he saw her. Under the hood of his robe his eyes widened visibly in his deep brown Amrithi face. He hadn't expected Mehr any more than she'd expected him.

Mehr moved first. She turned, breaking into a run. More figures emerged from the air around her. Until that moment, their brown robes had hidden them from sight. She stopped sharply, realizing with despair that she was surrounded. There was nowhere to go.

"Don't harm me," she said, holding her hands out, palms open. "I have no weapons."

Her words didn't stop them from drawing their own blades. The man who had first seen her strode up to her and held his dagger a hairsbreadth from her throat.

"How did you find us?" he demanded.

Mehr swallowed back her fear and said, carefully, "I'm sorry. I didn't intend to be here. The storm led me astray."

"Do you expect me to believe that?" The man's eyes narrowed. "Tell me who you are, or so help me—"

"Stop. Lower the dagger, Kamal."

That voice. Mehr knew that voice.

"But, Lalita—"

"Lower it."

As the blade lowered, Mehr turned her head. And Gods above, it was Lalita after all. Lalita was striding toward her, hood lowered. Her robe was faded, her dark hair loose over her shoulders. There was silver in her hair, no paint on her lips and no kohl around her eyes, but there she was, undeniably alive and whole.

"Oh, my dear one," Lalita said. Her voice trembled with joy. "What are you doing here?"

This had to be a dream—a mirage. But the pain in her chest, the ache in her feet, told her this was all too real. Lalita was here. Lalita was well.

"I thought you were dead," Mehr said, in a voice that trembled like a leaf. "I went to your haveli and I thought…"

"No, no," Lalita said, shaking her head. "I am sorry you saw that, so very sorry, Mehr. But I'm safe." Her eyes were bright with unshed tears. She managed a smile. "You didn't come here to find me, did you?"

"No," Mehr said softly.

"Look at her clothes," Kamal said in a low voice. "She's come from the temple."

Lalita was still looking into Mehr's eyes, her face full of wonder. She barely seemed to hear him. "That isn't possible."

"Perhaps you can't see what stands in front of you, but I see one of the Maha's creatures."

Lalita laughed faintly. "Mehr's father is Ambhan," she said. "She doesn't have the gift. The Maha would hardly trouble himself with her."

It was astonishing, how love could blind someone. Lalita was looking right at her, and yet Mehr had a sense that Lalita was not seeing her at all, that hope and love had reshaped Mehr in her eyes into someone softer, someone safer to love. Perhaps that was why she had never warned Mehr about *amata*, or sensed the gift that lay under Mehr's skin. Perhaps some part of Lalita had sensed the truth and shied away from the knowledge, far too aware that the only future that awaited most *amata*-gifted women lay at the end of a knife.

Mehr swallowed. "Lalita," she said. "Look at me."

Mehr's voice finally dispelled the wonder in Lalita's eyes. She took another step closer to Mehr, her gaze sharpening, taking in the sight of Mehr's faded clothing, her gauntness. Finally, her gaze settled on the marriage seal around Mehr's neck. Her mouth thinned.

"I'm sorry, Lalita," Mehr said quietly. "But I do. Have the gift. When the dreamfire came to the city, it showed itself. And the Maha, he..." She paused. Touched the edge of her seal. "He found me."

"She's been sent here to trap us," Kamal said, more loudly now. "I'm sure of it."

There were uneasy murmurs from the circle around them. She saw hands move back to their blades. For a long, painful moment, Lalita was silent.

Finally, Lalita spoke up. "Mehr is telling the truth. She has a good heart. I trust her completely."

"She belongs to the Maha," Kamal said. "She doesn't have a choice. Do you?"

"I'm not bound to the Maha any longer." A ripple of utter disbelief ran through the Amrithi at that, but Mehr held on to her courage and rallied on. "I don't expect you to believe me or—trust me. I don't. But I am not his property, and I am not subject to his whims. I'd never let harm come to my mother's people." She spoke fiercely, pushing her heart into every word, hoping he would believe her. "*Never.* But you needn't believe me. Just let me go, and I'll bring you no more trouble."

"Let you go so you can lead the monster directly to us?" Kamal said angrily. "We're not fools, girl. We've not survived this long by being half-wits."

Mehr laughed. She couldn't help it.

"Lead him where?" She raised her hands helplessly into the air. "I don't know where I am! Even now, I can't see a thing through the storm." She shook her head. "I have lived my entire life in the city. I know nothing of navigating in the desert."

"How can we trust your word?" Kamal said, just as Lalita snapped, "You think I'll let you wander off after a statement like that? You'll die out here on your own."

"Be sensible," Kamal said. "Think with your head, Lalita."

"I could say the same to you!"

A figure on the edge of the circle yanked their hood away from their face and said, "Must we watch you argue all day? Let her go, kill her, bring her with us—we don't care."

"*No one is killing her,*" Lalita said sharply.

"That's good to hear," Mehr said faintly, but no one was listening to her.

"Fine, fine, no killing. But..." Kamal raised a hand to his head, massaging the groove between his eyes as if the entire situation pained him physically. "A blindfold. We'll walk her away and let her go. That's all I can offer, Lalita, and far more than I should."

Lalita shook her head, mouth pursed.

"We can't let her go."

"She's the Maha's creature."

"Maha's creature or not, she's Ruhi's daughter."

That stopped him short. He gave Mehr an unreadable look, then drew his hood down over his face and walked abruptly away.

Lalita took Mehr by the shoulders.

"Ah, Mehr," she said, her voice choked. "I am so sorry, dear one. If I had known, I would have warned you."

"It isn't your fault," Mehr said gently. She touched Lalita's shoulder in return. Behind Lalita, she could see the Amrithi watching her with wary eyes.

"There is a place—an outpost—near here. You'll be safe there for now."

Mehr nodded, slowly. Then she said, "Lalita. Why did you mention my mother's name?" Mehr asked.

"Because Kamal—the others—they belong to her clan, Mehr." Lalita said the words gently enough, but they still dropped through Mehr like a stone. "Your mother is here."

CHAPTER TWENTY-EIGHT

Perhaps the veiled daiva hadn't been there to take her to her final rest after all. Trudging after the Amrithi, blinded with a cloth that Lalita had tied carefully around Mehr's eyes, Mehr only knew for certain that the ancient had been a harbinger of a great change in fortune. After months of living to a set routine of prayer and rites and service, her life free from the Maha's control was a whirlwind, a storm within a storm. She felt adrift. Only Lalita's hand on her arm, gently guiding her forward, kept her tethered.

"We're here," Lalita said. She didn't say where, or what, *here* was. But Mehr heard the heavy rustle of cloth, felt the ground change from giving sand to the firmness of pinned fabric, and knew they had entered a tent even before Lalita removed the blindfold from her eyes.

The tent was a low construction, barely tall enough for Mehr to stand without stooping. Its fabric was the same dun color as the world around it. It was likely easily concealed; from a distance, it probably looked like no more than an eddy of sand. It was a clever construction, but clearly not the home of all the Amrithi. It was barely larger than the tent she'd slept in, alongside Amun, on her journey to the temple.

She and Lalita were alone now, although Mehr suspected Kamal was still waiting just beyond the tent entrance. Lalita sat cross-legged on the floor, and Mehr sat across from her. Lalita pulled a skin of water from her robes and offered it to Mehr, who drank the warm water in careful sips, trying not to gulp it down greedily as she wanted to.

Lalita watched Mehr drinking for a moment, then began to speak. In a quiet, measured voice she told Mehr how she'd come to be in the desert with an Amrithi clan. She told Mehr that the restless nobility, stirred up by the Emperor's missives, had become suspicious of her. Even though Lalita had changed her birth name to a Chand one to hide her origins, even though she had embraced life among Ambhans, the truth of Lalita's origins had made it somehow to their ears.

Lalita had planned to move somewhere else for safety. But nobles who called themselves devotees of the Saltborn had come for her, and she'd been forced into Irinah's deep desert instead. She'd found her way to a place where she had known she would be safe.

"Mehr," Lalita said carefully, hope folded up in her voice. "Do you know—that is, did you see Usha? Is she well?"

Mehr's stomach dropped like a stone.

"I'm sorry," Mehr said, her voice soft. "I am so sorry, Lalita. The mystics killed her."

Grief flitted across Lalita's face. The hope in her eyes died away. "I should have known," Lalita said. "And yet, I hoped..." She swallowed, holding her grief back. "I hoped she had escaped somehow."

"On the night of the storm, I was looking for you," Mehr said. "I walked through the dreamfire, and I asked it to help me find you. I begged it..." She trailed off, squeezing her eyes shut, embarrassed at her past naïveté. "It brought me to Usha. I was with her at the end, Lalita. She wasn't alone."

"Ah, Mehr, I'm glad of that," Lalita said, her voice thick. "I'll dance a rite for her. A proper death rite. She would have liked that."

"She would have," Mehr agreed.

They sat in silence for a moment, both of them thinking of Usha. Grieving her. Mehr pretended not to notice when Lalita wiped her eyes, slowly calming herself.

"Tell me about my mother," Mehr entreated finally, breaking the silence.

"She'll be here to talk to you soon. You know we were friends once, when she lived in Jah Irinah?" When Mehr nodded, Lalita continued. "When she left, she asked me to watch over you and your sister. So I did. But when I ran, I knew she would take me in. In this clan, your mother is Tara," Lalita said, using the title for an Amrithi clan leader. "She took the mantle when she returned, after her own mother—your own grandmother—passed on."

"Tara," Mehr repeated. Stunned. "I hadn't expected that."

"She'll be very glad to see you, Mehr. Of that, I'm sure. But she will have questions too. We can't truly trust that you're free of the Maha. It isn't a thing that can be done, the breaking of vows." Lalita's voice was gentle, slow, as if she wanted to soften her words. "The vows we make are inviolable. When they are made, they bind forever."

Mehr shook her head. "In my case, the Maha made an error. He couldn't risk the ire of the nobles. To simply take me—my father would have revolted. It would have offended his honor. He realized I could not be bound as Amrithi are, although I have the gifts, without causing fury among the nobles. So he bound me the way Ambhan women are bound: marriage." She heard Lalita's sharp inhale. "He wed me to the last Amrithi he had, whom he'd bound as a child. That man...Amun. Amun is the reason I'm free."

She told Lalita about her life among the mystics: about the endless rote prayers and practice, about the Maha's cruelties, large and small; about Hema's kindness, and Hema's brutal death;

about Amun and the mercy he'd shown her. She spoke until her voice cracked, then stopped to take a sip of water. When she paused she realized how heavy the silence was, and how closely Lalita was hanging on her every word.

Then she began speaking again. There was so much to tell, and the telling was an act like forcing poison from a wound: painful but utterly necessary. She told Lalita, haltingly, that she and Amun had made their own vows to each other. Vows of love and flesh and choice, more sacred than any other vows they'd ever had inflicted upon them. And Amun had known: Amun had risked everything to set Mehr free.

"I ran," Mehr finished, when she had no more words. "In the end I ran, and you know the rest. You found me."

She didn't mention the daiva and her strange fever-dream of its veiled face, its humanness, its hunger for her tears. Somehow, despite the fact that she'd bared her soul to Lalita, the daiva felt like a secret. Even the thought of speaking of it made the words wither on her tongue.

"I want to believe you," Lalita said.

"Do you think I'm lying?" Mehr demanded.

"I think you believe your own words. But trusting that the vows you made to the Maha are shattered—Mehr, it's more than I dare hope for."

Mehr nodded. She couldn't argue with Lalita's belief. She could feel that the vow holding her to the Maha had been cleaved through, just as she could feel the ache of the bond between her and Amun, but these things were invisible to Lalita—to anyone but Mehr herself.

Lalita's gaze was soft with compassion. "I must leave you now," she said. "But your mother will be here soon. Prepare yourself, if you can."

"What is she like?" Mehr asked.

"A great deal like you," Lalita said.

For some reason, Mehr didn't find that particularly comforting.

It was Kamal who entered the tent first, carrying a lantern. He gave Mehr a level look as he settled the lantern on the ground in front of her and moved to sit to her left. His presence felt like a warning. Mehr wasn't to be trusted, not yet, and certainly not with their clan's Tara.

Tara. Mehr's mother. She couldn't quite believe it.

A moment later, a woman entered. The first thing Mehr noticed, as her mother ducked inside, her form half hidden by the shadows thrown by the lantern light, was how unassuming she was. She was average height, dressed in dun-colored robes, her face hidden by her hood. She wasn't dressed in the finery Mehr had come to expect of a leader, and there was nothing proud or regal in her bearing or in the way she looked slowly around the tent, head moving from side to side, before carefully lowering back her hood. She could have been any of the Amrithi who had circled Mehr earlier.

Then she stepped into the lantern light, hood lowered, and Mehr's heart nearly stopped. She was frozen between breaths, looking into the face before her.

Ruhi, her mother, Tara and Amrithi, was not exactly beautiful. Her face lacked the idealized Ambhan delicacy that beauty required. Instead she had the kind of bold looks that caught the eye and held it. Her cheekbones were high, her nose strong, her mouth full; her skin had the richness of soil after rain. There were hints of silver in her curling hair, and fine lines etched around her mouth, but that made the resemblance no less striking.

Mehr had seen her own reflection: in mirrors, in the oasis, in the dreamfire when she had seen through Amun's eyes. But she had never seen herself as clearly as she did in that moment, looking into the face that had shaped her own.

The Tara smiled tentatively. Her eyes were sad.

"Hello, Mehr," said her mother. Her voice was rich. It was exactly the voice Mehr remembered from her childhood. It was the voice that had sung her to sleep and told her stories she'd held dear all the long, long years since her mother had left her. Listening to her mother's voice made Mehr feel like a child, small and hopeful and helpless, heart an ache in her chest.

"Mother," she whispered.

Her mother's dark eyes traced every inch of her face.

"Oh, Mehr," she said. "You've grown so much. I knew you would, of course. But…you are a grown woman now, aren't you?"

Mehr swallowed. "Yes," she said.

"And Arwa? How is Arwa?"

"When I left Jah Irinah, she was—well." She thought of Arwa's warm weight in her arms. The smell of her hair, her curiosity, her solemnness and her playfulness. How could she possibly describe all of what Arwa was, to a woman who had not seen her since she was a baby? "She's a bright girl. Very sweet. Good-hearted."

"Good," her mother said, nodding. "That's good."

A brief silence fell. After a moment of hesitation, Mehr's mother kneeled down across from her. Mehr watched the way she clasped her hands tightly together on her lap.

"Lalita told me what became of you, among the Saltborn," her mother said. "Mehr, I am so very sorry."

"It isn't your fault, what was done to me."

"If I had known you had my gift…" Ruhi shook her head. "Ah, it's too late now. I won't force you to ease an old woman's regret."

"You have it too, then? The—gift?" Mehr asked. "You can move dreamfire to your will?"

Her mother nodded. "My mother had four children, and I was the only one to inherit it."

"I have aunts and uncles? A family?"

"We are depleted," Ruhi said, her voice subtly strained. "There have been difficult times. A great deal of hunger and suffering. Some vanished. Others chose to leave Irinah and never returned." She paused. "There are few of us left now."

Mehr clasped her own hands, letting that answer settle within her heart. She couldn't imagine how difficult life had been out here in the desert. The Amrithi had been hunted, their culture and their way of life decimated, their people stolen and forced to choose vows to the Maha or freedom at the end of their own blades. No wonder her mother didn't dress in finery; no wonder Kamal continued to stare at Mehr with narrow-eyed suspicion. They had so little hope left.

"Why did you leave us?" The question escaped her almost without her say-so. But now that she had spoken, she couldn't unsay it. She didn't want to. "You would have remained safe in Jah Irinah."

"Your father exiled me," Ruhi said. "I couldn't return to you."

"But you could have stayed with us. Arwa and me. He would have allowed that." Mehr stared into her mother's eyes, which were so like her own. "I remember."

Ruhi shook her head at that, her mouth thinning.

"I couldn't, Mehr. I was afraid."

"Of the Maha? His Saltborn?"

"Of many things," said Ruhi. "When I fell in love with your father...Mehr, I was an idealist. I had great dreams of what we could accomplish together, a Tara's daughter and the Governor of Irinah. I believed we could make the world better for the Amrithi. But I learned, soon enough, how little power an Ambhan nobleman has. Your father loved me, but he still obeyed his Emperor. When his nobles attacked my people, he turned a blind eye—for my sake, he told me, and yours. A Governor who refuses to obey the Emperor's will, he told me, does not remain a Governor for long. And what would become of us all then? What would happen to you and Arwa, without the protection of his title and power? The thought terrified me, Mehr."

Ruhi leaned forward, her gaze intent. She spoke as if she didn't care what Kamal heard—as if there were no shame in it, airing their family's grief before an audience. Mehr, raised behind walls and protocol, was frozen by her mother's honesty.

"I was afraid," Ruhi said frankly. "Afraid of what your father and I had done by loving one another. Afraid that no matter how well your father obeyed his Emperor and his Maha, one day their eyes would turn on him and they would see me, his *amata*-gifted Amrithi mistress, and steal me away, or punish him for loving me. And worse still, I feared they would punish you and your sister for existing at all."

"Is that why you left? To protect us?" Mehr's voice sounded small, so small.

"I had a duty, Mehr," said her mother. "My clan needed a Tara, my mother had passed on, and I..." She paused, then continued, slow and deliberate. "I chose to leave for your sakes, yes. But I also left for my own. For my people. My clan. Your father told me if I left, I could never return. He thought he could use you and your sister as a weapon, as chains to hold me. But I would not be caged, Mehr. I had made him no vows and no promises. I told him: I am Amrithi. I know the price of freedom." Her voice was flint, all its richness hardened to a fine edge. "I don't ask you to forgive me, Mehr. I have thought of you and your sister every day since I left the city. But I will not say I regret my choices. I believed that I left my half-Ambhan daughters well protected, and far safer than they would be in my care. I thought his blood would keep you safe; our gifts are so rare, after all. I never thought one of my daughters would inherit mine."

All Mehr could think of, as she listened to her mother speak, was of the grief she'd felt when her mother had left: the weight and the greatness of it, the way it had shaped her into what she was. She thought of her father's guilt-stricken face. She thought of all the things Arwa had never experienced, the love she'd never had and the stories she'd never been told, and now never would be.

"Now that you're here, I'll keep you safe. Whatever the Maha has done to you, whatever hold he continues to have on you, you will be protected," Ruhi said into the silence.

"Will you vow it?" Mehr asked.

Her mother's answering look was steady. "We don't make vows, Mehr."

There were many things Amrithi didn't do that Mehr had done. Mehr had made vows and manipulated the dreams of the Gods. She had done things that Ambhan women didn't do too. Knowing that she stood on the distant edge of both the world she'd been born to and the world she had always wanted to belong to left her heart cold. She lowered her head.

"Mehr," her mother said, her voice soft. She reached out a hand as if to comfort her.

"I can't look at you," Mehr said sharply. Her voice was full of all the bitter things she couldn't allow herself to think, feel. "Don't touch me. Please."

Ruhi dropped her hand. Mehr saw her hesitate, saw her clasp her own hands together, as Kamal shifted angrily in the corner.

"Lalita was right," Ruhi said ruefully. "You are very like me after all."

In the end she left with a promise to return, taking Kamal—and the lantern—with her.

CHAPTER TWENTY-NINE

Mehr was soon moved from the tent to a new hiding place, a moderately larger shelter carved into rock. The clan weren't willing to accept her in their own home yet, and it was possible they wouldn't be for a long time. Many, Lalita told her, were afraid she was still bound to the Maha; others feared that her presence would somehow draw the mystics to them. Mehr couldn't find it in herself to blame them for their fears.

Lalita also told her that the shelter that would now be her home had once been used by Amrithi preparing for the Rite of Dreaming, as a place to dress and pray and wait for the dreamfire to fall. Now it was abandoned. Not large enough to hold a clan, too enclosed by sand and its own walls to act as a guard post, it served no purpose to their clan.

For Mehr, it was perfect. It didn't have the honeycomb warren of corridors of the Maha's temple, or the gleaming, golden elegance of her father's household. Instead the structure was dark and secretive, its columns and walls all soft lines, flowing with the grace of dunes. It felt peaceful, but most of all, it made Mehr feel safe. She couldn't help but trace its whorled walls with her hands, thinking of what it must have been like when those with and without the *amata* gift walked the room together, ready to dance the Rite of Dreaming as a clan.

Lalita spent a few hours with her on the first day, talking to her and offering her comfort. She treated Mehr as if she were fragile, keeping her voice soft and her movements slow. The kindness aggravated Mehr to no end. Too full of feeling, she couldn't remain still under Lalita's eyes. Instead she walked the room in circles, bristling like a caged animal.

Lalita watched Mehr pace, back and forth across the shelter's floor, and said, "You need to rest, Mehr. Sit. You've been through an ordeal."

"I'm well," Mehr said, and that was true enough. She was as well as she could be, would be, when her chest ached, when Amun was not with her, when the Maha still lived and the echo of immortal nightmares still writhed under her eyelids.

"Just try not to think so much, then," Lalita said gently. "I can almost see you fretting. For now it's enough that you're safe, and you're here."

Lalita left eventually, assuring Mehr she would return when she could, but as the days passed with no sign of her, Mehr soon found she was glad to be alone. She was grateful, so very grateful, that Lalita was alive and well. But she wasn't the girl Lalita remembered any longer. That girl had believed in her own strength, but she had been soft, her resolve untested. Mehr had been tested, and she had shattered and remade herself. There was no going back for her.

Rest, Lalita had entreated. But Mehr couldn't allow herself to rest. Not yet, not even for Lalita's sake. She would need to regain her strength eventually, but for now the thought of being soft, even for a moment, pained her.

That night, after eating some of the food Lalita had left for her, Mehr lit a prayer flame. She told herself it was a much more economical use of fuel than the oil lantern, and also far less likely to draw attention from any Saltborn out searching for her. But really she simply liked the comfort of holding the small clay container in her palm and feeling the flickering heat of the candle flame. She sat on the floor and looked down at the marriage seal around her neck, the one Amun had carved for her long before he'd met her.

The light flickered on the seal, and on the whorls Amun had carved into it, the same whorls that decorated the walls of this Amrithi ruin around her.

Amun would have been so happy to be in this place, among these walls. Mehr imagined him by her side, kneeling on the cool ground, imagined him tracing the whorls of her seal, the only mark on it apart from his name, and speaking in that low voice of his. *I gave you a symbol of our people—*

She let the seal go.

Her heart ached for him, and for herself.

Amun had sacrificed so much to save her, and Mehr had found so much that she'd feared she had lost forever: her mother, Lalita, a surviving clan. She had no right to feel crushed by her own grief, and yet she was. Amun should have been here, not Mehr. This was where Amun belonged.

A noise from beyond the shelter made Mehr flinch, then tense abruptly. Straightening, curling her fists at her sides, she looked up—and saw her mother watching her from the doorway. In the light of the flame, her hooded face was largely shadowed, and Mehr was glad of that. She wanted no mirrors.

"I'll be on watch, if you'd like to join me," her mother said. She vanished back into the dark.

When Mehr finally followed, she found her mother seated facing the horizon. Her hood was thrown back, her hands clasped in front of her. She had no lantern of her own to illuminate the night, but she didn't truly need one. The stars were achingly bright above them.

Mehr looked up at those stars and shivered. They looked... wrong. They glittered like shattered glass, splinters of fury on the black surface of the night. They reminded her of the Maha's nightmare-flecked eyes. Sickened, she forced her gaze down, only to find that the sand was reflecting the starlight, wavering and strange.

"Come sit by me," her mother offered.

Mehr wrenched her gaze up.

"I don't need to be guarded," she said.

"It puts my mind at ease to do so," her mother responded. "Come."

Mehr sat down next to her. The air was painfully cold, but the breeze was blessedly faint. Her mother was silent beside her, eyes narrowed and watchful. At her left side lay her dagger. Unlike the one she'd given Mehr when she left Jah Irinah, this one was unornamented, with a bone handle worn smooth by countless hands. It seemed she really did intend to remain on watch.

Mehr followed her mother's gaze and stared out at the desert. Under the shattered sky, the flowing lines of the desert—its peaks and valleys, its sparse vegetation—glowed with subtle, off-kilter light. Only the horizon remained dark, a deep and fathomless blackness.

Under Mehr's gaze, the darkness shifted.

She flinched with surprise, then narrowed her own eyes and leaned forward, squinting through the darkness.

"The daiva are moving," said Mehr after a moment, awed. Now that she was looking closely, she could see them roiling upon the horizon, wild and seething.

Her mother was quiet for a long moment. Then she said, "Strong dreams give them life. Now that the Maha's grip has weakened, they dance." Ruhi leaned forward too; she laid one hand on her dagger hilt, the fingertips of her free hand pressed thoughtfully to her lower lip. "If not for the Maha, perhaps they'd still walk the earth like men."

"When I was little you told me stories about the daiva," Mehr said. "Do you remember?"

"Ah, Mehr," her mother said. Her breath gusted out of her. "Of course I do."

"I used to try to tell Arwa those stories. But I don't remember them as well as I should," Mehr admitted. "And I had little chance to tell her tales."

"Why?" Ruhi asked. Her voice was cautious.

"Our father's wife didn't care for Amrithi tales." Mehr kept her gaze fixed on the black horizon. Maryam seemed like such a distant memory, now. A creature from another time and another world. "She thought it would be best to raise Arwa as an Ambhan, ignorant of her heritage."

"Perhaps she has done Arwa a kindness," Ruhi said. "Perhaps she has given Arwa the chance to live a life without regrets."

Ruhi didn't sound as if she truly believed her own words, but Mehr shook her head anyway.

"I don't believe that," Mehr said. "Arwa is part Amrithi. It's part of her, just as being Amrithi is part of me."

You are part of us, like it or not, Mehr thought.

Mehr was so like her mother. She had always known she was. She'd seen the truth of it often enough in her father's eyes. It still made it no stranger to be confronted with the truth of it. Her mother's eyes, her face, the way she held herself like a creature always on the verge of flight—

Mehr was not so sure, anymore, that she was happy to be her mother's daughter. Her mother was so . . . hard. Hard as blade or bone, and she wore her feelings like scars that pained her still. She'd left her clan once, although she'd returned to them, to be their Tara. She'd left her daughters behind too, though she welcomed Mehr now with open arms. She wore her love for her clan and her love for Mehr like a grim wound, a thing that had to be borne. Looking at her made Mehr think of her own love for Arwa. Her love for Amun.

She'd left them both behind too. Ah, *Gods*.

She looked at her mother again, then looked away. It was so hard to acknowledge her, when the feelings she conjured in Mehr were a child's feelings, deep and grief-stricken and furious. So Mehr looked back at the daiva instead. Once the sight of them would have filled her with joy. Now the sight of them only made her heart beat faster and a cold sweat rise on her skin. Joy seemed a faraway thing.

"The desert isn't right," Mehr said. "Something is wrong. I know you see it."

"I do," Ruhi acknowledged. "But it will return to normal soon enough."

Ruhi spoke in a tone that suggested she didn't want to be asked any further questions. Instead of heeding her, Mehr said, "Why is the desert as it is now, then? Why will it return to normal?"

There was a brief silence. Then Ruhi said, "The night of the storm . . . you didn't perform the Maha's rite. Did you?"

"No."

"No one did." Her mother looked tense. "There is a balance, Mehr, to the world the Gods have woven. Death and life, sickness and health, dreams and nightmares. The Maha has altered the natural balance through his rite, ensuring that the Gods dream sweetly for his sake. Without the Maha demanding imbalance, holding their dreams in his hands, balance inevitably attempts to restore itself. The daiva grow stronger. And the dreams he has kept at bay so long begin to take shape." She sighed. "But he will find another Amrithi to wear his leash, as he always does. And everything will be as it has been all the years of the Empire."

"What will happen," Mehr whispered, "if he doesn't find another Amrithi to perform the rite?"

The temperature almost seemed to plummet at her words.

"What does balance look like?" Ruhi shrugged helplessly. "Mehr, we don't know. Who living can? But we fear that setting the world right will come at a terrible cost. The Gods have so much fury waiting to be unleashed. And..."

"Tell me," Mehr prompted, when she saw her mother hesitate, still watching the darkness whirl on the horizon.

"We fear the full anger of the Gods," she said. "We fear the worst: that they will awaken in their fury and shatter the world." Finally, she looked at Mehr. Her face was gray. "But Mehr, you needn't fear. Nothing will happen. The Maha will find another of us, as he always does."

"And if he doesn't, this time?"

"He has shaped the world into a place that is kind to him," Ruhi said shortly. "He will."

Mehr wasn't so sure. She thought of the way word of the Emperor's displeasure with "barbarians" had spread across the Empire, the way the Maha had stretched his eyes and ears across the Ambhan provinces, seeking gifted Amrithi far and wide, when he should have been able to thieve them from his own doorstep. She thought of the way she had been taken, despite the fact that she was Ambhan, and a nobleman's child, and the Maha had risked igniting the fury of the Emperor's most loyal followers. The Maha had been desperate when he'd claimed Mehr, and now that she was gone and Amun lay somewhere in an agony Mehr could barely contemplate, he would be more than simply desperate.

"If you truly believe he will find another Amrithi, why are you so frightened?" Mehr said softly.

"I'm not afraid."

Mehr looked at her mother. She met those dark eyes, set beneath straight, serious eyebrows. Oh, she knew that look. "I know that you are," she said.

For a moment her mother was utterly silent. Then, with visible effort, she held Mehr's gaze and spoke.

"I am afraid," she said slowly, "because when I danced the Rite of Dreaming with the clan the last two storms, I felt a fury grow. I can feel the Gods' anger, Mehr, as you must." She touched her fingertips to the nape of her neck, at the place where Mehr could still feel the cold touch of the nightmares in her own skull. "I know that their anger wears its own flesh and squats in the shadows, waiting for the dreamfire to breathe life back into it. I fear what immortals are capable of." Her voice lowered. "The clan are afraid too. And the fear makes them act— differently. Rashly. But when the next storm comes, and they see he has control again, they won't fear any longer."

The clan were afraid, and here was Mehr, a convenient tool to be returned to the Maha's keeping. Mehr understood then that it was more than distrust of Mehr's vows that had led her mother to keep her out here alone, far from wherever the clan resided. She was trying to keep Mehr safe.

Perhaps the Amrithi feared the Maha more than they cared to keep a fellow tribeswoman—a daughter of their own clan—safe. Perhaps they didn't think of her as Amrithi at all. The thought made anxiety knot in Mehr's chest, so she pushed it away.

"There will need to be a balance," Ruhi said. "But not today. And hopefully not in any of our lifetimes." She closed her eyes and opened them, a bleak look on her face. "He has created a trap none can escape from."

"You should send me back," Mehr said bleakly. "If he has no Amrithi to use when the dreamfire next falls…"

"You've paid more than enough," Ruhi said fiercely; her sudden fierceness, the depth of emotion in her voice, jarred Mehr. "More than enough! It's a miracle you're free, a *miracle*, Mehr. And he will take someone else—he always finds someone."

Mehr bit her tongue. *So I wait, then, for Amun to awaken, or another Amrithi to take my place? I let another suffer for me?*

She felt sickened.

"I'm going to rest," she said abruptly. She stood. Her mother turned her head away, nodding sharply.

"I'll keep watch a little longer," Ruhi said. "Just until sunrise."

Hours later, Mehr finally heard her mother go. Steeling herself, she breathed deep and slow and lifted her marriage seal from her skin. Then she touched her fingers to her scar.

The pain raced through her, fierce and all-consuming. But she resisted the urge to wrench her hand away from her scar. She clung on instead, letting the pain deepen its claws into her blood and her bones. It was Amun's pain, and it should have been Mehr's burden as much as it was his. She let it consume her, until she was floating in a red sea of agony, until she could feel every subtle element of his suffering: the conflicting weight of his vow to her and to the Maha, stretching him thin, clawing him apart; the way his pain went beyond flesh to the place where his soul lived.

There was nothing Mehr could do to save him.

Finally she wrenched her hand away and found herself curled up on her side on the ground, gasping for breath. She climbed laboriously up onto her knees and wiped her streaming eyes.

Oh, Amun. *Amun.* How long could he possibly survive, suffering as he was? There was no possibility that he would be able to perform the Rite of the Bound when the next storm came. Mehr was not even sure he would live to see it.

One thing, at least, was clear: If nothing changed, the Maha would soon have no Amrithi in his service at all.

Lalita

Would you really send a tribeswoman back into the great monster's grip?" a woman named Sohaila asked, disbelieving. "Jabir, elder, I never thought you would betray a fellow Amrithi. I'm ashamed of you."

"I never said I would send her back," the elder blustered. "I said *someone* may want to send her back. It's very different."

"I don't see how. I don't see—"

"Some people," Jabir cut in loudly, "might be worried what terrors the world will suffer if the Maha doesn't have one of our own to perform his rite. Some people might consider one girl a price worth paying."

"Why don't you hand yourself to him, then?" Sohaila countered.

"I don't have the *amata*."

"Then I don't think you're in a position to comment."

"Daughter, calm yourself," another woman said, placing a gentle hand on Sohaila's shoulder. "And Jabir, no one is handing a tribeswoman, never mind the Tara's very own daughter, to that monster. Be serious."

"Agreed," said another. "But I do fear that allowing the girl to join the clan would be premature, nonetheless."

A murmur of agreement ran through the circle of Amrithi

who surrounded the communal fire. In order of seniority, elders sat close to the warmth of the flames, with the youngest and newest members of the clan at the very edges. Lalita sat at the outer limit of the circle, wrapped up tight in both a heavy robe and a shawl tucked about her shoulders. She listened.

In their Tara's absence, the clan had gathered to discuss Mehr's fate. Although the Tara held the greatest power in a clan, the view of the clan as a whole held great sway, and a Tara could not easily deny her clan's united will.

The will of Ruhi's clan, tonight, did not seem particularly unified.

The question of whether to allow Mehr a full place in the clan was a fraught one. A great number of the clan feared that she was still vow-bound to the Maha. They feared he had sent her in search of others with the *amata* that he could take and bind to his service. Others—like Sohaila—argued that all Amrithi deserved a place in the arms of a clan. Lalita, new as she was, had done her best to merely listen and interject only rarely.

Kamal walked out of the darkness and touched Lalita on the shoulder.

"She's back," he said. With no little relief—she had never cared for the laborious business of Amrithi politics—Lalita nodded and stood up.

Kamal gestured at the inner circle, and someone reached a ladle into the pot simmering over the communal fire and filled a cup. They passed it back to Kamal, who placed it in Lalita's hands. She nodded her thanks and headed away from the circle.

Ruhi was walking up the curve of a dune, a defeated turn to her shoulders. Lalita walked toward her and handed her the steaming cup of steeped herbs, which Ruhi drank fast and handed back to her. Lalita held the cup tight. The night had been bitterly cold, and warmth was welcome.

"Go and rest," Lalita said.

"I will," said Ruhi. "But first, tell me what the others said."

"They're still arguing," Lalita said.

"Have they come to a consensus yet?"

"About allowing Mehr into the clan proper? Not at all," Lalita said with a sigh. "But they won't countenance giving her up to the Maha. They've agreed on that, at least." She saw Ruhi's shoulders slump and gave her a look of surprise. "Did you really believe they would make any other decision?"

"I don't know what to believe anymore," Ruhi said tiredly. "These are trying times, Lalita."

"Oh, I'm very aware. Now sleep," Lalita said pointedly. "I'll make sure someone else keeps watch."

"Will you go to her?" Ruhi asked abruptly. Her expression was raw. "Will you comfort her?"

Ruhi did not say, *because I cannot*, but there was no need. Lalita understood.

She was reminded of the day, so very long ago, when Ruhi had asked her to take care of Mehr and teach her the rites. Ruhi had been the Governor's concubine long before Lalita returned homesick to Jah Irinah, but becoming the mother of two half-Ambhan daughters had shattered something within Ruhi and tipped her from uneasy contentment into slow-moving, dreadful awareness. Lalita remembered pitying her. Ruhi hadn't married the Governor, hadn't made any vows, but the children were as good as a chain holding her fast within the palace walls. And Ruhi had come to understand, far too late, how ill-suited she was for Ambhan society.

Where Lalita had flourished, gaining financial independence and a modicum of security, Ruhi had become a shadow of the woman she'd once been. She'd had fire in her once. She'd been a Tara's daughter, and a headstrong one at that, determined to make a better life for her clan and her people. But her life in the Governor's palace had crushed the spirit out of her and filled her soul with terrible, unanswerable fears. Lalita remembered the way Ruhi had taken Lalita's hands in her own, her grip firm, her eyes blazing.

Take care of Mehr for me, Ruhi had said. *Teach her. Help her. I can't be the mother she needs. Please, Lalita.*

Lalita had known that day that Ruhi would leave eventually. She'd never blamed her for it. The clan had needed a Tara, after all, and Ruhi had needed to survive. If she'd remained in Jah Irinah, she wouldn't have.

"Of course," Lalita said gently. "You don't even need to ask."

CHAPTER THIRTY

Despite everything, Mehr's body healed and grew stronger. She slept—briefly, restlessly, her sleep riddled with dreams. She ate the food left for her, which wasn't plentiful but was still more than she'd been able to stomach in those last weeks of service to the Maha. Sometimes Lalita came and kept her company, and nearly every night her mother kept watch outside her shelter.

She had no idea when her mother rested, and didn't ask. Ever since the first night when they had spoken so freely to one another, Mehr had struggled to find the words to simply talk to her mother. All the words she had were raw, weighty, an echo of her wounded heart. She didn't dare let them pass her lips. Instead she sat by her mother in silence, watching the daiva writhe on the distant horizon until dawn broke the sky.

She saved her questions for Lalita instead. On one of Lalita's visits, Mehr asked her if there was any way she could assist the clan. "I'm just a burden as I am," Mehr said with a shrug, thinking of all the food she had eaten, the prayer flames she'd burned that could have been put to a better use. "I'd like to help if I can."

"How would you like to help?" Lalita asked her, quirking an eyebrow at her.

Mehr shook her head. "You know well enough I have nothing

to offer." She smiled. "I have a noblewoman's skill for doing nothing."

"Oh, hush."

"Let me contribute," Mehr said. "Teach me a skill, if you're willing." She thought of the way Amun had fixed her torn sleeve with those large, gentle hands of his. She swallowed and said, in a voice that was less even than she'd hoped it would be, "I can't simply sit here and wait. I feel—restless."

Lalita made a soft humming sound. "I can teach you to sew. When the clan accepts you, they'll be glad of the skill."

"You can sew?"

"There's no need to sound so surprised, Mehr."

"Forgive me," Mehr said. "It just doesn't seem like something that would interest you."

"It isn't. And yet here I am, darning day in and out." Lalita's laugh was strained. "And you wonder why I wanted a life in the Empire," she added wryly.

They spoke of other things after that, but Mehr noticed the way Lalita looked down at her own hands, studying the new calluses that had covered their old softness. Mehr was reminded, forcefully, that she was not the only one who was struggling to adapt. Lalita had chosen a life beyond the desert and flourished in it. Now she had been forced to return to a clan that wasn't her own by birth, to a desert haunted by strangeness, and a life defined by her blood and not by her choices. Her dear friend had been murdered. She was adrift, just as Mehr was adrift, struggling to carve a place in a world that was not fit for her.

When Lalita moved to leave, Mehr reached for her. She took Lalita's hands in her own, feeling their new roughness, and their new strength. Her heart was so heavy inside her.

You've always been my clan, Mehr thought. *Even when I didn't realize it, fool child that I was, you were more a mother to me than I understood or deserved.*

Thank you, from the bottom of my heart.

"What is it?" Lalita asked.

Mehr couldn't say all she wished to, not without splintering the brittle strength Lalita had drawn tight around her, keeping her tall. So instead she said, "I would love it if you taught me to sew."

Lalita laughed at that. "You'll forgive me if I doubt you."

"I would," Mehr insisted. "I've always found you to be an excellent teacher."

"Ah, well then, that's good." Lalita smiled. "Next time I come, I'll bring a needle and thread." She clasped Mehr's hands tight in return. "You've always been my favorite student."

"I'm your only student."

"That makes it no less true, dear one."

Mehr hadn't been joking when she had claimed she had a noble-woman's typical lack of practical skills. She was able to navigate an Ambhan household artfully. She'd learned long ago how to play the dutiful child while not-so-secretly transgressing. She could read and write, and knew how to dress appropriately to reflect her station. She could recognize beautiful art and make meaningless conversation. But she could not mend clothing or start a fire, or cook or heal or contribute in a way that would assist her own survival, or anyone else's.

The only skill she had that was of any worth here was her ability to dance the rites. So that was exactly what she did.

She began to spend the early mornings performing the rites out in the light, before the heat of the day became unbearable. When the sky darkened, before her mother came to keep vigil, Mehr would practice again for a half hour or so more, taking advantage of the cooler weather. She danced every rite she could remember, danced until exhaustion consumed her. She danced until the restlessness in her bones eased, until she could breathe without thinking of Amun and the red of his agony, the red of Hema's blood. She danced until she no longer had the strength to run, as she so wanted to.

Mehr blamed the distraction the rites offered for the fact that it took her far longer than it should have to realize the daiva had taken to watching her dance. They hung in soft shadows around the edges of the shelter, shaping themselves to the swinging arc of her own shadow as she moved through the sigils and steps of each rite. She froze the first time she saw them—saw the glow of their golden eyes, the whisper of their talons—and hesitantly offered them a gesture of respect. But when they remained unmoving, simply watching her, she returned slowly to her practice of the rites. When they remained complacent, unmoved, she grew more confident.

If they were content to leave her be, she would do the same for them in return. This was their desert, after all. Mehr was merely an interloper, as all humans were, on this land that belonged to sleeping Gods. If the daiva wanted to use their new strength to simply watch her, well then, that was their right.

The daiva finally acted when foolishness—foolishness and the force of habit—led Mehr to err.

She'd been dancing all morning, tracing the air with her limbs, stretching her strength. For a moment, she felt as if she were back in the Maha's temple, moving through the rites in the rote way she and Amun had grown to perform them: one rite after the other, warming up their muscles, preparing themselves for service. She felt the ghost of Amun at her back, remembered the way he'd move closer to her after the first hour of practice, his voice low and considering. She remembered the brush of his breath against her hair. *If you're ready, Mehr, then let go—*

Her limbs grew loose, and her breathing deep. She exhaled slowly, her body soft around the hum of her own thoughts, the beat of her heart. She could feel the morning's light against her skin, smell a faint sweetness on the air, a pale ghost of godly dreaming. She reached for the part of her that wasn't mortal in response, reached for the part of her that was ichor, that held a trace of immortality—

A howl echoed through the air. A heavy weight slammed into her chest and flung her to the ground. When she raised her head she saw the daiva circling her in a black cloud. Her heart thudded sharply in response, fire shooting through her blood. Ah, Gods. She was a fool.

The daiva did not like the rite. Amun had told her that long ago. And oh, silly child that she was, she'd begun to perform it, by instinct, by habit. And there they were, the children of those Gods she'd compelled, bristling at her, their darkness growing to surround her—

Just as quickly as they'd risen, they drew back, flinging themselves away in wisps of shadow. It was only then that she realized her lip was warm and wet. At some point she'd bitten her lip, or abraded it on the sand. The result was the same: She had bled, and her blood had reminded the daiva of their vows, banishing them away. She waited a moment, until she was sure the daiva had departed, then climbed shakily to her feet.

Without the daiva around her, the sand glittered menacingly. The sky was a blue so bright it burned. Gasping, she leaned against the wall of her shelter and thought: *There's a storm coming. I know it.*

The knowledge lay in her memories, in her dreams; it lay in her body, in her muscles and her bones and the way she moved when she forgot she was no longer a weapon for the Maha to wield. A storm was coming, and no matter how far Mehr had run, the knowledge of how to wrap the dreams of the Gods between her footsteps hadn't left her. The rite waited in her blood.

Steadying herself, she went back inside the shelter and sat

down on the ground. She held herself very still, painfully aware of the hum in her blood, a strange kind of foreknowledge.

With a dark sense of foreboding, she waited. As the sun rose to its zenith, the scent of incense rose with it. The hair at the back of Mehr's neck prickled.

There was no denying it now: A storm was coming.

Mehr went outside, holding a hand up to shade her eyes so she could watch the horizon. It wasn't long before a figure appeared in the distance, striding swiftly toward her despite the oppressive midday heat. The figure was too tall and broad to be her mother or Lalita. When it drew a little closer, she realized it was Kamal. His hood was drawn low over his forehead to keep the heat at bay, but Mehr could still see the tension in his jaw and in his narrowed eyes.

"The Tara sent me to check that you're still whole," he said tersely, once he drew close enough to see her. He crossed his arms. His hands were in fists.

"I'm well," Mehr told him. "Entirely whole."

"Good. I'll tell her so." He turned abruptly on his heel, ready to leave, when Mehr called out to him.

"Why did she send you?"

The look he gave her, as he turned back, was utterly incredulous.

"Don't you sense the storm coming?"

"Of course I sense it," Mehr said. "I'm merely wondering what my mother fears. What did she think could have happened to me?" She cocked her head to the side thoughtfully, looking at Kamal narrowly through the glare of the sun. "The Maha is unlikely to find me here."

His lips thinned.

"There are dangers in the storm. Apparently she wants to protect you from them."

"The nightmares," she said. "You mean the nightmares."

When he simply stared at her, uncomprehending, she touched her fingers to the nape of her neck. "The fury you feel at the back of your skull. The pale thing, the force that has flesh. You've felt it, haven't you?"

Mehr hadn't thought it possible, but somehow the look of dislike on Kamal's face seemed to intensify. No matter. Mehr didn't need him to like her. She simply needed him to listen to her.

"Go inside," he said in response. "Don't come out until you're told to."

"I could make them go away," Mehr told him. "You know that."

"I know that I've done what my Tara has bid me," he snapped. "And now I want to return to my clan. Are you finished?"

"My mother believes the Maha will find another gifted Amrithi to replace me," Mehr continued calmly, refusing to let him sway her. "But he hasn't, and he won't. I know my mother fears I'll try to return to him because of my vows, but that isn't what you fear, is it?" She met his eyes, unwavering. "You fear what the nightmares of the Gods will do, without someone to control them. You fear me *staying*."

"It doesn't matter what I feel," Kamal said, which was as good as a *yes*. "I do what my Tara bids. That's all."

"It does matter," Mehr insisted. "You're not wrong to be afraid. But I can make things better. All I ask is that you convince your Tara not to come here tonight. Tell her your clan needs her this storm. Please."

"So you can sneak back to your master? No." His voice was flint. But he didn't walk away.

Mehr crossed the sand toward him. She gazed at him steadily, thinking of Amun, of the deep red of his pain as he suffered far beyond her reach. She thought of the nightmares, their flat eyes, their malevolence. She knew what had to be done.

"Kamal," she said softly. "It's in all our best interests that I go back to him."

She stepped even closer, until she was looking up at him, raising her head to meet wary eyes. "The one who shared the burden of service with me is as good as dead, and if you fear the nightmares now, you have no grasp of how much worse they're going to become." Mehr didn't blink. Didn't allow herself to waver. "I know. I've felt them."

Kamal still looked wary, but some of the brittleness was gone from his voice when he spoke again. "I don't lie to the Tara."

"Her heart is leading her astray," Mehr said. "Her heart is lying to her. She loves me. She can't help her nature. But you understand. *You* know what needs to be done." Mehr pressed on. "Just tell her not to come. That's all I ask."

A moment passed. Another. Then finally, Kamal gave a small nod.

As he walked away, Mehr crossed her own arms, holding herself as if the day were cold instead of sweltering.

What am I doing?

Some part of her had known it would come to this. When her mother had told her the cost of her freedom—when the storm had fallen, and the daiva had whirled in their fury around her—she'd known.

Perhaps even before then. When she'd stood in the desert alone and told a distant Amun that she would come back for him, that she wouldn't leave him bound alone and in pain to the Maha's service. She'd rested long enough. It was time for her to finally face her reckoning.

She had to go back. For his sake. For her own. For everyone's.

"My choice," she whispered. "This is my choice."

Mehr waited until the desert had just begun to cool, the sun beginning to dip below the horizon, then left the safety of her shelter. She walked away from the shelter, her boots sinking into the sand, which shivered and clung to her as if it didn't quite know how best to behave. A heartbeat of time passed. She heard a voice call her name.

"Mehr. Stop."

She turned, throat tight, and saw her mother. Ruhi rose from the ground where she'd been kneeling, waiting for Mehr, hidden by her dun-colored robe and her own careful stillness. Behind her stood Lalita, her own face tight with grief.

"Where are you going?" Ruhi asked.

"I'm sure you already know," Mehr said.

"Did you truly believe Kamal would lie to me, Mehr?"

"I hoped he would do the right thing."

"He did." Ruhi's voice was a terrible, soft thing, full of love and pity. "He obeyed his Tara. He kept you safe."

Ruhi pushed her hood back from her face and walked toward Mehr. "Come with me," she said. Her eyes were liquid dark, her face gentle. "Please, Mehr."

"I have to go back," Mehr said, resisting the urge to step away from her mother. "You must see that."

"Your vows are misleading you," her mother said. "You don't truly want to return to the Maha."

Of course Mehr didn't want to return to him. The thought of him turned her knees to water, made her blood run cold. But her wants and her fears changed nothing. "It won't be long until the dreamfire falls," Mehr said, struggling to keep calm in the face of her mother's gentleness. "I need to go now. The price of me remaining here is far too high. You must see that."

"I told you he would find someone to replace you," Ruhi said, with the sureness of hope. "Most likely he already has." Ruhi took one of Mehr's hands between her own, holding on to her gently, her expression earnest with love. "You would not have spoken to Kamal if you didn't want to warn me. You want me to stop you."

"No, Mother," Mehr said. "No. I'm leaving. I have to."

Ruhi's grip tightened into a vise that made Mehr wince.

"I can stop you, Mehr. I will if I must." A beat. "Please, daughter. Don't make me do this."

Mehr looked at her mother. The veil of gentleness had fallen away to reveal the iron that lay beneath it, a desperation so pure and fierce that it took Mehr's breath away.

"You don't have the right," Mehr said.

"I'm the Tara. I protect the clan. I protect *you*."

Mehr swallowed. "The best thing you can do for the clan is let me go."

"I'm your mother." Ruhi's voice wavered. "I can't sacrifice you. I won't let you go. It's too much."

"This is my choice," Mehr said.

"Mehr, I can't allow you to do this."

"And what right do you have to decide for me?" Mehr demanded. Suddenly she was furious. Furious at her mother for loving her too much, far too late. Furious at herself for standing here, wasting time and courage when there was so much yet to be done. "You left me. You gave up your right to control me a long time ago, and you can't have it back." She wrenched her hand back, and this time her mother's grip faltered and released her.

The silence that fell was sudden and bitter. Her mother looked stricken.

"I don't want to hurt you," Mehr said, pained, as she rubbed her wrist. "I don't want to be angry at you."

"But you are," her mother whispered.

"How could I not be?" The words—all the words she had held back so carefully, for the sake of building the fragile peace growing between them—began to pour out of her. "Father used me and Arwa as a weapon against you, and instead of fighting him you left us behind. You *chose* to leave us. Arwa was a baby. She doesn't even remember you. I missed you more than I can say. I still miss you. I miss the mother I had, the mother I dreamed would come home to me." Mehr's voice cracked. "Of course I'm angry. I'm angry that I have been caged and sold and failed by the people who were supposed to protect me. I'm angry because I love you still, despite everything, and I want you to *let me go*."

She wouldn't fail Amun, as she'd been failed. She would save him. She couldn't allow anyone to stop her.

"I don't want to be angry at you, Mother," Mehr said, chin held high. "But I don't regret it."

She saw the moment the blow struck. Saw her mother straighten.

"You have a right to your anger," her mother said. Her voice was wooden, heavy with hurt. "But it changes nothing. I only want you to be safe. I always have. If you can't resist your vow, I'll resist for you. I'll do what's needful to protect you from yourself."

Mehr's stomach fell.

"No," said Mehr. She took a step back, and her mother followed her.

"I don't want to have to restrain you," Ruhi said, her jaw firming. "But I will if you don't come with me now."

Mehr's own hands curled into fists. Her blood was pounding in her ears.

Even now, her mother didn't trust her. She thought Mehr was a puppet on long strings.

"Ruhi," Lalita said. "Please."

"Quiet, Lalita," Ruhi said sharply. "This doesn't concern you."

"I'm sorry. I can't remain silent. I must speak for the clan."

Lalita stepped forward into the fading light. "The price of keeping Mehr safe is too high," she said to Ruhi. "The clan, the desert—even this forsaken Empire—must come first. She must return to the Maha."

Lalita looked at Mehr with a face wet with tears. "You're a good girl, Mehr," Lalita said softly. "Brave and good, as I've always known you were."

Mehr's mother stood still and silent, looking at Mehr with a face so full of raw feeling that it hurt to gaze upon it. Ruhi stood strong for a long moment, ever the survivor and soldier—and then Lalita placed a gentle hand on her shoulder and she crumpled into tears, her resolve shattered.

"Go, Mehr," Lalita said. "Go now."

Mehr hesitated for a moment. Her mother had her hands over her own eyes, as if she couldn't bear to look at Mehr, as if Mehr were already lost to her. Mehr forced herself to turn and walk away.

"I love you," she said. She didn't know if either woman had heard her.

She walked for a long, long time, until the sky was black and pricked with fractured stars. She walked into the pain of her bond with Amun, listening to the discordant song of his agony.

When she finally turned back, she saw nothing but empty desert behind her. She was alone.

CHAPTER THIRTY-ONE

It wasn't long before the storm began to brew in earnest, faster and fiercer than ever before. Dreamfire bled across the sky, swift as spilled ink on paper, its jeweled edges tinged with darkness. The daiva were everywhere, their black shadows flitting wildly across the sky and beneath the cover of sand, their howls filling the air. They no longer seemed interested in keeping their distance. More than once she felt them brush against her body, more solid than they'd ever been before, or shift the ground incautiously beneath her feet. She did her best to ignore them. When she stumbled, she simply straightened and kept on walking.

She couldn't allow herself to think too deeply on the dangers surrounding her. She didn't want her resolve to waver. Instead she focused all her energy on the fierce tug of agony inside her chest, using it to guide her forward, closer and closer to the source of her pain, the wound in her heart. When she closed her eyes, she could almost see the thread binding her and Amun together, drawing her inexorably toward the Maha's temple. She clutched her marriage seal with one hand, tracing the marks he'd carved there. Thinking of him gave her the strength to go on.

I'm coming, Amun. I'm coming. Please, survive.

* * *

It didn't take long for the mystics to find her. She saw the glint of their weapons long before she saw them running toward her, dark robes billowing around them from the force of the storm. The only thing that kept their weapons from being put to use was the roar of Bahren's voice.

"Careful! Hurt her and the Maha will have your heads!"

It was Bahren who pinned her wrists behind her. Judging by the hatred in the eyes of the other mystics, he did so far more gently than any of the others would have. Mehr didn't try to fight him. *I want to be here*, she reminded herself, as he steered her toward the temple by his grip on her hands, barking orders at the mystics around him, ordering one to run ahead to the temple to warn their master. *This is my choice.*

"Bahren," Mehr said. "Please take me quickly to the Maha."

Bahren laughed, an ugly sound without joy. "I wouldn't dare take you anywhere else."

The hands holding Mehr pinned were slippery with sweat. More than the storm had him scared.

"I'm glad you've come back," Bahren murmured. "I'm glad you've remembered your duty."

Mehr said nothing to that and kept her head lowered. She let herself be led through the honeycomb halls of the Maha's temple, passing nervous mystics, moving through the echo of their prayers. She could feel Amun's presence, could barely breathe through the pain and the longing.

"Where is my husband?" she asked.

"Dying," Bahren said grimly. "He broke his vow. Now his soul is paying the price for the both of you."

He took her to the Maha's chambers.

One of the mystics must have succeeded in warning the Maha, because Abhiman stood in the entrance of the Maha's chambers, waiting for them, his hand on the scabbard of his scimitar. When he caught sight of Mehr, his grip visibly tightened. "She's here, Maha," he said. He stepped back, allowing Bahren to shove Mehr forward into the room.

The Maha was standing at the balcony with Kalini by his side, watching the storm fall. As Bahren released Mehr, leaving her to stand alone in the center of the room, the Maha turned to face her. His expression was calm. His face was not simply riven; his skin was paper-thin, brittle with more age than a human body should have been able to carry. His hand on the edge of the balcony trembled faintly. But it was his eyes that revealed the true extent of what the storm had already done to him. They were black, deep black, the irises clouded and shattered beyond repair. Mehr shuddered at the sight of him. As he looked at Mehr, the brokenness within those eyes only seemed to deepen.

No doubt he could feel, just as Mehr could, that the bonds that had tied them together were broken. Mehr could sense only the barest shadow of his terrible strength, an echo of what Amun could feel passed to her through the vows they'd made to one another. Her bond to Amun ached, oh, it ached—but it reminded her, too, of why she had to be strong. It reminded her that she wasn't the Maha's creature any longer.

The Maha stared at Mehr silently for a long moment, an ugly tightness forming around his eyes, threatening to tear his skin clean. Kalini placed one hand on her own scabbard, and the other gently on the Maha's arm. Her gaze on Mehr was just as flat and unwavering. It took Mehr one long, absurd moment to realize the Maha was waiting for her to kneel.

"Maha," she said instead. "I have come to bargain."

Behind her Abhiman snarled and strode forward. She felt him grip her arm roughly, raising the other to strike a blow. Heart hammering, Mehr forced herself not to look away from the

Maha's face. "Will you risk seeing your last weapon with a sharp edge become dulled, Maha?" she asked.

His nostrils flared. "Stop," he ordered Abhiman. "Leave her for now."

Abhiman paused, then released her and stepped to the side.

The Maha kept his eyes on her, as if he were afraid that if he looked away she would vanish in a puff of smoke. "So," he said. "You think you can bargain with me?"

"I do," Mehr said.

He took one painfully slow step toward her, pain pinching his features. Mehr watched as Kalini's hand tightened on his arm, holding him steady. Kalini was looking up at him, her eyes full of fervent light.

"Vow yourself to me again," the Maha said, "and you will suffer no more than you deserve."

"I know what you think I deserve," Mehr said calmly. "My answer is no. I have no interest in being beaten for your pleasure." She took a step forward and watched Abhiman's hands curl into fists from the corner of her eye. "The dreamfire will fall soon, Maha. And if you want its strength, you must bargain with me."

"Don't be foolish, Mehr." The Maha's voice was a rasp of silk. "Vow yourself to me," he repeated. "Do what you know is right. Think of the Empire. Think of your family. Consider the consequences of your betrayal on the ones you love."

"I have made a sacred vow that leaves no room for you," Mehr said. She closed her eyes, just for a moment. Long enough for her to envisage that golden thread tying her and Amun together, that circle with no end. She felt the distant echo of a heartbeat and thought, *I am here, Amun. I'm here. And I will be strong for you.* "I made a vow in love, and I will not undo it for anything or anyone. But I will bargain. Will you listen, Maha?"

The Maha looked over her shoulder. He made a gesture, and Mehr felt a blinding pain shoot through her skull and her spine as Abhiman wrenched her arms high behind her back with one hand and took hold of her hair with the other. Fear, she knew from experience, made pain infinitely worse. But at least this time she was not the only one who was afraid. The Maha was afraid too, terrified that his power was slipping away from him. So she would be brave, brave—

Abhiman's hand closed around her throat. Mehr couldn't scream. She couldn't breathe. He was pulling her hair harder and harder. The air went white around her.

She almost vomited when he released her. She crumpled to the floor, holding herself up with a palm against the cool marble.

"Will you have him beat me now?" Mehr asked, her voice raw and pained. "Don't be a fool. You can't afford to damage me."

Light reflected on the marble, bright and deep. Mehr raised her head. "The dreamfire is falling," Mehr rasped. "You're running out of time."

"Your vow," the Maha said. His voice trembled.

"You know what will happen if the rite isn't performed, even if your mystics do not. The Gods will awaken. Their nightmares will tear the world apart." She coughed hard, fixing her eyes on his face. "You will fall. The Empire will fall. Your Emperor will fall." This seemed to hit him the hardest. His shattered gaze flickered, a hundred points of pain. "The world will fall." She rose to her feet, looking at their stricken faces through the ringing haze of her own pain. "Bargain with me or break me," she snarled. "Those are your options."

The mystics were silent. They watched her. Watched the Maha.

"Speak," he said.

"I will perform the Rite of the Bound alone, without a part-ner to dance alongside me. I'll keep the world whole. I will do this task of my own free will, although it is anathema and threatens to destroy me. I will not fail." She said this calmly. "And in return you will release Amun from his vows. You'll let him walk away free and whole. *That* is my bargain."

The Maha looked at her. A smile bloomed on his face.

"You did not have to come to me, to attempt to perform the rite," he said softly, as if he had her in his snare again. With his power over her restored, his fear abated visibly. The broken light in his eyes grew. "You could have tried to perform it alone, far from this place, but you came to me because you are a weak and foolish creature after all." He leaned forward, into the support of Kalini's hand. "You came for him."

"I did," said Mehr.

"If you refuse to vow yourself to me, if you refuse to obey me, he dies too," the Maha said, in the same slow, gentle voice. "Everything dies."

"I am not as much a fool as you think, Maha. I know. But I also know his heart. He would rather die than remain with you. If the world is the price, well." She swallowed. Raised her head high. "I will have his freedom, one way or another."

The brightness of the dreamfire was growing, growing. Beneath the howl of the daiva she heard the creak and skitter of new limbs. Fear, animal and raw, crawled down her spine. She heard the prayers of the mystics rise, somewhere far below them. The Maha turned to listen. His expression was hungry, utterly starved of the power that had kept him blessed for so many years. When the light filtered over his face, his skin looked as thin as gauze.

"Without the dreamfire, you're nothing but a man who likes to hurt people," Mehr murmured. "I see you, Maha. I know you won't deny me this bargain."

Kalini was looking at the Maha too, gazing at him with eyes that drank him in, that consumed the new hollows of his face, the thinness of his skin, the turn of his thin, starved lips. Her gaze never wavered. Her mouth was slightly parted, her hand soft on the Maha's arm.

The sound of screaming rose suddenly between the prayers. Bahren cursed, startling from his place by the door. Abhiman began to unsheathe his weapon. "What is that?" he shouted.

"Nightmares," said Bahren. He sounded sick. "They're here."

"I won't act before I see Amun's vow broken," Mehr said.

Abhiman wrenched Mehr to her feet with an oath. Mehr bit down on her tongue to stop herself from making a sound. She maintained eye contact with the Maha. There was nothing he could do—nothing she could hear—that would make her relent.

"Bring Amun here, Abhiman," the Maha said. He spoke through gritted teeth. "Bahren, you stay and watch the girl."

The Maha looked at Mehr, his fractured eyes full of fury and helplessness. "You have a bargain, Mehr."

Abhiman was stammering, protesting, but when the Maha snarled, "*Go*," he stumbled swiftly out of the room.

Mehr felt suddenly as if she could breathe. She tried to hide her relief, tried not to appear triumphant. Nothing had been won yet. First Amun had to be set free, had to *survive*. Then Mehr had to dance the Rite of the Bound—*alone*—without being destroyed by it. She had to face the nightmares without allowing them to coil their way inside her head and heart. Easier said than done. But Mehr would find a way. She would have to.

"Maha," Bahren said, into the bitter quiet. "Maha, our brothers and sisters are dying. I hear them. I fear for them. Please, give me leave to assist them—"

"No," the Maha said, his voice sudden and savage. "No, you stay here and protect me. I am your master. I am the reason the Empire stands. You stay."

"Maha," Bahren said respectfully. He spoke no more.

Kalini had bowed her head. She raised it then, looking up at

the Maha with eyes soft with light. Mehr saw her touch her fingertips to the Maha's wrist.

"Maha," she murmured. "Are you in pain? Do you suffer?"

"When the storm proceeds as it should, my pain will ease,"
he responded, his voice gentler, now that he was speaking to his
beloved one. "Everything will be as it should be." He smiled at
her, beatific. "I am not an old man yet."

"No, Maha," Kalini agreed, looking up at the gossamer of his
face. "You will never be old."

Her hand was still on his wrist, soft and tender, when she
drew her scimitar from its scabbard and slit the Maha's throat.

It was a dance, almost. She moved so beautifully, so econom-
ically, that she could have been moving through the steps of a
rite. She drew the scimitar in a fine, clean arc. Blood poured
from the gaping maw where his throat had been. He was dead
before he even had the chance to scream.

Mehr was frozen. Kalini looked over at her, cocking her head
to the side. The blade was still in her hand.

Bahren made an awful noise behind her, choked and heartsick. "What have you done?"

"He wasn't a God any longer," Kalini said to him, her voice
terribly calm. "Surely you saw the mortality creeping over him.
The taint of it. I spared him from suffering the foulness of begging scraps from a slave." She leaned down and gently brushed
his eyes closed. "I gave him a merciful death. I've kept him pure.
You would have done no less, if you had been brave enough,
Bahren."

"How could you, sister?" Bahren whispered, uncomprehending.

"I'm not your sister," Kalini said. "I had a sister. She died for
no less than a God. Now that will never change."

Kalini stood and walked calmly toward the door. "Let the
world burn," she said to Mehr as she passed. "None of it matters
any longer."

Bahren let her go. His hands hung numb at his side. Mehr listened to Kalini's measured footsteps fade beyond the doorway.

"The nightmares had her," Bahren said, his voice full of grief. "They must have forced her to do it."

Mehr pressed a hand to her face, breathed in her own skin deep and slow to blot out the smell of blood, and took him by the shoulder. "Bahren. You need to go."

He looked at her. His eyes were wet and shocked.

"What?"

"Run," Mehr said gently, "while you still can. I don't think the temple will be safe much longer, and I still have work to do."

CHAPTER THIRTY-TWO

The honeycomb corridors of the temple were dark, the lanterns snuffed out. Mehr could barely see. She walked slowly, tracing the walls with her fingertips. She was glad, now, that she'd worked so hard to learn the layout of the temple. She had nothing but her memory to guide her through the gloom. She saw none of the mystics, but as she walked she heard the occasional sobs and cries cutting through the howling darkness. She thought of the girls who had welcomed her and taught her karom, and shivered, dread for them coiling in her stomach.

Mehr was sure the mystics had marked the windows with Amun's blood to keep the daiva out, but the Gods and their nightmares had made no promises on Amrithi blood. There was darkness in the temple now, a smell of iron in the air. Mehr heard a skittering, drawing steadily closer. She froze.

The nightmares were walking the corridors.

She closed her eyes. Stayed very still. *You will not find me. Not now, not yet, not today—*

The noise passed. Mehr waited a moment, then kept walking.

Mehr found her way to their old room by memory alone. She walked up the stairs. The room was bathed in the light of the dreamfire pouring in through the open shutters. Abhiman was nowhere to be seen. She didn't know if Bahren had found him and told him to run, or if he had made the decision himself. She didn't know if the nightmares had caught him. She didn't really care.

"Amun," she whispered.

Amun lay on the divan. He was thinner than he'd been before, bruised and very still. She saw water with a ladle on the ground beside him. Someone had gone to some effort to keep him alive, but his skin was gray, his body soaked with sweat. His sigils were as faded as the rest of him. It was only when she placed her hand against his lips, her own fingers trembling, that she was sure he was still breathing.

It broke her heart and healed it over again to see him alive but so harmed. The Maha's death may have released him from his vows, but the bond between them was still hot with his pain. After all he'd suffered she wasn't sure, couldn't be sure, that he would recover from what had been done to him.

She wanted to lie beside him and feel the warmth of him beside her. But there was no time. Instead she placed a hand on his chest, on the place where the scar of their marriage vow lay. She leaned forward and kissed him, a bare brush of her lips against his own. The light of their bond was a golden knot binding them together, so bright it burned her fear clean away.

"I'm going to survive for you," she whispered. "Please, survive for me in return, my love."

She left him there. She had no choice but to do so.

She walked back down the stairs and made her way toward an exit that led to the desert. The doors were flung open. Mehr stopped and stared at the lashing dreamfire, the waves of sand rolling as swift as water with the wind. She had never seen a more awful storm.

The Maha was dead. His mystics were in disarray. Mehr would not have their prayers running through her to guide her or give her strength. Amun would not be with her, performing the rite at her side. She had no partner. No ritual clothing. No kohl around her eyes, no ornaments wreathed through her hair. She was just a woman, thin and hurt and tired. She was no more than human, no more than that, and that would have to be enough.

She kneeled down and took off her boots. Then she sucked in a breath, straightened her shoulders, and stepped beyond the temple walls.

The sand wasn't smooth beneath her feet. It didn't even cling to her strangely, as it had when she'd left her mother's clan. Instead it kept re-forming into new shapes beneath her, collapsing into hollows, then re-forming into jagged edges that made her stumble and struggle for balance. Around her the wind transformed from blistering heat into bitter cold. In the cracks between the dreamfire, the sky was a cavernous void, then a seething mass of pale things. It was as if the shape of the earth were constantly altering.

Mehr bit her lip and kept on walking.

The daiva surrounded her fast. They swept around her, not harming her, their golden eyes blinking in and out of sight between the gouts of dreamfire. Mehr took strange comfort in their presence. They made her feel a little less alone.

Deep in the storm, she stopped walking. She breathed in and out, trying not to choke on the sand around her. She reached for the seed of immortality within herself. There was no more time left to build up her courage, to remind herself of what needed to be done. It was time to act.

Mehr raised her hands. Set her feet against the ground. She began to dance the rite.

The dreamfire poured into her. It was an obliterating fire, too big for her body, too large to leave her soul whole. She let it come. It rose through her blood, filled her eyes and her ears and her throat with light, lifting her bodily with its power. She submitted to its power, bending with the storm, refusing to allow it to break her. She had to survive. She had to turn her will to the task of bending the Gods.

This time she did not have the Maha's will or the mystics' prayers. She did not have Amun to guide her or save her. The only hands shaping the dreams of the Gods were her own. She poured all her heart and soul into a rite that was no longer a two-person act of creation but an act of pure lonely desperation. She drew forward the dreams toward the only thing she desired: survival.

Do not kill us, do not end the world, oh Gods, do not send your nightmares for us, please, do not send your nightmares—

She was thrown back into her body. Her lungs ached. Her eyes stung. She was flat on the ground, arms pinned by clawed, pale fingers. A nightmare hung above her, its face a thousand pale, fractured shards around flat silver eyes. She turned her head and saw more of those eyes watching her. They were everywhere. The storm had breathed life into them.

Mehr wanted to laugh. She'd achieved the opposite of what she'd asked for. The Gods were angry indeed.

The nightmares were no longer simply a cold, creeping horror at the back of her skull. The fury of the Gods had carved them into flesh as hard as bones. It hung above her, but its whispers were inside her too, filling her skull with cold terror.

Images rose up in her mind, blotting her vision out: Hema's throat cut; Usha dead on the ground; Kalini's cold eyes; Amun gray and broken; the feel of Abhiman's hands around her throat; the Maha's fist against her face; Amun's eyes, starless and bleak. There was so much darkness inside her. She'd locked it away for so long. Feeling it now, rising up, nearly destroyed her. Sickened, she felt tears force their way from her eyes. A scream began to claw its way up her throat.

She forced her eyes to snap open. *No.*

She wouldn't be destroyed.

Mehr gripped one of the clawed hands that had pinned her to the ground. It was hard, but it had a brittleness like sandstone. As she dug her nails in, struggling to shift its hold, its surface crumbled a little against her skin.

She dug her fingers in harder. It wasn't enough. Not nearly enough. She couldn't escape it. She gritted her teeth and forced herself to focus on her body. Turning her wrist laboriously in its grip, she clumsily shaped the sigil for *banishment*.

The nightmare shuddered above her, then crawled slowly away from her. Mehr struggled up onto her knees, keeping her gaze fixed on the nightmare, on its lidless gaze.

She'd escaped, but it was no good regardless. Her lungs were heaving; her hands on the ground felt raw and abraded. The storm was too big and far too furious. The nightmares were inching in closer again. She couldn't do this.

It didn't matter if she had already failed. She still had to stand. She still had to *try*.

She was just beginning to rise to her feet when a hand reached for her own. The hand was pure smoke, dark and full of shadows. Mehr looked up. A daiva stared down at her. Veiled, its eyes glowed through the mesh.

The world around her was suddenly, blessedly silent. The howl of the storm had faded away. Daiva wings rustled, producing the barest, whisper-soft susurration. A circle of daiva surrounded them and, beyond it, the nightmares hovered like hungry scavengers, carefully held at bay. The sand beneath them was still and soft, and the howl of the storm seemed like a faraway thing, ancient as a childhood memory. The daiva had hollowed a place within the storm for Mehr to kneel and for the veiled daiva to watch her. For a moment, at least, Mehr could not feel the weight of the dreamfire, and the respite was desperately sweet.

The daiva was still holding out its hand. Mehr took it. The hand felt as solid as the nightmare's flesh had, cool and silken, no brittleness to it at all. Its veil was dusted with stars.

"You," Mehr whispered. "I gave you my tears."

"Yes," the daiva said. "You did."

The voice did not come from the daiva alone but from everywhere around them: from the air and the sand, from somewhere deep within Mehr's own soul. It rattled in her head, filling her with glorious warmth.

Mehr flinched, stumbling back.

"You spoke in my language," the daiva said. Its voice was a chorus, a hundred familiar voices—Lalita's, Amun's, Arwa's—bound together in an inhuman song. "Your master's control has shattered. Now we are stronger and can speak with your words." Mehr had a sense the daiva would have smiled, if it could. "Words aren't so hard."

"He's not my master," Mehr rasped.

"Of course," the veiled daiva said mildly. "Dead men master no one. He *was* your master."

"No," Mehr said, shaking her head. "No, no matter what he did, I always belonged to myself." She spoke reflexively, but in that moment, she knew it was true.

The circle of daiva rustled around softly, a whisper running through them that sounded like the chime of bells.

Mehr knew that sound. She'd heard it. Dreamed it, long ago.

"I have watched you a long time," the veiled daiva said.

Mehr thought of the daiva that had haunted her dreams, the chimes she'd heard in the desert, on the first night she and Amun had shared a tent under the stars. She shivered, not quite from fear.

"Why?" she asked softly. "Daiva, why me?"

It cocked its head to the side, quizzical as a bird. "You were a tool," it said slowly, as if grasping the words from a long distance.

"You were in the right place. Near the one you call Maha, but not yet his property. We haunted the edges of him, the man who made immortals small. Years and years, we haunted him." The veil rustled. "And there you were."

"I see," Mehr said. "You saw that I was a weak link in his armor."

"A strong one," the daiva responded. "A strong link to us. Your blood is our blood. You were still ours." The daiva held a hand toward her. Its hand transformed back into wisps—coiled, gently, against the edge of her jaw. "There is a little of my blood in that flesh of yours," the daiva said. "And in the flesh of your mother, and the flesh of your beloved. Blood has power."

"So I've always been told the daiva believe," Mehr said shakily.

"So humans believe too," the daiva responded swiftly. "The one you call Maha came to the Salt and bound his first Amrithi for the sake of his bloodline, after all. All this, he did for love of his children. He wanted an Empire for his progeny. He wanted to bless them with an everlasting throne."

An image bloomed in Mehr's mind through the daiva's touch: the shadow of the Maha from time long gone, an arrogant and charming commander of men with unflinching eyes and over-bearing charisma. She saw a small hand in his own, saw the terrible love in his eyes. In his child he'd seen himself, seen his glory stretching eternally into the future. His love was selfish and overpowering, a monstrous thing.

He would not have cared about the price he paid or demanded the world to pay for the sake of his own blood. He'd died sure of the glory of his own purpose.

Mehr felt nothing for him. Not even pity.

"Some men believe there is no greater immortality than blood," the daiva observed. "Even when they die, as they must, they hope their blood will survive."

The images faded. The daiva drew its shaded flesh back, coil-ing it back into a simulacrum of fingers. It watched her with its prayer-flame eyes, still and silent, as if a storm weren't raging in a great circle around. It watched her as if they had all the time in the world.

"Men," the daiva said, "are so often fools."

"Do you want to punish me for the heresy I have committed?" Mehr asked. She held her head high, trembling a little, the eyes of all those daiva and pale nightmares following her every movement. "I know that binding the dreams of your forefathers is wrong. Daiva, I am sorry for it, but I can't relent. I must try to perform the Maha's rite. I must try to keep this world whole. Please don't stop me. I beg you."

"We do not care about heresy," the daiva said. "That is a mortal concept."

"Why have you come for me, then?" Mehr asked.

"Because we care about balance," the veiled daiva told her. "We who are the sunrise and sunset, life and death, good and evil. We desire order. The man called Maha shattered the balance. He weakened us. He fed on the good dreams of our mothers and fathers and left their dark dreams caged, feral and alone. That was wrong of him."

"He did many things that were wrong," Mehr said in a small voice.

"The nightmares must be free," the daiva said. Its voice held the compassion of Hema's, the implacableness of Nahira's. "You should not stop that."

No. Mehr would not accept it, would not let the world burn.

"Should not or cannot?" Mehr demanded.

The daiva tilted its head again. It didn't appear angry.

"Do you respect the will of your ancestors?" it asked.

"I can't let the world die," Mehr said.

"All things want to live," the veiled daiva agreed. "So do we." A susurration ran through the watching circle. "So we ask you for a trade. Daiva to mortal."

The daiva was suddenly very close to Mehr, close enough that Mehr could discern the sunburst of its bright eyes and the ever-shifting contours of its face beneath the veil.

"Use the rite the Maha turned to his own purposes. Use it to return the world to balance, as it was always intended to be used."

"Can I do that? Return the balance with the rite?" Mehr asked, full of wonder. "The Maha told us the Rite of the Bound was for two people. That it was an act of creation, not an act of balance."

"You can," said the daiva. "You, the Amrithi with *amata*. Or you, alone, here and now, because there is no one else."

Mehr saw a great set of scales in her mind's eye, heavy with dreams. Good dreams. Ill dreams. A world balanced by unknowable forces, by waves of stars that sped beneath the closed eyes of sleeping immortals. Her breath caught.

"The rite was a gift once," the daiva said. Its voice was a woman's voice, soft with regret. "From an immortal mother to a mortal daughter. It was a promise that all darkness would pass, and all suns would set. It was a gift of hope. It can be a gift again."

The daiva opened its fist. An obsidian blade, Amrithi in design, sat upon its palm. A gem, pale as tears, lay embedded in its hilt. The daiva took the blade in one hand and carved open its palm. The shadows of its skin peeled back to reveal stars whirling under the surface, galaxies bursting into miniature life. Mehr's breath caught.

"My blood," the daiva said. "I make this vow on my blood. Make the Gods sleep, little daughter. Lull them back into slumber. Ask them for nothing but this. Do not cage their nightmares or demand their gifts. Teach them peace. Dedicate your life to this service. Maintain your vigil whenever the dreamfire falls, and when you are prepared, teach others with *amata* to share your burden. It will be a long vigil, but if you choose to serve, we will do more than forbid harming you. In return for your service we will protect you, and as the keeper of balance, we will enthrone you. You will be the first among Taras, the first in your own dynasty. We will give you the glory an Ambhan man once reshaped the world for." The daiva's blood dripped to the ground, shattering like glass. "Will you take my vow, small one? Will you take it to give you the strength to do what must be done?"

Mehr looked at the daiva's star-strewn blood. She looked into its eyes.

"What are you?" Mehr whispered. "You're no small bird-daiva. Nothing I've ever known."

"When we were worshipped, I was called Elder Mother," the veiled daiva told her. "I wept for my children, who were mortal and soon lost to me. Now I have no children, no tears, no name. But you may call me Elder, if you wish, because that at least is still true."

"Elder," Mehr said. "Forgive me. I can't bargain with you."

The daiva chimed around her. The nightmares howled. Mehr winced, closing her eyes, holding her strength close. She opened them again.

"I'll do as you ask," she continued. "I'll dance the rite. I'll beg the Gods for peace. I'll dedicate my life to the task, if I must. But I will not make a vow again. I will not bind my soul, not for anything. Certainly not for the hope of human glory." She thought of Amun: his blue-limned sigils, the deep darkness of his eyes. "My last vows...I hold them sacred. I will never hold any above them. That was a promise I made to myself, and I will not break it."

"You will face the storm with no promise of hope for the future?" the daiva asked. "You will face our mothers and fathers with nothing but your mortal hope?"

Mehr gave the veiled daiva a watery smile.

"Yes," Mehr said. "And I am afraid it will have to be enough."

Mehr bowed her head and made a gesture of thanks. Elder considered her carefully, then raised one hand up to touch the edge of her own veil.

"Then I will simply give you my blessings, little one," Elder said. "My blessings on you, and your mortal heart."

She raised her veil and pressed a kiss to Mehr's forehead. Mehr heard the great sound of fluttering wings, and the daiva were gone.

The dreamfire returned, fierce as ever, and it was swallowing her whole.

This time Mehr did not falter. She let the fire of the dreams and the nightmares both take her. She didn't fight. She yielded, with absolute trust.

She thought of the first time she'd danced with the dreamfire, in the storm when she'd tried to make her way across Jah Irinah to Lalita's side. She hadn't commanded the dreamfire then. She'd had no clan, no partner. She'd had no Rite of the Bound, no knowledge of her true gifts. She had pleaded with dreamfire, simply pleaded with all her heart for it to guide her to Lalita's home. And it had.

This rite was not a terrible act of creation. It was a gift of hope. A gift of balance.

She thought of balance. Even nightmares had their place. She remembered the sweetness of Arwa's laughter and Nahira's brusque kindness, the bitterness of Maryam's hatred and the loneliness of the women's quarters. She remembered the suffering the Maha had inflicted on her, and the scars it had left forever on her heart. She ached with the memory of Amun's love. All of these things had shaped her. They were part of her now.

So she didn't demand that the Gods shape the world into an image she desired. She didn't ask for their kindness. She didn't ask them to restrain their nightmares or their fury. She moved her limbs with the dreamfire, let it sing through her flesh and her soul. She held all her memories close and shaped the sigils of the rite. They flew from her fingers like birds.

Gods, mothers, fathers. I ask you, please do not awaken. Sleep. Let the world remain whole.

She poured all her will into the task, into the rite, into a dance that stretched beyond her limbs. She felt grace rush through her. It was an awe not born from fear but from true love, pure and good.

Sleep, and let your children live. Sleep, and let the balance return.

When the nightmares reached for her, she let them. She held her hope close to her skin. She didn't turn from the fear. Instead of swallowing her terror away, she accepted it and let it flow through her, with her. The fear, too, was part of the balance.

Sleep. Please, sleep.

For the sake of your children, your love—

She danced beyond exhaustion. Danced until the light of the dreamfire began to fade from the sky, and the sand was still and even beneath her feet. She danced and pleaded, heart and soul. And she *hoped*.

She danced until she could dance no longer. Her legs buckled. She fell, and kneeled in the sand, gasping for air, sweat cooling on her skin. Her hair was loose and wild, tangled over her shoulders. Her skin felt raw. Unable to even kneel any longer, she let herself collapse to the ground. She lay on her back and stretched her arms out at her sides, open to the vastness around her.

When she next opened her eyes, she saw nothing but blue above her. The sky had cleared. The dreamfire was fading. The sand was still and unmoving beneath her body. Somehow, she was alive.

She was alive, and the world was whole.

Mehr would have wept, would have laughed, if she'd had the strength. Instead she could only smile alone, helplessly joyful, at the sky.

"Thank you," she whispered. "Ah, thank you."

She could have happily continued lying there in the sand until unconsciousness claimed her, but her need to see Amun was a fierce thing, stronger even than her exhaustion. Mustering up all her remaining energy—of which there was precious little—Mehr clambered to her feet.

Ah Gods, it was hard! She was so tired. But she knew her own stubbornness now, and she pushed herself onward. Limping, she began to walk back toward the temple.

She hadn't walked far before she was forced to stop again. She froze in her tracks. She could go no farther. The way back to the temple was barred.

The mystics were waiting for her.

CHAPTER THIRTY-THREE

There were only ten mystics. There was no sign of Kalini or Bahren, or Hema's women. But the mystics waiting for her were all armed, and Abhiman was at the head of them, striding toward her with his sword unsheathed. His gaze was murderous.

Mehr was far too tired for this.

"What good will it do to harm me?" she yelled, stumbling back as he strode ever closer.

There were red scratches on Abhiman's face and a new bruise swelling up his left eye. "You did this," he snarled. "I know you did. I found the Maha dead. My brothers and sisters are gone, or scattered to the winds." His sword wavered in his grip. His face was stained with blood and sweat. "You've destroyed all that's pure and good. The Empire will fall. We will all fall."

Mehr shook her head. "No, Abhiman," she said. Her head was pounding terribly. She didn't want to die here, but Abhiman was weeping now, teeth bared, and she thought, *He will not let me go.* "I've saved us. That's all."

Abhiman howled. It was a sound of pure animal fury.

"You wretched bitch," he snarled. "I'll cut your heart out, I swear it!"

He ran toward her, swinging his sword with fury and no

finesse. Mehr tried to scramble away from him, tried to run—
and froze all over again.

Something dark shifted under the sand beneath her feet.

A daiva ruptured up from the ground between them. It was
a monstrous thing, vast, its shadowy body bristling with thorns.
She saw its vast array of teeth, its glittering stretch of eyes. It
stretched its body out between them, a great wall that blotted
Abhiman from her vision. Then it swooped down. Mehr heard
an awful sound: the snap of teeth meeting resistant flesh.

Abhiman was dead before he hit the ground.

Mehr bit her tongue hard enough to bleed, forcibly holding
back her instinctual scream of horror at the sight of the severed
remains of him. She didn't even shudder as the mystics shrieked
and recoiled, faces gray with terror. She curled her hands into
fists and stood stock-still.

The daiva curled itself up, small and sleek, its teeth carefully
tucked away. It glided across the sand to her. A tendril of smoke
wound its way gently around her wrist and uncurled her fingers.

A weight pressed itself into her palm. The daiva made a soft
sound, somewhere between a coo and chitter, and sank back
into the sand.

Mehr looked down into her open palm. On it lay the black
blade, its teary gem gleaming in the light. She stared at it, long
and wondering, then tucked it carefully into the sash of her robe.

Mehr had made no vows to the daiva. Apparently, they had
decided to protect her regardless.

Thank you, she thought.

"You should leave this place." She didn't bother to imbue her
voice with threat. She let the threat of the daiva act as her armor.
When she took a step forward, the armed mystics flinched. "Irinah has no place for the Saltborn any longer."

She knew her words were true. She'd felt the dreams of Gods.

She'd been in the presence of a daiva so ancient it spoke her tongue. Returning the balance of the world, allowing the Gods to dream naturally, would return the world to order. But balance did not have to be *kind*. Balance wore the face of a nightmare as easily as it wore the guise of a daiva veiled in stars.

The mystics had praised the Maha. The mystics had loved him. The mystics had helped him chain the Gods and weaken the daiva, and now with the Maha's death the world had slipped swiftly, brutally from their grasp.

Mehr looked at their feet, pressed to the sand. Beneath it, the Gods they had helped chain slept and dreamed their unleashed dreams. She thought of the shadow of the daiva and the way it had risen beneath her feet. She thought of the flat, silver eyes of nightmares too-long crushed beneath mortal heels. She thought, too, of Abhiman's death. His blood hadn't yet begun to cool.

They shouldn't be surprised, Mehr thought, *if the world shows them its teeth*.

They would be wise to leave Irinah swiftly. She did not think they would find what passed for balance, here on the backs of sleeping Gods, anything akin to a kindness.

She held her courage, held the iron in her spine, and walked toward the temple. The mystics parted like a sea to let her pass. Their weapons hung useless at their sides. She knew she would never see them again.

Amun was still unconscious. Mehr leaned over him. Sand had come into the room through the open shutters. His face glittered with dust, the loose curls of his dark hair etched with gold. Mehr brushed the sand from his eyelids. He didn't stir.

"Please wake up," Mehr whispered. She whispered it against his forehead as she kissed him, just once, as if her mouth could pass on blessings just as Elder's had. "I can feel you. I know you're not gone. Come back and see the world we've saved."

She took his hand. His skin was warm. "Please, Amun."

She was too raw not to feel her own fears. They washed over her. She feared that fighting his vows to the Maha had broken him irreparably. She feared that the Maha controlled him still, those vows extending beyond death. She feared having to let him go. She feared that it had all been for nothing, that the world would go on but Amun would not, and Mehr would be left behind, alone with nothing but her grief to sustain her.

It turned out that she had the strength left to cry after all.

She curled up beside him like she had so many times before. She wiped her tears on her sand-stained sleeve. She nestled herself against the crook of his shoulder and took hold of his hand again, taking comfort in the warmth of his skin, the roughness of his knuckles, the familiar softness of his palms. In a voice hoarse from all she'd been through, she sang to him. She sang the lullaby she'd sung to him that night when the pain had consumed him, when there had been no hope left inside either of them. She sang him the lullaby she'd sung on the night when they had made their own hope.

Eventually, her voice began to fade. Her eyes began to close, exhaustion claiming her.

When she felt him move, she thought she was dreaming.

Then his hand curled tight around her own.

She shot upright. Heart in her throat, she looked down at his face. His eyes were unfocused, pained by the light. Blinking hard, he slowly began to focus.

"Mehr," he rasped. "Mehr."

"Amun." She clasped his hand tighter in return. She was trembling. "I'm here."

"Mehr. The Maha. Can't—feel. Him."

"I know, Amun." Now that she was looking at him in the clear light of day, she could see that the scars of his vows had lost their color, had faded to thin white traceries on his skin. Their master was gone, and the power of the vows scarred onto his skin had gone with him.

"The Maha…"

"He's gone," Mehr said, her heart so full, so very full. "He's dead, Amun. We're free."

There would be time enough to tell him everything later. For now it was enough to see the smile that dawned on his face and the light that grew in his eyes. For now it was enough to have his hand reach up to touch her tangled hair and feel his mouth against hers, the vow between them humming with life, golden and strong.

They rested and ate first. Then, much later, Mehr told Amun all she could. Amun listened silently, asking no questions until Mehr's voice faded, until she shook her head and told him that she had explained everything she knew.

"The daiva protect you now?" he asked. "They won't allow anyone to harm you?"

"I made no vows to them," Mehr said. "But they made vows to me, and I think they've decided to keep them, bargain or no bargain."

Amun looked unbearably relieved.

"You could go home," he told her. "You could see your family. Your sister."

Mehr felt a pang in her chest. "No. I can't. I have to stay. I have to perform the rite again," she explained. "Every storm. The Gods' fury won't be so easily quelled, and the balance will take a long time to be restored. I need to maintain the peace. I'm the only one who can."

"You're not the only one."

"Perhaps one day I'll teach other Amrithi with the gift," she said, shrugging, looking carefully down at her hands so she wouldn't need to meet his eyes. She would need to. One day.

"But who would learn now? There are so few of us left, and it's an anathema act. Still, there will be time enough, I expect. I'm young yet."

"Mehr." Amun's voice was sharp. Mehr looked at him. "Don't pretend you misunderstand me. I can take up the burden. I've performed the rite all my life."

"No, Amun," Mehr said softly. "I would never ask that of you."

"I'm a free man now," Amun said. "It would be my choice."

His gaze was so steady, so clear. Mehr forced herself not to look away.

"You've sacrificed enough for me, Amun."

"My choice," he repeated. "Don't you consider choices sacred, Mehr?"

"Ah, Gods." She squeezed her eyes shut. Opened them. "You've been trapped in the heart of a nightmare since you were nothing but a child. And now you're *free*. Don't you see, Amun? The thought of you staying in this place, forcing yourself to perform the rite for my sake..." She paused, struggling to speak through her feelings. "Amun," she whispered finally. "It would shatter me."

Mehr stood abruptly. She didn't want to hear his protests. "You need more water," she said, "and more food."

She searched through the supplies they'd scavenged earlier. The mystics had taken almost everything when they'd fled, but there had been water and a little food left. Enough to last them a few weeks. She poured some water into their cups, then carefully peeled spiked fruit and carried it over to him. By the time she returned to him, she'd found some of the words she needed.

"If you had a choice, if it weren't for me," she said, "would you perform the rites—any of them—ever again? Would you set foot in this temple? Or would you go somewhere else, far away from here, and begin again?"

When he was silent, she said, "I thought so."

"Mehr," he said sharply. "We're vowed to each other. Does that mean nothing?"

Mehr's stomach plummeted. "Oh."

Amun straightened. "No. You don't understand—"

"I understand perfectly," she said, cutting in. "I never, ever wanted our vows to chain you. I didn't make those vows to trap you in a new cage."

"Mehr, no."

"Our vows set me free. Do you think I'd want any less for you?" She shook her head. "I love you enough to want to see you unchained, even if that means I remain here alone. I mean that, Amun. I want you to go."

Amun looked as if he wanted to argue. He held out a hand, reaching for her. He began to say her name—

A daiva flickered at the edge of Mehr's vision, just beyond the window. She turned her head sharply.

"What is it?" Amun asked.

"I'm not sure."

He followed her to the window. They both looked out.

An armed group of people was approaching the temple. Amun tensed at her side.

"Those are not mystics," he said.

"No," Mehr said, looking at the figure leading them. Her face was exposed, her body wrapped in dun-colored cloth, her braid whipping out behind her. "That's my mother."

The daiva were waiting when Mehr and Amun walked out of the temple into the sunlight. They clung to the temple walls and circled their feet. A few swooped through the air high above them.

The Amrithi were a small group. All adults, Mehr saw. They looked nervous, but not afraid, exactly. Their expressions were perilously close to hopeful. Only Ruhi's face was unreadable, her eyes shadowed.

Mehr saw Lalita standing just behind her mother. She smiled at her, tears threatening to overwhelm her again. "Welcome," she said.

"Ah, Gods," Lalita said. Her smile was watery. "It's good to see you alive, Mehr."

"Likewise," Mehr said, somewhat foolishly.

Mehr made eye contact with her mother then. "Why have you come?" Surely they hadn't come for her. Mehr didn't think her mother would have put the clan into such clear danger, not even for Mehr's sake. Certainly, Lalita wouldn't have allowed it.

"We saw the storm," said her mother. "We felt the nightmares come, the earth shudder, and we thought the world was coming to an end. But the storm ended, and we did not." Ruhi looked at the daiva flying above them. "The daiva came for us," she continued. "They beckoned us. We knew then that we had to take a risk and follow them."

"We didn't know they would bring us to the temple," Lalita said. "That was a pleasant surprise."

"The Maha is dead," said Mehr. An audible ripple ran through the Amrithi. "But I danced his rite, his anathema rite, which was never his to begin with. I reclaimed it, and I kept the world whole." Mehr felt Amun encircle her wrist. She took strength in that touch. "I don't regret it. I regret nothing I did for the sake of our survival."

Her mother's face remained expressionless. "Will you take his place?" she asked. "Rule the Empire as its quiet master, sequestered here among your worshippers?"

Mehr could see the same doubt in the eyes of some of the other Amrithi. She understood that her mother spoke not only for herself but for her clan.

"She has saved us all," Amun said, his voice rich with utter conviction. He looked at them with clear, cloudless eyes. "Tara, Mehr has ensured that no one will be bound to the terrible service the Maha demanded ever again. No one will wear the scars I wear. She is nothing like him. I know, better than any living creature, that she is the best of us. She is hope."

"The daiva wouldn't surround her if her path was evil," one of the Amrithi said. A woman, her face weathered, her hair pure silver. "She acts with their blessing."

"They have asked me to keep the balance," Mehr said to her, to them all. "And that is what I have chosen to do."

In response to her words, the daiva swirled up around her—somewhat ostentatiously, Mehr thought sourly. Still, a symbol was a symbol, and the joy growing in the eyes of the Amrithi was desperately beautiful to see.

"All I ask," Mehr said to her mother, as the daiva settled around them, "is that you don't try to stop me."

Her mother took a step forward, then another. In one swift motion, she kneeled.

"I am thankful, beyond thankful, that you have risked your own soul in order to save us all." Her eyes shone with barely contained emotion. She looked up at Mehr with a face that was all feeling, fierce and broken with love. "We owe you a debt of gratitude, daughter. We can never hope to repay it."

The Amrithi behind her touched their hands to their foreheads, their chests, in a gesture of respect. Mehr almost wept again at the sight of them.

Her mother stood. "I am so glad you're safe, Mehr," she said softly. "I was so afraid you were lost to me."

"I'm here," said Mehr. "I'm whole."

She felt it when Amun's hand released her own. Her mother embraced her, held her tight, and Amun walked toward the other Amrithi. She saw him murmur something about food and shelter to the silver-haired woman, and then he was gone. Just another robed figure in the crowd.

CHAPTER THIRTY-FOUR

Dear Arwa, Mehr wrote.

It's been so long, little sister. I hope you are happy. I miss you. Do you miss me?

I have a good life now, better than I once hoped for. One day I'll tell you all about it, but I'm sure you're having adventures of your own now...

Mehr sat in the library. Its shelves were half-ransacked, all the clever silver-dialed instruments long gone. She was sure Edhir had been the one to raid the library. The other mystics had taken useful things, food and fuel and clothing. But Edhir had loved his maps more than all of those things. He would never have left them behind.

She tried not to think too often of what had become of all those mystics: the young and the old, the ones who'd truly believed the Maha was their God and had loved him better than anything in the world. Their world had been shattered, their safe universe of prayer and service and glory utterly destroyed. Mehr did not want to have any sympathy for them, but despite herself, she did.

Hema had been one of them, once.

She sat by the window on a table, legs crossed, writing so hurriedly that the ink kept smearing. There was a daiva on the edge of the window, fluttering lazily, occasionally chirruping. She ignored it.

She told Arwa about her life. Only the good things, for now. Arwa was so young. Perhaps later Mehr would tell her the whole truth. For now she only wrote about the sand, and how it shimmered and spun itself into shapes, for the sheer joy of it. She described the daiva, and the way they were growing stronger, their shadowy forms growing more solid day by day, their numbers growing. She told Arwa that she hoped she would see her very soon. She was still writing when she heard footsteps on the stairs.

Lalita peered in. "He's ready to leave," she said. "Come quickly now."

Mehr picked up the letter carefully, trying not to smudge the ink any more than she already had. She followed Lalita down the stairs toward an exit that led to the desert. Kamal was waiting for them, a pack slung over his shoulder. He raised an eyebrow at the sight of Mehr flapping the letter as she walked.

"Is it dry?" he asked.

"It will have to do," said Mehr, handing it to him. He rolled it up neatly, placing it in his pack beside the letter she'd written for her father.

"If your sister is in Irinah, I'll deliver it to her. If she isn't..." Kamal shrugged. "Well, I'll do my best." He looked at her narrowly. "You could come as far as Jah Irinah with me, if you like. See if you can find her."

"I can't risk leaving," she said. "Besides, I doubt it would do any good. No doubt they're far away from Irinah now."

"No doubt," he agreed.

Mehr had learned some days ago from the Amrithi that her father was no longer the Governor of Irinah. He had left the province entirely. The news had hit her like a physical blow. Generations of her family had governed Irinah. Now their governance—the blessing they had earned through loyal service to the Emperor and his line—had ended.

She didn't know if her father had chosen to relinquish his position willingly or if politics had forced him from the role. All her knowledge was fragmented and secondhand; the brief gossip the Amrithi had imparted to her told her nothing of the games of power that must have been played in her father's court after her departure, or how well her father had fared. She desperately wanted the truth, but she had chosen to dedicate her life to a service that ensured the survival of the world. She couldn't step beyond Irinah's borders and seek out her family herself. Second-hand knowledge, then, was all she would ever have.

But ah—her heart ached for him, her father, who had governed Irinah loyally, who had loved her and Arwa so unwisely, who had promised to keep Arwa safe, no matter the cost.

So much was unknown to her now. She had little hope that Kamal would find her father or Arwa. But little hope was still *hope*, and Mehr had learned that even the smallest kernel of it, preserved in the darkness, could bloom into a miracle.

"Thank you," she said to him. "It was a kind offer regardless."

Kamal's smile was thin. She knew he still didn't care much for her.

"You'll be missed," Lalita told him gently.

"More Amrithi arrived this morning," Kamal said to her, his expression warming. It was hard to dislike Lalita. "You won't be short of company for long. And I'll send messages, of course."

Amrithi had been making their way to the temple for the last few days, following the guidance of the daiva, the whispers on the wind. Many seemed determined to stay, hungry for the security and promise the temple now offered them. But some— Kamal included—had decided to leave. *We'll need to know what's happening in the Empire, if we're to protect ourselves,* he'd told Mehr's mother, and she and the elders had agreed. But really, Mehr thought he simply wanted to see the world beyond Irinah's borders. The Empire was still far from a safe place for the Amrithi, but Kamal could travel through it now without fearing for the clan he'd left behind. The Amrithi had a home again: a safe haven, cradled on the backs of the Gods.

"Where will you go?" Lalita asked him.

"As far from here as I can," he said swiftly. "I've never been to Chand. Or perhaps I'll find the coast, cross the sea." A pause. Then: "You could come, Lalita. See the world with me."

"Not with you," Lalita said with a laugh, tossing her hair back. But Mehr could see the yearning in her eyes. Desert life wasn't one Lalita had chosen. Irinah wouldn't keep her forever.

They watched Kamal go. When he was no more than a dark speck on the horizon, Lalita let out a sigh.

"Do you think he'll be safe, Mehr?" she asked.

"I think the world is very changed," Mehr said. She shook her head. "I just don't know. I only hope he finds Arwa safe and well."

Lalita put an arm around Mehr for comfort. They stood like that for a long moment, watching Kamal vanish into the distance, the sunshine beating down on their heads. Then Lalita broke the silence.

"Your mother is looking for you, by the way," she said. "I hear there's a great deal to be done."

There was indeed a great deal that needed to be done. More Amrithi kept arriving at the temple, beckoned by the daiva, the gifted and ungifted alike emerging from hiding and seeking the temple's shelter. The oasis provided some sustenance, but work had to be done to ensure that the growing clan would be properly cared for. It was the kind of work Mehr knew nothing of and would never be able to assist with helpfully, but her mother seemed determined to involve her in it regardless.

Mehr listened semipatiently as her mother and the elders discussed how the growing conglomeration of clans would be governed, and shared what little fragments of news they'd managed to discover about what was occurring beyond the desert's borders. The Amrithi who had arrived so far had been by and large normal people. None were wealthy or well connected or in a position to know the direction of the political tides in Jah Irinah or the Empire beyond it. As a result, the clan elders—and Mehr—knew frustratingly little. Scraps. All they had were scraps.

The nobility mourned ostentatiously. In villages and cities across the Empire, its citizens, noble and common alike, buried faceless statues of the Maha and Emperor as one in graves and wept, and wept, and wept. There were rumors that the Maha had not died at all—no matter what wild-eyed mystics claimed—and the Emperor had put a handful of the Maha's own beloved Saltborn to death for reasons no one had yet been able to explain to Mehr or to the elders. Nightmares and daiva had begun to appear beyond Irinah's borders. An Amrithi man who'd lived for a number of years in Jah Irinah told Mehr, once, that soldiers had been sent into the desert to retrieve the body of the Maha, but none had returned.

Mehr had thought of Abhiman's death and asked him no more questions.

Even without scraps of news to guide her, Mehr would have known that the Empire was in tumult. The faith and law had been torn asunder. The strength the Maha had blessed the Empire with was fading. And yet, for all the Maha had done to her for the Empire's sake, Mehr couldn't be glad, not entirely, not when so many would suffer the consequences of the Maha's choices. Not when her own family lived in the Empire. Not when she loved the Empire still, despite herself.

But the Empire's fate—thank the Gods—was out of her hands now.

When the meeting ended, Mehr's mother took her hand. "Come with me," she said. "We should speak alone."

They walked out onto one of the balconies facing the oasis. Mehr could see Amrithi below, trying to make sense of the irrigation surrounding it. She leaned forward to watch them and saw her mother's eyes focus on the ribbon around Mehr's throat, the lazy shift of her marriage seal against the faded cloth of her tunic.

"The man," Ruhi began hesitantly. "Your fellow—servant..."

"Amun," Mehr said. "His name is Amun."

"Amun," she agreed. "Amun has been helping the sick and the young settle. The elders like him. I've been told he's a neat mender of clothes."

"He is," Mehr said, feeling a tug in her chest. It wasn't the bond. It was just pure affection.

"He's a gentle soul," Ruhi said.

"I know," Mehr said. "Mother, what are you trying to say to me?"

"If you don't want to see him," her mother said carefully, "you won't need to. No more than that. There will be clans who choose to leave here when they feel safe to do so. He could be encouraged to go with one of them."

"Why wouldn't I want to see him?" Mehr asked. "You said it yourself, Amun is a good person."

"Goodness doesn't erase bad memories, and I know you shared a dark time together." Mehr's mother looked away. "I only mean, Mehr, that no one would blame you if you wanted to begin again. I believe he would understand."

Mehr bit her lip. She and Amun hadn't spoken properly since the day she'd told him she wanted him to leave. Amun had kept his distance—a task that had become easier when the Amrithi had begun arriving and filling the temple—and Mehr had done the same in return.

I will not be the Maha, she reminded herself. *I will not keep him, if he wants to go.*

"I just want him to do what he wants to," Mehr said. "No more."

Even without the maps and instruments of the mystics, the Amrithi elders were confident they could predict the arrival of the next storm. They mapped the stars from memory, discerned their patterns with their eyes. They smelled the storm on the wind and watched the daiva for signs of growing restlessness. They had assured Mehr the next storm was coming soon. The Gods remained unsettled, their dreams rising far too easily to the surface. They would need to be soothed.

It was Mehr's duty to prepare for the next storm, so she went to do just that. No one stopped Mehr from walking out into the desert or offered to accompany her. They knew already that she preferred to practice alone. Even the daiva didn't hover around her, although she knew they were there. One day she would bring other *amata*-gifted Amrithi out here with her and teach them the rite, but the new peace was still far too raw and fragile to be disturbed by unwary students. For now, she would have to manage on her own.

She stretched her muscles, moving through familiar motions to warm her limbs and her blood. She manipulated her hands, shaping the ghosts of sigils on her fingertips. She was barely prepared to begin when she realized Amun was approaching.

She felt him long before she saw him. The golden thread binding them hummed with the warmth of him. It wound tight within her. She touched her fingers reflexively to her marriage seal. When she looked up he was there, watching her.

"Amun."

"Mehr."

He walked toward her. He was wearing a new pale robe. His face was still a little hollowed from his illness, but his scars were silver shadows, only an echo of the vows that no longer held him fast. He looked whole and alive, and Mehr could only drink the sight of him in.

"I hoped you'd be here," he said. "I've struggled to find you alone."

"Have you?" Mehr wondered if her mother had run interference, and cursed inwardly. "I thought you were the busy one. You've been making friends," Mehr noted, her tone gently teasing. "I never thought I'd see the day, but I'm glad of it."

"It's good to be among people I may one day trust," Amun said.

"One day?"

"Give me time."

She looked him over.

"Where did you get those clothes?" she asked. His hair had grown a little longer, she noticed. Her fingers itched to reach up and push one errant curl back from his face.

"Someone gave them to me."

"I gathered," Mehr said dryly. She found she couldn't help but smile. "You look nice."

Amun smiled back at her. It lit up his face and warmed her like pure sunlight. "Kamal gave them to me, before he left."

"He must have liked you."

"No. I think he felt sorry for me." The possibility didn't seem to bother Amun.

For the first time, he looked at ease in his own skin. It was as if the breaking of his vows had literally left him lighter.

"I thought you might go with him," Mehr admitted.

"I considered it," said Amun.

Mehr traced an idle circle in the sand with her foot. She didn't want to look into his face any longer.

"I told you," Mehr said. "I told you that you should do whatever you want to do. You could have gone. Seen the world."

"I don't want to see the world, Mehr."

"Don't stay here for my sake, Amun, that's all I ask." She hated how it left her feeling flayed bare, speaking to him so. "Don't stay just because..."

"Mehr?"

"Just because I want you to," Mehr admitted.

Amun strode toward her. When Mehr took a step back, shaking her head, he froze.

"Don't," she said.

"I know you fear what I may say," Amun said, his careful eyes tracing the contours of her face, reading it as if it were paper. "But I want you to hear me. Will you let me speak, Mehr?"

Mehr nodded.

Amun took a tentative step forward. There was only room for breath between them, but he didn't touch her. He tilted his head, speaking low and soft, his breath against her hair.

"I was trapped with vows as a child. I was told I would never escape them. So I served and I suffered, and I never allowed myself to dream of anything. Not of freedom, not of family, not of happiness. I accepted my lot." A deep exhale. "Then you came, and I began to dream again."

Mehr looked up at him then. His eyes, oh. The way he looked at her was like a brand to her soul.

"I imagined what it would be like to court you, if we were free."

"I know," Mehr said, remembering the night when they'd held one another, when they'd made their bond. "I remember."

"And now I'm free," Amun said. "I'm truly free. Because of you."

"Because of you," Mehr cut in, her voice fierce. "You were the one who tried to show me mercy. You were the one who risked your own soul to set me free. Amun, if it weren't for your courage, the world would still be in chains."

"You said you'd let me speak, Mehr," Amun said mildly.

"I didn't promise to let you speak falsehoods."

"True." He looked at her as if she were his moon and stars all at once. "Both of us then. We saved one another. And now, perhaps, I can have my dream."

It took Mehr a moment to understand.

"You want to court me?" she asked.

"If you'll allow it," Amun said.

"We're—we're married. We're vowed, we—Amun," Mehr said helplessly. "You don't need to court me."

"But I'd like to," he said, his gaze clear, his voice steady. "I want to court you every day. I want to choose you and ask you to choose me, and know that we are bound because we have chosen each other. I want to know we are bound because we continue to choose to belong to one another."

Mehr raised a hand. Amun took it. He twined his fingers with hers, a touch that made light shiver inside her.

"I don't want to see the world," Amun said. "I want to see our future. I want to see *you*."

She looked down at their interlaced fingers, at their strength and their scars. Her heart ached. Amun had saved her, and she had saved him in return. Mehr had chosen him, over and over again, and Amun had chosen her in return.

Choices. Choices were sacred, and Mehr had made hers long ago.

"No more," she said, her voice shaking. "You've courted me enough for today, I think."

When he began to pull his hand back, unsure, she held on more tightly.

"You've won me completely, you see," she said.

"Ah." A long exhale. "That's...good."

Mehr laughed. There was the taciturn Amun she knew so well.

"You can court me again tomorrow. And the day after that. And after that."

"And so forth?"

"Yes," Mehr said. "I'd like that very much."

She looked up at his face. She'd seen the promise of a better future in the daiva and their growing strength, in the growing presence of Amrithi, no longer hidden and afraid. But in Amun's face she saw something more: a future of love and of kindness. A future spun from the very best of dreams.

She reached her free hand up and finally pushed back that curl that had so vexed her. She cupped his cheek.

"Now," she said, "let me court you."

"And tomorrow," he prompted.

"And so forth," Mehr said.

In response he leaned down to meet her, their hands still twined. Mehr kissed her husband, the man she had chosen and the man who had chosen her in return.

Amun lifted her up, and Mehr laughed, twining her legs around his waist, utterly weightless with joy.

"Kiss me again," she said, and he did. His lips were warm, sweeter than wine. He kissed her fiercely, joy and love pouring from every inch of him, filling her up.

"I thought you were courting me?" Amun asked, pulling back.

"I think you're thoroughly courted," she said.

"Do you?"

"I know so."

Mehr touched a fingertip to his lower lip and watched the shiver that ran through him.

Amun. My heart.

There was training to do, Mehr thought distantly, and so much work to be done to keep the Amrithi alive. There were unknowable dangers ahead, and nightmares roaming free across the Empire. But whatever lay in the future, Amun would be by her side, steady and strong. Mehr couldn't be afraid, knowing that.

"I love you, Amun," she said softly.

"And I you." He met her eyes. "You're correct, of course. I'm thoroughly courted." His face was full of light. It wore a look of pure wonder. "Do what you will."

She cupped his face in her hands, leaned forward, and did just that.

The story continues in...
Realm of Ash
A novel of the Books of Ambha.
Keep reading for a sneak peek!

Acknowledgments

Writing may be solitary, but publishing is a wonderfully collaborative process. This book wouldn't exist without the hard work of many people, and I am grateful to all of them. My first thanks must go to my agent, Laura Crockett, who took a chance on me and my book, and has been a marvelous, kind-hearted advocate for my work from day one. Thank you also to the whole fantastic team at Triada US, especially Uwe Stender and Brent Taylor.

Thank you to my editor, Sarah Guan, who made this a far better book than it would ever have been without her guidance. Thank you also to the rest of Orbit, particularly Tim Holman, Anne Clarke, Ellen Wright, Paola Crespo, Gleni Bartels, Lauren Panepinto, and Lisa Marie Pompilio. Huge thanks also go to the UK Orbit team, especially my lovely UK editor, Jenni Hill, and publicist, Nazia Khatun.

I am lucky to have a family who have always been supportive of my weird desire to write books. Special thanks must go to my parents: my mum and fearless champion, Anita Luthra Suri, and my dad, Nishant Suri, who passed away a month before I found an agent but always believed I would be a published author one day. This book is dedicated to him.

Thank you to Alison Barlow for giving me beautiful books to read and for teaching me how on earth taxes work. Heartfelt thanks also to Shekar Bhatia for the wonderful author photo and to Gordana Radich-Pattni, who listened to all my stories for years and years without complaint. I hope you enjoy this one.

My final acknowledgment goes to my chosen family. Carly, thank you for believing in this book and in me. I couldn't have done it without you.

extras

orbit

meet the author

Shekar Bhatia

TASHA SURI was born in London to Punjabi parents. She studied English and creative writing at Warwick University and is now a cat-owning librarian in London. A love of period Bollywood films, history, and mythology led her to write South Asian–influenced fantasy. Find her on Twitter: @tashadrinkstea.

interview

When did you first start writing?

I've been writing for fun since I was pretty young. Apparently as a kid I had a full-blown tantrum when I learned about full stops, because I was mad no one had told me about them earlier, and now I had to fix all the stories I'd already written because they were *wrong*. You'll be happy to know I've become a little more relaxed about editing since then.

I've only been writing seriously for publication since leaving university in 2011. I wrote one book that wasn't very good but taught me a lot, and then I started working on *Empire of Sand*.

Who are some of your most significant authorial influences?

Juliet Marillier, Jacqueline Carey, N. K. Jemisin, Catherynne Valente... They're all very different from each other, but they've all had a huge influence on my writing. Valente's prose is gorgeous; Jemisin's books always rip my heart out and make me love it; Marillier's Sevenwaters Trilogy will always hold a special place in my heart; and Carey somehow manages to make giant, sweeping epics feel deeply personal. I feel like I've learned a lot from all of them.

How did you come up with the idea for Empire of Sand?

I've always wanted to write a fantasy that draws on India's history and epics and myths. I love Mughal art and architecture, and *Mughal-e-Azam*—a classic Bollywood film set in the Mughal court—was one of my childhood favorites. So finding inspiration for the setting was easy, really.

I'm not really sure how the plot and characters came together, but I do remember reading lots of books about the Mughal emperors and being fascinated by the women in their lives: their daughters and mothers and wives, who wielded huge power behind the scenes. The rest of the idea just came together, in its own time, like magic.

What, if any, research did you do in preparation for writing this book?

I read lots and lots of books about the Mughal Empire, and read any academic papers I could get my hands on. (When they were actually available to be read at all. Don't get me started on the open accessibility of academic research...)

The funny thing about research is that you can do a huge amount of it, and only use the barest fraction of what you find in the final story. I could probably write a thesis on the ways the Ambhan Empire differs from the Mughal Empire, as it ended up deviating in really big ways! But I wouldn't have been able to create it at all without diving into the intricacies of Mughal court politics and provincial governance, and I definitely wouldn't have been able to write *Empire of Sand* without looking at the lives of Mughal women.

The magic in this book, from the daiva to the dancing of Amrithi rites, is fascinating and unique. How did you develop this magic system?

Hindu belief and epics had a big influence on the magic system. Amrithi rites and sigils were influenced by Indian classical dance (specifically Bharatanatyam) and by the depiction of the god Shiva creating and destroying the world with dance and cosmic fire, which should sound familiar. Hindu epics are rife with vows made by mortals and immortals that have terrible consequences but can't be broken, and spirits that aren't quite gods, so they were a great source of material!

Honestly though, the magic system started off with me just throwing ideas I thought were cool on the page. It was only later that I realized I'd drawn a lot of inspiration from Hinduism, which isn't surprising, as I grew up with it.

A major theme of Empire of Sand *is sacrifice: the choice between familial and romantic love, between ambition and community, between different forms of government, etc. What compelled you to write about this?*

I think when characters are put in a position where they have to sacrifice something—when they're forced to choose between different, huge forces in their lives at a great cost—you get the most powerful conflict and character growth. I love reading stories that force their characters to make sacrifices and difficult choices, so of course I had to make all of that a big part of *Empire of Sand*.

Strong female characters are often portrayed as gun-wielding, ass-kicking heroines. However, in Empire of Sand, *the protagonist is a young woman whose strength manifests in less overt ways. What were your inspirations for Mehr's character?*

The Mughal women I read about were a huge influence on Mehr's character. I actually named her after one of the most powerful women in the Mughal Empire, Nur Jahan, whose birth name was Mehr-un-Nisa. Women at the highest echelons of Mughal society often held huge political and economic power, but as you'd expect in a patriarchal system, they needed to utilize the strength and standing of the men around them to achieve that power. I wanted to look at the kind of strength a woman raised in that world would have—and what kind of weapons she'd have in her arsenal.

Mehr is marginalized in lots of ways, but she's also a noblewoman and the daughter of a very powerful man, and because of that she has a strength honed to suit the environment she's been raised in. Women have historically fought in wars and led armies, and I love reading about women who *do* kick ass and take names, but it's been a joy to explore a different kind of strength that's been no less present—and no less admirable—in history.

Do you have a favorite scene in this book? Which part was the most difficult to write?

I love the scene when Mehr meets Elder in the desert, after the Maha's death. I feel like it captures the awe and magic and otherworldly power of the daiva better than anything else in the book, and it's a moment of powerful agency for Mehr. I also just really enjoyed writing it!

The most difficult scene to write was the one right after Hema's death, when Mehr and Amun consummate the marriage. I really, really, really struggled to write it. I tried to do anything *but* write it. In the end I had to eat some chocolate biscuits and cry and get it done. As a general writing tip: chocolate biscuits make everything easier.

What's one thing about either the world or the characters of **Empire of Sand** *that you loved but couldn't fit into the story?*

Oh, there was so much about the world I couldn't fit into the story, because *Empire of Sand* was tightly focused on Irinah. I would have loved to show more of the wider Empire, but I'll get to explore some of the other provinces in the next book, which I'm really excited about.

The one thing I would have loved to explore further in *Empire of Sand* is Suren and Ruhi's past relationship. Their idealism, their meeting of cultures, their doomed romance... it's all writer catnip. But it wouldn't have served the story to give their relationship any more attention than it had, sadly.

Empire of Sand *is the first book in the series. What's in store for us in future books?*

There's definitely going to be one more book in the series. That book will explore the consequences of the big, world-changing events at the end of *Empire of Sand*. The world is returning to balance, but that's hardly going to have pleasant consequences for the Empire, or for its people. The daiva are spreading across the Empire, growing stronger, and the nightmares aren't gone either.

The books in the series should all stand on their own and give different insights into the world and its magic, but the next book will bring back Arwa as a grown-up, so I hope it will be extra satisfying for anyone who read and enjoyed *Empire of Sand*.

If you could spend a day with one of your characters, who would it be and what would you do?

Oh, this one is easy. I'd spend the day with Amun, and I'd demand piggyback rides. He'd be too nice to refuse! Then

I'd feed him cake and make him tea, because my god, that boy needs some cake and tea.

Lastly, we have to ask: If you could have any magical power, what would you choose?

I've thought about this long and hard, and I've decided that I'd choose to have the power to make cats do my bidding. It would make my day-to-day life a lot easier, as my cat is a tiny disobedient hellspawn. Also, if anyone said to me, "It's like herding cats," I could say, "No, herding cats is very easy, actually." It's perfect.

if you enjoyed
EMPIRE OF SAND

look out for

REALM OF ASH
The Books of Ambha

by

Tasha Suri

Some believe the Ambhan Empire is cursed. But Arwa doesn't simply believe it—she knows it's true.

Widowed by the infamous, unnatural massacre at Darez Fort, Arwa was saved only by the strangeness of her blood—a strangeness she had been taught all her life to suppress. She offers up her blood and service to the imperial family and makes common cause with a disgraced, illegitimate prince who has turned to forbidden occult arts to find a cure to the darkness hanging over the Empire.

Using the power in Arwa's blood, they seek answers in the realm of ash: a land where mortals can seek the ghostly echoes of their ancestors' dreams. But the Emperor's health is failing, and a terrible war of succession hovers on the horizon, not just for the imperial throne, but for the magic underpinning Empire itself.

To save the Empire, Arwa and the prince must walk the bloody path of their shared past, through the realm of ash and into the desert, where the cause of the Empire's suffering—and its only chance of salvation—lie in wait. But what they find there calls into question everything they've ever valued...and whether they want to save the Empire at all.

CHAPTER ONE

Don't be sick. Don't be sick.

The palanquin jolted suddenly, tipping precariously forward. Arwa bit back a curse and gripped the edge of one varnished wooden panel. The curtain fluttered; she saw her maidservant reach for it hastily, holding it steady. Nuri's eyes met her own through the crack between the curtain and the panel, soft with apology.

"I'm sorry, my lady," said Nuri. "I'll tie the curtain in place."

"No need," Arwa said. "I like the cold air."

She adjusted her veil to cover her face, and Nuri nodded and let the curtain fall without securing it.

Arwa leaned back and forced her tense fingers to release the panel. Traveling through Chand province hadn't been so bad, but once her retinue had reached Numriha, the journey had become almost unbearable. A frame of wood and silk was a decent enough mode of transport on even paths, such as were found in Chand, but the palanquin was ill-suited for travel up a mountainside. And Numriha was *all* mountains. For two days, Arwa's nausea had ebbed and flowed along with the shuddering movement of the palanquin, as she was carried slowly up the narrow and treacherous southern pass through the Nainal Mountains.

Once that day already, she'd stopped to heave up her guts by the roadside as her guardswomen milled close by and her guardsmen waited farther up the pass, respectful of her dignity. Nuri had stroked her hair and given her water to drink and told her there was no need for shame, my lady, no need. Arwa had not agreed, and still did not, but she knew no one expected her to be strong. If anything, her weakness was a comfort to them. It was expected.

She was grieving, after all.

Arwa sank deeper into her furs, her veil a cloying weight against her skin, and tried to think of anything but the ache of her stomach, the heat of nausea prickling over her skin. She turned her head to the faint bite of cold air creeping in through the faint gap between the curtain and the palanquin itself, hoping its chill would soothe her. Even through the rich weight of the curtain, she could see the flicker of the lanterns carried by her guardswomen, and hear her guardsmen speak to one another in low voices, discussing the route that lay before them, which was made all the more treacherous by nightfall.

The male guards were meant to walk in a protective circle around her guardswomen, close enough to defend her, but far enough from her palanquin to ensure she was not directly at risk of being visible to common men. But the narrowness of the path and the dangers posed by following a cliff-edge road in darkness had made following proper protocol impossible. Instead all her guards snaked forward in an uneven, mixed-gender line, with her palanquin at its center.

She felt the palanquin jolt again, and this time she did swear. She hurriedly gripped the edge of a panel again as her retinue came a stop, voices beyond the curtain rising and mingling in a wave of indecipherable noise. Someone's voice rose higher, and then suddenly she could hear the crunch of booted footsteps against stone, growing louder and then fading away.

Her palanquin was lowered to the ground. The path was so uneven that it tipped slightly to one side as it touched soil, enough to make the curtain flutter and Arwa's weight fall naturally against one wall.

Arwa drew the curtain the barest sliver wider. She saw Nuri's silhouette in the darkness, saw her carefully adjust her own shawl around her head, lantern light flickering around her, as she kneeled down to Arwa's level.

"My lady," Nuri said, voice painstakingly deferential, "the palanquin can go no farther. We will need to walk the final steps together. The men have gone back down the path and will not see you, if you come out now."

When Arwa did not respond, Nuri said gently, "It is not far, my lady. I've been told it's an easy walk."

An easy walk. Of course it was. Most of the women who took the final steps of this journey were not as young or as healthy as Arwa. She adjusted her shawl and her veil. Last of all, she touched the sash of her tunic, hidden beneath the weight of her furs and her shawl and her long brocade jacket. Within her sash, she felt the shape of her dagger, swaddled in protective leather. It lay near her skin where it rightly belonged.

She pushed back the curtain of the palanquin. Her muscles were stiff from the journey, but Nuri and one of the guards-women were quick to help her to her feet.

As soon as Arwa was standing, with the cold night air all around her, she felt indescribably better. There was a staircase to the side of the path, carved into rock and rimmed in pale flowers, that led up to a building barely visible through the darkness.

She could have walked alone and unaided up those steps, but Nuri had already taken her arm, so Arwa allowed herself to be guided. The steps were blessedly even beneath her feet. She heard the whisper of Nuri's footsteps, the gentle clang of the guardswomen before her and behind her, their lanterns bright moons in the dark. She raised her head, gazing up through the gauze of her veil at the night sky. The sky was a blanket scattered with stars, vast and unclouded. She saw no birds in flight. No strange, ephemeral shadows. Just the mist of her own breath, as its warmth uncoiled in the air.

"Careful, my lady," said Nuri. "You'll stumble."

Arwa lowered her head and looked obediently forward. At the top of the staircase, she caught her first proper glimpse of her new home. She stopped, ignoring Nuri's insistent hand on her arm, and took a moment to gaze at it.

The hermitage of widows was a beautiful building, built of a stone so luminescent it seemed to softly reflect the starlight. Its three floors rested on pale columns carved to resemble trees, rootless and ethereal, arching their canopies over white verandas and latticed windows bright with lantern light. Within it, the widows of the nobility prayed and mourned and lived in peaceful isolation.

Arwa had thought, somewhat foolishly, that it would look more like the squalid grief-houses of the common people, where widows with no husband to support them and with family lacking in the means or compassion to keep them were discarded and left to rely on charity. But of course, the nobility would never allow their women to suffer so in shame and discomfort. The hermitage was a sign of the nobility's generosity, and of the Emperor's merciful kindness.

For that kindness, Arwa was grateful.

Finally, she allowed Nuri to guide her forward again, and entered the hermitage. Three women, hair cut short in the style of widowed women, were waiting for her in the foyer. One sat on a chair, a cane before her. Another stood with her hands clasped at her back, and a third still stood ahead of the rest, twisting the ends of her long shawl nervously between her fingers. Behind them, leaning over balconies and standing in corridors were...all the other women in the hermitage, Arwa thought wildly. By the Emperor's grace, had they *all* truly come to greet her?

She shook off Nuri's grip and stepped forward, removing her veil as the third, nervous woman approached her. Arwa forced herself to make a gesture of welcome, forced herself not to flinch as the woman's eyes grew teary, and she reached for Arwa's hands.

The woman was old—they were all old to her weary eyes—and the hands that took Arwa's own and held them firm were soft as wrinkled silk.

"My dear," said the woman. "Lady Arwa. Welcome. I am Lady Roshana, and I must say I am very glad to see you here safe. My companions are Asima, who is seated, and Gulshera. If you need anything, you must come to us, understand?"

"Thank you," Arwa whispered. She looked at the woman's face. The shawl she wore over her short hair was plain, as one would expect of a widow, but it was made of a rare knot-worked silk common only in one village of Chand, and accordingly eye-wateringly expensive. She wore no jewels but a gem in her nose, a diamond of pale, minute brilliance. This woman, then, was the most senior noblewoman of the hermitage, and the two others were the closest to her in stature. "It's a great honor to be here, Aunt," Arwa said, using a term of respect for an elder woman.

"You are so young!" exclaimed Roshana, staring at Arwa's face. "How old are you, my dear?"

"Eighteen," said Arwa.

A noise rippled through the crowd, hushed and sad. Noblewomen could not remarry; to be young and widowed was a tragedy.

Arwa's skin itched beneath so many eyes.

"Shame, shame," said Asima from her chair, overloud.

"I truly hadn't expected you to be *so* young," Roshana breathed. "When I heard the widow of the commander of Darez Fort was coming to us—"

Arwa flinched. She could not help it. Even the name of the place burned, still. It was just her luck that Roshana did not see it. Instead, Roshana was still staring at her damply, still twittering on.

"...have you no family, my dear, who could have taken care of you? After what you've been through!"

Arwa wanted to wrench her hand free of Roshana's grip, but instead she swallowed, struggling to find words that weren't cutting sharp, words that would not flay this fool of a woman open.

How dare you ask me about Darez Fort.

How dare you ask me about my family, as if your own have not left you here to rot.

How dare—

"I chose to come here, Aunt," Arwa said, her voice a careful, soft thing.

She could have told the older widow that her mother had offered to take her home. She'd offered it even as she'd cut Arwa's hair after the formal funeral, the one that took place a full month after the real bodies from Darez Fort had been buried. Maryam had cut Arwa's hair herself, smoothing its shorn edges flat with her fingers, tender with terrible disappointment. As Arwa's hair had fallen to the ground Arwa had felt all Maryam's great dreams fall with it. Dreams of renewed glory. Dreams of second chances. Dreams of rising from disgrace.

Arwa's marriage should have saved them all.

You could come back to Hara, Maryam had said. *Your father has asked for you.* A pause. The snip of shears. Maryam's fingers, thin and cold, on her scalp. *He asked me to remind you that as long as he lives, you have a place in our home.*

But Roshana had no right to that knowledge, so Arwa only added, "My family understand I wish to mourn my husband in peace."

Roshana gave a sniffle and released Arwa's hands. She placed her fingertips gently against Arwa's cheek. "You must still love him very much," she said.

I should weep, Arwa thought. *They expect me to weep.* But Arwa didn't have the strength for it, so she simply lowered her eyes and drew her shawl over her face instead, as if overcome. There was a flurry of noise from the crowd. She felt Roshana's hand on her head.

"There, there, now," said Roshana. "All is well. We will take care of you, my dear. I promise."

"She should sleep," Asima quavered from her seat. "We should all sleep. How late is the hour?"

It was not a subtle hint.

"Rabia," said a voice. Arwa looked up. Gulshera was speaking, gesturing to one of the women in the crowd. "Show her where her room is."

Rabia hurried over and took Arwa's hand in her own, ushering her forward. Arwa had almost forgotten that Nuri was present, so she startled a little when she heard Nuri's soft voice whisper her name and felt her hand at her back.

Roshana's outpouring of emotion had both embarrassed Arwa and left her uneasy. She'd treated Arwa the way a woman might treat a daughter or a longed-for grandchild. She wondered if Roshana had either daughter or grandchild somewhere beyond the hermitage. She wondered what sort of family would discard a woman here to gather dust. She wondered what sort of family a woman would, perhaps, come here to hide from.

She thought of her mother's hands running through her own shorn hair. She thought of the way her mother had wept, as Arwa hadn't: full-throated, as if her heart had utterly broken and couldn't be mended.

I had such hopes for you, Arwa. Her voice broke. *Such hopes. And now they're all gone. As dead as your fool husband.*

Arwa followed Rabia through the crowd into the silence of a dark, curving corridor.

The widow Rabia was dying—nearly literally, it seemed, from the way she kept spasmodically pursing and loosening her lips— to ask Arwa questions that were no doubt completely inappropriate to put to a freshly grieving widow. Accordingly, Arwa kept dabbing her eyes and sniffling as they shuffled forward, mimicking tears. If the woman was going to ask her about her husband—or worse still, about what happened at Darez Fort— then by the Emperor's grace, Arwa was damn well going to make her feel bad about it.

"You must not mourn too greatly," Rabia said, apparently deciding to put her questions aside for now and provide unsolicited advice instead. "Your husband died in service to the Empire. That is glorious, don't you think?"

"Oh yes," Arwa said, patting furiously at her eyes. "He was a brave, brave man." She let her voice fade to a whisper. "But I can't speak of him yet. It's far too painful."

"Of course," Rabia said hurriedly, guilt finally overcoming her. They fell into silence.

Arwa's patience—limited, at the best of times—was sorely tested when Rabia piped up again a moment later

"I know some people say the Empire is cursed and that—the fort, you know—that it's proof. But *I* don't think that. This is your room," she added, pushing the door open. Nuri slipped inside, leaving Arwa to deal with Rabia alone. "I think we're being tested. One day the Maha is going to come out of hiding if we prove our worth against evil forces, if we show we're worthy. And what happened to your husband, his bravery, it's *proof*—"

"Thank you," Arwa said, cutting in. Her voice was sharp. She couldn't soften the edge on it and had no desire to. Instead she bared her teeth at Rabia, smiling hard enough to make her face hurt.

Rabia flinched back.

"You've been *very* kind," added Arwa.

Rabia gave a weak smile in response and fled with a mumbled apology. Arwa didn't think she'd be bothered by her again.

It was a nice enough room, once Rabia had been encouraged to leave it. It had its own latticed window and a bed covered in an embroidered blanket. There was a low writing desk, already equipped with paper and a lit oil lantern ready for Arwa's own use. One of the guardswomen must have brought in Arwa's luggage via a servants' entrance, because her trunk was on the floor.

Nuri kneeled before it, quickly sorting through tunics and shawls and trousers, all in pale colors with light embellishment, suitable for Arwa's new role as a widow. The ones that had grown dirty from use would be washed and aired to remove the musk from their long journey, then refolded and stored away again, packed with herbs to preserve their freshness.

Arwa sat on the bed and watched Nuri work.

Nuri was the perfect servant. Mild, discreet, attentive. Arwa had no idea what Nuri truly thought or felt. It was no surprise, really: Nuri had been trained in her father's household, under the keen of Arwa's mother, who demanded only the best from her household staff, a clean veneer of loyal obedience, without flaw. She'd been sent by Arwa's mother to accompany her on the journey from Chand to Numriha, as Arwa had not had a maidservant of her own any longer.

"The guards," said Arwa, "are they camping overnight?"

"The hermitage provides accommodation not far from here," Nuri said. "They'll leave in the morning, I expect."

"Does the hermitage have servants' quarters?"

Nuri was momentarily silent. Arwa watched her smooth the creases from the tunic on her lap. "I thought I would sleep here," Nuri said finally. "I have a bedroll. I would be able to care for you then, my lady."

Care for me as my mother ordered you to, Arwa suspected. The thought made her both sad and terribly angry. Her feelings concerning her mother—and her mother's brand of love—were far from straightforward. But her choice today, at least, was clear.

"I don't want you to stay," said Arwa. "Not here in my room tonight or in the hermitage at all. You can accompany the guards back tomorrow. I'll pay for your passage back to Hara."

"My lady," Nuri said quietly. "Your mother bid me to stay with you."

"You can tell her I made you leave," Arwa said. "Tell her I refuse to have a maidservant." *Blame my grief*, Arwa thought. But Nuri would surely do that without being told. "Tell her I raged at you, that I wouldn't be reasoned with. She'll believe it."

"Lady Arwa," Nuri said. There was a thread of fear in her voice. "You...you need someone to take care of you. To protect you."

From yourself, went unsaid.

"She won't cast you out for leaving me," Arwa said tiredly, ignoring Nuri's words. "She'll know it was my choice. I'll write and tell her so. I expect she'll be glad of your help with Father anyway."

Arwa reached into her sash and removed a purse. She held it out. "Take it," she said. "Enough for your journey to Hara, and more for your kindness." She could have given Nuri jewels—she had little need for them anymore, after all. But a maidservant with jewels would inevitably be accused of theft. Coin was different. Coin could come from anywhere.

Hesitantly, Nuri held out her hand. Arwa placed the purse on her palm, and watched Nuri's fingers curl over it.

"I should finish sorting your clothes," said Nuri.

"There's no need," said Arwa. "You should go and rest. You have a long journey tomorrow."

Nuri nodded and stood. "Please take care, Lady Arwa," she said. Then she left.

Arwa kneeled and sorted through her own clothes. She would have to arrange for one of the hermitage's servants to have them washed in the morning. When the job of sorting through her clothing was done, Arwa latched the trunk shut and closed the door.

She placed the oil lantern on the window ledge, sucked in a fortifying breath, and took her dagger from her sash.

She held the blade over the heat of the oil lantern's flame. Her hand rested comfortably on the hilt of the blade, where the great teary opal embedded within it fitted the shape of her palm in a manner that brought her undeniable comfort. She counted the seconds, waiting for the blade to warm, and stared out of the window. The dark stared back at her, velvet, oppressively lightless. She couldn't even see the stars.

She lifted the blade up and waited for it to cool again.

She'd been too afraid to use the dagger on the journey, with Nuri always near, with her guards ever vigilant. Once in her palanquin, she'd made a small cut to her thumb, and daubed blood behind her ear, in the manner mothers daubed kohl behind children's ears to keep the evil eye at bay. She'd hoped it would be enough, and perhaps it had been. She'd seen no shadows. Felt no evil descend, winged and silent.

Once the blade had cooled, she placed its sharp edge to a finger, and watched the blood well up. The cut was shallow, the pain negligible. She placed her finger against the window ledge and drew a line across its surface.

The lantern flame flickered, caught by a faint breeze. Arwa watched it move. She thought of her husband. Of Kamran. Of a circle of blood, and a hand on her sleeve, and eyes that gleamed like gold. Her stomach felt uneasy again, roiling inside her. Her mouth was full of the taste of old iron.

Curious, how even when the heart was silent and the mind declined to recall suffering, the body still remembered.

She wiped the dagger clean on an old cloth and pressed the material to her finger finally to stem the last of the bleeding. She looked at the window. The blood was still there, illuminated by her lantern, a firm line demarcating the dark and the light, the safety of the room, and what lay beyond it.

She sat on the bed, curling up her knees. She placed the dagger by her feet and watched the flame move. Waiting.

The night remained silent.

Nuri's voice rose up in her. *You... you need someone to take care of you. To protect you.*

What a nice idea, Arwa thought idly, as sleep began to creep over her. If only someone existed who truly could.

CHAPTER TWO

The walls of the hermitage were thinner than they first appeared. Arwa was woken from an uneasy sleep by the sound of women chattering as they headed to breakfast. The widows, it seemed, were early risers.

Once the corridors were quiet again, Arwa dressed and left her room. The night's bitter chill had softened, and now the indoor air of the hermitage felt no more than pleasantly cool on her skin. She drew her shawl loosely around her head and her shoulders, her bare feet moving soundless across the stone floor.

She found the prayer room much more quickly than she'd expected to. It was set farther down the corridor from where she'd slept, the scent of incense wafting from its open doors inviting her in. She had hoped it would be quiet, now that many of the women were breaking their fast, and it was. Two very elderly ladies were asleep against one wall, leaning against each other with their shawls tucked up to their chins. Apart from them—and their gentle snores—the room was empty and silent.

Arwa did not know if the women had come to pray at dawn as the most pious did and fallen asleep shortly after, or if they'd come here to surreptitiously share the carafe of wine she could see tucked between them. Although her guess was firmly on the latter, Arwa was just grateful they were not awake to speak to her, to question her or pity her with soft eyes.

She was tired of people and their pity.

One of the walls was a latticed screen carved to resemble tree roots and great sprouting leaves. The light poured through it in honeycomb shadows. Before the screen stood a statue as tall as Arwa herself. She drew her shawl tighter around her and approached it.

The statue was of a male figure, garbed in a turban and robes. Its upraised palm held the world inside it.

It was a statue of the Emperor—of all Emperors, past and future—and their blessed bloodline. It was a statue of the Maha, the Great One and first Emperor, who built the Ambhan Empire and then raised a temple upon the sands of Irinah province, where his power and piety had ensured the blessings of the Gods would shower for centuries down upon the Empire and grant him a lifespan far beyond mortal reckoning.

The sight of the effigy's blank face—of the eternity of its varnished, bare surface—brought Arwa an immense sense of comfort that she couldn't fully explain. Perhaps it reminded her of kinder times during her childhood, when she'd prayed at her mother's side for the sake of the Empire and for its future glory. Perhaps it merely helped her believe that all suffering was finite, and even the anger and grief coiled within her now would one day fade to the void.

There was no one to see her or to scold her. So Arwa took another step forward and placed her hands against the smooth face. The feel of it reminded her of the opal in her dagger hilt: smooth and somehow achingly familiar against her palms.

She let out a slow breath. Some of that awful tension in her unfurled. She stepped back and kneeled before the altar.

The ground was cold. She sang a prayer, soft under her breath so as not to disturb the sleepers behind her. At the feet of the effigy was incense and a cluster of flowers, freshly picked. Tucked discreetly at the base of the statute were tiny baskets, woven of leaves and grass. Filled with soil. Arwa paused in her prayer, thoughtful, and touched one with her fingertips.

She knew what they were. She had seen them on dozens of roadside altars during the journey through Chand to the hermitage.

Grave-tokens.

Tokens of grief. Symbolic burials, for the Maha, who had died when Arwa was only a girl. Four hundred years he'd lived, some claimed. And then he had died, and the Empire had been falling to curse and ruin ever since.

Or perhaps he'd risen to the Gods. Perhaps one day he would return. Perhaps he had not died at all, and was simply biding his time, waiting for the people of his Empire to prove their faith and their strength before he would deign to return and guide them once more.

She'd heard all the arguments before, at the celebrations and dinners she'd attended in her brief time as a married woman. Politics and faith, tangled together as they were, were never far from the minds—or tongues—of the nobility.

She wondered sorely if she was going to be privy to heated exchanges of faith here, too. No doubt a hermitage of widows was rich soil for questions of death and mourning. Rabia was clearly one of that hopeful number who believed the Maha was not truly gone, and she was also clearly stupid enough to announce her views to strangers like Arwa, who didn't care a whit what she thought about anything. The grave-tokens were

extras

proof enough that many widows held the opposite view and weren't afraid to profess their faith, or their grief.

Well, when the arguments began, Arwa would just follow the lead of the snoring friends behind her and turn to the quiet comfort of a prayer room—or wine, if required.

A noise startled her out of her reverie. Someone had rapped their knuckles deliberately against the doorframe, startling one of the elderly women mid-snore into wakefulness.

"Wh-what is it?"

"Nothing, Aunt," said Gulshera. Her eyes met Arwa's. "I've come for the girl. Rest."

The woman mumbled and subsided back into sleep. Arwa stood.

"Please come with me," Gulshera said.

Arwa followed her out.

In the morning light, Gulshera's hair was as pale as snow, her skin the lightest shade of brown. As a young woman, she must have been considered the epitome of Ambhan beauty, despite the severe shape of her mouth and the way she held herself, with a ramrod straight posture reminiscent of a military-trained nobleman's.

"You ate nothing this morning," Gulshera said, gesturing for Arwa to walk with her down the corridor. Arwa obeyed. "Roshana worried."

Arwa did not think it would take a great deal of effort to worry Roshana.

"I'm sorry. I didn't mean to worry anyone. I only wanted to pray."

"You'll have plenty of time for prayer here," said Gulshera. "Right now, we need to get you some food. The tables have been cleared, so we'll see what the cooks have left."

464

"If you direct me to the kitchens, I can go on my own," Arwa said with studied politeness.

"Ah, I see." Gulshera's voice was terribly matter-of-fact. "You want me to leave you alone."

Yes, thought Arwa.

"Not at all," she said. "I simply don't want to trouble you."

"Indeed. Well, perhaps I want to be troubled."

She took Arwa's arm imperiously.

"Come," she said. "A servant always brings hot tea to my room in the morning. You'll share it with me."

There was no way to refuse her now, so Arwa didn't try to. She allowed herself to be led.

Gulshera's room was a cluttered, lived-in space, with a low dining table by the lattice window and large sheaves of paper stacked neatly on her writing desk. Arwa saw silk-bound parchments, marked with the unfamiliar seal of a noble Ambhan family, balanced precariously on the edge of the bed. A set of bows hung on the opposing wall.

The largest of them caught Arwa's attention and held it. It was taller than her—tall as a grown man—its surface gilded with mother-of-pearl. Arwa itched to hold it. Its ends were shaped like the mouths of tigers, with serrated teeth stretched into an open snarl.

"It's a relic," Gulshera said, startling Arwa back to reality. "It takes a full-grown man all his strength to string and shoot an arrow from it. My husband was full proud of it. But of course, it's only good for display now."

Gulshera was already seated by the window. There was a tray set before her. "Sit," she said. "You can pour the tea."

There were herbs steeped in water, a small bowl of honey, and a shallow tray of attar-scented water. Next to the tea were

465

vegetables fried golden in gram flour. Arwa poured the tea and heaped in honey for both her and Gulshera, then took a quick sip from her own cup that was burning sweet.

"You didn't sleep," said Gulshera.

It wasn't a question. "I slept a little," Arwa said anyway.

"No food, and no sleep." Gulshera sipped her own drink; steam rose up around her face in coils. "I see."

Arwa picked up a fritter and bit into it pointedly, resisting the urge to bristle. No doubt Gulshera thought she was a fragile creature, a young and witless thing fueled by love and religious fervor, shattered by what she had seen that day and night at the fort a mere handful of months ago.

Let her think it. It was better than the truth.

She waited for Gulshera to begin lecturing her. She stared down at her oil-stained fingers in silence as Gulshera sipped her tea and took one of the fritters for herself.

Instead, Gulshera said, "Eat. Drink your tea. Then go, when you like."

"Go?"

"When you like," Gulshera repeated. She soaked her fingers in the attar-water, then stood, leaving Arwa alone with her tea and the cooling fritters, under a pale slant of sunlight pouring in through the window. She heard Gulshera settle at the writing desk. The sound of rustling paper followed.

Arwa hesitated.

A memory came to her, unbidden, of the feral cat she'd found in the gardens of her first home in the province Hara, where she had lived as a girl of ten. She'd been determined to make a friend of that cat, with its one bad eye and fanged teeth, but it ran and hid in the foliage whenever Arwa approached it. She'd gained a number of scratches before she'd learned that if she left slivers of meat on the ground near her, it would come and eat by her warily, as long as she studiously ignored its presence. In the end, it had grown warm with her, following her around the gardens, sleeping on her lap if she sat in the right patch of sun. Indifference and food had won it better than any straight-forward affection ever could have.

Arwa had the discomforting sense that Gulshera was treating her with the same studied, indifferent regard Arwa had once shown that cat.

She wants something from me, Arwa thought.

She ate another fritter, and drank her tea, before she murmured a suitably gracious thank-you and moved to leave.

"Come back whenever you like," Gulshera said, not raising her head as Arwa left the room. "I always have enough for two."

Arwa had liked the brusqueness of Gulshera's care, somewhat despite herself. But as time went on—as she walked from Gulshera's room across the hermitage, passing rooms and other widows—the memory of Gulshera's words began to feed her disquiet.

You didn't sleep, Gulshera had said. It hadn't sounded like a guess. Perhaps Arwa was simply that transparent, but she went to her room regardless, checking the undisturbed line of blood on her window ledge, hidden carefully beneath her own miniature effigy of the Emperor. No one had searched her room. And her dagger was in her sash, concealed where no one would find it and recognize it for what it was.

Arwa looked out of the lattice window. Without the dark of the night beyond it, she could see that the hermitage stood above a deep valley studded with rich swathes of flowers. The hermitage curved like a crescent moon, following the shape of the valley below it. Arwa's window faced another, far at the other edge of the building.

Gulshera's room lay at the other end of the hermitage. She'd walked the journey between their bedrooms and knew that now. No doubt she must have looked out of her own window in the night and seen Arwa's oil lantern burning. Perhaps she'd looked for a moment only, then gone back to bed. Perhaps she'd watched for a long time, marking the constant flicker of light in Arwa's window, wondering what dark thoughts kept Arwa far from rest.

Either way, she knew the exact location of Arwa's room. She'd stared through the press of the dark at Arwa's lantern light, deliberately, thoughtfully. It disturbed Arwa to be so watched. She stepped back from the lattice and sat on her bed, hands clenched, searching for calm. She thought of how she'd listened to Gulshera's words without discerning their full import, and stared about the older woman's room wide-eyed without using any of the thought and cunning a noblewoman should sensibly employ. Fool. She was a fool.

What else, she thought, *did I miss?*

After a midday rest, some of the women apparently liked to go for a walk, or so Roshana told her as she dragged Arwa out to join them. Roshana spoke to Arwa anxiously, asking how well she was settling in and how she liked it here in Numriha so far from her old home. Arwa clamped down on her instinct to be waspish and tried to be gracious in response. Still, she was glad when Asima commandeered her, demanding that Arwa walk by her side instead.

There was a gentle avenue that followed the edge of the hermitage, not quite dipping into the steeper territory of the valley.

extras

It was a smooth enough path for the widows of varying levels of health to walk it comfortably. From here, Arwa could see the valley, and also glimpse the guardswomen who walked the roof of the hermitage, on the lookout for bandits who'd normally consider a house of noblewomen a ripe target.

"Pick some of that for me," demanded Asima, pointing to some gnarled vegetation.

"Not the flowers?" Arwa asked, leaning down.

"No, no. Not flowers. What do I need them for?"

Arwa picked Asima green vegetation and long grass. It took her a moment to realize the purpose of Asima's commands. In Arwa's defense, her thoughts were somewhat distracted. Her visit to Gulshera's room was still running in small circles inside her brain, tying her insides into ever tighter knots.

"Can you weave them together?" Asima asked.

When Arwa shook her head, Asima clucked in response.

"Oh dear, oh dear," she said, shaking her head. "A noble girl who can't weave a simple basket! The Empire has truly fallen to shit, Gods save us."

Her words drew a startled laugh from Arwa, quickly quelled by Asima's gimlet-eyed stare. "As you say, Aunt," Arwa said quickly.

"Can you embroider?" Asima demanded.

"Yes, Aunt."

"But you can't *weave*?"

What followed was a demonstration of how to make a grave-token. It was a simple enough lesson, and one Arwa could follow without paying it all her attention. As she followed Asima's directions, taking green roots into her hands, winding them into a miniature braid, she worried over the thought of Gulshera watching her lantern-bright window. She worried over the thought as one worries over a sore tooth, incessantly, unable to soothe the irritation away.

Something had to be done.

Gulshera was not in her room. The door was locked. Arwa waited outside it for the woman to return. Eventually, Gulshera appeared, striding along the corridor. She hadn't been attending to prayer or to mourning or ambling gently along a well-trodden path, as the other widows had. Her bow was at her back, her face flushed with the heat of the day.

"Arwa," Gulshera acknowledged, tipping her head.

"You watched my room last night," said Arwa, without preamble. "Why?"

She saw Gulshera's forehead furrow into a frown.

"Did your mother not teach you subtlety?" Gulshera asked incredulously. "They would eat you alive in Jah Ambha, by the Emperor's grace! Come inside."

Arwa followed Gulshera into her room, shutting the door behind her as the older woman swiftly divested herself of her boots and her bow and the long jacket she wore over her tunic. Finally, when Gulshera was done, she sat by the window and gestured for Arwa to join her.

"I looked out of my window and saw the light in yours. For a *moment*," Gulshera stressed. "No longer. I had no darker motive. I only cared about your welfare. Are you satisfied?"

No, Arwa was not satisfied. Far from it.

"In my experience," Arwa said steadily, "people don't just simply care about one another's welfare. All actions have a purpose. I may be a child to you, Aunt, but I've lived long enough to know what people are."

"Then you've lived a terribly sad life," Gulshera said, not

mincing her words. "You'll learn that we have to look after one another here. We're not like the noblewomen you left behind, we have no need to play political games and tread on one another for the sake of our husbands or children or even ourselves. Our time of power and glory is finished.

"Perhaps you don't understand yet," she continued, "that when your husband died, the part of you that shared in his world died with him. We all came here, by choice or by necessity, because we Ambhans hold our marriages more sacred than the lesser peoples of the world, and we respect our vows beyond death. We are the ghosts of who we once were, and accordingly we must take care of one another. No one else will." Gulshera's gaze was fixed on Arwa's, her voice unrelenting. "You'll think me dramatic, Arwa, but I assure you I am a realist. You must be one too. For your own sake."

Fine words. Strong words. But Arwa could not let the barefisted blow of them mislead her.

"I know what I know," she said. She raised her head higher, jaw firm.

Her mother had tried to teach her subtlety. But the art of folding secrets inside words and smiles, and hiding the knife of her anger until it was already in someone's gut, too late to be escaped—those things had never been Arwa's strength. *Flighty*, she'd been called as a child, and *mercurial*. She wore her heart, fierce and changeable as it was, right on her skin.

For a handful of liminal years, she had learned to feign a veneer of placidity, for the sake of making herself an attractive prospect as a bride. She'd learned to smile and to be soft, to say gentle words when sharp ones came far more easily to her tongue, and in the end her hard-won calm—and her youth— had granted her the older, powerful husband her mother had hoped for her. For a time, she had been better than her true, barbed self. She'd been a commander's wife. She'd been a noblewoman worthy of respect.

But that was before the circle of blood and the eyes like gold. Before Kamran's death.

"I know," Arwa said, "that you have scrolls that were sent to you by an Ambhan noble family. I didn't recognize the seal upon them, which suggests to me that the seal is not real." Before her father's disgrace, he'd been a governor of a great province of the Empire. Her husband had been a commander of renown. Of course Arwa knew the seals of the great families; she'd learned them by careful rote as a young girl. "Someone of noble blood communicates with you but seeks to hide their true identity. I know you own a man's bow more expensive than anything I have possessed in my lifetime, embellished in a manner intended to please the eyes at court. Your husband, then, was a politician and a courtier. You wear no jewels but I suspect it is not Roshana who is truly of highest standing in this hermitage. You are."

Arwa leaned forward, not allowing her gaze to falter.

"You're not a ghost of a woman, cut off from the world," said Arwa. "You serve someone. You answer to someone powerful. And you seek to take care of me, of all people. Forgive me, if I do not think your motives are entirely benevolent."

"Well," Gulshera said finally. "If we're talking bluntly..." She leaned forward, intent, mirroring Arwa. "I am under no obligation to tell you anything. You have no power here. No standing. And if you truly believe I have so much influence, then you shouldn't have spoken to me like that."

"I meant no disrespect."

"Now that is a lie," Gulshera said.

"Then I apologize," said Arwa. "I know you don't have to tell me anything. I know I have no power. I could have been patient. I could have waited for you to reveal what you truly require, in the fullness of time. But I am tired of games, Lady Gulshera. If you do truly care of my welfare, then do me a kindness: Tell me what you want, then leave me alone to mourn."

"If you have a choice between being blunt or being patient in the future, then choose patient," Gulshera said. But there was a thoughtful light in her eyes. "Come back here tomorrow morning, after breakfast. We'll take a walk together."

Arwa let out a slow exhale. *This,* after she'd asked for no more games...

"We'll go down to the valley," Gulshera said. "Just the two of us, where we can't be overheard. And there, you can tell me about Darez Fort."

if you enjoyed
EMPIRE OF SAND

look out for

TORN

The Unraveled Kingdom:
Book One

by

Rowenna Miller

In a time of revolution, everyone must take a side.

Sophie, a dressmaker and charm caster, has lifted her family out of poverty with a hard-won reputation for beautiful ball gowns and discreetly embroidered spells. A commission from the royal family could secure her future—and thrust her into a dangerous new world.

extras

Revolution is brewing. As Sophie's brother, Kristos, rises to prominence in the growing anti-monarchist movement, it is only a matter of time before their fortunes collide.

When the unrest erupts into violence, she and Kristos are drawn into a deadly magical plot. Sophie is torn—between her family and her future.

1

―――∞―――

"MR. BURSIN," I SAID, MY HANDS CONSTRICTING AROUND THE
fine linen ruffles I was hemming, "I do not do that."

"But, miss, I would not ask if it were—if it were not the
most pressing of circumstances. If it would not be best. For all
concerned."

I understood. Mr. Bursin's mother-in-law simply refused to
die. She was old, infirm, and her mind was half-gone, but still
she clung to life—and, as it turned out, bound the inheritance
to her daughter and son-in-law in a legal tangle that would all
go away once she was safely interred. Still.

"I do not wish ill on anyone. Ever. I sew charms, never
curses." My words were final, but I thought of another avenue.
"I could, of course, wish good fortune on you, Mr. Bursin. Or
your wife."

He wavered. "Would...would a kerchief be sufficient?" He
glanced at the rows of ruffled neckerchiefs lining my windows,
modeled by stuffed linen busts.

"Oh, most certainly, Mr. Bursin. The ruffled style is very
fashionable this season. Would you like to place the order now,

or do you need to consult with your wife regarding style and fabric?"

He didn't need to consult with his wife. She would wear the commission he bought from me, whether she liked the ruffles or not. He chose the cheapest fabric I offered—a coarser linen than was fashionable—and no decorative embroidery.

My markup for the charm still ensured a hefty sum would be leaving Mr. Bursin's wallet and entering my cipher book.

"Add cutting another ruffled kerchief to your to-do list this morning, Penny," I called to one of my assistants. I didn't employ apprentices—apprentices learn one's trade. The art of charm casting wasn't one I could pass on to the women I hired. Several assistants had already come and gone from my shop, gaining practice draping, cutting, fitting—but never charm casting. Alice and Penny, both sixteen and as wide-eyed at the prospect of learning their trade as I had been at their age, were perhaps my most promising employees yet.

"Another?" Penny's voice was muffled. I poked my head around the corner. She was on her back under a mannequin, hidden inside the voluminous skirts of a court gown.

"And what, pray tell, are you doing?" I stifled a laugh. Penny was a good seamstress with the potential to be a great one, but only when she resisted the impulse to cut corners.

Penny scooted out from under the gown, her pleated jacket bunching around her armpits. "Marking the hem," she replied with a vivid crimson blush.

"Is that how I showed you to do it?" I asked, a stubborn smile forcing its way onto my face.

"No," she replied meekly, and continued with her work.

I returned to the front of the shop. Three packages, wrapped in brown paper, awaiting delivery. One was a new riding habit with a protective cast, the second a pelisse for an old woman with a good health charm, and the third a pleated caraco jacket.

A plain, simple caraco. No magic, no spells. Just my own beautiful draping and my assistant Alice's neat stitching.

Sometimes I wished I had earned my prominence as a dressmaker on that draping and stitching alone, but I knew my popularity had far more to do with my charms, the fact that they had a reputation for working, and my distinction as the only couture charm caster in Galitha City. Though there were other charm casters in the city, the way that I stitched charms into fashionable clothing made the foreign practice palatable to the city's elite. The other casters, all hailing from the far-off island nation of Pellia by either birth or, like me, ancestry, etched charms into clay tablets and infused sachets of herbs with good luck or health, but I was the only charm caster in the city—the only one I knew of at all—who translated charms into lines of functional stitching and decorative embroidery.

Even among charm casters I was different, selling to Galatines, and the Galatine elite, who didn't frequent the Pellian market or any other Pellian businesses. I had managed to infuse the practice with enough cachet and intrigue that the wealthy could forget it was a bumpkin superstition from a backwater nation. Long before I owned my shop, I had attempted charming and selling simple thread buttons on the street. Incredibly, Galatines bought them—maybe it was the lack of pungent herb scents and ugly clay pendants that marked Pellian charms, or maybe it was the appeal of wearing a charm no one could see. Maybe it was merely novelty. In either case, I had made the valuable discovery that, with some modifications, Galatines would buy charms. When I finally landed a permanent assistant's job in a small atelier with a clientele of merchants' wives and lesser nobility, I wheedled a few into trying a charm, and, when the charms worked, I swiftly gathered a cult following of women seeking my particular skill. After a couple of years, I had enough clients that I was able to prove myself and open my own shop. Galatines were neither particularly superstitious nor religious, but the novelty of a charm stitched into their finery captivated their interest, and I in turn had a market for my work.

"When you finish the hem, start the trim for Madame Pliny's court gown," I told Penny. The commission wasn't due until spring, but the elaborate court gowns required so much work that I was starting early. It was our first court gown commission—a sign, I hoped, that we were establishing a reputation for the quality of our work as well as for the charms. "And I'm late to go file for the license already—the Lord of Coin's offices have been open for an hour."

"The line is going to be awful," Alice said from the workroom. "Can't you go tomorrow?"

"I don't want to put it off," I answered. The process was never sure; if I didn't get through the line today, or if I was missing something the clerk demanded, I wanted several days to make it up.

"Fair enough," Alice answered. "Wait—two messages came while you were with Mr. Bursin. Did you want—"

"Yes, quickly." I tore open the two notes. One was an invoice for two bolts of linen I had bought. I set it aside. And the other—

"Damn," I muttered. A canceled order. Mrs. Penneray, a merchant's wife, had ordered an elaborate dinner gown that would, single-handedly, pay a week's wages for both of my assistants. We hadn't begun it yet, and so, per my own contract, I would have to agree to cancel it.

I glanced at our order board. We were still busy enough, but this was a major blow. Most of the orders on our slate were small charmed pieces—kerchiefs, caps. Even with my upcharge for charms, they didn't profit us nearly as much as a gown. Early winter usually meant a lull in business, but this year was going to be worse than usual.

"Anything amiss?" Penny's brow wrinkled in concern, and I realized that I was fretting the paper with my fingers.

"No, just a canceled order. Frankly, I didn't care for the orange shot silk Mrs. Penneray chose anyway, did you?" I asked, wiping her order from the board with the flat of my hand. "And I really do need to go now."

Alice's prediction was right; the line to submit papers to the Lord of Coin was interminable. It snaked from the offices of the bureau into the corridors of the drafty stone building and into the street, where a cold rain pelted the petitioners. Puddles congregated in the low-lying areas of the flagstone floor, making the whole shabby establishment even damper and less welcoming than usual.

I held my leather portfolio under my fine wool cloak, only slightly dampened from the rain. Inside were the year's records for my shop, invoices and payment dates, lists of inventory, dossiers on my assistants and my ability to pay them. Proof that I was a successful business and worthy of granting another year's license. I traced my name inscribed on the front, tooled delicately into the pale calfskin by the leatherworker whose shop was four doors down from mine. I had indulged in the pretty piece after years of juggling papers bound with linen tape and mashed between layers of pasteboard. I had a feeling the ladylike, costly presentation, combined with the fashionable silk gown I wore like an advertisement of my skills and merchandise, couldn't hurt my chances at a swift approval from the Lord of Coin's clerk.

I was among a rare set of young women, not widows, with their own shop fronts when I opened almost ten years ago, and remained so. My business survived and even grew, if slowly, and I loved my trade—and I couldn't complain about the profits that elevated my brother, Kristos, and me from common day laborers to a small but somewhat prosperous class of business owners.

"No pushing!" a stout voice behind me complained. I stiffened. We didn't need any disruptions in the queue—any rowdiness and the soldiers posted around the building were likely to send us all home.

"I didn't touch you!" another voice answered.

"Foot's not attached to you, eh? Because how else did I get this muddy shoeprint on my leg?"

"Probably there when you hiked in from the parsnip farm or wherever you came from!"

I hazarded a look behind me. Two bareheaded men wearing poorly fitted linsey-woolsey suits jostled one another. One had the sun-leathered skin of a fisherman or dockworker; the other had the pale shock of flaxen hair common in the mountains of northeastern Galitha. Neither had seemed to think that the occasion warranted a fresh shave or a bath.

I suppressed a disapproving sigh. New petitioners, no doubt, with little hope of getting approval to open their businesses, and much more chance of disrupting everyone else. I glanced again; neither seemed to carry anything like enough paperwork to prove themselves. And their appearance—I tried not to wrinkle my nose, but they looked more like field hands than business owners. Fair or not, that wouldn't help their cases.

Most of the line, of course, was made up of similar petitioners. Scattered among the new petitioners who were allowed, one week out of the year, to present their cases to open a business, were long-standing business owners filing their standard continuation requests. It grated me to have to wait in line, crawling at a snail's pace toward the single clerk who represented the Lord of Coin, when I owned an established business. Business was strictly regulated in the city; careful ratios of how many storefronts per district, per trade, per capita were maintained. The nobility judged the chance of failed business a greater risk than denying a petitioner a permit. Even indulgences such as confectioners and upscale seamstresses like me were regulated, not only necessities like butchers and bakers and smiths. If I didn't file for my annual permit this week, I could lose my shop.

As we moved forward down the corridor a few flagstones at a time, more and more dejected petitioners passed us after unsuccessful interviews with the clerk. I knew that disappointment well enough. My first proposal was rejected, and I had to wait a whole year to apply again. I took a different tack that second year, developing as much clientele as I could among minor nobility, hoping to reach the curious ears of nobles closer to the Lord of Coin and influence his decision. It worked—at least, I assumed it had, as one of the first customers when my shop opened a year later was the Lord of Coin's wife, inquiring after a charmed cap to relieve her headaches.

The scuffle behind me escalated, more voices turning the argument into a chorus.

"Not his fault you have to wait in this damn line!" A strong voice took control of the swelling discontent and put it to words.

"Damn right!" several voices agreed, and the murmuring assents grew louder. "You don't see no nobles queuing up to get their papers stamped."

"Lining us up like cattle on the killing floor!" The shouting grew louder, and I could feel the press of people behind me begin to move and pulse like waves in the harbor whipped by the wind.

"No right to restrict us!" the strong voice continued. "This is madness, and I say we stand up to it!"

"You and what army?" demanded the southern petitioner who had been in the original scuffle.

"We're an army, even if they don't realize it yet," he replied boldly. I edged as far away as I could. I couldn't afford to affiliate myself, even by mere proximity, with treasonous talk. "If we all marched right up to the Lord of Coin, what could he do? If we all opened our shops without his consent, could he jail all of us?"

"Shut up before you get us all thrown out," an older woman hissed.

I turned in time to see a punch thrown, two men finally coming to blows, but before I could see any more, the older woman jumped out of the way and the heavy reed basket swinging on her arm collided into me. I stumbled and fell into the silver-buttoned uniform of a city soldier.

I looked up as he gripped my wrist, terrified of being thrown out and barred from the building. He looked down at me.

"Miss?"

I swallowed. "I'm so sorry. I didn't—"

"I know." He glanced back at the rest of his company subduing what had turned into a minor riot. They had two men on the floor already; one was the towheaded man who had started the argument. "Come with me."

"Please, I didn't want to cause trouble. I just want to file—"

"Of course." He loosened his grip on my wrist. "Did you think I was going to throw you out?" He laughed. "No, I have a feeling that the Lord of Coin will close the doors after this, and you're clearly one of the only people in line who even ought to be here. I'm putting you to the front."

I breathed relief, but it was tinged with guilt. He was right; few others had any chance at all of being granted approval, but cutting the line wouldn't make me look good among the others waiting, as though I had bought favor. Still, I needed my license, and I wasn't going to get it today unless I let the soldier help me. I followed him, leaving behind the beginnings of a riot truncated before it could bloom. The soldiers were already sending the lines of petitioners behind me back into the streets.

orbit

Follow us:

f /orbitbooksUS

🐦 /orbitbooks

▶ /orbitbooks

Join our mailing list
to receive alerts on our
latest releases and deals.

orbitbooks.net

Enter our monthly
giveaway for the chance
to win some epic prizes.

orbitloot.com